About the ʹ

Clive Hart lives iʳ
spends as mʹ
on horseback.   .dl
   community ͺ   ͺeval
   mounted comͺ   ͺally was.

ww   ͺ.net

Also by Clive Hart:
The Rise and Fall of the Mounted Knight

The Legend of Richard Keynes series:
Book One: Golden Spurs
Book Two: Brothers in Arms
Book Three: Dogs of War
Book Four: Knight Errant

Cover photo by Sam Gostner, of the Spanish stallion
Icaro and his owner Dominic Sewell

Second Edition

Contents

EVICTION

England, 1166

Richard scratched his white feathered quill across the stiff yellowed parchment to mark out two questions:
What makes a man?
What happened to my father?

The young man used his knife to saw the parchment apart around each question, then rolled up each slip into a tight tube and tied them shut with a thin lace of leather. He plaited them into the base of the blonde mane of his yellow coated horse, and those questions were to stay suspended there until Richard had found the answers. That is what the wise woman from the village had told him to do when he'd come to her asking about the fate of his father. 'He will never leave the Holy Land,' the old woman had said out in the circle of sacred trees as the light faded. 'You will need to become a man to uncover the truth, your family will depend on you,' she had croaked in the crisp air beneath leaves that whispered.

Later, on a very different day, a gentle breeze brushed through the foliage around a different clearing. Beams of light danced through the canopy and onto the undergrowth. A trio of female red deer grazed. They pulled and chewed the grass, the grind of their teeth the only sound above the faint rustle of leaves in the morning air. The eldest deer froze. She threw her head up into the air and her nose twitched. The other deer copied. An arrow whistled through the foliage. It glanced off a tree behind them and disappeared back into the woodland.

By the time the arrow had vanished, the deer were gone too, leaving the clearing empty. In the distance a groan rang out. 'Adela, I thought you had it,' Richard said. The teenage girl next to him lowered her bow. 'So did I.'

'Dawn has broken, we can try again tomorrow,' the boy said as he stretched his arms out and yawned. 'Come on, brother, we can find them again,' Adela said.

'You can't have everything your own way. The deer are gone, and I still have two horses to exercise today,' Richard said as he patted her on the back and started to walk away. Both youths were of an unremarkable height and shared the same dark hair, although Richard's was cut short. They also shared the same straight nose. When they were much younger they had been able to confuse their parents. Neither were heavy, but Richard looked slightly more rounded underneath his tight blue tunic than Adela did under her long light blue dress. His cheeks still had what his father had called child-fat. 'I can't believe you went to the old lady,' Adela said. 'Mother always forbade it. What will Father Adam say?'

'I asked the priest first but he couldn't give me any answers. He could only tell me to pray. Father Adam forbids lots of things and he doesn't make sense to me. He doesn't allow us to read about Arthur and Merlin either, even though he taught us how to read in the first place,' Richard said.

'I like Merlin, but mother says reading that book is a bad influence.'

'Maybe she's right, I would never had gone to see the old woman if I hadn't read about a pagan wise man,' Richard laughed.

'Did you ask her about me?'

'No, my visit was serious. I told you that I think father is dead, which means I'll have to look after you. He should have come home by now.'

'Our family has coped perfectly fine without him for more than a year,' Adela said.

A crow cawed sharply in the distance three times. Richard looked up for it in the trees. 'That means death,' he said. 'I told you, he's gone, even the crows know it. We need to go home.'

'Fine,' Adela said and followed him to their horses which

were tied to a tree. Both animals were asleep. The larger one, a palomino with a yellow coat, jolted awake when they approached. The stallion hit his head on a branch above him and snorted loudly at it although he didn't scare himself.

'Idiot,' Richard said. He patted the now very awake horse on its neck. Two rolled up pieces of parchment hung from his mane.

'He's not an idiot,' Adela said. 'He stood there the whole time and didn't make a fuss.'

'This time,' Richard untied the stallion. He tightened the saddle's girth strap up and put his foot into the metal stirrup.

'Won't you help me up first?' Adela looked at him with her hands on her hips.

'Why, do you need help?' He grabbed a handful of mane and jumped up swiftly into the tall wooden saddle. The saddle was painted white with a high curved back piece, the cantle, where a blue horizontal line had been painted across the middle.

Adela raised her eyebrows towards her brother. She slung her bow over her shoulder without bothering to unstring it and mounted her small brown gelding. A long row of colourful beads hung around the base of its neck. Their father had carefully selected them based on the latest advice for horse charms.

'See, you do not need my help,' Richard said.

'That doesn't mean you shouldn't offer it,' she arranged her dress in the saddle. Both of them laughed.

'I think you need more help with the dress than the saddle,' Richard said.

'We should have someone to tuck it in for me, like the Fitzwilliam's do. We need a larger household, Richard, other families don't hunt on their own.' Adela said. Theirs was a small but close family. Although they benefited from a few servants, they were as poor as could be while still being called noble.

'Maybe when father returns he will bring riches from the Holy Land,' Adela said.

Richard frowned. 'I told you, he isn't coming back,' and turned his shoulders towards home. His stallion turned in sync with him. 'Anyway, if we had more income, I would hire a trainer of horses first.'

'Do you think he will bring back any gifts for us?'

'If he does come back I expect he would,' Richard looked up through the leaves above him, some glowed as the sun shone through their fragile skin. 'I would love to hear about it. The Holy Land sounds so different to here, I can't imagine it.'

'Maybe someone will sing a song about him?'

'They already do, don't they,' Richard followed a track flanked by hazel and oak trees. 'Although it didn't come with any riches.'

'I just want to see him,' Adela said. The sun started to beat down and Richard began to feel its warmth. Even in the shade the cool of the morning had almost burnt off.

They rode for a while until they left the woodland. Ahead were the strip fields and small houses of the village attached to the manor of Keynes. Villagers worked together to clear a ditch of mud around some of the fields. They took no notice of the two riders. Their horses made their way through the village, a village that was actually just a row of houses on either side of the dirt track that passed locally for a road. Piglets squealed in play in one house with a hole in its roof. Richard's horse's ears swivelled towards the noise, but he'd heard it many times before.

The road followed a slight incline up to a grassy mound on which the fortified manor sat.

'If we had more money, I would build a keep of stone and call it a castle,' Richard said as it drew near. The manor centred around a hall which had a chamber behind it for the family. Around the yard were a collection of secondary buildings for cooking, stabling, storage and praying. All the buildings were wooden and a low wooden palisade ringed the site for protection. They rode through the main gateway. Richard could make out at least a dozen horses inside.

'Who is visiting?' Adela asked.

Richard looked at the high wooden saddles and the leather breastplates on the horses which were muscular and lean. 'Warhorses' he said.

'Maybe father is home?' Adela kicked her horse on.

A few men in woollen tunics milled around the horses. Some

refilled the water trough that sat outside the stable block. A few pack horses had bundles of cargo unloaded from them by others.

'I think I recognise a few of them, they look like uncle Luke's men. They wear the family colours,' Richard said. 'None of them are father's men though, I don't see Old Tom, John or Ralph.' Some of the men wore white tunics with a horizontal blue line across the middle. The rest wore tunics of yellow and red in a chequerboard pattern. 'I've never seen those tunics before. They must be expensive to make,' Richard said to himself.

'Let's go inside,' Adela jumped from her gelding. 'We can untack our horses later.'

'What would father say?' Richard dismounted. They led their horses to the entrance of the stable building and put them back inside, saddles still on.

Adela ran over to the hall as soon as the stable door slammed shut behind her. Richard carefully removed the bridle from his horse and hung it up before he followed his younger sister.

Richard walked across the interior of the small yard towards the high beamed hall. He knew it would be nice and cool inside even as the day heated up. Richard thought of what the old woman had said about his father. Uncle Luke had gone on pilgrimage to the Holy Land with his father William, and Luke had now returned. That meant either the old woman with her herbs was about to be proved very wrong, or very right. A tight feeling gripped his stomach and his head echoed with the cawing of angry crows.

The hall of Keynes was a single storey, single room structure. A hearth smouldered in the centre of its modest space, grey smoke spiralling upwards. Around it were several wooden benches. The hall only had two tables to furnish it, and the cups on them were wooden.

A large man pushed his way over from a crowd of strong and well tanned men who poured drinks from a pottery jug. Adela stood just inside the doorway, as if frozen to the spot. Richard looked at the large man. His shoulders were broad and tall and his eyes stared back at Richard with green eyes that pierced him. Dark hair hung down the man's shoulders, but it was those eyes that made the man. Father Adam said green was the Devil's colour, and these green eyes stopped Richard in his tracks.

'Is there any food in this place at all?' The man asked. Richard swallowed.

'Well, boy, don't you know?'

'The kitchen?' Richard replied.

'Are you asking me or telling me?' The large man's eyes moved on to Adela. 'Who do we have here, a beauty fit only to increase my hunger I think?'

'That's my sister,' Richard said, even though his voice tripped over the words.

'Is my father here?' Adela said quietly.

The man stopped and considered the faces of the two youths before him. 'Boy, your uncle has gone to speak to your mother, you should go to them. I will look after your sister.' The man's grin made Richard twitch. The hearth started to die, soon it would become nothing more than a pile of ash and glowing embers. The pall of light grey smoke that rose up to the rafters began to turn darker. Richard thought the man's eyes gleamed and pulsated the same way the embers did.

'Who are you?' Richard asked him.

'Eustace Martel,' the large man said. The group of men refreshing themselves from his family's heavily watered wine started to drink it. They complained about it. The throng included a number of men in his family's colours, so Richard decided to push his uncertainty of Eustace to the back of his mind. He turned towards the door and his sister. 'Wait here, I won't be long,' he went outside. The family chambers were in a two storey building behind the hall. The ground floor was mostly a store room and a wooden stairway led up to the private rooms. Richard put a foot on the staircase and heard a shout from above. He stopped.

'I will never let you into my bed, let alone give you an heir,' a strong female voice cried. His mother's voice.

'That is the only thing I need from you. Then you can rot in a convent for all I care,' a male voice shouted. It sounded almost like his father's but Richard knew it was Uncle Luke.

'I shall never remarry,' his Mother said. 'This is against the law and the natural way of things.'

'The law of the land is the law of the sword, and I have the sword. This is surely not so much to ask of you.'

'You ask a woman to give over both her body and her children's rights. Those are the only two things that women have in this world,' his mother shouted.

Richard stepped slowly up the stairs. Luckily he knew exactly where they creaked.

'I care not for your rights, the church teaches us that woman are the stem of sin, so why should I care for your rights?' Luke said.

His head level with the first floor's floorboards, Richard craned his neck to see through the doorway.

'They are your kin and Richard is the rightful heir to Keynes. This manor is now his, by all laws and customs. For what you desire, he would have to be dead,' his mother said. Those words rang in Richard's ears. He could see his mother's back but Luke stood out of view behind the wall.

'I am offering you the chance to make sure the future lords of Keynes have your blood,' Luke said. 'Can't you see how generous I am?'

Richard wished he had a sword, but then he'd never had his own.

'You will never have me,' his mother screamed and ran out of sight. The two unseen voices cried out and something wooden thudded onto the floor. The sound of fabric tearing shook Richard into life and he decided he had to help his mother. He took another step just as his mother hurtled back into view. She tripped sideways and fell onto the corner of the wooden bed. A loud crack curdled Richard's blood and stunned him to a stop. The pile of linen and wool that was his mother didn't move at the foot of her bed. Her feet stuck out of her blue dress.

'That was your fault,' Luke shouted, still out of sight. Richard breathed shallow and fast. This couldn't be real. He knew what he'd just seen but how could it be? His world shifted before his eyes. Hair stood up on Richard's neck and he remembered how all the men in the hall had swords around their waists.

His uncle would too. 'I offered you everything,' Luke shouted at the motionless body. 'This was not my fault, you did this to yourself.'

Richard backtracked as fast as he could. He avoided all the creaky stairs and was about to jump onto the beaten earth of the ground floor when the last stair creaked. It had never creaked before. Richard abandoned stealth and fled out of the door and outside into the yard. He heard the stomp of rapid footsteps from the floor above. Richard looked around the courtyard of Keynes on that quiet summer's day, and knew he wouldn't get back to the hall unseen by his uncle. If Luke saw him running he'd know what Richard had seen. Then Richard would die. So Richard stopped running and tried to breath normally. He clenched a fist and concentrated on that, then turned into the doorway and tried to walk back in calmly. Uncle Luke jumped the last two steps and ran head first into Richard. 'Oh Christ,' he said and slammed to a halt.

Uncle Luke's face appeared a hand's breadth away from his nephew's. His face shared the straight family nose. His skin had darkened and his cheeks had sunk since Richard had last seen him. That had been when he had left on pilgrimage to the Holy Land with his father. Luke was of average height, but his body had a sinewy strength to it. His uncle looked a lot like his father, but Luke had been the first to carve Richard a real looking wooden sword when he'd been a young boy. Richard pushed the memory aside for he could sense the presence of a real blade without having to look down. 'Uncle,' he said as flatly as possible.

'Richard? You have grown.'

'Is my father with you?' Richard held his breath but his heart thumped in his chest.

His uncle took a step back. 'I have bad tidings from the east. I'm afraid your father died there.'

'How is my mother?'

'I had expected you to be more surprised?' Luke said.

Richard remembered the ceremony of the old woman in the woods and his ears rang with the clamouring of crows.

'There have been bad omens,' he said. 'But how is my mother?'

'She has taken the news very badly,' Luke walked through the doorway, put an arm on Richard's shoulder and gently pushed him outside.

Richard had an urge to pull his shoulder away, the touch of his uncle stirred up darkness. 'We should go to the chapel and say a prayer together for your father. I think you need to think about what I've told you. Maybe you need time to understand it,' Luke said. He walked Richard towards a small wooden building on the far side of the yard. Around the stables, Luke and Eustace's men still tended to the horses and continued to unpack their baggage.

'Keynes is not much, is it?' Luke looked around the basic fortifications.

Richard glanced at his uncle's hand that rested on his shoulder but something inside him told him he had to control himself. 'But it is home,' Richard said. It had never been home for Luke, who was a second son. His father had told him that second sons should go into the church.

Luke, who had not gone down that path, sighed and removed his hand. 'It will be better than sitting at another man's hearth any longer,' he said.

'You are coming to live with us?' Richard asked, aware that Luke's face grew red through his tanned skin. Luke had never spent much time with them at Keynes, he'd preferred to stay at his elderly father's larger manor. While that was far better than toiling in the fields, such a nobly born man living at another's hearth would hear whispers behind his back.

'I live here now,' Luke said as they reached the small timber chapel. 'It is a time of change.'

The chapel had only ever just been big enough to fit the family in to pray in together. It was lit via a single beam of sunlight which streamed in through the only small window. The hair stood up on Richard's neck again as they crossed the threshold. He shivered, and once the door closed behind them he could no longer hear the outside world. He said a silent prayer to the family's single piece of silverware, a mildly ornate candlestick, then turned to his uncle. 'Is he really gone?'

'Yes, my boy. I truly am very sorry,' Luke said.

'What happened?' Richard asked, reminded of the question rolled up in parchment on his horse's mane. He felt tears build up in his eyes.

Luke looked at him for a moment. 'He died a martyr's death in service to God.'

Richard tried to sniff back the tears. 'But how?'

'His time came,' Luke said.

'But how did he die?'

'He fought a rearguard to allow the rest of us to escape a trap. It was a good death and it is now done. Let us say a prayer for him.'

Richard's stomach turned. His instinct said that the question on his parchment was not yet answered. Richard concentrated on keeping his breathing steady. He turned to the simple altar, put his hands together and closed his eyes. Richard said a silent prayer, but not for his father. He asked the Lord, and any other spirits who may be there, to deliver him from his uncle and to allow him to rescue Adela.

'You have taken this news calmly,' Luke watched his nephew in silent prayer. 'It is fitting that your father died so well, it should give you comfort.'

'It matters little how he died, uncle, it matters that we are now without him,' Richard said. His eyes opened again. 'I will arrange for prayers to be said for him.' Those words were the right ones for a son to say, but Richard's voice wavered and cracked all the same.

Luke sighed and his eyes fell away. 'That will not be your responsibility, my boy, and you should be thankful of it.'

Richard stood still for a moment. He felt the same rush in his stomach that invariably appeared when a boar turned to face him out hunting. Danger faced him now. Hunter circled prey inside the chapel, and he was the prey. The thought of it made him want to curl up in the corner and cry. That thought needed to be pushed aside. Richard knew hunting, and he knew that the prey could turn around and become the hunter when cornered. Richard was the unarmed prey in the corner and he knew it. He could cry and accept whatever his uncle planned for him, or turn and face the hunter.

Richard's palms sweated. 'So you would be lord here?' he asked, his tone steadier than he'd expected.

His uncle looked back at him and said nothing. The only thing that moved in the chapel were the specks of dust that drifted down through the beam of light from the window.

Richard swallowed. He knew he was still a boy, but had David not slain Goliath? 'How is my mother?' he turned to look Luke in the eyes.

His uncle swallowed and took a deep breath. 'She did not react well, her heart burst.'

In the dim light, Richard noticed how pale his uncle's skin looked around his eyes. The colours on his face were all wrong. Everything was wrong. Luke continued to speak but Richard didn't hear the words. He knew what they were though, they were the thread of his life unravelling. He felt the wetness of a tear leave his own eye and knew it fell for his mother. Everything had changed and everything was gone. Maybe there would be no more happy hunting trips with his sister. Richard nodded because the time had come for the prey in the corner to chose to submit or fight. He turned towards the wooden bench that acted as the altar.

'Are you well?' Luke asked.

'You mean to be lord here,' Richard said. He exhaled and felt red anger pulsate through his veins. His mind stilled and he pictured the first question he'd scrawled onto the parchment.

'It is a thing,' Luke began, but Richard moved fast. He grabbed the family's silver candlestick and spun round. Before his uncle could finish Richard swung the silverware at his head. Luke didn't comprehend and the candlestick flashed through the blade of light from the window. The silverware cracked into the side of his uncle's head and he crumpled to the floor.

Richard stood over him, the candlestick tainted by a smudge of blood. No sound came from anywhere except Richard's lungs.

He looked down at his uncle and saw that his chest moved up and down. He went to return the candlestick so it could stand ready for the next mass, but stopped himself. The last mass for his family had already been said. Richard wiped the blood off his holy weapon onto Luke's own tunic then tucked the silverware under his clothing.

He paused for a moment with his hand on the door handle, then walked out of the dark room and back into the daylight. He squinted at the glare of the sun and felt the warmth of it wash over his face. Richard looked over to the stables where his horse stood saddled and ready, then back to the hall and Adela. The men who tended to Luke and Eustace's horses went about their business slowly and quietly, and the gate out into the village sat wide open. The hall or the stables then, that was his next choice.

Richard tightened his grip on the candlestick hidden in his tunic, and nodded. He marched off towards the hall and Adela. He had let his mother die so he had to save his sister. Richard got half way across the yard before the tall and bulky silhouette of Eustace Martel appeared in the doorway of the hall. A bundle hung over his shoulder. Eustace strode off and around the hall towards the family chambers and Richard saw that the bundle was Adela. She hung limply, her long hair nearly down to the earth. A few of Eustace's men followed him out. They shouted and laughed. Richard stopped still, there were five of them. That meant six swords. And he had only a candlestick.

No one looked in his direction as they all made their way out of sight. Richard knew a desperate boar could kill a single hunter, but rarely would it survive two or more. 'I'm so sorry Adela,' he whispered and turned towards the stables. His stomach knotted up. Richard walked past the two dozen horses of the visitors and into the building that held his horse. The stallion whinnied when he heard him and his head popped up from behind his stable door with a mouthful of straw.

'Come on Solis, I need your help now,' Richard eased open the door.

Solis snorted and watched him pick up his bridle. The horse lowered his head to help Richard put it on. He wrapped the candlestick up in a linen blanket and tied it to the back of his white and blue saddle. Richard took Adela's bow and bundle of arrows and tied the arrows on top of the candlestick. He held the bow as he led Solis from the stable, put his foot in the stirrup, and hoisted himself up.

One of Luke's men walked past and Richard stopped, his heart loud in his chest. The man nodded at him and continued on his way. Richard exhaled so hard he thought the whole world would hear. He asked Solis for a walk and rode away from the stables towards the gateway. As he reached it he glanced back. The chapel door swung open. That was bad, it would be better if Luke was dead. Without waiting to watch a presumably furious Luke emerge from it, he urged Solis into a canter. The palomino launched into his stride and a cloud of dust followed his heavy hoof beats out of the gateway. Richard didn't hear if there were cries or shouts behind him, he just rode away. Away from his home, his family and his old life.

FUGITIVE

Richard flew down the village road as fast as Solis's hooves could take him. He rode by the ditch and its repair party, disappeared into the woods and kept going. Solis cantered for as long as Richard wanted although he dropped his head to snort. Richard could ride to a monastery and become a monk, or get help, but that choice never entered his mind. Richard had only one family member he could go to, and that was his elderly grandfather Sir Hugh. Sir Hugh was the head of the family and away in London on legal business. Richard rode south because he knew the city was that way. Soon the sun reached its peak. He rode as fast as he could through villages and uncultivated areas of wasteland.

Eventually he asked Solis to walk and the stallion happily slowed down. The horse sweated and his nostrils flared. Richard could feel his lungs try to catch up underneath him. He gave the horse respite for as long as he dared, then pushed him into a canter again despite the oppressive midday sun. After some more hard riding, Richard saw the stony shape of Berkhamsted Castle emerge from the trees ahead. A river ran alongside the road so he stopped Solis and let him have a long drink. Richard's heart still thumped and his mouth tasted dry. He remembered his father had always stressed to him the importance of looking after your horse instead of riding it into the ground, so he allowed Solis to graze on the grassland by the river for a while. Some ducks drifted down the waterway, and away on the far side a shepherd slowly moved his flock. A cart pulled by a lumbering ox trundled towards him from the direction of the castle. The man driving it went on his way without even a glance, so Richard took the chance to drink from the river himself. He gulped the fresh water and as it ran down his face it cleaned away a layer of dust. Richard watched as the water flowed by, distracted as it glittered in the sunlight. The thought occurred to him that London was further away than he could possibly manage that day. All he could do about that would be to look out for a remote piece of woodland to hide in when the sun started to set.

Richard remounted Solis and followed the road around the castle, beyond which he knew lay the town of Hempstead. The town, he thought, offered an opportunity to steal himself some food. Solis stopped walking and his ears shot up. The horse turned his head around to look behind and Richard followed his gaze. The cart from earlier trundled away in the distance, but behind it were figures that moved at speed. Horsemen, and they were coming his way.

'Sorry, Soli,' Richard spurred the stallion on. They reached a full gallop in four strides. The track beneath them reverberated so hard as the hooves crashed into it that it sounded like a drumbeat. They rode into a wooded area, pressed through it quickly, then out onto open ground. Richard crested a small hill and before him the town spread out along the river. Solis dropped out of a gallop, so overworked that white foam congealed on his yellow coat. Richard could smell him, a smell that reminded him of better times.

Richard descended the hill into the town. Hempstead was big enough to get lost in, and Solis barely managed a laboured trot as they entered its main street. Richard looked back and could see his pursuers crest the hill. They moved a lot quicker than he had, too. Richard dismounted at a two-storey stone building that looked like a guest house and tied Solis to a wooden railing outside it. The group of pursuers entered the outskirts, so Richard ducked into the nearest large side street and started to run. Carts headed to and from its central square and Richard nearly tripped to avoid some oncoming traffic. A man shouted at him to get out of his way. Richard darted into an alleyway, pressed himself against a wall, and tried to catch his breath. He heard the background noise of the town around him, the rumble of carts and loud voices. Further away geese honked and dogs barked.

As Richard's breath settled that background noise didn't change. No one ran into the alley and no pursuers rode past it. He wished he'd thought of taking the bow or even the candlestick with him, his hands felt empty.

Richard edged towards the main street and looked around. Someone in the house opposite threw a bucket of grey liquid into the street which splashed his leather shoes. It make his nose wrinkle. He heard footsteps behind him and turned to see a man walk towards him. He wore a red and yellow tunic. Richard swore and ran out into the main street. A horseman ambled down it towards him, a horseman who also wore a tunic of the Martel family. Caught between them, Richard turned and threw himself at the pursuer in the alley. The man was young, although still older than Richard, but he was surprised by the sudden attack. Richard's fists connected with something and the youth staggered sideways. Richard grabbed his head and slammed it into the mud wall. The boy's nose exploded and a stain of blood smeared onto the wall. The horseman reached the alley, which was too narrow for him to ride into, so he jumped off his horse.

Richard leapt over the fallen youth and ran away. He shot out of the alley and nearly slipped over as he cornered. Another man with a yellow and red tunic ran towards him from another direction. Richard felt a surge of energy as he realised he still had to escape two assailants. He raced along the street and took a turn at a junction. Richard sprinted past a yard where children enjoyed a cockfight, and almost ran into a horse being ridden by a startled woman.

Richard saw a group of men stood drinking in the street ahead and bumped his way through them as they cursed him. He kept running but looked back to see one of his pursuers run into the same crowd. One of the Martel men knocked a tall drinker to the ground. His blonde hair sunk into the mud and came up brown.

Richard ran. His chest heaved and sweat streamed down his face and back. He rounded a corner into an alleyway and skidded to a halt.

It was not an alleyway.

A wall stood across it so he turned to get out. The two men with yellow and red tunics appeared at the entrance together and halted.

Trapped.

All three of them stood still for a moment, chests trying to recover air. The taller of the two assailants smiled and drew a knife from its leather scabbard. The length and sharpness of the blade caught Richard's eye. He looked back but the wall behind him was still a wall. The second man started to draw his sword.

From the main street another man appeared. A tall, burly man with blonde hair covered in mud. He smashed a pottery drinking cup into the knife-wielding man's head. The man fell to one side and his friend twirled around in surprise. The blonde man pushed him towards Richard and his half-drawn sword fell from his grip and thudded onto the dried mud. Richard caught the man as he stumbled into him and pushed him away. The assailant tripped and fell to the ground at the feet of the blonde man.

'Pick up the sword, boy,' the blonde stranger said.

Richard scrambled to get his hand around the hilt of the sword on the ground. The other pursuer staggered to his feet and reached to retrieve his knife.

The blonde man drew his own knife and in a flash he buried it into the neck of the man at his feet. The Martel man screamed out his last breath before his lungs started to fill with blood.

The other man pointed his knife at Richard and lunged.

Richard raised the sword and slashed. Richard was clumsy and both of them missed.

The blonde man straightened up and laughed. 'Ever cut a man before, boy?'

The knifeman lunged again.

Richard jumped back and the knife cut only air. His body and arm reacted by themselves and he swatted down with his blade. The sword dug into his opponent's arm and he dropped the knife with a howl.

The blonde man pulled his red knife out of his victim whose mouth gurgled. Life lingered in him as he drowned. 'This one is mine,' the blonde man plunged the knife down into his victim's neck again. 'That one is yours.'

Richard's opponent howled and looked at him with wide eyes.

'Go on, boy,' the blonde man said. 'Something tells me he deserves it.'

Richard swallowed. 'I'll let him go,' he said.

'Does he have friends?' the blonde man asked.

'Yes,' Richard said.

'Then he's still yours.'

The assailant yelped and made to run past the blonde man, who grabbed him by his wounded arm and threw him right back in front of Richard.

A local man appeared from the street and poked his head into the alleyway. His startled face considered the corpse and growing pool of blood.

'Quickly, now,' the blonde man said as the shocked townsman ran off.

'I beg you,' the injured pursuer raised his bloodied arm, 'let me live.'

Richard felt a heat grow inside and he thought about his mother and sister.

'If he lives, we die,' the blonde man shrugged.

Richard's eyes darkened and he raised the sword. He cut down and the sword buried itself in the wounded man's head. His expression froze as his skull opened. Richard withdrew the blade with a great tug and the body crumpled.

The blonde man chuckled. 'Truth be told, I was not sure you would do that.'

Richard looked down at the two dead men and felt an urge to throw up.

'No time for that, boy. Take his scabbard and let us be gone.'

Shouts and cries started to rise up around the town and dogs started to bark.

'The Hue and Cry,' Richard said.

'We better be quick then, lad.'

Richard unlaced the sword belt from its former owner and followed the blonde man out of the dead-end alley.

'Come on,' urged the blonde man.

They both ran from road to road as Richard's heart pounded in his ear. Calls and yells rang out behind and around them. Richard followed his companion down a side street and through a house doorway.

The blonde man shut it behind them. He leant against the inside of the door and slid down it until he sat on the floor. He coughed loudly and took a deep breath. 'I have not run like that for a long time. I almost enjoyed it,' he grinned.

Richard looked at him and recovered his breath. 'Who are you?'

'That would depend very much on who you are, my young lord.'

Richard took a deep breath. Outside he heard a rush of feet and voices but it passed by. He let the breath out. 'I am Richard of Keynes.'

'Am I supposed to know who that is?' The blonde man smiled.

Richard blushed. 'Do you know of Keynes?'

'No, otherwise I would know who you are, wouldn't I,' the blonde man pulled himself back to his feet. 'I don't actually care who you are, but I am curious as to why men in those colours were chasing you.'

'They wanted to kill me.'

'I noticed that. Why?'

Richard looked around but the building they were in contained nothing but pigs. Two of them slept in a corner on a bed of straw spread out across the floor. It was mostly brown and wet and the smell started to reach into Richard's nostrils. He sighed. 'They killed my mother and have taken my manor.'

'Aren't you are a bit young for a manor?'

'It was only mine from today. The men in yellow and red brought word of my father's death in the Holy Land.'

'A lord for a day,' the blonde man chuckled and wiped some mud from his hair.

'Why did you help me?' Richard asked.

'They spilt my beer.'

'Seems to be a slight cause for a murder,' Richard said.

The blonde man laughed again. 'True, but I know those yellow and red colours and I have little love for them. Tell me boy, which Martel has taken over Keynes?'

'It was Eustace Martel. He came with my uncle Luke, and it is he who stole my manor and killed my mother.'

'Eustace,' the blonde man spat on the straw.

Richard's legs felt weak and empty so he sat himself down on the straw with his back against a wall. He put his head in his hands and closed his eyes. 'I don't even know if my sister is alive or not.'

'Does Eustace have your sister?'

Richard looked up at him. 'Yes.'

The blonde man grimaced. 'That is a shame, for sure. I am very sorry, young lord,' he said.

'Will he kill her?'

'No, boy, he will not. But what he will do may be worse than death. May God save her soul.' The blonde man made the sign of the cross.

Richard felt a knot tie itself in his stomach. 'How do you know that?'

'Experience, boy. He is a monster, but a god-fearing one all the same. He thinks it wrong to kill a woman. There is little you can do unless you have an army or the king's favour behind you.'

'Then I need an army,' Richard said.

The blonde man laughed. 'Start praying then, young lord. It appears to me though, that survival is your concern today. If you ask me, you should seek family.'

'I'm not asking you,' Richard said, then regretted his tone. 'You never answered who you are though, did you?'

The blonde man smiled. 'My friends call be Bowman, and now that we have killed together, we are friends.'

'We are not together,' Richard said.

'If that mob out there calling the Hue and Cry finds us, we'll be hung together,' Bowman said.

'Then we need to leave the town,' Richard said. He'd heard the Hue and Cry once before, at home when a visiting singer had been caught stealing in the village. The cry had gone up and the singer had been chased from house to house until cornered. His father had told him that by the time he'd arrived, the singer had been almost cut in two by furious villagers wielding knives and farm tools.

'I have nothing but what I am wearing to my name, young lord, I certainly have no horse with which to escape on,' Bowman said.

'I can get you a horse,' Richard smiled.

The blonde man raised his eyebrows and brushed down his green tunic with his hands. 'Can you now.'

'I can. Can we trust those men you were drinking with?'

'As long as we don't need them to do an honest day's work,' Bowman grinned. 'If they have not already taken up the Hue and Cry, that is.'

Richard smiled. 'Then let's get you a horse.'

Richard and Bowman peered around the corner of the building next to the guest house where Solis had been tied up. The horse still stood there but had been joined by four of the five horses of Eustace's men. Two of those men were still there on guard, their hands rested on the pommels of the swords that hung from their waists. The building lay at the edge of town and although the noise of the Hue and Cry could be heard, it wasn't close enough for anyone to make it out. 'I hate horses,' Bowman said under his breath.

'How can you hate horses?'

'You can't reason with them,' Bowman said, 'and I hate falling off them.'

Richard suppressed a laugh. 'That's not reason to hate them though.'

Bowman opened his mouth to answer but his drinking companions walked down the road into view.

'Call the Hue and Cry, there's been murder,' one of them shouted towards the guest house.

The two guards in their yellow and red tunics came together and exchanged words. The group approached them. They spoke to the guards and pointed towards the centre of town.

The guards protested. They argued louder and rapid gestures flew. The two guards conferred again before then their shoulders slumped. They joined the rear of the small mob and were taken away along with it back through the town.

'The Lord above smiles on you today, my young lord,' Bowman said as the street became quiet.

'He didn't at the start of it,' Richard started to walk towards the now unguarded horses.

'Hurry up,' Bowman started to jog.

'Don't run up to horses,' Richard said, 'no wonder you hate them. I think they just hate you.'

Bowman slowed down and scowled. 'Just hurry, they could be back at any moment.'

Richard ignored him and walked over to Solis and stroked him on the neck. The horse still dripped with sweat.

Bowman went to the nearest Martel horse and unbuckled its leather breastplate, a strap that was attached to the saddle on both sides and went around the horse's chest. It had some small metal decorative fixings studded along the leather, and he collected two more from other horses. Then he ran back to the alley and threw them into it.

'I hope they find those,' Richard said.

'Oh, they will,' Bowman said on his return, 'those are very good payment for very little work.'

'It's not really work, though,' Richard untied two of the Martel horses.

'It is for us, and what do you know of work anyway, young lord?' Bowman asked.

Richard frowned but just for a moment.

Bowman untied a horse and heaved himself up into its saddle.

Richard watched him fumble around with the stirrups which were too short for him. 'I thought we were in a rush?' he said.

'The Devil take you,' Bowman managed to re-buckle the second stirrup.

'If we take these horses, those two men will take longer to follow us. Can you lead one of them while you ride, or do I have to lead all three?' Richard asked.

'You are very demanding for such a young lad,' Bowman said, 'I can take one, don't you worry.'

Richard handed him the reins of one of the Martel horses, and Bowman took them in his free right hand.

Richard mounted Solis. The stallion put his ears back and went to kick at the Martel horses.

'Soli, no,' Richard shouted.

Solis stopped and snorted loudly but his ears stayed pinned back. Richard gathered his reins and they went to leave, stolen horses in tow.

'The road to London is through the town, so we will need to go north for a way to go around it,' Bowman said.

'Good idea,' Richard turned back to ride up the hill he'd entered the town over earlier.

They trotted up the hill, beyond it, and only then relaxed into a walk. After a while they turned east and skirted around the town, all the while in silence as their ears searched the distance for the sound of hooves.

They walked quietly until the sun started to dip and stopped only occasionally to allow the horses to drink or graze for a moment. Richard felt his heartbeat slow to near normal, but constantly turning around to look for pursuers had made his head ache. His stomach rumbled, too. He looked at the bundles of wool tied to the horses. 'I think we have enough blankets to spend a night outside tonight,' he said. Bowman looked around at the vegetation, a mix of grass and scattered trees. 'We do, should be some hobbles here for the horses too. Although I still do not trust a horse in hobbles to be nearby when we wake.'

Richard laughed. 'They will. Soli won't go far and I'm sure he'll keep the others in order.'

'We can ride until dusk,' Bowman said, 'we should put as much distance between us and them as we can.'

'Those Martel men won't get far on foot,' Richard said.

'No, but if we can steal horses, so can they.' Bowman said.

Richard sniffed. 'Shame we haven't got any food,' he said.

Bowman looked at Solis's saddle, from which hung Adela's bow. 'Got any arrows for that?' he asked.

'A dozen.'

Bowman smiled. 'Tonight boy, you hobble the horses, and I'll deal with your hunger.'

SMITHFIELDS

Before morning broke, Richard and Bowman breakfasted on the remains of the rabbits the blonde man had managed to shoot the previous night. The horses were gathered up with ease as they hadn't gone far, and their saddles buckled on. Their sweat had dried on in matted messes and their coats were uneven and caked in dried dirt. 'Have you ever been to London?' Bowman asked once they were on their way again, leading their Martel horses southwards.

'No.'

'There is a market at Smithfields, a field outside the walls,' Bowman said, 'it will be busy as they say the horse fair is on for the next few days. We can lighten ourselves of these extra beasts and make a pretty penny from it.'

Richard thought about it. 'I would like to keep a spare horse but I suppose I will need the money. We can sell them if we get a good price.' The sun hovered half way to its peak, the morning crisp but pleasant. Richard could smell that it would be a calm and warm afternoon. 'How do you know London so well?'

'I know everywhere, young lord. I have spent nearly twenty summers travelling this country,' Bowman said.

'What exactly do you do? You aren't a farmer and you are no carpenter or merchant.'

Bowman laughed. 'My trade recently has been to avoid notice. At least until the Martels reappeared and spilt my beer.'

'What did they do to you?'

'Spilt my beer.'

'Before that, you know what I mean,' Richard said.

'For now, be satisfied that you and I have a common grudge.'

'Fine then, once we've sold the horses, I will buy you another beer in London,' Richard said.

Bowman smiled and looked over at the scrubland they rode through.

They rested for a while as the sun hung at its height in the blue sky. The horses were all still hungry and pulled up grass as if they were starved. Richard dared not rest long enough to let them recover fully, so soon they were on their way again. As the afternoon went by the track became wider until the ruts from carts became entrenched. Other traffic going to and from London started to become more common. Eventually they joined an old Roman road and their pace could quicken as the road became stone. When the sun started to wane, Bowman suggested that they spend another night for free before they reached the city, seeing as they had missed the market that day anyway.

Richard spent the evening cleaning the sweat off the horses and attempted to smarten them up for sale the next day. The ritual of wetting them, wiping the sweat off and rinsing them allowed him to forget the things he wanted to forget.

Bowman watched him clean the horses two or three times more than he needed to, but just set himself down under a tree, closed his eyes and went to sleep.

The following day was cloudier, but the horse's coats shinned, and they walked with higher steps and brighter eyes. Richard felt excitement at going to a horse market. He'd heard about them from his father and travellers, but had never been. They rode towards Smithfields and saw buildings in the distance with fenced pastures protected by well maintained ditches. The pastures were full of breeding herds of horses, and Richard had never seen so many equines in once place in his life. 'That's a royal stud,' Bowman said, 'those horses will not be at the market.'

'Good, our horses are not as good as they are,' Richard said.

They entered the outskirts of Smithfields. Traffic bustled, herds of horses came in and out, and carts heaped with produce rolled in every direction. Groups of riders made their way to and from the city, and Richard heard the distant hum of urban life. The road became a newly cobbled street lined with buildings, and those buildings became larger and more numerous.

'Here we are,' Bowman said as the street opened out into a smooth field. It was huge, the boundary almost as far as the eye could see.

Richard decided it would take two whole minutes to gallop across it.

'Horses are over there,' Bowman pointed to one end. He moved his gesture to another corner. 'Swine over there.'

Richard nodded.

'And cows and oxen over there,' Bowman pointed to the far end of the field. The market teemed with livestock and all their calls and noises. Every time a horse went by Solis pinned his ears back at it. Richard watched him sniff the air. 'There are mares in season here,' he said.

'Of course there are, everything is here,' Bowman said. A herd of mares with foals were shepherded by, the foals ran loose but never strayed from their mothers. Solis shouted at the mares, his neck arched and his legs started to lift higher than normal. Richard had to jab him in the ribs to snap him out of it, but once the mares and foals were gone Solis calmed down. 'I think we need to get this done quickly,' Richard said.

'Your stallion is not so well behaved as you thought, young lord?' Bowman smiled.

'He's just a stallion, he is in hand,' Richard replied.

They rode over to the part of the field where horses were being traded. There was no order to it, herds or single horses were brought onto any area of the field, and sellers wandered between them, making offers where they saw fit. Richard and Bowman stopped in a space and waited.

Horses milled around, sometimes they kicked out. Some shouted at separated friends who had just been sold, and mares and stallions called to each other incessantly from one end of the huge field to another. In the distance a stallion broke lose, lunged at some horses with its teeth bared, and before long the nearest mare was newly pregnant.

'I hate horses,' muttered Bowman.

'You can't complain, your stallion is quiet,' Richard said.

Bowman looked at his horse. 'It hasn't tried to kill me yet, I'll grant you that,' he said.

'Why can't you tell me why you hate horses?' Richard asked

Bowman sighed. 'Many years ago there was a dispute over my horse. Someone stole it from me so I took it back. They chased me around a town but I was well hidden behind a cart full of logs. They would never have found me had my horse not decided to pull one of the logs from the cart. It spooked at the log as it fell, even though the dammed horse had been the cause of it himself. His hooves clattered on the cobbles, which the whole town heard seeing as it was the dead of night.'

'So they took the horse from you?' Richard asked.

'They took a lot more than that,' Bowman frowned.

A group of men appeared and inspected the Martel horses. The men were well dressed in rich tunics of mustard yellow, blue and red. Each and every one of them had full cloaks lined with furs around their shoulders. The head of the group motioned to the Martel horses and a spokesperson came forward and started to negotiate with Bowman.

Richard thought about getting involved but left Bowman to it. A flurry of bids flew back and forth, and before he knew it the three Martel horses were gone.

Bowman held a bag of coins.

'Did we get a good deal?' Richard asked.

'Not really, but it was fairly clear the horses were stolen,' Bowman smiled, 'but now we have coin.'

'We can go at least,' Richard said as Solis snaked his neck at a horse that walked by.

'Where to? Where is this grandfather you are looking for?' Bowman asked.

'God only knows,' Richard said, 'wherever the lawyers live, probably.'

'I know where that is.'

'Of course you do,' Richard turned to follow Bowman as he rode towards the ancient walls of London.

On they travelled to the city. They had to avoid carts that had lost wheels, and groups of travellers who gathered inconsiderately outside Saint Bartholemew's Hospital and its priory. They rode up to the stone walls of London, which Richard knew were Roman. Parties of builders worked with blocks of stone to make them taller, rubble strewn from their activities lay all around.

'This is the Aldersgate,' Bowman said of the gateway as they entered the city.

Richard looked up at the high stone arch and felt a nervous excitement.

London was busy, loud and smelt of fish. Over that there were wafts of stale water and human waste. Richard felt glad to have Solis between him and the ground, and looked warily at everyone who moved along the roads as his excitement waned. People entered and left houses and shouted at each other. Street vendors sold food, from buttered peas to hot pies. Richard examined some hot sheep's feet with caution.

'I'm not having those, I hate sheep,' Bowman said. He found a seller of pies more to his liking.

'Father never let us eat from street sellers,' Richard's mouth watered and he took a warm pastry pie and ate it.

Deeper into the city, Richard saw a square with a pit dug into it where a bear tethered to a stake faced snarling dogs to the cheers of a crowd.

Church spires seemed to rise above the rooftops in every direction, but soon enough Bowman brought his horse to a stop and Richard stopped sightseeing.

'If you want lawyers, this is where you want to be,' Bowman said. They rode down the street Bowman pointed at.

Richard looked at some buildings and the brightly coloured banners that hung from some of them. They were limp and crumpled in the still air, but he could make out a white one with a horizontal blue line across the centre of it.

'I thought it would be harder than that,' Richard said, 'that's him just there.'

'I best stay outside with the horses, you can do what you need to do, young lord.' Bowman said.

'That's fine with me,' Richard dismounted. He patted Solis on the rump on his way past and knocked on the wooden door of the building. A good time later the door opened and a grey haired woman peered out.

'Lord Richard?' Her prematurely wrinkled face shifted from a frown to a smile. 'What are you doing here? Come in, come in.'

He entered the house that sat over two floors, the lower of which was a hall with some extra rooms attached to the back of it.

'I am so sorry to hear about your father, may God keep his soul,' she said.

'Thank you, Edith, where is Sir Hugh?'

'He can no longer take the stairs, follow me,' Edith shuffled through the hall where its large hearth fire crackled away. Beams lined the tall ceiling, partly obscured by the pall of smoke that hung there waiting to fade away.

Richard walked through the hall and into a small chamber at the end.

Edith shut the door behind him and left Richard alone with his grandfather.

Sir Hugh lay in bed under a grey woollen blanket with his head propped up on a straw filled linen bag. His hair was long and white, and his face looked like his father's had, but with deeper lines.

'My boy,' the old man said softly, 'praise be to God for sending you to me.'

'Grandfather,' Richard bowed his head.

'I am afraid you will have to be louder, my boy. My ears are not as good as they used to be,' Hugh said.

'Grandfather,' Richard shouted so loudly that the nearby candles flickered.

'Not that loud, boy, I am yet alive,' his grandfather winced. He coughed. 'What brings you all the way to London? How is your mother?'

'Uncle Luke and Eustace Martel came to the house,' Richard said, picking his words carefully.

'Ah yes, they were here just the other day,' Hugh said. His expression hardened.

'What did they tell you?' Richard asked.

Hugh frowned. 'That my firstborn son is dead, may God have mercy on his soul.'

Richard made the sign of the cross. 'Did they tell you how he died?'

'Did they not tell you?' Hugh asked.

Richard paused. 'No.'

'They mollycoddle you, boy. You deserve to know, especially if you are to be the lord of Keynes now.'

'Yes grandfather.'

'It seems that my son went to he Holy Land and got himself indebted to some southern French lord. He then died of some ghastly foreign disease. Luke asked me for a large amount of money to clear the debt and the family name.'

'Did he?' Richard's eyes narrowed, 'did you give him the money?'

Hugh laughed although it turned into a cough. 'Of course not, boy. Why do you think I am here trying to have my case put to the royal court?

'Because you have no money?'

'Precisely. I sent Luke away with nothing. Luke is a second son still, and the family money is really yours. You will be the head of the family soon, my time is nearly over.'

'Don't say that,' Richard said.

'I have found that being alive is rated too highly,' Hugh coughed a few times.

'What disease did uncle Luke say my father died from?'

'He did not tell me, he was rather more interested in squeezing money out of me. Luke always was jealous of his older brother, but usually in a healthy way. It was that fear of inferiority that drove him to learn the ways of the sword. I prayed every day for twenty years that he would go and find his own lands somewhere.'

Richard sighed and crossed his arms. 'I have something to tell you about uncle Luke and my mother.'

'Speak up, boy. What?'

'Luke and Eustace Martel came to Keynes, but they killed my mother and have carried away Adela.'

Sir Hugh's faced remained perfectly still apart from his pupils, which widened. Richard thought his skin paled but it was already almost white so he couldn't be sure.

The old man took a sharp breath and grabbed his chest.

Richard rushed to him.

Sir Hugh gasped for air and Richard wondered if he was

about to lose another relative. A while later his grandfather recovered himself.

'They sent men to kill me, grandfather, I barely made it here,' Richard said once the old man's eyes were bright again. Those eyes bored into Richard's and he felt an urge to turn away.

'My boy, this is very serious,' Hugh said faintly.

'What do we do about it?' Richard asked.

'You seem to be managing well enough, you are still breathing after all,' Hugh said.

Richard raised his eyebrows. 'What else is there to do other than escape and come here for help?'

'A little more mourning might be expected,' Hugh said, 'but if you are alive then the family is still intact. If that hearth son of mine wishes to run the manor, then there is little you can do about it until you are a full man. He told me that all of your father's men remained in the Holy Land, so you are but a lonely boy.' Hugh coughed badly. 'That manor was your father's and it shall be yours. However, my land is no richer than Keynes and I have no men to help correct matters. I will start legal matters against Luke, but you must stay alive in the meantime.'

'How long will that take?'

'Two, maybe three years,' Hugh said, 'if I live long enough to see it through.'

'Two years?' Richard said. He kicked out at nothing in particular.

'Be patient, boy. If what you say is true you must stay away from your uncle. The royal court will rule in our favour, but you have to be alive to return to Keynes.'

'Can you do nothing to help my sister? Or me? Where am I supposed to go?'

'Patience, young man. There is nothing to be done for young Adela, what would you have me do? Mount my warhorse and charge into Keynes brandishing my walking stick?'

'I would go with you,' Richard said.

'And who with us? A dozen of my men who have not fought a battle in fifteen years, against the crusading knights with Luke and his rude friend?' Hugh pushed himself up so he could sit upright.

'I can't just abandon Adela,' Richard said.

'You abandoned her when you rode here,' Hugh said. The old man shook his head. 'But it is better to be alive to avenge her than to be killed trying in vain to save her.'

'She might not be dead yet, we have to do something,' Richard said.

'What you can do is pour me some wine,' Hugh said.

Richard walked over to a wooden table and poured wine from a jug into an undecorated pottery cup. He passed it to his grandfather. 'What would you have me do then, where can I go?'

'I have heard that the Chamberlain of Normandy is seeking to expand his retinue of knights again. He, that is Lord Tancarville, is known as the father of knights because he also keeps a company of aspiring boys whom he turns into knights. He fixes golden spurs onto the best of them. He will give you bed, board, and a place to grow strong. I will use the law to regain Keynes. Only then will you be able to act.'

'Normandy? I've never been to London before today, let alone across the sea.'

'My dear boy, respect in this world is not gained by the timid, no matter what the priests say. Learn how the world works and find a place in it. If you want to find a woman worth marrying, you need to be worth marrying yourself. You must learn courtesy and you must become a man.'

A man. Richard thought of the rolled up parchment that hung from Solis's mane and wondered if Normandy was where he should go to answer that question. He sighed. He didn't really have any other options, so Normandy was as good as anywhere. 'How do I get to Normandy then? How do I pay for the voyage?' Richard asked. He shut his eyes and wished his father was back.

'You have no money?' Sir Hugh asked.

'Actually I have some, but is it safe to travel to the coast with it on my own?'

'Of course not,' Hugh said. 'But you can get a letter of credit from the Templars here in London. They will redeem it for you at Dover if you show the brothers there your letter. Then you can buy passage without getting robbed on the road to the coast.'

Richard sat down on the lonely wooden chair in the chamber. 'Is there another way?' he asked.

'Richard, prudence is key a principle for a knight. If you wish ever to be knighted, then you would do well to learn when to retreat. Although you have shown no fear of running away so far.'

Richard leant back in the chair and held back the response that first came into his head. 'Very well, grandfather. I will go to Normandy.'

'You will go to Castle Tancarville and seek to the service of Lord William Tancarville. He knows who I am, that may be enough if he likes you.' Sir Hugh finished the wine in his cup and held it up. When Richard didn't take it, his grandfather shook it.

Richard got up from his chair, retrieved it and placed it back onto the table.

'I should have a letter of introduction written for you to give to Lord Tancarville. Unfortunately Edith does not write, I have no one else here, and you cannot write your own letter of introduction.'

'No, grandfather,' Richard said.

'Pay a Templar clerk to write one, they will do anything for a coin.'

'I will.' The room smelt stuffy.

'I grow tired. Take your leave, my boy. Will you pray for me at Canterbury?'

'Of course, grandfather, but I will return,' Richard went over to the bed. He leant over and embraced the old man, who barely managed to embrace him back.

'May God grant you bravery and luck. Now go,' Hugh said.

Richard nodded back to his grandfather and left him alone. The hall was empty so he walked straight past the hearth that had almost gone out. The acrid smoke caused him to pick up his pace.

Richard stepped back onto the street where Bowman still held both of their horses.

'So?' he asked.

Richard frowned. 'I'm going to Normandy.'

'Normandy? Who would want to go there?' Bowman asked.

'You can keep that horse and half the money, and I'll be on my way. Thank you for your help, you don't have to go anywhere,' Richard said.

Bowman looked at him. 'Do you even know the way to Normandy?'

'My grandfather said to ride to Dover,' Richard took Solis's reins from his companion.

'Do you know how to get to Dover?' Bowman asked.

'No,' Richard scuffed the ground with the ball of his foot, unable to meet Bowman's gaze.

'Then I will show you, young lord.'

Richard's face lit up. 'But why?'

'Why not? I can't go back to Hempstead anyway, that man saw my face good and clear. Maybe my luck will turn in stinking foreign land.'

'We are to go to the household of William Tancarville, he is recruiting and looking for men who can fight,' Richard said.

'You wish to be a knight?'

'It is the only way. My grandfather will take my case to the courts for me.'

'I see. And until that is settled, you are nobody. Or an outlaw if that man from Hempstead recognised you and told the shire reeve.'

Richard frowned but his companion laughed. Richard ignored him and put his foot in the stirrup to mount Solis.

Bowman nodded to himself. 'It is ironic really, young Lord. But there is always war in the north of France which means there is money to be made and land to be had. Damned this country anyway, nothing good happens here. I shall ride with you.'

'Can we leave the city now, I want to be in the countryside again,' Richard said.

Bowman got on his horse and nodded. 'Very well.'

'We just need to find the Templars here so we can swap our money for a letter of credit,' Richard said.

'Their house is on the Strand,' Bowman frowned, 'but I do not trust them, monks should not wield swords.'

'Their services are known to be reliable, and everyone knows the roads are dangerous. I don't want to be robbed. This much money is more than my manor produces in two years.'

'Your manor? Don't get ahead of yourself, young lord. Fine, we can do as you wish, the money is more yours than mine anyway,' Bowman put a hand on the pouch that held the coins

Richard looked at him. 'We can keep enough to get to Dover, how far is it?'

'Three days ride, so we best move on lest your uncle is clever enough to guess you would come here,' Bowman said.

They walked their horses on and went to find the Templars of London.

PILGRIMS AND PALOMINOS

Crossing the Thames focused Richard on his immediate future rather than his recent troubles. They kept up a decent pace and Richard found that the urge to look back nagged him less and less. Ahead lay the unknown, but as they pressed south and east into Kent, he at least found the countryside to his taste. The tree lined avenues were quiet and he could think. Bowman rode next to him on his black stallion.

'What are you calling him?' Richard asked.

'I do not name horses,' Bowman spat onto the ground.

'Just because of your horse dispute?'

'That didn't help, but the good ones die on you and the bad ones try to kill you.'

Richard patted Solis's neck. 'The good ones will look after you.'

'I do not know which sort this one is yet, young lord,' Bowman said.

'If Soli is tolerating him, then he's probably a good sort,' Richard said.

Bowman snorted.

Richard leant forwards slightly in his saddle as they walked up a hill, Bowman didn't bother. The hills here were bigger than back at home and the land somehow greener. They carried on all day until the sun started to drop and their shadows started to lengthen across the rutted tracks.

'We are nearly at the Medway,' Bowman said as they climbed another wooded hill.

'Is Medway a town?'

'A river. We have to cross it at Rochester but we can spend the night there,' Bowman said.

'Is it safe for us to be in a town?'

'It is, young lord. The Hue and Cry will have broken up once they got bored. The dead men were not local so the townspeople will not care enough for them to chase us around the country.'

'I just mean that if my uncle has more men after us, they will look in the towns,' Richard said.

'If this sir Hugh of yours has any honour and loyalty in him, he will send them the wrong way,' Bowman said.

Richard nodded as Rochester came into view. The castle's large stone tower loomed up on the far side of the river and a tall cathedral spire pierced the sky next to it. The town spread around them along the river, and many palls of smoke rose up into the darkened sky. As they rode closer Richard could smell the burning wood and realised how much he wanted to sleep near a fire. Richard sniffed the air.

'Not a lover of sleeping outdoors, then?' Bowman asked.

'I've slept outdoors on hunts enough times, but always with my family. These past few days haven't been the same.'

'I imagine they have not,' Bowman yawned, 'come on, let us find a nice cosy fire for your delicate young bones.'

Richard scrunched his face up but didn't reply. They rode into town, both yawning now, and the chill of the evening began to seep through their woollen clothing. Bowman found stables for their horses attached to an inn, which boasted a large hall with a long central hearth. The fire crackled, bright and large, and embers drifted up into the roof. Shadows flickered along the walls as travellers rested on whatever space on the floor they could find. After paying a bitter looking man for entry, Richard and Bowman found the last free corner and laid out their blankets. Richard wrapped his sword up in its belt and tucked it between his bed and the wall. He crawled under the blankets, pulled them over himself and rested with his head looking at the fire.

Bowman looked down at him. 'I will get food, you stay here and rest, young lord.'

Richard closed his eyes and when he opened them Bowman was gone. He felt heavy and his back ached. He closed his eyes again and fell asleep.

Richard woke up when Bowman put two bowls of watery stew down next to him. Chunks of carrots and peas bobbed around on the surface of the grey liquid.

'There will be less meat in here than you're accustomed to,' Bowman said.

Richard looked at the food. 'It's just water with some peas floating in it.'

'More for me, then,' Bowman started to eat. After he finished the first bowl, and as the other guests in the hall started to go to sleep, he turned to Richard.

'I did see someone I know outside,' he whispered. He leant in closer. 'Someone who should not really see me, if you know what I mean.'

'Who?' Richard asked.

'That matters not,' Bowman said, 'all these travellers are pilgrims and they will leave at first light. I would prefer if we let them all leave before we do, just to avoid trouble.'

'What did you do to this person?' Richard asked.

'I said it matters not. You said you needed sleep, what's the harm in having a bit more in the morning?'

'Fine,' Richard replied.

Quiet conversations between guests rumbled on in the background. He heard talk of journeys, catching boats, France, Spain and the Holy Land. This was a very different place to home. His stomach rumbled.

'Sure you are going to turn this down?' Bowman said.

Richard pulled the woollen blanket up to his eyes and shut them.

'Suit yourself,' Bowman tucked into the second bowl.

Richard thought about giving in and eating the peasant food, but the next thought he was aware of occurred when he opened his eyes and he saw people get up from their beds. He couldn't see outside but everyone's movements were energetic so it must have been morning.

Bowman snored next to him. The fire had been tended and still flickered, crackled and popped as pilgrims packed up and slowly left the hall. Richard was tired and his limbs didn't feel like they were ready to move quite yet.

Bowman opened his eyes as the last group of guests rolled up their bedding. He yawned.

'Good timing,' he said, sat up and stretched his arms out.

Richard stared into the fire and watched the flames flicker and dance. He thought about Adela and his mother. He wondered what had really happened to his father. He wondered if Sir Hugh would fix everything for him. The more violent flames made him think of the skull he'd cleaved in two, in the alleyway that hadn't been an alleyway. That thought at least banished Richard's hunger.

Bowman got up onto his knees and started to roll up his blankets.

'Do we have to go today?' Richard asked.

'I was all for leaving a little late, young lord, but you cannot stay here forever.'

Richard sighed and pushed his blankets aside. He yawned for what felt like the thousandth time and forced himself to roll away his bed. After a good stretch he followed Bowman out of the hall, still half asleep, as they made their way to the stables. The skies were cloudy and the wind steady.

Bowman looked up. 'Today will not be as good a day as yesterday.'

They rounded a corner and entered the stables. Richard walked past Bowman's black horse but the stable next to it was empty. His white painted saddle wasn't where he'd left it either, and Richard immediately felt a pang of regret that he hadn't brought it into the hall with them. But the loss of the saddle paled in comparison to the empty stable.

'Soli is gone,' he said.

Bowman peered into the stable. He swore.

Richard looked around, but no loose horses wandered about, let alone his palomino stallion.

'God's teeth, his tack is gone,' Bowman looked at where the saddle and bridle had been. 'Someone has taken him.'

Richard looked into the bare stable. 'I can see that.' Tears welled up in his eyes. He felt the emptiness of the stable and looked into each corner as if the horse could be hiding there. Richard sat down on the straw and could smell Solis on it. He could see where the horse had flattened the bedding lying down overnight, too.

'I am so sorry,' Bowman crouched down with Richard.

Richard started to cry. He tried to hold it but there was no use. The tears came faster and faster and he buried his head into his hands. Tears dropped down onto the straw.

Bowman looked around and shifted himself awkwardly. 'Now, young lord, everything will be alright.'

'Will it?' Richard snapped, the words muffled from beneath his arms.

Bowman swore again. 'Christ looks after us,' he said.

Richard started crying harder. 'They're all gone,' he said, 'all of them. Everyone. Soli was the last one I had left.'

Bowman leant down and little by little wrapped his arms around Richard. Bowman gingerly patted his head. 'Take as long as you need, young lord,' he said.

Richard stopped when his tears ran out. He sniffed loudly.

'I might as well go to a monastery now,' he wiped his face with the sleeve of his tunic.

Bowman got up and looked around. 'No need for that,' he said.

Richard blew his nose and put his head back in his hands.

'I thought you had been handling everything too well. I think you needed that,' Bowman said.

Richard took a deep breath and got to his feet. He sniffed. 'We should have left earlier,' he glared at Bowman.

Bowman pursed his lips. 'Aye, we should have. That was my error,' he said.

'What can we do now?' Richard asked.

Bowman looked over to his black horse. It kicked the door of its stable and called out, steamed-breath flew from its nostrils in the morning chill. 'I suppose that is why they did not take him,' he said.

'He has bonded with Soli, he wants to find him,' Richard said.

Bowman half rolled his eyes but Richard didn't see. 'I would wager all our coin that your horse was taken by a pilgrim, and they are all going the same way,' he said.

'To Dover?'

'Exactly, young lord. We still have one horse, and you barely weigh a thing,' Bowman said. He went over to the black stallion who let him into the stable.

Richard brushed the straw off his tunic as Bowman prepared the horse. They attached their bedding to its saddle and Bowman mounted up. He took Richard by the hand and swung him up to sit behind the saddle.

'I hate doing this,' Bowman said.

Richard put one hand around Bowman's waist, grabbed his tunic and cursed his uncle for causing all of this.

They rode through Rochester, past the castle and cathedral and headed south.

'Worry not, young lord, we only have to catch up with whoever took your horse and we will get him back. Mark my words, we will do so before we reach Canterbury.'

Richard looked around as the track started to wind through the countryside. 'Why did you want to avoid that person?' he asked.

Bowman paused and then sighed. 'The last time I was in these parts, I may have taken some cattle from a man who owed me money.'

'You stole cattle?'

'He owed me and they covered what he owed. I do not call that stealing. Was more of a settling.'

'Everyone else would call that stealing,' Richard said.

'That may be,' Bowman said.

'Was he a man of rank?'

'A shire reeve,' Bowman said quietly.

'By the Lord's grace, we would both have hung if he had seen us,' Richard said.

'That's why I wished to avoid him,' Bowman said, 'I never thought I would see him again, truth be told.'

Richard groaned and buried his face in Bowman's dark cloak.

'The good news, young lord, is that the ground is soft here and tracks are clear. We probably will not need to even resort to tracking, but we can if the need arises.'

'It better not,' Richard said. They soon started to overtake pilgrims on foot who journeyed south east. Usually in small groups, they mostly walked with staffs. They trudged on and on and paid little notice to the horse with two riders who passed by. Before long Richard started to overtake the carts of traders, and soon up ahead they made out their first group of mounted travellers. They followed the road into a wood and Bowman and Richard increased their pace.

'Stay quiet if you see him,' Bowman said.

Richard clung on and looked around Bowman's large frame, he tried to spot Solis in the group ahead when they came back into view.

'No palominos,' he grimaced. They rode on and overtook the party.

Bowman nodded the occasional cautious greeting as they went. Richard felt ill and a headache grew above his eyes. He heard ravens in the distance and hoped it didn't mean anything.

A few hours passed and they had checked and overtaken a handful of parties of mounted pilgrims. Still no palomino horses. The sun hung at its peak for a while and as they entered a forest of ash and beech, it began its decline. The road wound its way through the trees and Richard couldn't see very far ahead. He mumbled a prayer under his breath.

'What was that, young lord?' Bowman asked.

'An offer to spend a whole day at prayer in the cathedral at Canterbury if the Lord would see fit to return Soli to me,' Richard said.

Bowman shuddered. 'You will do so alone if it comes to it,' he said.

Richard didn't care if Bowman went in with him or not. In the distance he could see a hint of bright colours through the trees ahead. A moment later he made out a party of a dozen horses being held to the side of the road in a clearing. Pilgrims enjoyed a rest stop around them. Bowman eased his horse to a halt.

'There is a yellow horse there,' he said quietly.

Richard's heart jumped. He squinted his eyes and thought he could see a blonde mane amongst the blacks, browns and greys.

They rode closer and the suspected blonde mane was definitely blonde. The neck it grew on lashed through the air and other horses tried to get away from it.

'That's Soli,' Richard said.

'Quiet. Don't let on,' Bowman said, 'we can ride with them for a long time and wait for nightfall to take him back. Do you understand?'

'Yes,' Richard felt a pain twist his stomach. He licked his lips as Bowman walked his black horse into the clearing.

'Good noon pilgrims,' Bowman said. A few of them greeted him back.

Richard slid off the back of their horse and looked over at Soli. He felt Bowman's gaze on him so he walked away to a tree and emptied his bladder. No one took any notice and when he finished Richard walked back towards Bowman.

'Where are you heading?' Bowman asked the nearest pilgrim, a man in a faded blue tunic and full grey beard. He had pewter pilgrim badges pinned to his felt hat.

'Santiago de Compostela,' he replied.

'That sounds grand,' Bowman said.

The pilgrim narrowed his eyes.

'I am sure you will all have a lovely time,' Bowman added.

The pilgrim whirled away and stomped off. Bowman chuckled to himself. 'I know what I am going to call this horse,' he said to Richard.

'Yes?'

'Pilgrim.'

Richard laughed with him, a laugh that cracked his melancholy. A sound of kicking hooves erupted behind him. Horses squealed. Richard spun around to see some of the resting horses throw hooves at each other. A loud crack of hoof hitting horse rung out. The three pilgrims who held them shouted and struggled to regain control. Horses started to leap and bounce everywhere. Solis was in the middle of the herd, his ears pinned back. He spun and launched both back legs at a grey horse next to him. They connected and the grey horse sprang away in fright. It pulled back from the man who held him and ran free. Another horse turned to kick at Solis.

'Soli,' Richard shouted.

A few of the pilgrims turned and looked blankly at him.

Bowman sighed and his hand went to his dagger hilt. Solis either ignored or didn't hear Richard, and proceeded to bite the horse who attacked him on the rump. It bucked away with a squeal and broke free. Pilgrims rushed in from around the clearing to grab the loose horses.

'Who are you, boy?' the pilgrim with the pewter badges asked.

'Just a traveller,' Richard said. The horses were caught one by one, pushed apart, and brought under control. Solis pawed the ground and snorted. Some of the pilgrims started to walk over towards Bowman and Richard.

'We will be on our way now,' Bowman beckoned for Richard to jump up onto his horse.

Richard looked back. 'But Soli.'

'He said it again,' one pilgrim said, 'what is that?'

A pair of pilgrims who had hung back from the chaos pushed through the others. They looked to be in their prime years, but had jagged lines etched into their faces. They wore mustard coloured tunics and cloaks that were soiled and heavily patched.

'Have you something to say to us?' one asked Richard.

'No,' he replied.

'Maybe he thinks we have something of his,' the second mustard pilgrim said to the first.

'Maybe they have other things we'd like?' the first said. Both grinned.

'Lads, we don't want any trouble,' Bowman said.

The two pilgrims started to walk closer.

Richard looked at his horse. 'Soli,' he shouted.

The horse's ears pricked up and it turned around.

'Soli, come,' Richard said and took a step towards his horse. The stallion pulled away from the man who held him with the swing of his muscular neck. The man swore loudly as the rope slipped from his fingers, leaving him with rope burn and no horse. He yelped and cursed.

'For the love of,' Bowman drew his knife.

Solis snorted and walked towards Richard. Richard smiled.

One of the two disgruntled mustard pilgrims turned to their

comrades. 'He wants to steal our horse,' he cried.

The second one ran at Richard.

Bowman kicked his horse on and it slammed into the mustard pilgrim, sending him sprawling to the ground with a thump. Cries rang out all around.

Solis cantered over to Richard and came to a halt by him.

'Watch out, boy,' Bowman shouted.

The second mustard pilgrim drew a knife and ran towards Richard. A number of other pilgrims ran over too. They wielded their walking staffs in two hands like weapons. Richard broke his gaze from Solis when he noticed.

'Stop in the name of all that is holy,' a voice boomed out. A flock of birds flew up from the trees around the clearing and the pilgrims stopped dead. They looked back to a lone figure who emerged from behind one of the trees. He wore a long brown mantle with a brown hood attached to it. He did up his underclothes.

'What is going on? This is supposed to be a pilgrimage,' he shouted.

Most of the pilgrims shrank back.

Bowman pointed at the two instigators. 'They stole my young lord's horse,' he said.

One clutched his ankle on the ground, but the other one pointed at Richard. 'That's our horse, the boy is stealing it.'

The man in the brown mantle sighed and walked over. He was tall, the same age as Bowman looked, and sported a head of short dark hair.

'Can anyone prove whose horse it is?' he asked.

'I called his name and he came over,' Richard said.

'There we are, what more proof do you need?' Bowman smiled.

'That could have been the Devil's voice,' the mustard pilgrim who nursed his ankle said.

'Yes, it was the Devil's voice, I'm certain of it,' his companion said to the mantled man. 'It's our horse, Sarjeant,' he added.

'Soli's mine,' Richard said.

The man they called Sarjeant rearranged the mantle that covered his large frame. 'Whispering to horses can indeed be the Devil's work, but horses know their masters too,' he said.

Richard's eyes lit up. 'They do. I can prove it.'

'He can't prove it,' the mustard pilgrim went to tug on Sarjeant's mantle. He was batted away.

Richard pointed back to Solis's saddle. 'The saddle is white with a blue line across it, those are my family colours.'

'We don't know who you are, my boy, you need to do better than that,' Sarjeant said.

'The horse has two parchment bundles plaited into its mane,' Richard said.

'We can all see that, do better,' Sarjeant said.

Richard knew he was committed now, but no one was going to keep his horse from him. 'See there, in the bundle behind the saddle. If you unwrap that, there is a silver candlestick inside,' Richard said.

'Ha,' Bowman returned his knife to is sheath with a flourish.

Sarjeant walked over to Solis, and Richard had a momentary worry that the thieves may have moved the silverware already.

'Who are you, anyway?' Bowman asked the mantled man.

'For my sins I am their guide,' Sarjeant said. He removed the bundle, placed it on the earthen ground and unrolled it. At the end of the roll the silver candlestick was revealed and Richard released a breath he hadn't been aware he'd held.

'Witchcraft,' the first mustard pilgrim shouted.

'Nonsense,' Sarjeant rolled the bundle back up. He picked it up and handed it to Richard.

'Thank you,' he said.

'You have all made a mockery of the institution of pilgrimage,' Sarjeant shouted across the clearing. His blue eyes pierced holes in each man he looked at. Some pilgrims shuffled their feet, they all bowed their heads.

'You can find your own way to Santiago de Compostela, ungrateful swines,' he said, 'our contract is over.'

Richard stroked Solis's neck, but then thought it wise to get on him. He shortened the stirrups back to his length and jumped up into the saddle. Sarjeant walked to the herd of horses and snatched the reins of one from the attending pilgrim. He mounted his slight and old grey horse as Bowman rode over to Richard.

'Better be off now, young lord,' Bowman said.

Richard nodded after he'd checked the candlestick bundle was secure.

'Men will kill for that silver,' Bowman looked around at the assorted pilgrims who peered back up at him. 'We should press on.'

'May I join you?' Sarjeant rode over. 'My previous company had been grating me anyway, and I would be glad to be rid of it.'

Bowman laughed as he walked his horse off. 'Why not? What do you say, young lord?'

'Having a man of God with us for even a while can only be a good thing,' Richard said.

Both Bowman and Sarjeant let out a bout of laughter then stopped and looked at each other.

'He has a sense of humour, so he can be no man of God,' Bowman said.

'I am not worthy of that description, no,' Sarjeant said. The corners of his mouth edged up into a faint smile.

Richard furrowed his brow. 'You must be for those pilgrims to have listened to you,' he said.

Bowman rode up alongside Sarjeant and looked at his clothing. 'Ha, I see the stitching,' he said.

Sarjeant looked down at his mantle and swore.

'He used to be a man of God, young lord, but it looks to me that he has fallen from grace,' Bowman said.

'Oh?' Richard said as they left the woods and started to ride across some wasteland. The wind blew cool gusts into them from the side.

'Do you now see, boy?' Bowman jabbed his finger into the mantle. 'He has a brown mantle and has ripped off a cross. That the pilgrims called him Sarjeant reveals all.'

Richard remembered seeing men with brown mantles with red crosses sewn on in London. They had been amongst the Templars.

'You're a Templar Sarjeant?' Richard asked.

'I was,' Sarjeant sighed.

'If you wanted to hide it you probably should have gone by another name,' Bowman said.

Sarjeant looked at him.

'It is not my name is it, it is just what those thieves and fools called me.'

'What is your name, then?'

'I would rather not say,' Sarjeant replied.

'Fine then, my fallen friend, Sarjeant it is,' Bowman grinned.

Sarjeant groaned. He looked over at Richard. 'This man is clearly not yours, he has no respect whatsoever. You are young to be travelling alone for one born above the masses. What are you doing here with this single rude man?'

Bowman snorted.

'He is my friend,' Richard said. He looked into the wind and had to narrow his eyes for comfort. 'He is travelling with me to Dover to see me onto a ship.'

'A ship, you go abroad on your own? Men will kill you for that candlestick,' Sarjeant said.

'I just told him that,' Bowman shrugged.

'It is God's will, what choice do I have?' Richard said.

'I very much doubt that. I will wager it was the will of men alone. Greedy men or violent men though, that is the question?' Sarjeant asked.

'Both,' Richard said.

'Both? What is your name?'

'Don't tell him,' Bowman said.

'Well, what is your name, then?' Sarjeant asked Bowman.

'They call me Bowman.'

'And you mock me?' Sarjeant snorted.

'Why can't you tell us?' Richard asked Bowman.

'Because it isn't a real name either, is it,' Sarjeant said. He pulled his mantle fully around himself.

'Which of course he will not tell us because he is clearly some degree of criminal.'

Bowman knotted up his face and spat onto the passing ground, missing the bush he'd aimed at.

Richard looked at him. 'It doesn't matter to me, he saved my life,' he said.

'That was an accident,' Bowman broke a smile.

'I am Richard from Keynes.'

'Boy,' Bowman said.

'Worry not, I mean no harm to anyone,' Sarjeant said. 'All I want is enough honest work to pay for me to have a few good drinks each night. Have either of you ever travelled across the sea?'

Bowman stayed silent and Richard shook his head.

Sarjeant smiled. 'Well then, for a shilling every now and again I can find you passage and help you reach your destination. That is what I do, I guide people. Where are you headed?'

'We are going to see William Tancarville in Normandy,' Richard said.

'Really? I see now. Something has gone very wrong at home, and you young Richard are off to make your fortune in France. Are you a second born?'

'First born.'

'Interesting. And you believe you can impress Lord Tancarville enough for him to knight you so you can make money with violence on the tournament circuit.'

'I suppose so,' Richard said.

'You suppose? Do you know what you are doing at all?' Sarjeant said.

'Not really.'

'He really has no idea,' Bowman smiled, 'other than going to Dover because he was told to.'

Sarjeant laughed and patted his grey horse who strained to keep up. 'I have passed through Castle Tancarville before,' he said, 'I can find a ship going to Harfleur, which is an easy day's ride to Tancarville. Tell me Bowman, does our young lord show enough promise with a sword or lance for us to invest our time in him?'

'Well, I have not seen him couch a lance, but I have seen him bury a sword into a man's head, so I would say he has some promise there.'

'Dear God,' Sarjeant said.

'I will pay you,' Richard said.

Bowman's eyes rolled. 'We can find our own way, young lord, we barely have enough coin to get to Normandy as it is.'

'I'll pay him from my share then,' Richard said.

'Excellent,' Sarjeant said, 'although I fear to ask what money the two of you have to share. Say nothing on it, my boy, I do not wish to know what your scheme was.'

Bowman laughed. 'Those who lost out deserved to. They were as bad as your pilgrims,' he said.

'I very much doubt it, those so called pilgrims are a laughing stock. Half of them were on the road to Santiago because of ordered punishments and the rest were using it as an excuse to see the world. You are not supposed to enjoy going on pilgrimage, the suffering is the whole point.'

'They seem to have caused you suffering,' Bowman said.

'Indeed, with their blasphemy and horse charms, I will be extremely glad to never see another pilgrim again in all my life,' Sarjeant said.

Richard laughed from nowhere, and both men looked at him. He recovered himself. 'Bowman just named his horse Pilgrim, so you'll see a Pilgrim every day you're with us.'

Bowman muffled a laugh. 'Maybe I will like this horse after all,' he said.

Sarjeant shook his head. 'I am regretting this already,' he said and with a smile the trio continued their way towards Canterbury.

A SACRED VOW

Richard had become annoyed by Sarjeant's company.

'Can we rest a while? This horse feels like it is going to drop,' the former Templar said.

Richard sighed. 'That's the fifth time you've asked,' he looked at the grey horse.

It lifted its hooves up as if iron weights were attached to them. Richard wrapped his cloak around himself. 'Although I wouldn't mind getting out of the wind for a bit,' he said.

The clouds had darkened as the day wore on and the wind pushed them across the sky with a constant howl.

Bowman glanced up. 'It may rain tonight, we should get to Canterbury as soon as we can.'

'Please, just a short rest,' Sarjeant asked, 'otherwise I am afraid that I will be walking on foot from Canterbury to Dover.'

Richard looked ahead. 'That's easy for you to say, you're not the one being chased by people,' he said.

'Chased? Who is chasing you?'

'Your former employers for one, but other unpleasant people too,' Richard said. Saying that, Richard thought, they were on the main road, so a slightly different route would be safer. They'd just gone through a village and there was another area of woodland ahead that looked to stretch on forever.

'No one back there,' Bowman noticed where Richard's gaze lay. 'You two soft flowers can rest a while hidden in the trees.'

No one argued so they continued on until the undergrowth got thicker on one side of the road. Bowman turned down a well trodden branching track and they followed that for a while.

'Should be far enough,' he said when they reached a stream that trickled over the track. Everyone dismounted and offered their horses a drink. They grazed for a while and Solis started to rip branches from the nearest tree with a rattle of foliage. The twigs snapped loudly in his mouth as he chewed them.

'Could you stop him doing that, it will be heard for miles,' Bowman said.

'Only if you can find him some grass,' Richard said.

'I hate horses.'

Richard ignored him and stretched his legs out. The wind blew over the top of the trees, mostly birches, but the air at ground level was still. Richard could see a small way through the undergrowth, but not far.

'A shame we do not have that bow,' Bowman said to Richard.

He nodded, but hadn't even noticed it hadn't been on Solis's saddle when they recovered him.

'How far is there left to go?' he asked.

'An hour at most,' Sarjeant said.

'Then why have we stopped?' Bowman put his hands on his hips.

'I thought you'd been everywhere?' Richard asked.

Bowman looked at the young man and raised his eyebrows. 'I have, but that does not mean I remember it tree by boring tree,' he said.

Bowman froze and looked back up the track.

Richard looked too but didn't hear anything.

Solis stopped eating and pricked his ears in the same direction, a huge branch motionless in his mouth.

Richard looked and waited. He wondered if his uncle's men could have tracked them down.

'Maybe there is an animal?' Sarjeant whispered.

Richard's hand went to the hilt of his stolen sword.

Bowman turned around and looked the other way. He swore. 'They are on both side of us, no point trying to be quiet,' he said.

Richard heard footsteps from up the track and the snap of twigs from across the stream ahead. The first pilgrim to emerge from the woods wore a tattered mustard tunic.

'I hate pilgrims,' Bowman said.

'You and me both,' Sarjeant sighed.

'They aren't taking my horse,' Richard said.

'There are too many, boy, leave the sword where it is,' Bowman said.

He was right, Richard realised as a dozen pilgrims appeared on either side of them. They stood ready with staves in both hands, all of them with grins on their faces.

'Now, then,' Sarjeant said loudly.

'We have decided that we don't need to listen to you no more,' the pewter badge pilgrim stepped forwards.

'Come now, John,' Sarjeant said, 'this is hardly the expected behaviour of a pilgrim.'

'The way we see it,' Pilgrim John walked towards them, 'is that you still have our money, and that our fee for collecting it should be all three of these horses.'

Richard felt anger rise within and started to slide his sword out slowly. He wasn't going to lose Solis again.

'Now, now, little one, put it back in like a good boy,' Pilgrim John said.

Bowman nodded to him so Richard paused. He noticed that one of the pilgrims, a man with an undyed tunic, had a bow drawn and pointed an arrow at him.

'Adela's bow,' he said in suprise.

'That is the least of our concerns,' Bowman said.

'You are all fools,' Pilgrim John walked closer to Sarjeant. He pointed his staff at him.

Their former guide sighed and drew his reins over his horse's neck, handed them to Pilgrim John, and backed away.

'This track is the one the nobility take to avoid the common people. We thought you might think yourselves very clever and go this way. But we didn't actually believe you were stupid enough to do it. Yet here you all stand.'

'How did you get ahead of us?' Bowman asked.

'You are slow and predictable,' Pilgrim John laughed as he rearranged the reins of the grey horse. 'This may not be a very good horse, but still worth a pound,' he said.

Sarjeant growled.

Richard didn't know what Solis was worth in coin, but with no horse for transport, he was worth Richard's life. His started to draw his sword again.

Bowman noticed and saw the young man's dark face and furrowed brow. Bowman spat onto the ground. 'God's legs, I never thought I'd die over someone else's horse. These horses will fetch you some silver for sure, but they are going to cost you a fair price in blood first,' Bowman drew his knife.

'Now lads, there can be a peaceful way out of this,' Sarjeant said, but he tightened his grip on his pilgrim's staff anyway.

Pilgrim John touched his pewter badges one at a time then approached Sarjeant with his own staff lowered.

Richard remembered how he'd felt back in the chapel at Keynes, but this was different. This time he had a sword. He fully drew it and held the blade out. The mustard pilgrim who had tried to kill him before ran at him.

Behind him Sarjeant clouted Pilgrim John in the stomach with his staff but four pilgrims closed in on him fast.

Richard stepped sideways and cut at the mustard pilgrim, who thought better of it and backed off. A trickle of blood sprouted from his chin where the tip of Richard's sword had nicked him.

'You will pay for that, boy,' he said as he touched his face and came away with a red hand.

The noise of more hooves thundered from up the track. Richard let out a sigh and tightened his sword grip.

The pilgrims looked to each other with nervous eyes. Pilgrim John lay on the floor winded. He gasped for air and peered back up the track with his hand on his stomach.

'Whoever that is, this lot are worried about them,' Sarjeant said.

The pilgrims who were still on their horses turned them, jumped over the stream, and fled away out of sight. A dozen horseman burst through the woodland at a canter and slammed to a halt in the middle of the confrontation. Horses snorted and iron horseshoes dug into the ground as they stopped from speed. Mud flew up and dirt covered Sarjeant and Pilgrim John. Sarjeant wiped his face clean.

The horsemen were well dressed, Richard had seen clothes as richly coloured as theirs only a few times in his whole life.

'What is the meaning of this?' one asked. He was tall and had a frown on a face. There were wrinkles on his forehead but not around his mouth. His clothes looked a bit like the bishop who had once visited his grandfather's manor, but shinier.

Solis bit in half the branch he'd been holding during the encounter and it fell to the ground in two pieces.

The man who looked like a bishop looked at him, then burst into laughter. 'That horse thinks he's a dog,' he said.

All his companions exchanged a glance then laughed along with him.

'Oh Christ, save me,' Sarjeant dropped to a knee, 'that is the archbishop himself,' he hissed.

The remaining pilgrims followed his lead and knelt.

Bowman looked around, shrugged and did the same.

Richard's anger subsided and he copied everyone else.

The archbishop surveyed the scene. 'Why are pilgrims fighting each other?'

No one spoke. The leaves at the top of the canopy rustled in the wind and somewhere a crow squawked.

'You,' said the archbishop to Sarjeant. 'Why do you wear a Templar mantle with the cross torn off?'

Sarjeant swore under his breath. 'I left the order, your grace.'

'Why?'

Sarjeant waited a moment before replying. 'I served out my term of penance, your grace.'

'Penance for what?'

'Drink, your grace.'

'How ordinary. How very mundane,' the archbishop said. He looked at Bowman briefly before his gaze fell on Richard. 'Are you on pilgrimage? You are very young for that.'

'No,' Richard said.

'Then why are you here with these pilgrims?'

'I'm not, they are trying to steal my horse. That man already has my sister's bow.'

The archbishop's eyes followed Richard's pointed finger towards the bow.

The pilgrim who held it laid it down beside him and backed away with wide, skittish eyes.

'It has an A carved into it, because my sister always thought I'd steal it from her,' Richard added, feeling that recent history was repeating itself.

The archbishop gestured and two of his men rode over. One dismounted and picked it up. He looked it over.

'There is an A, my lord,' he said.

The archbishop shook his head and frowned. 'What is the world coming to when pilgrims turn to theft? Clear those wretches from my sight.'

The horsemen obeyed and herded the pilgrims away at speed. They all ran, grabbed their horses, crossed the stream and disappeared into the woods.

On his way, Pilgrim John spat towards Sarjeant who stayed still, his eyes on the archbishop.

'Young man, what is your name?' the archbishop asked.

Richard glanced over to Bowman who this time just shrugged. 'Richard of Keynes.'

'Keynes near Berkhamsted?' the archbishop asked. He walked his horse closer and peered down at Richard.

'Yes, your grace,' Richard said slowly.

'I knew a Sir William of Keynes, he was a poor man but brave and loyal. Is that your Keynes?'

'Yes, your grace.'

'A shame, I heard he was killed in the Holy Land,' the archbishop said.

'He was my father.'

'Was he now?' the archbishop's face softened ever so slightly. He looked Richard up and down.

'You have his face. I will say a prayer for him tonight for he did God's work. I remember well the song they sung about him. I was told it was even true.'

Bowman and Sarjeant looked at Richard.

'Yes, your grace,' he said and met their eyes with an awkward smile.

The horseman with Adela's bow walked over and handed it to Richard who thanked him. Richard started to unstring it.

'The light will fail soon, you will all come with me back to Canterbury. My men will give you lodgings and wake you in the morning. You will see me then.'

'Of course,' Richard stowed the bow on his saddle. He mounted up along with everyone else and they followed

behind the archbishop's horsemen as they made the final part
of the journey under their protection. Richard rode in silence,
unsure of what to make of their narrow escape, and wondered
whether or not they were now in the clear. The party reached
Canterbury as dark fell and a steady rain set in that saturated
his woollen cloak.

Richard and his companions were taken to a newly built
stable block and shown to a chamber with fine furniture
around the hearth. It even had silver drinking vessels on the
tables. All three of them were worn out and made the most of
a peaceful night, safe in the knowledge that the archbishop's
stables had actual guards. Even so, Richard brought his saddle,
bridle and breastplate into the hall for the night and slept with
his sword and candlestick in his bed.

The chamber they had been given was certainly a cut above
the hall of the inn at Rochester. It had three windows with
narrow vertical panes, each glazed with thin slices of horn to
keep the wind out. The pieces of horn were clear or yellowed,
and when the first rays of sun for the day hit them, it sent
dappled beams of soft light across the chamber. Richard was
pulled from his deep sleep by an attendant who nudged him
and his companions awake. They were taken to the archbishop
who was already holding court with a queue of supplicants
stretching out of his audience chamber. A collection of scribes
sat to one side of that grand chamber and took notes with
furious energy. The hall was large and well lit by stained glass
windows, the walls made entirely of stone. Tapestries adorned
with biblical scenes hung from the walls. Richard joined the
queue and promptly his eyes started to droop down again.
They waited for some time in sleepy silence. Once at the
front of the queue they were ushered in and bowed before the
archbishop.

'Ah, the pilgrims who weren't,' he said, 'young Richard, I have
something for you.'

'Me?' Richard blinked his sleep away, 'thank you, your grace,'

'You can call me Thomas, I knew your father quite well, did I
mention that yesterday?'

'Yes, your grace, sorry, your, sorry. Lord Thomas.'

The archbishop laughed as an aide brought over a richly decorated manuscript. The cover was studded with precious stones and liberally covered in gold leaf.

'Your father was adequately educated if I remember correctly. Some grasp of Latin, not enough, but some. I am assuming he took measures to educate you also?'

'He did, Lord Thomas,' Richard took the manuscript and turned it over in his hands. It was heavy, heavier than the manuscripts he had at home, but then none of those had stones embedded in their covers. Their library at Keynes had contained precisely three items, which thanks to Richard were now tattered and faded.

'Eric and Enid,' the archbishop said, 'I picked this up while I was in France. Your father would have enjoyed it. It teaches what a knight should be and I believe Christ put you in my path so I could give this to you. It is a fiction too. Did you know fiction has not been done since the ancients? This is one of a few copies I've had made of the original, which of course I am keeping.'

'Thank you, Lord Thomas,' Richard couldn't believe the luxurious artefact in his hands was just a copy.

'Thank me by working for the church and glory of our God. I urge you to take the cross and follow in your father's footsteps. Serve in the Holy Land and save your soul. Sew a cross onto your tunic.'

'I will, Lord Thomas,' Richard said.

Next to him Bowman groaned.

Sarjeant turned his head to whisper in Richard's ear. 'I hope you know what you just did.'

Richard blinked, then realised. He had heard his mother complain to his father when he'd announced he was going to the Holy Land. She had cried for days. That had been five years ago, and like his father, he knew it didn't mean he had to go tomorrow, or even next year. But he had to go.

'Where are you going to find the money for that?' Bowman hissed.

Richard realised he'd been holding his breath and let it out in one go.

'Now you,' the archbishop said, a bony finger pointed at

Sarjeant.

Richard took the chance to take a step back.

'Yes, your grace?' Beads of sweat made their way down Sarjeant's face even though he'd left his brown mantle behind and wore only a grey linen tunic.

'Pray tell me, what is your name?'

'John of Lincoln,' Sarjeant said.

'John of Lincoln. I believe you had a problem with intoxication.'

Sarjeant kept his eyes down. 'I turned to wine instead of my faith. My superiors took a dislike to me and punished me for things I had not done,' he said.

'Were these superiors in the order?'

'Yes. I have since realised I should have used their suffering to become closer to Christ,' Sarjeant said.

'Yours shall be a path of redemption. I bind you to this young man. Accompany him on his own journey and that shall be your eternal penance. Guide him towards prudence, temperance and fortitude. Ensure he learns from your mistakes.'

'Yes, your grace,' Sarjeant tugged the neck of his tunic around to let some air out.

'I know nothing of you,' the archbishop said to Bowman.

Bowman stayed quiet and still but his eyes were set on the churchman.

The archbishop waited a moment but nothing was forthcoming. 'Your name?'

'Robert.'

'Anything else?'

'Just Robert.'

The archbishop frowned and shook his head. He opened his mouth to press further but looked up at the lengthy queue of supplicants that awaited him.

'Very well. Are you travelling with young Richard too, a guardian of some sort?'

'Of some sort,' Bowman replied.

'Fine. Good. Where in France are you heading, Richard? Did I say I had just come back from there?'

'You did, Lord Thomas,' Richard took a tentative step

forwards. 'My grandfather suggested to go to Lord William Tancarville.'

'Ah, the Chamberlain of Normandy. An interesting man. A strong man. Too strong for our king's liking, which makes him a friend of mine. Learn from him, young Richard, stay close to him. I instructed him to take the cross some time ago, see if you can jog his memory of it.'

Richard inclined his head but didn't know what any of that meant, so held his tongue.

The archbishop nodded slowly. 'You will be allowed into the cathedral. God be with you,' he waved them away.

The three of them quickly took their leave and left the room. No attendants followed and from then on it was as if they didn't exist anymore.

'I don't like him,' Bowman exhaled once they got back into the corridor.

Sarjeant wiped his brow. 'I think I am going to be sick,' he said.

Richard looked at his book. 'He seemed nice.'

His companions laughed.

'Careful who you say that to, young lord,' Bowman checked they were unobserved. 'His popularity ends at the entrance to the royal court.'

Richard didn't care, he wanted to read.

Sarjeant looked at the book. 'Another expensive item we will need to keep hidden.'

'We?' Bowman said.

'Like it or not, the Archbishop of Canterbury has bound me to the boy so it is we now,' Sarjeant said.

'I hate churches. Read it once if you must, young lord,' Bowman inspected the jewelled cover, 'but then we can sell it. It will keep us fed for a year.'

Richard scowled at him. 'I need to pray for my grandfather and father.' He wondered if the archbishop knew how his father had died.

'Fine, you can get that out of the way first,' Bowman said.

Richard hid the manuscript under his bed roll back in their sleeping chamber and the trio made their way to Canterbury cathedral.

Even after London's abundance of ecclesiastical buildings the cathedral was impressive. It reached up into the heavens, pillars and arches of stone that Richard thought must have been crafted by God himself.

The scaffolding around it suggested otherwise.

Bowman stayed outside, arms folded as he leant on the stone wall, so Richard and Sarjeant went in without him. Inside, sweet incense tickled Richard's nose and Latin prayers confused his ears.

Their lack of importance confined their prayer to the central nave, far away from any relics or particularly scared spaces. The nave, the long part of the cathedral, was open and devoid of any seating. Richard stood, took in the majesty of it all, and prayed.

He closed his eyes and saw his family, saw how they used to eat, hunt and live together. As the Latin prayers echoed off the walls down from the altar of the cathedral, he reflected that his old life was surely over. He begged Christ for forgiveness for leaving Adela behind, an act which he had been doing his best not to think about. He swore to God that he would go back for her one day. Richard continued to avoid thinking about his mother for that was too painful. He did pray for sir Hugh, and repeated the prayer over and over again until he'd lost half the day in a moment.

He opened his eyes and immediately felt faint. Once his body had adjusted, faintness was replaced by hunger and thirst.

Sarjeant sat with his eyes closed on the cold stone floor. He snored.

Despite his need for a decent meal, Richard felt energised and alive.

Sarjeant woke with a snort and looked up at the young man. 'Back with us then?' he said.

Richard nodded. 'I know what I need to do.'

'And what would that be, my boy? Would it be whatever the archbishop told you to?'

Richard frowned. 'Well, yes, but he's the archbishop so who else should I listen to?'

'Yourself, perhaps,' Sarjeant pushed himself off the stone floor and to his feet. 'Make your own way with Christ. There are those who believe differently than what you will hear between these walls.'

Richard looked around. 'To say something like that is heresy,' he said.

'Maybe, but you can listen to yourself and keep what you hear to yourself, too.'

'It doesn't matter.' Richard admired the stained glass window at the far end of the enormous building. 'I need to rescue my sister and reclaim my manor, which means I need money and men.'

'Aiming low, then,' Sarjeant sighed and put a hand on his shoulder. Unlike his uncle's hand, this one warmed him. Richard trusted it.

He took one last look at the interior of the cathedral to lodge it in his memory. He'd never imagined so much gold could even exist.

'I think Christ brought me this far for a reason. He means for me to rescue Adela then make a pilgrimage to the Holy Land,' Richard nodded slowly.

Sarjeant grimaced. 'You sound serious.'

'I am, what else can I do?'

Sarjeant looked at him and Richard met his gaze. 'We are prisoners of fate, then,' Sarjeant began to walk outside, 'I suppose we need to find a ship to Normandy.'

THE SEA

Richard had never seen the sea. From the wind-battered hill above Dover he could see the grey water stretch out in what seemed like every direction. Richard was taken by its vast flatness. On the horizon it met the equally grey sky and they smudged together at a point Richard couldn't pick out. The wind whipped his cloak around him and he could smell salt. On another hill far to their left, Dover castle sat watch over the entrance to the country. This castle was mostly wooden but it was also a building site with blocks of stone visible even from as far away as Richard was. Men moved about it in the distance like busy ants.

He was glad when they descended the hill and into the port town. His face, blasted icy cold by the wind, had a chance to warm up a little. Houses and warehouses clustered under the high ground around the docks, which were full of masted ships. A few flat bottom galleys from the Mediterranean were moored and tied together. Next to them were some single masted longships, with low hulls and decorated prows. The rest of the vessels were much shorter, but tall and with big bellies.

'Those are the new kind of trading ships,' Sarjeant said.

Richard just nodded.

Sarjeant pointed to them. 'They are called cogs, and it will be on a cog that we will seek passage to Normandy.'

Richard rode behind Sarjeant who repeatedly said he knew the way, but all they needed to do was follow the carts laden with wool which slowed down traffic on the road to a crawl.

Most of the wooden carts held big bags of wool which were being taken to Flanders.

'This is how England makes its money,' Sarjeant said.

'I hate sheep,' Bowman said as they approached the wooden wall that separated Dover from the rest of England.

Richard stared at him. 'How can you hate sheep?'

'They are impossible to keep alive. They have been the ruin of many men,' Bowman's face looked dead ahead.

'I think not, the men selling all this wool are a long way from ruined,' Sarjeant said.

Richard looked up at the town walls as they rode through them. Some decomposed heads were stuck on spears either side of the gateway. 'What did they do?'

'Something King Henry did not like,' Bowman didn't even look, 'and his laws have just changed, young lord. We step into a new world, a better world.'

'Why is it better?' Richard asked.

'Because he's banned trial by fire,' Bowman shivered, 'I never much liked the idea of going through one, I have to say.'

'They were pirates, but we might face our own trial by water if the weather gets any worse,' Sarjeant wondered out loud as he looked up at the now almost black sky.

The wind howled above them, shot off the clifftops and out to sea, and Richard thought he felt a drop of water on his face. Seagulls whirled overhead and screeched at each other while they fought against the wind.

They made their way to a small building marked with a cross on the door.

'That mark shows they are free from the king's taxes,' Sarjeant told him.

Richard knew that already so ignored him as they entered the building. A fire roared along a back wall, but the rest of the room was filled with desks.

A clerk in a brown tunic looked up from one of them.

'Yes?' he said briskly in an accent Richard found thick to his ears.

'I'd like to redeem a letter of credit,' Richard looked for the letter he'd been given in London.

The clerk sighed. 'You redeem those in the Holy Land, boy. Be on your way.'

'My grandfather said I could redeem it here so we could pay for a ship.'

'He may have said that, but saying a thing does not make it true,' the clerk said.

Sarjeant took a step forward but Bowman put a hand on his chest to stop him. 'Calm it.'

The clerk looked up and squinted at the brown mantle. 'Where did you get that?' he asked.

'You really need to put some time into removing those broken stitches,' Bowman let Sarjeant go as he stepped back.

The former Templar sarjeant turned red. 'I was given it by a Brother Templar,' he said.

The clerk narrowed his eyes and scrunched up his face. 'Stealing from the Templars is a hanging offence,' he said.

'I stole nothing, unlike some others,' Sarjeant said.

'Do you accuse the Temple?' the Clerk pushed the desk away and got to his feet. He had a long face that Richard thought resembled a rat he had once found squashed in Solis's stable.

Bowman raised both his hands up to calm the clerk. 'He does not, he loves the Temple and all of its wise and honest brothers.'

Sarjeant's eyes were unblinking.

'All of them, he loves all of them,' Bowman put a hand on Sarjeant's shoulder.

The tall man brushed it off and spun on his heels.

Richard watched Sarjeant stomp out through the door and slam it behind him. It knocked a hinge loose.

'You will have to pay for that,' the clerk said to Richard.

'For what?' Bowman asked.

'The hinge.'

'Jesus Christ,' Bowman ran his hand through his blonde hair, 'no wonder everyone hates you lot.'

The clerk looked at Bowman. 'You broke it, you fix it,' he said.

'Not out of my half,' Bowman patted Richard on the shoulder, smiled, and followed Sarjeant out of the building.

Richard looked at the clerk who had his hands on hips and looked back at him. 'I need to go to Normandy.'

'Well, go on then,' the clerk said.

'I need my money to pay for the voyage. I don't have enough without the money I gave to the Templars in London.'

'This is not my concern,' the clerk folded his arms, 'my concern is that these accounts need to be finished by the end of the day.'

'Accounts? What are they?' Richard asked.

The clerk went to speak but instead groaned and sat back down. He dipped his quill in ink and started to write on the page on his table.

Richard watched him.

The clerk continued to scribble and scratch.

'I still need to get to Normandy.'

'I still need to complete these accounts,' the clerk didn't look up.

'I don't have another way to cross the sea, so I'm going to stand here until you give me my money,' Richard said.

The clerk went to throw down his quill but stopped himself. 'Please just get out, boy. We do not have a store of money here, we are not an Italian bank. The letters of credit exist so that pilgrims can withdraw their money in the Holy Land. They do not work in Dover.'

'That doesn't help me though, I need to...'

'Yes I know, you need to get to Normandy,' the clerk sat back in his chair and looked up at the young man in front of him.

'I need a way to get my money. Is there anything you can do to help me? The Archbishop of Canterbury is sending me to Normandy,' Richard said.

'Is he now,' the clerk snorted. He crossed him arms. 'I really do not have any money for you.'

'I have taken the cross, I swear it on my own soul. Your order exists to help pilgrims get to the Holy Land, that's what I'm trying to do. If you help me, I'll leave,' Richard said.

The clerk studied the young man. He sighed and closed his eyes for a moment. 'We do have one ship in the harbour here. I can make an adjustment to your letter of credit for the value of the voyage. If you travel on our ship that way, then you do not need to take the money out at all.'

'Yes, thank you,' Richard smiled.

The clerk went through the rear door in the room, and for a

while Richard wondered if he was actually coming back. When he did, he shuffled over with a piece of parchment in his hand. He handed it to Richard then went back to his desk.

'What do I do with this?' Richard asked.

Without looking up the clerk replied, 'Hand it to someone on the Templar ship.'

'How do I know which ship that is?'

The clerk groaned and looked up. 'Do you know why I joined the Templars?'

'To serve God?' Richard suggested.

'No, because I am one of nine children, eight of which were younger than me and by the time I was your age, I was surrounded by screaming babies and young children asking stupid questions. There are no children in the Templar Order. Get out.'

Richard didn't know what to say.

The clerk went back to his accounts.

Richard looked at his parchment, which just had an order on it. 'This doesn't have my name, I haven't even given you my name.'

'I do not know how I can make this any clearer, boy. Count your blessings, it is free passage because you are annoying me so much. Get out.'

Richard grinned and didn't need telling twice, so he left.

He met Bowman and Sarjeant outside where it was overcast and had started to rain. Despite that, he waved the parchment with a big smile on his face.

'What's that?' Bowman asked. Only half of his face protruded from his thick woollen cloak.

'Looks very little like your coin,' Sarjeant said. His face was as dark as the weather.

'Passage, we've got passage.'

'How?'

'I annoyed that clerk so much he gave us a pass onto their ship.'

Bowman and Sarjeant exchanged glances.

'I threw the archbishop's name in too,' Richard added.

Bowman laughed. 'You might be a good investment after all,' his face softened, 'you might just have what it takes to play the courtly games, my young lord.'

Richard smiled and felt taller than before.

'I am not stepping foot on a Templar ship,' Sarjeant said.

Bowman groaned, his smile vanished and he turned to Sarjeant. 'We aren't crossing the sea any other way. Have you got any better ideas? No? Then finish taking that dammed stitching out so they don't burn us as apostates, and get on their dammed ship.'

Richard didn't know what an apostate was, but Sarjeant glared at Bowman with such force he dared not ask.

Richard reached into the leather pouch that hung inside his tunic and produced a few coins.

'Here, is this enough to buy wine so that you don't remember the journey?'

Sarjeant's eyes brightened. He held his hand out and Richard poured some of the money into it.

Sarjeant clenched his fingers around the coins. 'If I remember any of it at all, you will owe me.'

Richard nodded and shrugged. He let Sarjeant go off with his horse and look for wine while he and Bowman rode down to the docks. Wagons lined the streets, draped in covers to protect their valuable cargo from the driving rain. Puddles grew everywhere and the street turned to mud.

Bowman pulled up the hood on his cloak and leant over to Richard. 'No ship is leaving in this weather, young lord, and we should not leave the horses on a ship overnight if we have any choice about it. Let's find a warm and dry place to spend the night.'

Solis walked with his head down and looked about as happy as Bowman did.

Richard agreed, so they found a wall to hide behind that blocked half the rain.

Sarjeant reappeared with two wooden barrels strapped to his horse, one on each side.

'That poor horse,' Richard said as he approached, 'that looks heavy.'

Sarjeant agreed to Bowman's plan, so they found somewhere to stay and Sarjeant began to reduce the weight his horse needed to carry by starting on the wine.

They slept by a fire and relaxed once the hall was full and no pilgrims they recognised had entered it.

This time Richard slept surrounded by everything he owned.

In the morning they left the hall and walked out into a calm day, much more pleasant than the previous night's downpour. The puddles and mud remained however, so they had to pick their way back down to the harbour where cargo was already being loaded onto ships. Their horse's hooves slipped in the mud which covered their fetlocks in brown sludge.

Bowman asked around until a seaman pointed to a cog that was being loaded with sacks of wool.

Richard presented his parchment to the captain in charge, an old man wearing a brown mantle with a red cross sewn onto it. He ushered them onboard and ordered his men to load their horses. 'Get below decks, you will be in the way otherwise,' he told them.

Richard wanted to watch everything but went into the small cabin with Bowman and Sarjeant after the captain told him to get out of his way again.

The cabin was basic, wooden floors, wooden walls, wooden ceiling, all with no decoration or furniture. They unrolled their bedding and sat down. 'Is this it for the voyage?' Richard asked.

'You can go onto deck when the crew are less angry,' Sarjeant said.

'I want to see the sea when we sail,' Richard said.

Bowman laughed. 'I was keen on my first trip across the sea too, young lord. Eat no food this morning is my advice.'

Richard wasn't sure how that would help him, but was interrupted when the door flew open and two sailors holding a woman marched in and threw her into the cabin. They slammed the door behind them when they left.

The woman had a worn face and her hair was a mix of grey and mousy brown. She wore a pale blue dress, maroon cloak, and a facial expression like thunder. She pulled herself up.

'Bloody sailors think they know everything,' she brushed herself down. 'These Templar sailors are the worst, especially when you aren't a man.'

She unpinned her cloak and laid it down as far away from the men as she could.

Bowman lay down and pretended to be asleep.

Sarjeant stared at the woman with an expression Richard wasn't sure about, but she ignored him and silence filled the cabin.

A while later the captain opened the door. 'You may come on deck now, if you please,' he said.

Richard noticed that his eyes didn't even flicker in the woman's direction.

Richard went out onto the deck, which in length was only as long as he could throw a spear, and went to the wooden railing.

The crew unfurled a large white canvas sail above him, exchanging loud shouts Richard didn't understand. The canvas unrolled and fell down towards him with a whipping sound. It revealed a large red Templar cross at its centre. The harbour was busy and the hustle and bustle excited Richard now that he was set apart from it.

The cog set out to sea slowly, which gave Richard plenty of time to look up at the castle on the hill, and soon the white cliffs of England as they started sailing southwards.

'I always wonder if I will see them again. You would be surprised how many die on pilgrimages.' Sarjeant stood next to Richard. He had his brown mantle wrapped around him, and Richard noticed the errant red thread had now been taken out.

Bowman inspected a wooden cart that had been tied down onto the deck.

'Get away from that,' the woman from the cabin said as she appeared on deck.

'I mean no harm,' Bowman stepped back, 'just curious how having a cart on deck is a good idea.'

'That is none of your business,' she walked over, her heavy footsteps thumped across the wooden deck which creaked.

The cog lifted with a wave for the first time and Richard grabbed the railing.

Horses shouted below deck.

'These waters are calm,' Sarjeant grinned, 'once we get further out you will need to hang on tighter.'

Richard's eyes widened.

Solis shouted, but not a shout of worry, it was the same shout he had bellowed at Smithfields.

'Who let a stallion onboard,' the woman shouted in the direction of the captain. 'That was the one thing I was promised at the Templar office. No stallions.'

Richard looked at the woman. 'Was it a clerk who made you the promise?' he asked.

The woman whirled away from the captain, who took the chance to skulk away.

'It was, who are you, boy?'

'My name is Richard, and the clerk I met didn't seem to care about very much other than his writing.'

'That weasel,' she said.

'I thought he looked more like a rat,' Richard said.

The woman paused, then burst into laughter. 'Bloody Templars,' she glanced up at the sail. 'They take your money quickly enough. The stallion is yours, yes?'

'He is,' Richard said as the sound of hooves striking wood could be heard from below.

'Your stallion and my mare will be exhausting themselves talking to each other this whole voyage. She will be in no fit state to travel once we make land.'

'I'm very sorry,' Richard said.

The woman walked over and peered at him. She smelt of cheese.

'You have a kind face,' she said, 'not like those two men you are with. It is not your fault the clerk lied to me.'

'What is your name?' Richard asked.

The woman laughed. 'No one ever asks me that anymore, not since my hair turned grey.'

Richard noticed that Sarjeant leant on the far side of the cog, but watched them instead of the sea.

'I am Nicola,' she said.

'Where are you sailing to?' Richard asked.

'The same place as you, obviously. Harfleur. I take wool from England to Flanders, and clothing from Flanders to Normandy. Then silver from Normandy to England, which I use to buy wool.'

'Why are you sailing from London to Normandy then?' Richard asked.

'I preferred it when no one asked me anything,' Nicola said

dryly.

The waves grew in size and the cog pitched for the first time. Richard started to feel sick as the deck rose and fell under him.

'Stay near the side, boy,' Nicola said.

'Why?' Richard asked. A big wave made the cog roll and Richard leant over and threw up into the sea.

'That's why,' Nicola said.

Sarjeant laughed. 'He was excited for his first sail,' he said from across the cog.

Nicola ignored him. 'It will get worse, young Richard, but then it will get better,' she said.

'Really?' he said as he wiped his mouth on his tunic.

'Usually, although sometimes the sickness kills,' she said.

Richard's already pale face turned whiter still.

Bowman laughed. 'Your legs will learn to be at sea, young lord,' he said.

Richard hoped so. The cog rode the waves. Its hull cut through smaller ones and heaved up and dropped over the larger ones. Richard was soon sick again.

'Glad you didn't eat?' Sarjeant asked a few hours later.

Richard wasn't hugely aware of the question and retched over the side again. The cog sailed over towards the French coast and once close, it stayed within sight of it.

Sarjeant pointed out Boulogne, a French port town, and later identified the estuary where the sea met the Somme river.

The wind died down after that and by nightfall the cog barely moved. The waves lapped gently onto the hull and the cog's movement calmed.

That suited Richard well as it meant he could sleep.

Once rested he started to read through the manuscript the archbishop had given him. He got lost in the story of knights, chivalry and courtly love, and imagined that Lord Tancarville would be a man who lived in the same way as the knights on his pages did.

The sun rose the next day to a stronger breeze, which soon picked up into a wind that pushed the cog westward. Richard began to feel stable enough to go below deck and visit Solis. The palomino hung in a canvas sling that wrapped under his belly and was attached to the ceiling. His legs could touch the creaking wooden boards below, and kick the wall in front, but he couldn't do any damage to himself or anyone else. The other horses were transported in the same way and at least the crew had put Pilgrim and Sarjeant's horse between Solis and Nicola's mare. Her chestnut horse was stocky and hairier than Solis, but both were obsessed with each other. Solis barely ate the hay hung up for him, but snatched occasional mouthfuls when Richard tried to force it into his mouth. His nostrils foamed and his eyes were wide.

Richard spent the rest of the day trying not think about his horse, but images flooded his head of what it would be like for the horses if the ship started to sink. He was almost ill again. To try to take his mind off it, Richard leant on the port side railing and watched the coast go by in the distance. Soon enough it disappeared altogether and the cog turned towards the newly empty horizon.

Sarjeant pointed to it. 'Round that headland is the Seine, my boy. They call this the Creek of Rouen, as that is where the Seine takes you.'

Excitement and nervousness filled Richard.

'Not long now, my boy,' Sarjeant said.

The cog sailed into the mouth of the Seine which narrowed and narrowed from an estuary into a river. Both banks were filled with greenery and the southern bank rose up gradually to higher ground. The cog headed for the north bank and towards the port town of Harfleur.

As the cog sailed up the channel that led towards the port, Richard could smell land again. He could smell earth and smoke. They headed towards the tall town walls that sat in the sea and created a fortified harbour. The clang of blacksmiths and the chime of church bells floated over the water.

'That's the sound of safety from the sea,' Bowman said.

'I hate ships,' Richard said.

Bowman laughed. 'Me too.'

'Obviously,' Richard grinned.

'I've never been here, though,' Bowman studied the wall and the roofs he could see over it. 'What do we watch out for?' he asked in Sarjeant's direction.

'Nothing much,' he replied.

'Thieves. Thieves and men of God. Men of drink and men of war,' Nicola said.

Sarjeant blushed. 'I have had no trouble here.'

'I have, my horse was stolen here ten years ago,' she replied.

Richard groaned as he remembered his own recent trouble with horse thieves.

'Do not worry, young Richard, I learnt a lesson from it. Now my horse looks cheap and is angry. It makes the thieves think twice.'

'What is she called?' Richard asked.

'Three Legs.'

Bowman erupted into laughter. 'A good for nothing horse.'

'Exactly,' Nicola flashed a toothy grin, 'men as dumb as you will pass her by.'

'Amazing,' Sarjeant said.

Richard chuckled. 'What would you tell us of Normandy?'

Sarjeant crossed his arms and looked away towards Harfleur as Nicola answered.

'It is a good place for trading wool, for they have few sheep. They have wine and better food than England. The English king is wary of his powerful Norman lords, and the Flemings and French jealously eye the whole land.'

'How does a woman know all that?' Bowman put his hands on his hips.

Nicola winked at him and he rolled his eyes.

'Watch this one, young lord, she is trouble,' Bowman said.

'Men always say that,' Nicola spat overboard.

The cog sailed gently through the sea wall of the town and into the man-made harbour. The mostly wooden walls were painted white and smoke drifted up from every part of the town. Seagulls flew overhead, squawked at each other and harassed anyone with food on the port-side.

They docked and a crane was used to hoist the horses out of the hold. Solis had his ears flat back the whole way, and bit the sailor who untied the sling under him.

Richard put his bridle on and led him away from the ship.

'I will try to never do that to you again. No more ships,' he stroked him behind his ears, which slid forwards. Solis snorted and coughed as the other horses were released from their captivity and staggered onto the firmer footing of the dock.

Richard swayed a bit on his feet but soon could walk normally again.

Nicola's cart was manhandled off the cog with great effort and much cursing, but eventually she was able to hitch up her mare and rolled off into town.

'I don't think I should ride him yet,' Richard said as Sarjeant walked up to him with his thin grey horse.

'Probably not, he looks angry,' Sarjeant replied.

They walked their horses into the town. Richard felt hungry and took full advantage of a street where meat was being roasted in many of its houses. As he chewed the last of the food, he started to notice that although the people were speaking French like at home, it didn't sound quite right.

'This isn't France,' Bowman said as he saw Richard watch at townspeople in conversation. 'They don't speak French, they speak Norman. In England the commons speak English and the lords speak Norman because they are not English. In France everyone speaks French, unless you're in the south then they speak something else. Here everyone understands French even though they are Norman. And even though you think you are an English Norman, the English commoners think you are foreign, and the Normans will think you are English. Get it?'

'Not really,' Richard said.

Bowman laughed. They bought a sack of horsebread before they reached a gate in the town wall. A cart blocked the way and the owner argued with the guards on the gate.

Richard recognised the cart and the mare who pulled it before he heard Nicola.

'I have given you the right amount, let me through,' she shouted.

A man with a single drooped eyelid and a red fur trimmed tunic gestured at the cart.

Richard didn't understand him and then Nicola drifted into what he assumed was Norman, and she spoke so quickly that he didn't understand her either.

Sarjeant walked over with his horse in hand and started to shout at the official. The official shouted back and Nicola shouted too, and Richard didn't think anyone was actually listening to anyone else.

Suddenly they all stopped, Nicola cracked the reins and her mare walked off.

Sarjeant beamed a smile but she didn't look back at him.

'Come on,' Bowman said and they followed the cart out of the town.

'What was that?' Richard asked.

'She paid her tax on the wool but the official wanted a bit more. So she parked her cart in the gateway and blocked the road. Eventually he gave up and let her go. If you don't stand your ground, young lord, these parasites will bleed you dry.'

They followed Nicola out of the town and into the lush unkept countryside along a well worn road. When they found a pond they all stopped and let the horses drink and eat some of the horsebread.

Sarjeant gave Nicola's mare some, which she crunched away on happily.

The four of them stayed as a group on their journey east towards Tancarville, along hedge-lined lanes that seemed deeper than the earth around them, as if the tracks were older than in England and therefore more worn down. Later on they all spent a quiet night surrounded by dense hedges. Accompanied by the hoots of owls in the warm Norman sky, the sun set in the west. Richard fell asleep knowing that the next day would be the start of the rest of his life.

CASTLE TANCARVILLE

Richard caught sight of the Seine before he saw the castle. They'd ridden all morning through sunken lanes which they could see neither through nor over. The sky was blue above them but due to the hedges they travelled in the shade. Around midday they rounded a gentle bend and the hedgerows gave way to a sweeping view of the Seine valley. They were on the north bank and when he looked out to the south, Richard had to squint because the sun was right in his eyes. He thought that Normandy wasn't too different from England, but then he noticed the stone keep that protruded above the treeline ahead.

'We have arrived,' Sarjeant said, 'that's Castle Tancarville. It is older than all the castles you have ever seen before, boy.'

The castle they could see was a square keep of bright white limestone on top of a hill overlooking the river.

When they got close enough Richard could see that the walls were stone and bright white like the keep. He'd just seen the Roman walls of London which could compare with these, and he looked up at the crenelated ramparts with wide eyes. England was the New World, this was the Old. The main gate sat between two large round towers that funnelled visitors between them. Richard glanced up and saw slits for crossbowmen as well as large red flags. At the centre of each red flag was a white shield, and around the red border were numerous white wheels that Richard recognised as star shaped spur rowels. He wore prick spurs, spurs with a point, but he had seen some men in London wearing the rowelled, wheeled, spurs.

Two crossbowmen stood next to the wooden gate in conversation with each other. The gate was shut.

Richard heard them as they rode up, he could understand them but he had to concentrate.

'They look foreign. If they're Norman let them in, if they're English let them wait. Too many English here already,' the crossbowman with a short brown beard said.

The second laughed.

'They know we are English,' Sarjeant dismounted. He greeted them and requested entrance.

'Come back tomorrow,' the bearded guard said.

'Our young lord here has been instructed by the Archbishop of Canterbury to see your lord,' Sarjeant said.

The second crossbowman looked over to Richard. 'I'm not sure Lord Tancarville cares about some snivelling English boy,' he said.

'I am sure,' the bearded guard added, 'and he doesn't.' Both crossbowmen laughed.

Richard saw a stack of pottery behind them, some cups upright, some rolled over.

'The archbishop,' Sarjeant began but the bearded guard cut him off.

'Where was he the archbishop of?'

'Canterbury.'

'Where's that?'

'In England,' Sarjeant said.

'So not Normandy?' the second guard asked.

'No.'

'Then why should we care what he says?' The first crossbowman said to yet more laughter.

'I am getting tired of this,' Bowman looked down at the scattered pottery, 'I could do with a drink.'

'Couldn't we all,' Sarjeant said quietly, then loudly, 'let us in.'

The guards laughed again and the second clutched his stomach and doubled over.

'I need to piss,' the bearded one said to him and slapped him hard on the back.

From behind Richard and Bowman there was a crack of reins and Nicola's cart rolled forwards up to the gate.

'Is that you, Nicola the Frank?'

'The Frank?' Richard asked.

She turned back and said to Richard, 'not really accurate, but these two don't react well to things like truth or honesty.' Nicola reached back into her cart under a blanket. She pulled out two bottles and held them out. 'Come on then.'

'Open the door, Jean, you idiot,' the bearded crossbowman said to his companion who massaged his own belly. Jean did so and swung the big wooden doors open slowly to reveal a passageway into the castle. The bearded guard took the bottles and held them up to the sky. 'No bits or anything,' he said.

Nicola clicked her tongue and her mare moved off.

Sarjeant glared at the crossbowmen as he led his horse past.

Richard watched them crack open a bottle each. Solis paused at the entrance way and looked down it as the cart and hooves echoed along what was really a tunnel. Richard squeezed his legs and the palomino exhaled and walked forwards. They emerged into the wide inner yard of the castle. The yard, and therefore the castle, were in the shape of a tall triangle, with the two towers of the entrance on a long side. To the right, at the base of the triangle, was a raised cliff, and atop that sat the stone keep which was many stories high. A variety of stone and wooden buildings hung off the keep and down the slope into the yard. That yard was full of men and horses, some stood in clusters to observe the others who rode and fought with swords.

'Is this every knight in Normandy?' Richard wondered out loud.

'No, young lord,' Bowman dismounted, 'this is Lord Tancarville's household, or mesnie, and those who wish to be promoted into it. Out there are your idols and your rivals.'

As Richard watched, two riders rode towards each other, shields on their left side and pine lances in their right hands. They wore steel helmets, painted in red with nasal guards, but their eyes and cheeks were exposed. The lances were blunt shafts only and as they cantered together, Richard breathed in.

Just as the lances were lowered one horse jinked to the right, away from the other, and no impact was possible.

'Use your legs, boy,' a man shouted from close by. 'Again.'

The horses turned around, and so did the man who noticed the newcomers. He had a dark face and black hair and was only slightly taller than Richard. His face had the same depth of lines as Bowman did, but this man had a slight hunchback and his head protruded forwards.

'Who are you?' he asked.

Richard's father had told him it was polite to dismount when greeting a new person on foot, so he did. He patted Solis on the neck once his feet were on the ground.

'I am Richard of Keynes in England.'

'England?' the man inspected Richard, 'I do not remember any more English aspirants being sent for, or offered.'

'My grandfather told me he knew Lord Tancarville and that I should seek an education here.'

'Did he now,' the man replied in an English accent.

'Who is your grandfather?'

'Sir Hugh of Bletchley,' Richard said, 'he is old now.'

'Ah, that old man from the midlands. I always thought he was too grumpy. Was he the one with the son who was at Lincoln.'

'Yes, William was my father.'

'Why didn't you say? I am Roger de Cailly and I was at Lincoln. If you can ride like your father then you are welcome to try your luck here.'

Richard decided not to tell him about his father. De Cailly wore a dark orange tunic, held together at the waist by a white leather belt from which hung a sword that glimmered in the sunlight. He wore golden spurs.

'Ah, that is what everyone comes here for,' de Cailly smiled. The knight considered Bowman and Sarjeant. 'Are these your men?'

'Yes,' Richard said.

Bowman looked back at him with raised eyebrows and said nothing.

Richard licked his lips. 'This is my bowman and my sarjeant,' he said.

Bowman stifled something that could have been either a

cough or a laugh.

In the yard two men, both younger than Richard, tumbled to the ground in a clang of metal. One screamed out.

De Cailly looked over briefly. 'Not one of mine,' he said. 'How many years do you have, boy?'

'Seventeen,' Richard said.

'No, how many years learning the way of the horse, spear and sword. I notice you do not have a pack horse, so no mail coat, no shield. So I ask in case you were raised badly and have never swung a sword or hunted a boar. We have some standards of entry.'

'I've done both,' Richard jutted his chin out involuntarily. He noticed himself and pulled it in.

'I have heard that before. We shall see what you can do, have you eaten and rested well today?'

'No.'

'Good,' a smile cracked across de Cailly's dark cheeks, 'get back on your horse.'

Richard checked Solis's girth was tight then remounted.

De Cailly shouted a command that echoed off the white castle walls that surrounded the yard and it began to clear. The combatants went to one side, unlaced their helmets and made the most of their break to drink some water.

'Sir Gobble, to me,' de Cailly ordered.

Richard frowned and watched as a tall and swarthy faced young man with short brown hair mounted a dark brown horse and rode over. His face was plain but when Richard locked his gaze into Sir Gobble's brown eyes, he had to fight an urge to look away. The young man exuded a certain intensity.

'This new boy is an Englishman,' de Cailly said to him, 'and he says he can ride.'

Sir Gobble smirked. 'We race?'

'Race the square,' de Cailly shouted and the resting knights and aspirants cheered.

They dragged four wooden barrels out onto the grassy yard and placed them in a large square.

'You start side by side, race around the barrels, and first one back here wins,' de Cailly said, 'and the loser spends the night in the stables.'

Sir Gobble's horse was slightly taller and wider than Solis, but Richard hadn't seen it move so couldn't judge its speed. He walked up to Sir Gobble, who grinned.

'You're sleeping on straw tonight,' he told Richard.

Richard pursed his lips. 'We'll see,' he said.

Solis lunged out and tried to bite his opponent's horse.

De Cailly laughed. 'The horse will fit in here, let us see about the boy,' he said.

Richard had never played this game, but he noticed that Sir Gobble had placed his horse right next to the starting barrel which meant Richard would have further to travel.

De Cailly raised his arms. 'Go!'

Richard used his spurs as well as his body and Solis launched into a canter.

Sir Gobble raced off too, and in a few strides they reached the first barrel side by side.

Richard tensed his stomach muscles to slow Solis, turned on the spot and launched off again to the next barrel.

Sir Gobble did exactly the same, but was already a horse's neck in front. They stormed to the second barrel, grass flew up about them, and hooves drummed on the earth. Richard did better on the second turn but couldn't gain any ground.

Sir Gobble set his spurs to his horse and the stallion put his head down and accelerated.

Richard shouted at Solis and the palomino responded, they reached the third barrel only a head behind Sir Gobble. Both riders slammed to a stop, spun around the barrel and kicked on again towards the finish mark. They rode hard towards de Cailly, who jumped out of the way as both horses crashed past him and ended the race.

Richard pulled Solis up behind Sir Gobble, who grinned.

'I hope the grooms put fresh straw out today,' Sir Gobble whirled his horse around.

'Now, what did I say about how to act in victory, William?' de Cailly said to him.

Sir Gobble paused, then turned to the crowd and waved, gaining a cheer from some of them. Others shook their heads.

Richard pretended to scratch his face as he wiped away some water from his eyes.

'My boy,' de Cailly walked over with a smile, 'Lord Tancarville will wish to see you stay with us.'

'Really, but I lost?' Richard said.

Solis's body expanded and contracted beneath him so much that Richard moved up and down on his back. The stallion snorted.

'Young William there has never lost the square race. Even then, he usually wins by over a horse length. What was your name again, boy?'

'Richard.'

'Our lord will wish to speak to you, that is him walking down from the keep,' de Cailly nodded over towards the cliff at the far end of the castle where the tall stone keep kept watch over the yard.

William Tancarville, the second of his name, was not like Richard had imagined. In his thoughts, whilst looking at the Norman coast from the cog, Tancarville was tall, had a dark kingly beard and moved with elegance and grace. The short man who strode down the embankment looked like nothing of the sort. His chest was as wide as the barrels Richard had just raced around, and he had short red hair with no beard. Tancarville wore a full length mail shirt, the small metal rings glinted in the sunlight and made a telltale metallic rustle as he strode into the middle of the grass.

The laughing and joking of the spectators subsided.

Tancarville walked fast despite his short legs.

'My lord,' de Cailly said.

'Roger,' Tancarville replied in a gruff voice, 'who is this? I do not need another one, does gold fall from my arse when I relieve myself?'

'No my lord, but this young lad has promise,' de Cailly said.

Tancarville turned to Richard who blushed. 'Do you have promise? You look too young to me. It will be at least two years before you can ride in the line next to me,' Tancarville said.

'My lord,' Richard struggled to hold his voice together, 'I do have promise.'

'He does, does he?' Tancarville said to de Cailly and burst into laughter. 'He has balls to speak to me at all, let alone with such bravado,' he added.

'He just raced Sir Gobble, and barely lost by a head,' de Cailly said.

Tancarville peered back at Richard in silence. He looked at Solis. 'A decent horse, is he yours?'

'Yes, since he was born,' Richard said.

Tancarville stepped closer and Solis put his ears back.

'Careful, that one is a proper warhorse,' de Cailly said.

Solis snaked his neck and made a half hearted attempt to bite Tancarville on the arm he held out. The Chamberlain of Normandy didn't even flinch, let alone move his hand. Solis snorted, backed away and started to fall asleep.

'A warhorse, yes,' Tancarville smiled, 'but he knows some manners too. Good. The horse can stay, I am not decided about the boy.'

De Cailly looked around. 'Are you good with the lance and sword?' he asked Richard.

'I'm well practised with the lance, but not the sword,' Richard replied. In his father's absence, he'd tried to fight with Adela in the woods where no one could watch, but she wasn't strong and he decided not to mention it.

'Then we will test your sword,' de Cailly looked over to the spectators. 'Bring me a mail shirt, shield and helm for the new boy.'

Two servants who had been on the sidelines ran off into one of the stone buildings.

Richard dismounted and another servant appeared to take Solis. 'Your horses will be stabled with those from my contingent,' de Cailly said. 'The English company. In Normandy they call companies conrois.'

As Solis, Pilgrim, and Sarjeant's grey horse were led away, de Cailly's attendants appeared, one held a mail shirt in his arms. The other carried a helmet and an undyed woollen tunic.

Richard looked at the small iron rings on the shirt as it was brought to him. He ran his fingers over it and the shirt rippled like a magical fabric.

'Have you never seen a mail shirt before, boy?' Tancarville snorted.

'Yes, but only my father had one at home, he couldn't afford one for me yet,' Richard said.

'Ah, so you are a poor hearth son,' Tancarville said more than asked.

'No, my lord, the first son of a poor knight,' Richard took the woollen tunic and put it on over his normal one. Instantly his body temperature went up and he was handed the mail shirt. The attendant lowered it over his head and Richard jumped up and down as it fell down over his body. It was too big for him and the sleeves were too long.

Tancarville laughed. 'I will call him Sir Stubby.'

De Cailly laughed and Tancarville turned to the crowd. 'Sir Stubby,' he announced loudly and they all erupted into laughter.

Richard felt his cheeks heat up and he placed the nasal helm on his head and laced up the leather straps beneath his chin.

De Cailly gazed at the onlookers. 'Who shall we match with him?' he asked Tancarville.

The short man inspected the options. 'We shall choose my son, he could do with an opponent he can actually beat,' he said.

'Very well,' de Cailly replied. Then he turned to the crowd. 'The Little Lord,' he shouted.

A short boy with a round face and red hair stepped forwards, picked up a kite shaped shield and strode over. The shield was flat at the top and tapered off just above the youth's foot. It was red with a white shield in the middle, and in the red border were many silver spur rowels.

Richard gulped, but at least the youth was his height, although broader.

'I asked for a shield. Someone get the boy a shield,' de Cailly said and an attendant ran back off inside. 'Honest to God,' de Cailly groaned. 'They have no initiative.' He turned to Richard and looked at the hopeful warrior. 'Sir Stubby is appropriate,' he said.

Tancarville roared with laughter. 'Come my son, this new boy is English, show him how Normans fight.'

The Little Lord drew a sword with a round pommel that was gold plated.

Richard's sword was functional and the blade was no longer shiny. Black stains on the metal ran along the final third of it where he had forgotten to clean it after he'd caved in the man's skull in Hempstead.

'The previous master of that sword no longer needs it, but by God did he use it,' de Cailly nodded in appreciation.

Richard didn't feel the need to enlighten him. A shield arrived for Richard so he put it on. Richard widened his feet and faced the Little Lord. The shield hung around Richard's neck on a strap, but his left hand was hooked under two leather straps on the inside, so he had a grip on it.

The Little Lord raised his shield so only his eyes and helmet showed above it.

Richard's eyes were glued to the sharp edge of his enemy's blade as it swooshed through the air towards him. His shield took the blow which Richard felt with a thud on his left arm.

He slashed out with this own sword but didn't step into it and the Little Lord was confident to let it hit him. The sword bounced off the Little Lord's mail, who had already leant into a new strike. His blade smashed into Richard's helm. His vision went black and his left ear rung like his head was inside a church bell. Richard reeled away from the blow and when he regained vision he felt the breeze on his hair and knew his helmet was gone.

The crowd cheered and the Little Lord pressed his attack, blows hammered into Richard's shield and forced him to stagger backwards.

'Use the dammed sword,' Tancarville shouted.

Richard did. He lunged forwards, ignored his opponent's sword as well as his own bare head and attacked. His sword bit into the side of the Little Lord's shield, then the top a finger's length from the young Tancarville's eyes. The red haired youth jumped back wide-eyed. Both combatants took a few breaths.

Richard couldn't get the air in quick enough.

'Your enemy won't rest in a real fight,' Tancarville said. 'Go again.'

The Little Lord tucked his head back down behind the shield and swung his sharp sword at Richard's head.

Richard ducked behind his own shield and pushed forwards. He crashed into the Little Lord who yielded a step then pushed back.

'He isn't meant for this,' Tancarville threw his hands up into the air. 'You should never duck.'

Richard heard him and swung a foot in between his enemy's legs, then pushed. The Little Lord tripped backwards and crashed to the earth with a cry. Richard swung his sword down but the young Tancarville brought his own sword up to parry it.

The Little Lord rolled over and was almost to his feet before Richard put all his might into a downwards blow. It glanced off his opponent's shield and cut through the leather strap holding it around his neck. The Little Lord partially lost his grip on it so he threw the shield at Richard.

Richard had to dodge it but that was enough for him not to notice the attack that floored him. He hit the ground and banged the back of his head on the dirt. A sword flashed and a heavy blow smacked his own shield down onto his face. He tasted blood and his nose burst into pain.

'God's teeth, that is enough,' de Cailly said.

'Not yet,' Tancarville roared, 'let us see if the boy really has any balls.'

Richard got to his feet but the Little Lord batted his sword out of the way, gripped Richard's shield and used it to pull him back down onto the dirt. This time Richard hit it face first and his nose exploded with even more pain. Grass in his mouth, he pushed himself up. A foot kicked him in his stomach and Richard was thrown onto his back.

The Little Lord appeared before him, his sword carved down.

Richard brought his arm up in time to save his face, but the sharp sword dug into his forearm. It stung and he cried out. Another blow came down but Richard's right arm didn't respond to his command to block it. He managed to lift his shield up though, but not enough to fully stop the blade which sliced into the top of his head.

He thought he heard cheers but his ears still rung. Richard kicked a foot out and caught the Little Lord who hit the ground beside him. Richard rolled over and brought his shield down into his opponent's face, the leather rim connected with the Little Lord's chin and he screamed. Richard repeated it but this time the Little Lord caught it with his left hand and went to carve Richard's head in two with his sword.

'Enough,' Tancarville yelled.

Both men froze.

Richard's chest stung and the air was painful as he breathed it in. His head hurt and he knew he was bleeding there. He put the sword down and flexed his fingers. Luckily they worked, even though it hurt to move them.

'He was gone until that kick,' Tancarville said to de Cailly, 'that showed the guts I am looking for.'

'Indeed,' de Cailly gestured to Bowman and Sarjeant. 'He is your lord isn't he? Help him up.'

Bowman crouched down by Richard and felt his head. 'Not broken, you'll be fine,' he said.

When Richard looked up, Bowman grinned. 'Hope you enjoyed yourself. Here you go,' he said. Bowman hoisted Richard onto his feet.

Sarjeant took his shield and inspected his right forearm. 'This is good mail,' he said.

'How is his arm?' de Cailly asked.

'How should I know,' Sarjeant said, 'but the armour is good.'

Bowman laughed and de Cailly cocked an eyebrow at them both. 'You can ride well enough already and fight a little. Can you read though?' Tancarville asked Richard.

'Of course,' he said.

'Latin?'

'A bit,' Richard answered.

Tancarville laughed. 'Those English, none of them can read Latin. Roger,' he said to de Cailly. 'He can stay with your group, seeing as he's English and uncultured like you,' Tancarville said.

De Cailly bowed. 'Very well,' he said.

Tancarville looked at Richard. 'Your sword skills are inadequate. Sir Gobble is responsible for teaching you how to fight. You use a sword like you have only ever fought women.'

Richard spat some blood out and looked over at Tancarville's son.

The Little Lord frowned back at him through teeth that were ringed in bright red blood. It ran down his face from his nose too. 'I had you,' he said.

Richard wanted to walk over and punch him in the face, but he knew his right arm wasn't up to it.

'Not worth the bother, young lord,' Bowman said.

'What was that?' The Little Lord asked.

Bowman turned back. 'Nothing concerning you, my lord,' he said.

'Father, he disrespected me,' the Little Lord pointed at Bowman, 'let me fight him too.'

Tancarville laughed. 'My boy, what spirit you have, but you cannot fight a lowly man. What would it prove?'

Richard saw Bowman smile with his mouth, but his eyes were hard.

'Find one of your lower born peers to fight him instead,' Tancarville added.

Bowman froze.

'One older than you though. It should be a fair fight,' de Cailly said.

Sarjeant took Richard and sat him down on the grass to wash, then left him to fetch some water.

Tancarville looked at Bowman, whose smile had gone and his jaw clenched.

'Have you ever used a sword?' he asked.

'I have,' Bowman replied.

'God grants us two surprises today, a boy who can ride, and a peasant who can fight,' Tancarville roared.

The Little Lord wandered back to the crowd of fighting men who were happy with their unexpected entertainment. He spoke to a tall young man, who followed him back over.

A chill shot down Richard's spine when we saw the man's shield. It had a red and yellow chequerboard pattern. Many families probably used that pattern, he thought to himself, but as the man came close he was struck by his bright green eyes.

'Ah, Simon,' Tancarville said to him as he arrived.

Simon greeted his lord and Bowman sighed before he walked over. He noticed the shield and stared at it.

De Cailly went to Richard. 'How is your arm?' he asked.

'It works but it hurts,' Richard said, 'aren't they giving Bowman a mail shirt?'

'Of course not, he has probably never worn one. Wearing one

now would probably hinder him,' de Cailly said.

Richard had only ever worn his father's armour before and that had been big and heavy. The shirt he now wore was in comparison light and easy to wear.

Simon took off his mail shirt to even the contest. He bent over and wriggled his torso until it came free and slid over his head into a pile of metal on the grass. He put his shield back on and drew his sword.

'I would wager a horse that this Englishman doesn't even know which end to hold,' the Little Lord said.

Bowman scowled and Richard watched as he looked straight into Simon's eyes. Bowman's expression was fixed, hard as stone and his eyes narrowed.

'To first blood?' de Cailly asked the lord.

Tancarville chuckled. 'That would be no sport at all, over in a moment. They fight until one yields, as is proper,' he said.

The Little Lord's round face was taken up by his red toothy grin. 'Take him down, Simon,' he said.

Bowman was handed the shield Richard had used and given a sword. Richard spotted rust on the pommel.

Simon stepped forward and attacked.

Bowman parried the sword aside with his shield, stepped into Simon and pushed him off balance. His sword flew at the fresh faced young man, whose eyes widened as it clattered into his helm. Simon was knocked back but stayed on his feet.

The Little Lord's smile vanished.

'Interesting,' Tancarville said.

Simon raised his shield higher this time and waited.

'Hit him,' the Little Lord ordered. The man with the Martel colours ignored him and waited.

Bowman went to cut at his head and Simon raised the shield to block, but the blow never connected. Bowman feinted and instead stepped around the shield to cut a vicious blow into the younger man's shoulder.

Simon doubled over from the strike and cried out. He tried to raise his shield but his shoulder didn't obey. Simon's eyes were still wide and he started to back away.

Bowman chased him down.

'This is not as much of a contest as we had thought,' de Cailly said, 'should we stop it?'

'Of course not, in war it ends when you yield,' Tancarville said as Bowman lifted his sword.

Simon blocked the next attack with his own sword but Bowman struck a second time, and harder. His sword snapped in two when Simon blocked it, leaving it half length but with a wickedly sharp point.

'Get him now, you have more reach,' the Little Lord cried.

Bowman's face hadn't changed expression the whole time and he brought his sword back to thrust. Simon threw his sword up to parry but Bowman pushed it aside as if he'd been a mere child.

Simon staggered backwards and dropped to one knee. 'I yield,' he said.

Bowman lunged anyway.

Simon closed his eyes.

Bowman's sword stabbed forwards but was knocked to one side by another sword.

'Not so quickly,' Tancarville's blade stretched out before Simon.

Richard hadn't even seen him draw it.

Simon opened his eyes when nothing happened to him. The young man's face was white as milk and Richard felt pity.

Bowman withdrew his sword slowly and backed up.

'He's your bowman you say?' De Cailly said to Richard.

'When a man yields,' Tancarville said to Bowman, 'you stop killing him, make friends with him, and sell him back to his family.'

'That is what lords do,' Bowman replied, 'but I am no lord, am I?'

Tancarville burst into laughter and Richard wondered how the short man had any more laughter left.

'If your opponent is poor, then whether you kill or not him matters little, but if he is rich, then for your own sake you need to learn to stay your hand,' Tancarville said.

'Is he rich?' Bowman asked.

Tancarville raised his eyebrows. 'A curious question,' he said.

Richard noticed a wet feeling on his forehead and wiped away a trickle of blood. His head started to sting and his forearm was mostly numb.

De Cailly called Bowman over and told him to tend to Richard. He also took away the broken sword.

'Useless,' the Little Lord said to Simon as he pulled him to his feet.

'A good lesson,' Tancarville told Simon. 'To feel what it is like when a man means to kill you.' He left them and went over to Richard,

'Have you tasted the iron in your mouth from real blows before, boy?'

'No.'

'Then now you know the way of our work, our iron work,' Tancarville said. He then spoke loudly so all could hear. 'This is what we are training for, the iron work. They call me the Father of Knights, and so I am. If you keep working, I will knight some of you and give you your golden spurs. But you will bleed first, some of you will break, and some of you will die. You need to be able to stand up to the aggression that this peasant showed today. Do not underestimate the lowborn, they can drive a spear into your chest as well as any knight can. This peasant,' Tancarville pointed to Bowman, whose face was still stone, 'laid low a noble boy. And he's English.'

Two thirds of the onlookers roared with laughter and Richard noticed that Sir Gobble and those around him were amongst those who did not.

Tancarville continued. 'England is a land for nobility who fight taxes and harvests instead of wars. They stay at home when war breaks out in France. There is no war in England to hone these men, nor even any tournaments to sharpen them. Yet this man, who is likely a poacher, nearly killed a man from a famous Norman family who has been training daily for ten years.'

A hush fell over the watching fighters who started to look down at the grass or finger the tiny rings of their mail shirts.

Richard noticed that a small crowd had gathered on top of the cliff under the keep, and some of them were young women in bright full length dresses.

'It is best that your eyes do not linger there too long,' de Cailly said softly into Richard's ear.

Tancarville had finished his speech and ended it by shouting at everyone to get back to work. The crowd broke up, remounted their horses, and re-slung shields over their necks.

Richard finally caught his breath, but he'd never felt as battered as he did now.

De Cailly looked at his head wound and poked around in Richard's hair. 'Nothing serious here. I would avoid mentioning it to the priest though, he has a habit of turning wounds like this into fatal ones,' he said. 'You will need to rest,' de Cailly added, 'all the aspirants will hunt before the feast of Saint James, so you have a day to recover your strength for that. Lord Tancarville likes to use the hunts as a competition, so you will need perform. I will place you with Sir Gobble, but of course as you lost to him, you will have to spend tonight in a stable.'

BIRDS

Richard managed to lift his wooden saddle onto Solis's back but his right arm twinged doing it. He had been able to rest for a day, happy to lie on the straw by Solis and read his gift from the archbishop. No one had bothered him from sunrise to sunset. Today though, he had set out before dawn with Sir Gobble and Bowman into the marshes of the Seine estuary. Sarjeant trudged along behind on foot with a falconer and his assistants. There were two of them, and on the leather glove of each perched a bird of prey.

The hunting party left through the castle gate and ignored the grumpy guards who they woke up on their way out. Sir Gobble led the way and Richard and Bowman rode side by side behind him as they travelled down from the castle towards the river.

'He sits well in the saddle,' Richard looked at the tall Englishman ahead.

Bowman grunted. 'It is hard not to,' he said.

'You ride like a sack of wool,' Sir Gobble said loudly without turning around.

'Obviously our glorious leader hears like a cat, too,' Bowman said.

Sir Gobble slowed his horse so he was level with Richard. 'Although I'll grant you weren't bad in the race,' he said.

Richard smiled. 'I'm sorry they asked you to help me with the sword,' he said.

Sir Gobble smiled back. 'It will be no hardship for me, it means I'm allowed to hurt you a lot. It will be like fighting a wooden post, not a hardship at all.'

Richard frowned and looked down at Sir Gobble's feet, around which were iron spurs rather than golden ones. 'You aren't a knight, are you?' he asked.

'No, not yet,' Sir Gobble replied. The smile on his face hardened. He reached into the linen bag that hung around his neck and withdrew an apple. He crunched into it. 'Can you fly birds?' he asked Richard with his mouth still full.

'I have, but only kestrels,' he replied.

'Kestrels? Were you born in a village?'

'No,' Richard snapped. He paused. 'Well, yes actually. I've just never flown sakers.' He looked back at the two birds behind them with their brown wings and white and brown dappled bodies. Their beaks curved downwards at the end and their talons were sharper than swords.

'Not many have,' Sir Gobble took another bite from his apple. 'Lord Tancarville was gifted these from some relative who picked them up in Sicily. They are not like kestrels though, different prey. Whatever you do though, don't lose one. Tancarville will kill you.'

Bowman leant over to Richard. 'I can fly yours if you prefer, young lord?'

'Really?' Richard said.

Sir Gobble laughed. 'So we have a poor noble boy who can't fly a noble bird, and a peasant who can?'

'It is not difficult,' Bowman said, 'I have been on many a hunt. All you do is hold the bird out and take care not turn left too fast so the bird does not fall off your hand backwards. Then you just caste it and it flies off. Nothing to it.'

'There's a bit more to it than that,' Sir Gobble frowned.

'Whatever you say, a Sir who is not a knight,' Bowman replied.

'Enough,' Richard said.

Sir Gobble snorted. They rode down a track that descended then levelled out at the base of the rocky outcrop the castle stood on. They rode under it and west, back towards the sea as the sun breached the horizon behind them. A golden glow stretched out from the east and started to push the darkness back down below the skyline ahead. The early morning chill soon started to give way too and Richard unwrapped part of his cloak.

'How much do we need to hunt to avoid sleeping in the stable tonight?' he asked.

'Sometimes a few waterfowl is enough,' Sir Gobble said. 'Sometimes a single rabbit if the other group is terrible. The problem is that the Little Lord has a female peregrine, so we'll be hard pressed to match him.'

The Little Lord was in another hunting party with his friend Simon, and they had left the castle before Richard's party.

'One of the stable boys said Lord Tancarville has four gyrfalcons,' Richard said.

'A scandal apparently,' Sir Gobble replied, 'when King Henry visited he brought three gyrfalcons, and when they all went hunting, Lord Tancarville came strutting out with his four. I'm told the king raged for three days.'

'I have never seen a gyrfalcon at all,' Bowman said.

They rode into the wide open air of the marshes and Richard sniffed the air for salt, but sensed none. The horizon flattened out until just small grassy knoll could be seen above the endless reeds and waterways. The trackway dwindled and became just a patch of dried mud that was uneven and slowed the horses down.

Solis stopped still and turned his head around. Richard followed his gaze and behind them he saw small figures in the distance behind them. Four mounted figures.

Sir Gobble looked too. 'Everything is training here,' he said.

'Training?' Richard asked.

'Tournaments are judged by the ladies. They decide who has shown the most prowess that day and wins the prize. So Lord Tancarville sends ladies out to judge us hunting,' Sir Gobble said.

Richard swallowed. He'd met young ladies at Berkhamsted Castle a few times on special occasions but he had never spoken to them.

'Don't worry about them,' Sir Gobble said, 'one is out to get the Little Lord's attention and the other is soon for the church.'

Richard walked Solis on and Sir Gobble led them to one of the grassy hills. From the top of it Richard could see even further along the wetlands. He heard bird calls he didn't recognise and watched as formations of large birds swept overhead.

'I can't see the Norman hunting party,' Sir Gobble said, 'I'd like to know where they were.'

Richard couldn't see any potential prey amongst the reeds that rustled in the breeze below them. He would have been much happier hunting deer.

Sir Gobble gestured to the falconer. 'Bring me a bird,' he said.

One of the saker falcons was brought over and Sir Gobble was given a leather glove. He slid it onto his left hand and the bird of prey was transferred onto it. He held it out away from his face and scanned the marsh.

'What are you looking for?' Richard asked.

'Ducks. Geese are too big for the sakers. And Tancarville likes duck,' Sir Gobble replied.

Richard could see a white sail drift up the river in the distance but couldn't see the hull.

Sir Gobble pointed the bird in a deliberate direction and threw it into the air. The saker spread its wings and flew. It flew effortlessly at head height across the marsh.

Richard was surprised by its speed and it covered a long distance before it dipped. It dropped out of sight below the reeds ,then returned. It had a duck in its talons, but then it dipped again.

'Off we go,' Sir Gobble said loudly. He kicked his horse on and Richard followed behind. He assumed everyone else would follow, too, and pressed Solis to keep up with Sir Gobble. They cantered along the rutted pathway and both horses tripped on the uneven parts of the parched ground.

Richard couldn't quite keep up and by the time he reached the saker, Sir Gobble had swapped the fresh kill for another, smaller, piece of meat. He retrieved the duck from the mantling falcon and put it in a bag. He looked up at Richard and grinned. 'This is a good start,' he said.

Bowman trotted up a few minutes later. He smiled and shared a laugh with the group of ladies who rode with him.

The taller of the two ladies rode up to Sir Gobble. She rode a small but fine looking horse, one that Solis sniffed in the direction of.

Richard thought she looked younger than him, and having not been married off yet, she couldn't have been older.

'I am not surprised that you are good at catching food,' the young lady said to Sir Gobble.

He ignored her as he collected the saker and tied it to his glove.

'My name is Richard.'

'Ah, the boy who couldn't use his little sword,' she said and the other young lady behind her giggled. The first lady was tall with a darkened complexion and long black hair. She wore a long yellow dress that had plenty of fabric in its skirts.

'What's your name?' Richard asked.

'I am Matilda de Cailly,' her gaze fixed on Sir Gobble, 'is it a big duck?'

'Big enough,' he remounted his horse.

Matilda looked over to her companion. 'Come now Edith, let us see if the Little Lord can catch something bigger.'

Edith looked over to Richard for a moment, her pear shaped face studied his. She was much shorter than her friend and had blonde hair and a red dress.

'Edith,' Matilda turned her horse away.

Richard watched Matilda go.

'You want to be doing less of that,' Bowman said to him as he rode up.

'I wasn't doing anything,' Richard said.

'Keep it that way, young lord.' Bowman said.

'You let your man speak to you like that?' Sir Gobble turned his horse towards them.

Bowman glanced over to him but thought twice of replying.

Sir Gobble mumbled something and rode back the way they had come.

Richard turned Solis to follow and rode passed Bowman. 'It's going to be easier if we keep up that you are my man, so you should behave like it,' he said.

'That is easy for you to say, you are playing the lord,' Bowman said.

'And you're the wanted man,' Richard replied. 'Did you nearly kill Simon because you think he's a Martel?'

Bowman turned his horse away instead of giving an answer

and followed Sir Gobble at a slow walk.

Richard caught up. 'Well?'

'The colours were right and his eyes are right,' Bowman said.

'Maybe we should check who he is before you kill him? I need to find out if he knows anything about my father.'

'Why would he? He clearly has never been to the Holy Land,' Bowman said.

They walked on between the reeds, the sun rose higher into the sky to their right.

It felt warm on Richard's face. 'He may have heard what really happened,' he said.

'That is true,' Bowman started to smile, 'so I will refrain from separating his head from his body for now, seeing as you are now my lord.'

'What did they do to you?' Richard asked.

Bowman continued to look straight ahead and didn't reply.

In stubborn silence they followed Sir Gobble who had met up with the falconer and his assistants. Sir Gobble found another grassy mound, this time one far from the river, which Richard couldn't see anymore. When they caught up to him, Sir Gobble finished off a piece of bread.

'You took your time,' he said. He scanned the horizon, which to the north now had a leafy treeline. 'That's the end of the marsh,' Sir Gobble added, 'I think the Little Lord will be over there.'

Richard looked but couldn't see anyone. He glimpsed the ladies above the reeds riding in that direction though.

'Your turn,' Sir Gobble said to Richard, and he was given a saker.

Richard had always loved the birds, but when their beaks were right next to his eyes he always felt weary. To make matters worse, the beaks on these falcons were bigger than his old kestrels. He took up his reins with his right hand and held the saker steady on his left.

He couldn't see any prey, no ducks, and just a few seagulls flying in the distance.

Sir Gobble couldn't see anything either, so they waited.

They waited as the sun reached its height in the clear blue sky and the insects started to come out to feast on them and their horses.

Richard's arm was heavy with the bird by the time they saw the ladies riding back over from the edge of the marsh. They rode up to join them and Matilda peered around.

'No more ducks?' she asked.

Sir Gobble pressed his lips together and looked away.

'We're waiting,' Richard said.

'I can see that,' she nodded to the treeline, 'the Little Lord has a number of ducks and some pigeons from the woods,' she added.

Sir Gobble cursed.

'Another night on the straw then,' Bowman said to Richard.

Richard felt an insect land on his neck, but he didn't have a hand free to swot it. He felt it bite.

'I have slept in the knight's chamber for the past year. I'm not going back to the stables now,' Sir Gobble said.

'Should we go to the woods and hunt there?' Richard asked.

'We don't have time to catch up,' a grin started to spread across Sir Gobble's face, 'not fairly anyway.'

'What do you mean?' Richard asked.

'Put the saker away and follow me,' Sir Gobble said.

Richard returned it to the falconer and followed Sir Gobble as he galloped across the marsh towards the treeline.

Solis put his head down and Richard let him run through the reeds. The rush of air through his hair made him feel alive. He'd missed galloping.

Sir Gobble followed the track as it left the reed bed and led up to higher ground. Soon it became flanked by trees and their bright green leaves obscured the river estuary entirely. When they halted it was far away from the marsh.

Solis bounced to a halt more than stopped and let out a great series of snorts. White foam sprayed out and Richard himself had to catch his breath. The lane opened out into woodland and Sir Gobble peered into the dense foliage ahead.

'What are we doing?' Richard asked.

'Hunting,' he replied.

Bowman cantered up behind them and came to a more gentle halt.

'Come on,' Sir Gobble walked his horse into the trees. Richard followed and soon had to sit deep into his saddle to avoid low hanging branches.

More than once he was hit in the face by one and a large branch dragged across his head and scrapped into the sword wound that had only just begun to heal. Once Solis had caught his breath, the horse pulled branches from trees to eat as they went. This made a great snapping noise as the tree limbs broke and pinged back, each time drawing a glare from Sir Gobble.

It was cooler in the shade but the mosquitoes if anything were denser, and Richard had to constantly brush them off his face.

A while later Sir Gobble stopped and pointed ahead.

Richard strained his eyes to see through the leaves and bushes, and he could just make out the bright colours of tunics.

'Their Peregrines hunt from high up, then dive,' Sir Gobble said.

Bowman nodded. 'Are you planning on stealing their falcons or their catch?' he asked.

Sir Gobble looked at him and smiled. 'I'm not sleeping in the stables,' he said. He looked at Solis and Pilgrim. 'Will your horses stay here if we leave them?'

'Solis will, we don't know about Pilgrim. I suppose we'll find out,' Richard said.

'Fine, when they fly the peregrine, I'll beat them to it ,and while they chase after me, you and your bowman go and take all their catch. Those poor servants won't resist, they are just peasants dragged in from their fields for the day. Flash your sword if they argue.'

'Won't Lord Tancarville be upset if we steal from his son?' Richard asked.

'Our Lord values one thing above all else,' Sir Gobble said.

'What's that?'

'Success.'

Richard crouched in the undergrowth a few paces from the Little Lord's falconer and his assistant. The Little Lord and Simon were mounted beyond them and faced away. The pair looked down the meadow that sloped away from Richard's view. On Simon's left hand was a peregrine, larger than the saker and grey where the saker was brown. The peregrine had yellow around its eyes and on its beak and feet. Simon threw his arm forwards and the bird of prey sprung into the air, dropped momentarily then spread its wings. It climbed up and up until it was barely a speck in the sky over the meadow. Richard knew that Sir Gobble was already down the hill and near the bottom of the meadow. The falconer and his single companion put down two bags which must have been full of hunted game. Richard waited for his moment. As he did, he wondered if his right arm was up to dragging away the bag of dead birds when the time came.

The time came. The Little Lord shouted and he and Simon began to race down the hill. In a puff of dust they were gone and the falconer ordered his attendant to pick the bags of birds again.

Bowman put a hand on Richard's shoulder.

Richard tensed his body then jumped up from the bushes. He drew his sword, raised it into the air and ran at the falconer.

The falconer was a middle-aged man with a jagged scar that ran down his face. His mouth gaped at Richard for a moment. Then he turned around and ran away down into the meadow after his lord.

His attendant froze on the spot. He was a grubby man with green clothing, but when Bowman walked out of the trees, indecision left him and he dropped the bags and followed his master.

Richard stopped by the hunted game and sheathed his sword.

Bowman picked up one bag so Richard picked up the other with his left hand. As they turned to rejoin their horses, the ladies rode into the clearing.

'I told you he was up to trouble,' Matilda said to Edith. The stocky lady nodded and looked at Richard who was rooted to the spot. He wondered if Tancarville cared more about the quantity of game they came back with than the judgement of the ladies.

'Is this how noble born men behave in England?' Edith asked.

Richard shrugged.

'Come on, young lord,' Bowman said, 'we need to be going. I tied Pilgrim to a tree in the end, and I don't know if he will stay there.'

'Not to mention escaping from your crime before the Little Lord comes back,' Matilda said.

Edith giggled. 'You're going to get into trouble when you get back,' she said.

'Richard,' Bowman swung his sack of ducks into Richard's back to move him along.

Richard blinked and looked up at Matilda as he stumbled into motion. 'I think we're just following the rules,' he said.

Bowman Laughed. 'I hope so,' they walked back into the trees and found their horses where they'd left them.

'Pilgrim is still here, do you still hate him?'

'It's more of a toleration now, we shall see how it goes,' Bowman smiled.

They tied the game bags to their saddles then rode north until they found a sunken lane. It was the same road through which they had originally arrived at the castle two days earlier, so they followed it back east.

Richard allowed Solis a quick graze from the hedges that lined the lane. The horse's ears pricked up and he bent his neck around to look behind them.

Sir Gobble burst around the last bend, his horse's head low and its hooves pounded the ground as fast as it could. Sir Gobble himself had a peregrine falcon on his left hand and had his right hand around the bird, trying to stop it from falling. His reins were looped over a hook on his belt.

He covered the ground between them in three heartbeats. 'You fools, move,' he shouted as he sped past.

The rush of air upset Bowman's horse and it threatened to rear up. Dirt flew up and hit Richard in the eye, but Solis had already locked on to Sir Gobble's horse and started to chase it without being asked. He launched into a gallop as the Little Lord and Simon flew around the same corner in pursuit.

Richard leant forwards and let Solis run how he liked, the horse with its ears pinned back found an extra pace and the hedges and trees whipped by as quickly as they appeared. They couldn't gain on Sir Gobble though, and when he looked back the Little Lord was still giving chase.

They galloped around a bend and straight into a group of

travellers. Solis galloped right between two of their horses who spun and reared before they crashed into the high hedges on either side of the track. Richard's left knee hit one of them and he grimaced in pain.

The travellers swore as Richard carried on but he never really saw them. He hoped they'd get in the Little Lord's way, too.

Richard rounded another bend and saw the white keep above the trees. They skidded to a halt by the castle gate and nearly thudded into the bearded crossbowman who stood in front of it.

The guard fell back and bounced off the stone wall. 'You children should be beaten for this,' he shouted.

Richard could see Sir Gobble as he trotted through the tunnel and into the castle.

Richard ignored the guard and followed, turning to check that Bowman was still behind him.

The Little Lord had almost caught up with them as he exploded out from the end of the hedgerow and into the gateway.

Richard pushed on through to the castle yard, where Sir Gobble rode right up to the cliff below the great stone keep.

Richard could hear the peregrine squawk even as he trotted over. Solis pulled up by Sir Gobble and went to sniff the bird of prey. Richard had to tell him off before he bit it.

Bowman caught up and swore.

'He's not going to take kindly to this,' Sir Gobble said as the Little Lord and Simon cantered through the gateway. 'You might want to draw your sword,' Sir Gobble added.

Richard's face drained of colour. He grabbed his sword but the act of retrieving it from its scabbard sent a shooting pain up his forearm.

Sir Gobble drew his sword and still rode with his reins on his belt, the bird of prey on his left hand.

Richard knew he could do that too, but not quite as well.

Sir Gobble lined up with Richard as their opponents rode up and came to face them.

'What need is there for swords?' The Little Lord asked as he slid his own silently out of its scabbard.

Simon was out of breath and glared at Bowman as he armed

himself too.

The Little Lord's round face was as red as his hair, and his lungs still puffed as he looked at the three riders opposite him.

'Give me back my peregrine and my father doesn't need to know about this,' he said.

'Come and get it,' Sir Gobble grinned.

Bowman started to walk his horse forward towards Simon. 'I will kill that one,' he said.

'Don't,' Richard hissed.

Bowman's eyes looked darker than normal but he stopped Pilgrim nonetheless.

No one moved and people started to come out of the buildings to watch. The most prominent of them wore a blue tunic with a fine yellow linen cloak. He had curly blonde hair framing a cleanly shaved face on top of a short stocky body.

Richard noticed his polished golden spurs that caught the sunlight.

'You are supposed to be hunting animals, not each other,' the man said in a low voice that was almost a growl.

'Sir John, they stole my peregrine,' the Little Lord told him, his voice pitched higher than usual.

'He left it unattended,' Sir Gobble said airily, unable to take the grin off his face. 'Besides, the hunt was for animals, and this bird is an animal.'

'Who are you?' Sir John asked Richard.

'Richard.'

'Are you the new English boy?' Sir John's nose wrinkled up.

Richard nodded, his breath yet to return to him.

'Is that the lord's peregrine?' Sir John asked.

Sir Gobble nodded, but his smile started to fade.

Sir John sighed. 'Why is it always you, boy?' he said to Sir Gobble.

'Because the English have no manners,' the Little Lord said.

'You have your sword drawn in anger too, young William,' Sir John said, 'our grandfather would be ashamed of you.'

The Little Lord's red face couldn't get any redder, but it seemed to withdraw in on itself.

'Put the weapons away,' Sir John said.

Everyone did, although Bowman hesitated first.

'Now give the bird back,' Sir John said to Sir Gobble.

'But I won it,' he protested.

'He stole it,' Simon said flatly, his green eyes switched from Bowman to the falcon.

Richard felt the hair on his neck stand up. He looked around and saw Lord Tancarville stride down from the keep, half a dozen knights and attendants in tow.

'That is not the bird you left here with,' he boomed across the yard across to Sir Gobble.

'No, my lord,' he answered.

Tancarville walked up to his son. 'Why do you not have the bird, have you forgotten how much it is worth?' he asked.

'I know, more than my horse,' the Little Lord replied and Richard noticed that he rolled his eyes back at his father.

Tancarville's face started to redden like the red fabric of his tunic. 'I am taking that horse from you as a lesson in carelessness,' he said.

'But father.'

'Quiet, boy,' Tancarville turned to Sir Gobble, 'what happened?'

To Richard's surprise, Sir Gobble told him the truth.

Tancarville looked back at his son then burst into laughter. 'The rules were that whichever party returned with the most prey will sleep in the knight's hall tonight, and the other in the stables. You are in the stables, my son,' he said.

'But we caught those,' the Little Lord pointed at the two bags that hung from Richard and Bowman's saddles.

'You did, but you lost them, didn't you. In a tournament, what happens if you capture a knight and leave him unguarded?' Tancarville asked.

'He can escape.'

'Which means?'

'Which means you can't ransom him or keep his horse and armour,' the Little Lord replied.

'Which means you lose. What is the point being good at fighting or hawking if you cannot keep what you've won?' Tancarville shouted.

Sir Gobble's smile came back all full of teeth.

Richard felt his muscles relax and he put his sword away.

'You could learn from Sir Gobble, son. Use your head. Which you will have plenty of time to do in the stables. I do not want to see you until tomorrow morning.'

The Little Lord's face dropped. 'Yes, father,' was all he could muster and he turned his horse round to ride towards his bed for the night.

Simon followed.

Tancarville walked over to Richard and peered up at him. 'You were lucky today boy, but I hope you learnt something.'

'I did,' Richard said.

'You will learn more tonight, a storyteller has arrived and maybe he can teach you what a man should be.'

THE DANCING MONK

The hearth crackled as an extra log was placed on it by the boy tasked with its attendance. The fire was three strides long, one wide, and radiated so much heat into the knight's chamber that the red-faced boy ran away once his task was complete. This was the hall where the knights and in-favour squires could spend the night. Lord Tancarville and his family slept in their own chambers but ate with everyone else. The stone walls were painted white and shadows cast by the flames danced along them. Tallow candles on tables around the room lit the corners, although the hearth was so bright it had driven away the darkest of the shadows even from those.

Richard sat at a table far away from the fire. It was the darkest but also coolest spot and he didn't mind being there. The hall was full of noise and people.

Tancarville sat on a table at the far end with his closest knights, and on the tables nearest them sat everyone else with golden spurs. Between them and Richard were the aspirants who had managed to avoid spending the night in the stables.

'There is a lot of silver here,' Richard said as women walked around and served food in silver basins. He thought plates would have been more practical. A basin with a roasted wood pigeon was placed before him but Sir Gobble swooped it up first.

'Our Lord is the Chamberlain of Normandy, remember, that

means he gets to wash the King's hands in a silver basin,' he said.

'So Lord Tancarville likes silver basins?' Richard said.

'He really does, so much so that he keeps the basin each time he washes the King's hands so the King has to get a new one. It is a hereditary right, although his father didn't bother to enforce it.'

'I see,' Richard said as Sir Gobble started to devour the wood pigeon.

'You'll get your turn,' he said to Richard through a mouthfull.

The high table had already finished eating and had started their business of the night. Red wine was poured and cups refilled. The wine had not even reached half of the knights yet, let alone Richard.

'I could eat another one of those,' Sir Gobble threw some bones onto the floor of beaten earth. A large shaggy dog sauntered over and inspected them with a black nose. The hound was huge, its back was level with Richard's head, but it had friendly eyes and it sniffed his tunic hopefully before it wandered off. The noise from the high table ended abruptly and Tancarville waved two men into the middle of the room.

'They've been here before,' Sir Gobble said, 'a story teller and a musician. Do you recognise them?'

'No, should I?' Richard said.

'God's toes you are dense, you don't remember nearly knocking some travellers off their horses earlier?'

Richard's face dropped. 'Yes but I don't recognise those two.'

'No, there were four travellers. You rode straight into those two monks,' Sir Gobble gestured over to the very end of the high table where two monks clad in brown robes ate.

Richard hadn't seen anyone speak to them yet. 'Mother of God help me, meeting a monk on the road means misfortune for me,' he said.

Sir Gobble laughed and grabbed a roasted wading bird Richard didn't recognise from a passing silver basin.

'You can have the next one,' he said.

Richard's mouth watered as the storyteller started his performance. The teller had a voice that rose and fell, but Richard couldn't hear him because he was at the far end of the hall.

'It's the Song of Roland,' Sir Gobble said, 'a shame, I remember that one well.'

'How long have you been here?' Richard asked.

'Since I was younger than you. Maybe six years,' he replied as he stripped the last of the meat from the waterfowl.

'Why are you here?' Richard asked.

'I didn't want to be a hearth son,' Sir Gobble threw a pair of small bones over his shoulder. 'My older brother will inherit from my father so I need to carve out something of my own. You have started to learn our business late, you are nearly too old. What brings you to Normandy?'

Richard thought for a moment. 'My uncle took over from my father so I also need to carve out something for myself,' he said.

'Why Normandy, do you have no family in England? Why come over the sea?' Sir Gobble asked.

'I could ask you the same thing.'

'Lord Tancarville is a relation, or at least that's what my mother said, and he didn't care enough to argue when he watched me learn how to swing a sword. I can better anyone here who still wears iron spurs.'

Richard listened as the musician started to play a lute in accompaniment to the story, which he still couldn't hear the words of.

'Why haven't you been knighted yet?' Richard asked.

'Timing, we need a war to start or his tournament team to take some losses before I have a chance. I'm sure I'll be next. You could be years from earning those golden spurs though,' Sir Gobble's eyes searched the room for a servant with food.

'How many knights are here?'

'Eighteen here with him in his personal mesnie, but when there's a big tournament he can summon fifty extra. We get left behind. No iron spurs on the tournament field, Richard. I need to be one of those eighteen knights so I can win some money there. Then I'll marry a rich heiress. I tell you Richard, I'll be an earl one day, and then the songs will be about me.'

Richard burst into laughter. 'You and me both,' he said. Another silver basin came round and Sir Gobble swiped it away so quickly Richard never had a chance.

'Yours is the next one,' he said.

Richard's belly rumbled, a situation made worse by the extra wine being lavished on Lord Tancarville and his favoured retainers. They included a Templar Brother who was drinking as much as anyone else.

Richard saw Matilda near their table, talking to de Cailly who was seated to Tancarville's left.

'You know that's his daughter?' Sir Gobble pointed a roasted leg at the young woman. 'She's too good for you.'

Richard looked down. 'You don't have to keep telling me that.'

'Even her fat little friend is out of your reach, she's the daughter of Sir John.'

Sir John de la Londe sat on Tancarville's right. Tancarville still wore his mail shirt, a habit that had spread to de Cailly and de la Londe too.

'Why do they bother staying in armour?' Richard asked.

'Armour is only heavy if you don't wear it,' Sir Gobble replied. There were several large pops from the hearth and a few flames reached up into the high beamed roof of the hall. The musician swapped from his lute to a flute and its haunting tones washed over Richard.

He shivered.

'Also,' Sir Gobble watched a silver basin be taken past them, 'the rumour is that he fears being murdered.'

'Murdered? By who?'

'King Henry. Every now and again a merchant or teller arrives who asks us about our lord and if he plots rebellion. The men who question us think they are subtle but we know what they speak of. There is a woman merchant who does the same job, she is smarter. She said the king sees him as a rival, another William the Conqueror who could invade England from Normandy. It doesn't help that the king of the French holds him as acceptable and dear.'

One of the monks Richard had almost unhorsed walked over to Tancarville, pushed de Cailly out of the way, and started to speak to him.

Richard noticed the lord's gaze momentarily meet his, but soon he waved the monk away. Richard watched, partly to distract his empty stomach, as the monk conversed with his companion and Tancarville said something to de Cailly. They all kept looking back at Richard.

Sir Gobble picked up another roasted pigeon from a silver basin, thought about eating, then handed it over to Richard.

Richard snatched it from his hands.

'Don't forget your courtesy,' Sir Gobble said as he withdrew his hand. The pigeon tasted as good as anything Richard had ever eaten. He finished quickly but it only seemed to make him more hungry.

De Cailly took his leave from the high table and made an indirect path towards Richard. He had brief conversations with various men on the way. The nobleman looked sternly at Sir Gobble when he arrived at their table, who yielded and moved along on the wooden bench.

De Cailly sat down next to Richard. 'Are you always trouble, boy, or is it a new habit?' he said.

'I don't know what you mean,' Richard replied.

De Cailly sighed. 'Knocking monks from horses is not courtly behaviour,' he said.

'I didn't knock them from their horses, I just bumped into them by accident. My leg still hurts from it.'

'That is not the story they are telling,' de Cailly frowned. 'And who are we to believe, two men of God, or a boy who arrived only a few days ago?'

Richard grimaced and looked down at the uncovered wooden table. He ran his fingers around a dark knot in it.

'The courteous thing to do, if you really did frighten their horses, would have been to stop and wait for them to recover. Then give them a gift,' de Cailly said.

'I will next time.'

'That is not why I am here though,' de Cailly said.

The musician switched back to his lute and the teller continued his account of the legendary Frankish invasion of Spain. Richard glanced at the mail clad warrior next to him and tried not to stare too long at his hunchback.

De Cailly sniffed. 'The monks did not just complain about someone nearly killing them. One monk is looking for a young man from England who is accused of murdering his mother. His name is Richard Keynes, and it occurs to me that no one else other than me has bothered to ask where in England you are from.'

Richard remembered giving de Cailly his full name, yet he hadn't been hauled off for murder. The empty pain in his stomach faded from Richard's thoughts and his stomach tightened up instead. For a moment he thought the pigeon might come back up, but he steeled himself and swallowed it back down. He wondered if it was best to pretend he was someone else entirely, to try another name and see if de Cailly remembered.

As de Cailly waited for his reply, Richard contemplated mixing the truth with a lie to cover himself.

When de Cailly sighed and went to stand up, he made his choice.

'I am from Keynes,' he said softly.

De Cailly settled back down. 'Good,' he said, 'so what do you have to tell me?'

Richard told him everything. Or almost everything. He started when his father left for the Holy Land two years before, and ended when he rode out of the manor at Keynes. He left out the altercations with Eustace Martel's men and the pilgrims in Kent.

De Cailly nodded throughout and didn't interrupt him. When Richard stopped, his eyes welled up and his nose threatened to run. The image of the man in the alleyway whose head he'd torn apart flashed through his mind and Richard had to choke it away.

'Quite a tale,' de Cailly said.

Richard watched the teller on the opposite side of the hearth. The man's arms told the story as much as his voice.

'Our lord has not given you away to the monk. Mostly because I did not tell him who you are, but also because he does not really care,' de Cailly said.

Richard looked at the knight, who was about his father's age. 'What will happen?' he asked.

'I have an idea,' de Cailly's eyes twinkled and reflected the hearth's light. 'We can tell a story of our own. It could be rather fun.'

Richard waited. He had no idea what the knight meant.

De Cailly's fingers drummed the table which sent a ripple up the small metal rings on his arm armour.

'We cannot change your name from Richard, but the world is full of Richards so we shall just give you another surname. Sir Gobble grew up further west in England that you did, but to the Normans it is all England. If you were part of his extended family, that would explain why you are here, as well as your English accent. Say you are from Newbury. One of Sir Gobble's most common stories about himself is based there, people will make the link themselves.'

Richard nodded along as de Cailly rattled off his impromptu plan, his voice raced faster and higher as he went. He noticed Richard stared blankly at him.

'This is a game, a game to be enjoyed, young Richard. It is no less lethal that the game of the tournament, but it tests different parts of you,' he said.

'What if the monk doesn't believe us?' Richard moved his gaze to the flames that darted out of the fire. Smoke congregated in a thick haze in the roof of the hall.

'Fully commit in all actions,' de Cailly grinned, 'make a choice and stand by it. On horseback, pick your target and drive the lance home. In the court, pick a strategy and follow it through.'

'What reason do I give if the monk asks why I crossed the sea?' Richard asked.

In de Cailly's eyes he could see the fire dance.

'Ha. I know, we shall say I have summoned you to judge if you are fit for marriage to my daughter.'

Richard's eyes involuntarily went over to Matilda.

'That should be an easy part for you to play, I see,' de Cailly said. A smile beamed over his face as he watched Richard's discomfort.

Richard's cheeks warmed up and he looked back into the fire.

Sir Gobble had been perfectly still throughout, but he was as close as possible to de Cailly without being noticed. De Cailly spun his head around to him only when he failed to stifle a laugh at Richard's expense.

'What a surprise, Sir Gobble has stuck his beak in.'

Sir Gobble straightened up and looked straight ahead, stock still.

'Do not fear,' de Cailly's softened his expression, 'you will need to play your part here too, but if you think of a reason to betray young Richard here, I will throw you out of the castle. Understood?'

Sir Gobble nodded then turned to Richard and smiled. 'Before you arrived it was getting a bit boring here anyway,' he said.

'Good for you,' Richard said.

De Cailly laughed and slapped him hard on the back, the rings of his shirt rattled roughly together as he did so.

'The monk will ask around, and everyone will point to you seeing as you have just arrived and fit his description,' de Cailly said. 'So prepare yourself. Show nothing on the outside, have a face of stone. If you succeed in that, then a future in someone's court may be possible for you. Sir Gobble is distressingly good at it, let him do the talking.'

Richard grunted in approval and was extremely thankful when some cider finally reached their table.

De Cailly pushed himself up and returned to the high table.

'The old man is enjoying it too much,' Sir Gobble said as he went.

'He isn't that old,' Richard said.

'Older than us,' Sir Gobble drained his wine in one go.

The teller moved through the Song of Roland and had evidently reached a boring part as the high table had gone back into full conversation.

Richard tried to listen to the tale for a while, his eyes glued to the reds and oranges that roared in the fire. The teller told of Charlemagne's paladins, of which Roland was one, and heard of the dastardly doings of the infidels in Spain. He drank more cider, and then some wine, which for their table was well watered.

A monk rose from the high table and went to sit at another.

Richard watched him move from table to table.

The second monk soon began to do the same thing. As they moved around the hall he felt hemmed in, like a deer running from the hounds only to land in a net and become fatally trapped.

'See, anyone with half an eye can see what they are,' Sir Gobble said.

De Cailly enjoyed his wine and requested another refill. He whispered into Tancarville's ear for a time. The lord chuckled and clinked glasses together with de Cailly.

Richard wondered who was providing more entertainment to the lords of the castle, the teller or him.

Richard decided he was too warm, the heat of the fire now stretched even into their corner of the hall, and the laughter and shouting made him sweat. Richard longed for the quiet of the hall at Keynes. He told Sir Gobble he was going to pass water and walked out of the hall.

Once he was out in the crisp evening air, he gulped down smoke free air and sighed. The castle yard was peaceful as the last of the sun's orange rays reached across the sky to the west. In the distance an owl hooted so he made the sign of the cross and said a prayer in response.

Servants pushed past Richard to get into the hall with either wine or silver basins, so he walked out of their way to do a circuit around the grassy yard.

Halfway around, the warmth from the hall started to seep from his limbs. He looked back to the hall and its welcoming hearth when he saw one of the monks exit it. Richard stopped and watched the monk. It was the monk who hadn't spoken to Tancarville.

The monk stopped in the dark shadow of the kitchen building and seemed to have a conversation with the shadow.

A serving woman walked past the monk, who stood still, stopped his conversation and adjusted his robe.

Once the serving woman had gone, the monk walked away, followed by a figure from the shadow who didn't walk as quickly as he did. Richard squinted in the gloomy light and thought it walked with a female manner. The monk and the figure went around the corner of a stone building and disappeared.

Richard glanced around the yard but everything else was silent and dim. He felt as if he was being watched and suddenly the warmth of the hearth became overwhelmingly attractive.

Richard walked back into the knight's hall, but couldn't relay the strange episode to Sir Gobble because the lady Edith sat next to him. Behind her stood an older lady with a sour face who monitored the discussion closely.

Edith turned around. 'Richard, so good of you to come,' she turned completely away from Sir Gobble, who frowned and looked over her shoulder accusingly at Richard.

'If you say so. Can I help you?' Richard asked.

Edith crossed her arms over her stocky body. 'I wished to introduce myself properly,' she said.

'I am Richard of Newbury,' he said.

Behind Edith, Sir Gobble smiled and nodded.

'Is your family of great importance in England?' she asked.

Richard could see the monk in the hall now interrogated a nearby table.

'Some. Well, not much,' he replied.

In the back of the hall Matilda said something loudly to her father and stormed off. Edith saw her leave, but turned back to Richard. 'Are you promised to anyone?'

'Promised?' Richard asked.

A reasonably well dressed woman walked over from the high table and whispered something in the ear of Edith's sour faced minder.

'To be married, obviously,' Edith said.

Her minder leant forwards and spoke into Edith's ear. The young woman's pear shaped face turned pink.

Richard went to speak but Edith shot to her feet, growled at Richard, and stomped off out of the hall. The aspirants on the nearest table all turned to look at the commotion, including the monk.

Sir Gobble moved over on the bench to take Edith's place. 'That went well,' he said.

'I'm not even sure what that was,' Richard said.

'Edith is already old to be wed, but Sir John has been dallying around and hasn't found a match. People say it's because he is poor and can't afford the dowry,' Sir Gobble said, 'you want nothing to do with her,' he added.

'You didn't seem to mind her,' Richard said.

Sir Gobble grinned. 'It's practice, one day I will need to speak well enough to impress a lady.'

'That rich heiress,' Richard said.

'Exactly,' Sir Gobble chuckled.

Richard wasn't sure what to say to that, but it didn't matter because the monk had gotten up and approached them. He wore a black robe with a hood which hung on his back and he had a tonsured head with a ring of dark brown hair around the side. He was a small man with big round brown eyes and soft face. He sat down next to Richard.

'Good evening, how are we finding the teller's tale tonight?' he asked in a gentle voice.

'It's boring until they get to the battle,' Sir Gobble said over Richard, who just nodded in return.

'Ah yes, of course,' the monk said, 'how long have you been in Lord Tancarville's service?' he asked Richard.

'Over six years now,' Sir Gobble interjected, 'who are you?'

The monk frowned for a split second. 'Brother Geoffrey of Cluny,' he replied.

The flames of the hearth dropped and parts of it smouldered instead of burnt. More smoke than before drifted upwards.

'What is the name of this fine young man?' Brother Geoffrey asked Richard.

'Don't you want to hear my name?' Sir Gobble asked as loudly as he could.

The monk pressed his tongue into his cheek. 'Of course, you are another fine young man,' he said.

'My name is William Marshal,' Sir Gobble said with his chin up in the air, 'and when I was five years old, King Stephen took me as a hostage from my father.'

'Very good,' Brother Geoffrey said and looked at Richard, 'and you are?'

He wasn't allowed to answer because Sir Gobble hadn't stopped. 'My father was holding a castle, and King Stephen put a noose around my young neck in front of the walls, but my father wouldn't surrender it even then,' he said.

'A fascinating story,' the monk said.

'It is,' Sir Gobble continued, 'the next day, King Stephen put me in the cup of a catapult and told my father he'd send me back over the walls if he didn't surrender.'

'Of course he did,' Brother Geoffrey sighed.

Richard could see one of his feet tapped on the beaten earth, beating it down some more. The monk coughed loudly and Sir

Gobble ceased, although he smiled.

Brother Geoffrey took his chance. 'What is your story, young man? Can it rival the scarcely believable tale that this talkative oaf is spinning?'

'I am Richard of Newbury,' he said.

'I know, you told me that,' the monk said, 'you sound like you are not Norman, where do you come from?'

'Newbury,' Richard said flatly. His eyes looked into the monk's.

Brother Geoffrey briefly shut his eyes. 'The youth today are not as they once were,' he said.

The musician returned to his flute and played a melancholy tune that wafted over the hearth and through everyone in the hall. The notes hung in the air with the smoke.

'How long have you been at Castle Tancarville?' The monk tried again.

'Six,' Sir Gobble started, but the monk whirled round and hissed at him,

'I know, six years, you have made that quite clear.' He turned back to Richard and his big brown eyes bore into him. The monk didn't seem to ever blink.

'A few weeks ago, around the Day of Saints Peter and Paul,' Richard said.

'On it, or after it?' Brother Geoffrey said.

'I'm not sure why that matters,' Sir Gobble said.

The monk kept his gaze for a moment then broke it to look at the teller who gestured with his arms and shouted above the noise of the hall.

Richard took a few shallow breaths and checked his cup for wine, but it had none.

'He's getting to the good bit,' Sir Gobble said, 'I think we should listen to the teller now.'

'Yes,' Richard said, 'this is the good bit.'

The monk looked at both of them, let out a barely perceptible sigh and got up off the bench. Once he'd walked out of the hall, Sir Gobble leant over. 'That was fun wasn't it?'

'Not really,' Richard said.

'He acts like he's your friend, but he is a serpent,' Sir Gobble said.

Richard nodded and tried to listen to the story. The tune the flute played made him think of home, of the sister he'd left behind. A wave of sadness started to creep up on him.

Sir Gobble picked up his cup of wine and went to drink it. He stopped, put it down and pushed it over to Richard.

Richard looked at him, smiled, and drank the wine.

'Is your name really William?' Richard asked.

Sir Gobble chuckled. 'My name is whatever Lord Tancarville says it is, and his name is William, and his son's name is William. There are five other William's here apart from them and me.'

'That was an impressive story to come up with so quickly,' Richard looked around for someone serving more wine.

'Was it?' Sir Gobble said, his eyes bright and his smile broad.

Richard was about to reply when the tall figure of Sarjeant entered the hall and approached.

'Where have you been all day?' Richard asked.

Sarjeant's blue eyes narrowed. 'Being your servant. Running around the marsh after you, then collapsing onto the straw in the stables because my legs hurt so much, then checking that the stable boys looked after our horses properly,' he said.

'Oh,' Richard said.

'You always like to say how much you like your horse, but have you checked him tonight?' Sarjeant asked.

'No.'

'Well luckily for you I have. Solis didn't eat the grass they brought in this afternoon to begin with. He spent the late afternoon shouting at Pilgrim, who he can't see from his stable. He's eating it now, but no thanks to you,' Sarjeant said. The lines on his face looked a little deeper than before.

'Have you eaten?' Richard asked.

'Yes, although we have to go to the kitchen and fight over scraps,' he replied.

Sir Gobble yawned. 'I'm going to bed,' he said.

'It's early for that, the teller is still singing his song,' Richard said.

Sir Gobble stood up. 'I'm tired, that's all, so I'm going to bed. It's just down here anyway,' he gestured to the wall behind their bench. A pile of bedding rested up against the wall and Richard realised he could move his own bedding out of the stables now. Sir Gobble sunk into his bed on the ground and rolled over to face the wall.

Sarjeant moved closer to Richard and leant over. 'There is a strange monk in the stables, he has gone to talk with young Simon,' he whispered.

'Why Simon?'

'Yes, that's what I thought. Luckily Bowman is up on the ramparts drinking with some crossbowmen, otherwise he'd be in the stable slitting Simon's throat.'

Richard groaned. 'The monk was asking about me, we told him I'm from where Sir Gobble is from, but it might be unsafe here for me very soon. If I can find out if Simon is a Martel, I can ask him about my father and then we can leave.'

'Where would we go?' Sarjeant asked.

'I have no idea, Christ will guide us,' Richard said.

'He might,' Sarjeant checked no one could hear them, 'but if you are sure then let us get on with it.'

Richard took one last look at the flames of the fire as a new log caught, then stood up.

Sarjeant led the way through the now pitch black yard towards the stables. Stars twinkled above Richard and smoke rose from the roof of the knight's chamber as well as most of the other buildings. A few braziers burned around the walls but light was scarce.

'Was Simon alone with the monk?' Richard asked as they walked.

'Yes, my boy, the Little Lord left the stables as soon as his father went into the knight's chamber.'

The stable buildings were made of stone and stretched out along the bottom of a length of the castle wall, using the wall itself as the back of the buildings. They walked past one entrance, a brazier flickered away in the corridor, and some aspirants sat around it wrapped up in cloaks. The next entrance had no brazier and Sarjeant stopped in the doorway and blocked what remained of the light. He pointed inside. 'There. I will stay here,' he whispered.

Richard put his hand around his sword handle and walked in. He hoped he wouldn't have to find out how strong his arm was.

A corridor ran along the front wall and the wooden stalls came off it. Horses chewed hay. Their teeth grinding was the only sound that came from the stalls until a horse snorted.

Richard peered into one box and saw a black horse. He checked the next one and saw a fine horse inside. It looked up and started to walk over so Richard moved on. In the next box he saw straw but no horse. He was about to leave when he heard the sound of twisting straw inside. He looked closer into the stable and could see a shadow.

'Hello?' came from the shadow.

'Good evening to you,' Richard said. He opened the door and entered. The stable smelt slightly damp, which it shouldn't have, and he looked down to see a pile of blankets.

'Who is it?' the shadow asked.

'Richard,' he squatted down. The blankets unfolded and he saw Simon's green eyes. Broad shoulders emerged next.

'You? What are you doing here?'

'I just thought I'd check on the horses,' Richard said.

'There are boys for that,' Simon said.

'I like the horses and I needed some air anyway,' Richard sniffed the air. Too damp. 'How are you doing?'

'Why do you care, your man tried to kill me,' Simon said, hurt in his voice.

'I apologise for that. He is, well, he can take things too far,' Richard said, 'maybe he thought you were someone else.'

'Someone else? Why would you say that?' Simon asked.

Richard thought about that himself. 'Did you notice the two monks while you were chasing us back to the castle earlier?' he asked.

Simon blinked a few times. 'Yes, why?'

'They are in the castle, have you seen them?' Richard asked.

Simon's mouth curled down at the sides and his eyes narrowed. 'Just say what you came here to say, you are a terrible liar.'

Richard picked up a piece of straw and absent-mindedly snapped it in two.

'The shield you fought with when I arrived, was that your shield, in your family's colours?'

'It was,' Simon sat up.

'A man owed my father a lot of money, and I was told that a family with your colours might know where he is,' Richard said.

'And what family might I be?'

'Martel.' The words hung in the air like the smoke in the hall.

Simon took his arms out of his bed. 'That is my family, who owes you money?'

'William of Keynes,' Richard said. He watched for a reaction and saw a twitch.

'I want you to leave,' Simon said.

Richard shook his head. 'My family is poor, we need him to pay what he owes. Do you know where he is?'

'He's dead,' Simon said.

Richard was almost used to hearing it now but it still hurt. 'What happened to him?' he asked.

'I was told he converted to the religion of the infidel so the Templars killed him as an apostate,' Simon said.

Richard's face twisted into clear disbelief.

Simon gave him a strange look.

'Who told you that?' Richard asked.

'My uncle is in Boulogne and sent a message to me,' Simon's green eyes were dark but still drew Richard's gaze. 'But I'm more interested in who you really are.'

'Richard from Newbury,' he said as Simon started to push his blankets aside. He was bigger than Richard, and likely to have his weapons nearby.

'See, the problem I have, Richard from Newbury, is that I was also told that William Keynes had a son.'

Richard pushed himself back up to his feet.

Simon did the same, but Richard got there first. He lashed out and hit Simon in the face in the same place that Bowman had on their arrival.

Simon fell against the stable wall with a great thud.

Sarjeant's large frame appeared in the doorway.

'I'm not looking to hurt you,' Richard said, 'I just had some questions.'

Simon touched his lip and blood came off on his fingers. 'You'll hang, you murdered your mother,' Simon spat.

Sarjeant stepped towards the young man and gave him an

almighty clout around the head.

The tall youth slumped back onto the wall and slid down onto the straw. Silence surrounded them. A series of thuds came from a horse that scratched its neck on a wooden door frame.

Sarjeant turned around as he heard a noise outside. Footsteps running away. Sarjeant reacted first and ran out of the stable.

Richard followed him and ran out of the building. Sarjeant chased a dark figure away from the stables towards the nearest tower on the wall.

Richard ran as fast as he could. He followed Sarjeant into the tower and ran up the stone spiral staircase. His lungs burnt after two floors, but he kept going up and round and round until he passed Sarjeant, bent double with one hand on his chest.

Richard went up and onto the roof of the tower. The roof was circular with crenelations around the top. A brazier burnt in the middle. It cast light all around and flickered in the gentle night breeze. It also illuminated a monk.

The monk struggled to breath. It was not Brother Geoffrey though, which surprised Richard, but his companion. The monk's belly protruded from his black clothing.

'What do you want, boy?' he asked between rasped breaths.

Richard swallowed. 'You were spying on us,' he said.

'Me? No?'

'Then why did you run?' Richard asked.

'Because you chased me,' the monk said.

'We chased because you ran,' Richard said.

The monk said nothing.

Richard took a step closer and the monk backed off.

'Who are you?' he asked.

'No one,' Richard said. He thought of what Simon had told him. This monk must be the Martel's man, the man spreading lies about his father and looking for him. If the monk left the tower alive, Richard was as good as dead. He gripped his sword and edged it out of the scabbard.

'Why are you doing that?' the monk took another step backwards.

Richard drew the weapon and held it up, the golden light

from the brazier cast dancing patterns along its length. Richard's forearm ached, but the blade was good. Sharp enough for wool and flesh, he thought. Richard took a breath and stepped forwards.

The monk backed up onto the wall around the tower, his hands felt backwards into a gap in the crenelations. Richard's hands felt hot, his lungs heaved and his mind swirled. A bat swooshed by overhead and dove down the side of the tower.

'You are Richard Keynes,' the monk's lips twitched in the light of the brazier. The flames reflected back onto his face.

Richard edged forwards.

'You are a murderer, what abomination kills their own mother?' the monk asked.

'Who sent you?'

'Our Lord above, now put that sword away, boy.'

'You're here to kill me, aren't you?' Richard asked. He stepped by the brazier and his shadow fell across the monk.

'No, not me. I'm a man of God. Your uncle though, he means to see justice done. Put down the sword and surrender yourself to God's judgement.'

Richard hesitated. The brazier heated his back as he searched for an alternative.

The monk saw and straightened up. 'You'll hang, even if you drive your sword into me here, they'll hang you for murder. Give me your sword, and we can arrange a painless death.'

'I will surrender to no one,' Richard moved quickly, 'this is for my mother,' he lunged forwards. He didn't use his sword, instead he lowered his shoulder to push the monk upwards. Up and onto the crenelated wall. The monk clung to the stone for a split second, face to face with Richard.

'A Devil,' the monk whispered.

Richard looked into his wide eyes and pushed.

The monk lost his grip and fell backwards off the fortification. Richard heard a scream but didn't look down from the tower. Instead, he stood back and sheathed his sword. He turned to the brazier, staring into its white hot core. It crackled and embers floated up into the now peaceful sky.

Richard felt numb. Battling voices in his heard screamed either murder or triumph, and Richard couldn't pick which he thought was right.

The clatter of footsteps came up the stairs.

Bowman appeared in the doorway, the two crossbowmen who had been guarding the front gate behind him.

'What happened?' Bowman said.

'Here? Nothing?' Richard said.

'Nothing?' Bowman panted and held the wall, 'I was down the steps with these two fine men, taking a piss out of the window, when this man falls down outside, through my piss, screaming all the way. That is not nothing.'

Richard looked him squarely in the eye. 'A Martel man,' he said.

Bowman's face froze and he blinked away some of his drunkenness.

'What's going on?' the bearded crossbowman asked.

'I'm too old for this,' the second crossbowman said as his chest laboured to breath. He shook his head and went back down the steps.

'One of the visiting monks had too much to drink, he was dancing on the wall,' Richard said.

'And then he fell,' Bowman added, 'a terrible pity, but accidents happen.'

'Accidents do happen,' the bearded crossbowman went over to look down the tower.

'Shame I don't have a drink to toast to that,' Bowman walked over and slapped him on the back which made him jump. 'Shall we fetch one, then we can toast to dancing monks?'

'Grand idea,' the crossbowman said.

Bowman turned him around by the shoulders and marched him back down the way they'd come.

'An accident,' Richard mumbled, alone again in the night, as he gazed back into the flames. They seemed to roar back at him.

SCRATCH MARKS

After being left alone at the top of the tower the night before, Richard had gone back for wine. A lot of wine. He didn't sleep much afterwards either, and for a while he stayed in his bed looking up at the old, smoke stained rafters of the knight's chamber as one by one everyone else went to sleep. When he got out of bed in the morning, his head ached and his stomach felt uncertain. The grogginess subsided after a while and everything came flooding back.

He'd pushed a man off a tower.

Richard ran outside and threw up. Then he went to see Solis, which usually made him feel better. On the way he thought to look in and see if Simon Martel was alive, or if he had two murders to feel sorry about. Richard poked his head into the stable in the early morning light and saw that Simon snored. Alive then. A voice inside his head told him Simon would have to be dealt with, for he knew Richard's truth, but in the calmer moment of the morning, Richard decided against cold blooded murder. Whatever will happen will happen, he thought, his head too foggy to think much more about it. After greeting his horse, Richard went back to the hall to wait for some food, but also because that was the least suspicious thing to do.

Sir Gobble still slept when Richard got back. Servants cleaned away debris from the night before, while some aspirants had woken up and spoke amongst themselves. Brother Geoffrey had slept in the hall too and he came over and sat opposite Richard. The heath fire continued its never-ending service, two large cauldrons hung over it and their contents bubbled.

'Your greedy friend likes his sleep,' the monk said to Richard, who nodded a vague reply.

'We seem to have been badly met yesterday, I wish to be on better terms,' Brother Geoffrey said.

'Fine,' Richard said.

Brother Geoffrey's big round eyes seemed softer in the morning. 'My companion has had me asking after a boy called Richard you see, and you are the only boy here that fits his description. I have spoken to your lord, and you are most certainly not him,' he said.

'No,' Richard said.

'I am worried about my companion though, he did not return to the hall last night. I have asked around but no one has seen him. It is most strange, I cannot think where he could be,' Brother Geoffrey said.

'Very strange,' Richard fixed his eyes on the cauldrons as the flames licked their black round undersides.

'In the meantime, while your rude sleeping friend cannot interrupt us, I would like to ask your opinion of this castle. How do you find it here?'

'Pretty good,' Richard said.

'I see. I enjoy stories, gossip and rumours, these show the nature of a place. I am curious as to how Castle Tancarville differs to other places that I have visited.'

'As a travelling monk?' Richard said, half asking.

'Exactly. Tell me a story about this castle,' Geoffrey said.

'I haven't really been here long enough to hear any,' Richard replied.

'What do you think of the great men of it? Roger de Cailly for instance?'

'Sir Roger? He looks after the aspirants he is responsible for. He seems wise,' Richard said.

'Does Lord Tancarville listen to him?'

'I don't know, I think our lord probably does whatever he wants,' Richard said.

'Fascinating,' Geoffrey stroked his bare chin, 'what of your lord, does he speak of other lands?'

'I don't understand. He only seems to care about training knights for himself,' Richard said.

More aspirants and knights started to wake up and the morning hum grew.

'Why does he need so many knights, I heard he can call on nearly a hundred of them,' the monk said.

'Ask someone else about that. Lord Tancarville speaks about tournaments a lot, that's all I know.'

'Tournaments? Everyone knows they are a hotbed of irreligious thought and treason.'

'I've never seen one,' Richard picked at a splinter of wood that stuck up from the table, 'nor ever really spoken to our lord,' he added.

Brother Geoffrey sat back and said nothing for a while. A young aspirant, a boy that Richard thought looked a few years younger than himself, ran into the hall.

'The monk is dead, the monk is dead,' he shouted.

Brother Geoffrey sprung to his feet. 'What? Where? Show me.'

The aspirant ran out with the monk on his heels. Almost everyone else rushed out too. Except for Sir Gobble who didn't stir.

Richard ripped up the loose splinter and flicked it onto the floor. He didn't want to see the monk, but knew he had to at least go outside and join the crowd.

By the time Richard got half way across the yard, the body had been carried inside the castle and a gathering had converged around it.

Bowman found Richard. 'How is your head, young lord?' he asked.

'The cut or the hangover?' Richard replied.

'Either? You were a sorry sight when you left our little get together in the tower.'

Richard had forgotten about that. The memory of drinking the previous night came back clearly to him. What else had he yet to remember? Richard had stayed up late with Bowman and the two crossbowmen before going to the hall, drinking more, and passing out. Richard felt sick again but it passed.

'You will get used to it,' Bowman said as he decided against slapping Richard on the back.

Richard winced in anticipation of it anyway.

One of the crossbowmen, the one with the beard, stood in the crowd and Richard heard him shout that the monk had been dancing on the battlements. This rippled round the crowd and quickly became its favourite theory. Once they'd seen the body most of the onlookers got bored and went away.

'This is of little interest to them, death surely visits this place often,' Bowman said glumly.

Richard and Bowman went back with the disinterested mass.

'Sarjeant is getting old, he is still fast asleep,' Bowman said.

'He didn't seem to like running up the staircase,' Richard said.

'No,' Bowman laughed, 'he was complaining about that last night, which I am thinking you do not remember either.'

Richard shook his head. His stomach rumbled but at the same time he was unsure if he should eat anything.

The knights and aspirants sat down in the hall when Tancarville strode through the doorway. He brushed it with his mail sleeve on the way which scratched it.

'If your spurs aren't golden, arm yourselves and get on your horses immediately.'

Groans erupted around the hall. The knights were excused from whatever Tancarville has planned, so they jeered at the younger men as they trudged out to ready themselves for whatever their lord had in store.

Richard landed in his saddle. The familiarity of it and the morning breeze made him feel better. Solis pawed at the grass and tried to move when he was supposed to stand still. Richard wore the mail shirt he'd been given and had his sword around his waist. He wore a shield in Tancarville colours around his neck, and held a spear with an ash shaft and wickedly sharp point. The two dozen other aspirants were likewise arrayed, including Sir Gobble, who had been woken up when de Cailly had kicked him out of his bedding.

Mounted, Sir Gobble yawned with his eyes closed. 'I'm glad I went to bed early,' he said.

Richard looked at him, aware that his own eyelids were half shut. 'Did you hear that one of the monks danced on the castle wall last night, and fell off?' he said.

'Really? I missed that,' Sir Gobble said, 'was it the annoying monk?'

'No, he's still being annoying,' Richard replied.

The Little Lord rode into the mass of mounted warriors on a smaller horse than the day before. It was black and looked decent enough, but it didn't move as cleanly as the horse his father had confiscated.

Simon led his horse out of the stables last. His hair was matted and wet.

Sir John stood in the yard and watched him. 'Where is your helmet? No knight has ever gone into battle without one,' he said.

'My head has swollen up so much it doesn't fit,' Simon replied.

'Did you bang your head waking up under a cow?' Sir John asked.

Simon blushed. 'I don't remember. Nothing from yesterday at all,' he said.

Richard closed his eyes and said a silent prayer of thanks. He watched Simon mount up slowly before he took his place next to the Little Lord. Simon never so much as glanced at Richard, whose head suddenly felt clearer.

The stable-boys dragged out a wooden structure with a wide cross base and tall post. On the post sat a spinning arm. On one end of each arm was a square piece of wood about the size of a man's head.

'A quintain,' Richard said.

'Of course,' Sir Gobble replied.

'I've never seen one before, only heard about them,' Richard said.

Sir Gobble laughed at him. 'You really are a poor boy aren't you. It's really very simply though. Ride past it on your left and hit the wooden square with your lance. Sir John and Sir Roger count the misses, and whichever side misses the most.'

'Spends the night in the stables,' Richard said.

'Yes, you're getting it,' Sir Gobble smiled, 'but don't worry, our side is much older and our horses more sensible, so we always win the quintain.'

Orders were shouted and both teams lined up to take their

turns.

The Little Lord went first. He cantered towards the quintain but his horse shied away from it at the last moment and his spear missed the target.

Laughs went up from Richard's comrades.

Sir Gobble went next. The Englishman cantered full speed at the quintain. His lance lowered only at the final moment and the point hit the middle of the square. The arm spun round three times before it stopped. Richard's side cheered. Solis pawed the ground and started to dig up the turf.

Riders from both sides took their turns at the quintain, most hit, until it was just Simon and Richard left. For his turn, Simon's horse dropped out of his canter into a trot. Simon's hit was disqualified.

'You can't trot with the lance,' Sir Gobble said to Richard, 'those strikes won't go through mail. You need the force of the canter.'

Richard knew a canter would not be a problem. He pushed Solis on, who chewed his bit with impatience. The stallion coiled up and exploded forwards. They powered across the grass. Richard's shield bounced and smacked him in the left knee, which hurt, and he had to use all his stomach muscles just to stay upright. The quintain appeared too quickly and Richard lowered his lance late. The point tore a splinter from the top of the target, which didn't spin around. A stable-boy found the splinter in the grass and held it up to a great cheer from de Cailly's half of the field. Richard only just managed to pull Solis up before he cantered into the castle wall. He didn't care though, he just felt glad that he hadn't entirely missed.

'Not bad,' Sir Gobble said when Richard returned on a warmed-up Solis, 'although not that good either.'

De Cailly and Sir John sent everyone round again as Lord Tancarville went to fetch his new horse. He rode out in full armour, including tightly fitted mail on his legs. His war saddle gleamed with new red paint, decorated with painted silver spur rowels. His helmet shared the same blood-red paint as his saddle. The shield on his left side was a Tancarville shield and the leather breastplate round the chest of the horse was painted red too, the leather tooled with yet more spur rowels.

'That's his new horse,' Sir Gobble said, 'he's training him for campaign rather than the tournament field.'

The horse had a high stepping action and an arched neck and its body shone a bright white. Its ash coloured mane covered the thick neck and it already frothed at the mouth when Tancarville approached.

Solis looked at the new horse and shouted.

'That is the finest horse I've ever seen,' Richard said.

'It's the one that Tancarville put on his seal. It's from Spain.'

'Spain? That's a long way to get a horse,' Richard said.

'I prefer Lombard horses. Lord Tancarville's one was a gift from the king of France. Stay away from it though, it is a warhorse and it kicks. Bit my horse a while ago,' Sir Gobble patted his own horse on the neck.

Tancarville rode at the quintain. The Spanish horse cantered in a straight line but its body jinked left and right as it went. As difficult to steer as it was, the stallion rode true enough for its master to dig his lance into the target. Tancarville broke off a chunk of wood and everyone cheered.

Richard did better on his second attempt. Solis settled down and went fast but calmly, which meant Richard could place his lance and strike the target cleanly. The blow sent the quintain arm spinning around. The aspirants continued until the square wooden target was a mangled stub on the arm, splinters and chunks of wood lay scattered on the grass below.

De Cailly's team won just as Sir Gobble had promised, and the stable-boys dragged the destroyed quintain off the field.

Bowman had stood amongst the onlookers and he and others came and collected the rider's lances.

'Well ridden, young lord, you almost fit in with this arrogant lot,' he said. He took the lance away and de Cailly, still on foot, shouted at the riders. 'Form two sides.'

Richard felt a surge of excitement. His quiet upbringing had never allowed him to fight as part of a group. This was going to be the closest thing to a tournament or battle he'd ever been in.

The dozen Norman aspirants lined up under the wall on one side of the castle, Tancarville at the centre with his son to his right. The Spanish stallion tried to bite the Little Lord's leg and his new horse jumped away from it.

Sir Gobble positioned himself in the centre of the opposing line, five riders on either side of him. Richard placed himself next to him.

Sir Gobble turned to him. 'Move to the end of the line, you don't want to be near our lord,' he said.

Richard backed Solis out of the line and rode over to an end. The two opposite sides were arrayed in good order. Even the youngest aspirants, barely teenagers, had placed themselves in a perfect line without thought. De Cailly inspected them.

'What are the rules?' Richard asked the young man next to him.

The wiry, light skinned rider didn't turn his head to answer. 'Fight until one side has yielded. Try not to hit their faces. Hitting a horse means a night in the stables,' he said in a thick accent Richard didn't know.

Richard drew his sword and licked his cracked lips. Solis pawed the ground again, but he wasn't the only horse doing it, for they knew what was about to happen.

De Cailly nodded. 'Go,' he shouted.

All the riders leapt from a standstill into a canter. Solis squealed as he accelerated, his ears pinned back. The two lines closed quickly and rode through each other. There was a flash of swords, metal rung on metal.

Richard had never swung his sword at a man from his horse before, and misjudged the distance. He was late and cut air. Richard turned. He looked across the yard and saw other horses wheel around and swords slash. He instantly knew he'd made a mistake in not remembering who was on his side. He noticed Simon and the Little Lord together in the middle of the fray so made for them.

Richard cantered through the swirl of the melee. Simon and the Little Lord got bogged down and dropped to a walk trying to overwhelm one of Richard's companions.

Richard kicked Solis on and as he cantered past them he delivered a blow to Simon's back with all the strength he had. He heard the young man cry out and he turned Solis to attack again. Richard's eyes went fuzzy for a moment and his ears started to ring. Then his head exploded in bright lights. Someone had hit him in the head.

'Don't fixate on your target,' the elder Tancarville shouted as he turned away from him and attacked someone else.

Richard urged Solis to get him out of the press so his eyes could return to normal. He could still hear a high pitched whine in one ear. He shook his head but it didn't go away.

Richard caught sight of Sir Gobble, he had hooked his reins onto his belt and had grabbed an opponent's shield with his left hand. His Norman victim wobbled off balance and was beaten around the head with Sir Gobble's sword pommel. The blow stunned him and he fell from the saddle as Sir Gobble moved on.

A young Norman spotted Richard and cantered towards him, sword raised in a high guard.

Richard saw the gleam in his eyes and was offended that the youngster saw him as an easy target. He gripped his sword and urged Solis on. As they encountered each other, Solis snaked his neck at the opposing horse, which put it off balance. Richard's sword met his enemy's in anger, he was stronger and pushed it backwards. He turned to his right almost on the spot as the young Norman slowed to a walk and started to turn right to match him. Richard knew he'd outridden him. He got behind him and tensed his body as he delivered a blow to the boy's head. It struck the helmet and pushed it down over his eyes. Richard slammed to a halt and with Sir Gobble in mind, smashed his pommel into the dislodged helmet.

The youth yelped. 'I yield,' he cried and tried forlornly to duck his head out of the way.

His first victory.

Richard felt the same rush he felt when he brought down a deer.

He turned his horse around and looked back though the melee. The Norman team had dwindled down to the Tancarville's and Simon, who stuck to the Little Lord's side and acted as a living shield.

Sir Gobble engaged Tancarville, both of them cantered in the tightest circles Richard had ever seen, blades flashed non-stop between them. Sir Gobble turned the other way and his horse pushed backwards into Tancarville's. It kicked twice at the Spanish stallion and both horses screamed the blood curdling roar that only fighting stallions can make. Tancarville's horse hopped a few strides with its front left leg held up in the air.

Tancarville slowed it to a stop. 'If you have hurt my horse, I will kill you,' he shouted.

Sir Gobble was being attacked by the Little Lord, and either didn't hear him or ignored him.

Simon tried to outflank Sir Gobble while he was busy.

Richard saw his chance and rode at Simon while he was concentrated on Sir Gobble.

Solis knew what Richard intended. The horse leapt up towards Simon with his jaws open. The stallion tried to bite Simon's face.

Simon hadn't seen it coming and his eyes bulged as white teeth and yellow hair appeared from nowhere. Richard pulled Solis's head to the side just in time, but Richard was still able to strike Simon across the chest before they disengaged.

Tancarville had dismounted and shouted at some stable-boys to come over.

Sir Gobble and the Little Lord broke apart.

Simon, slumped in his saddle, halted next to the Little Lord in pain.

Richard's right arm burnt again and he wasn't sure how much power it had left.

The Little Lord's horse lowered its head down and its eyes half closed.

'I'll still take you both,' he shouted over to Richard and Sir Gobble.

'I want to yield,' Simon said to his companion through gritted teeth. His face pale and his eyes dim.

'You'll do no such thing,' the Little Lord spat at him, 'I'm not losing again, not to these two poor upstarts. Who do they think they are?'

'You do ride well,' Sir Gobble said to Richard, 'if you can finish Simon, we'll take the loudmouth together.'

Richard nodded and entertained a passing thought that he should try to tip the helmet-less Simon head first onto the ground. The young man looked so pathetic that Richard decided on another tactic.

He spurred Solis on, which surprised everyone, especially

Simon, who recoiled as Solis careered straight at him. Richard purposely aimed his horse right at his target, who started to turn to escape. Richard cantered at him and pushed the willing Solis into Simon's horse. They collided together, horse into horse and man into man. Richard hooked his arm around his opponent's neck. He tensed his core and arm and as Solis broke away, Simon was wrenched from his saddle. The young Martel hung for a moment in the air before he was dumped onto the floor.

Richard heard cheers and shouts and turned Solis in case the Little Lord chased him.

He did. The Norman's sword flashed by but only dug into the top of Richard's shield. He turned Solis much quicker than the Little Lord could turn his tired horse, and Richard put in a blow that cut across his sword arm. The Little Lord dropped his sword and went to canter away. Richard pushed Solis on to chase him and rained down blows onto the red shield and the Little Lord's back as they flew around the yard together.

'Someone give me a sword,' the young Tancarville cried.

De Cailly went to forbid it but one of the young Norman aspirants ran over to offer theirs regardless. The Little Lord grabbed the sword and knocked over the boy at the same time. The aspirant fell flat on his rear and skidded across the grass. The Little Lord barely parried Richard's next attack as they closed.

The pair turned a circle together, right side to right side, and tried to beat each other into submission. Richard's arm struggled to raise the sword anymore and his blows were not as strong as he meant them to be.

The Little Lord slashed him across his chest and he heard his mail shirt rattle. Some rings had been sheared. The blow left pain when Richard took a breath. He raised his sword but his arm didn't lift above his shoulder.

The Little Lord smiled. 'I won't stop when you yield,' he snarled, 'I'll hurt for trying to steal what's mine.'

His sword pulled back for a hit Richard knew he wasn't going to be able to parry. Instead of trying, Richard threw his sword at him. The Little Lord's eyes followed it as it thudded into his chest without harm, but when he looked up, Richard had already grabbed his reins. The Little Lord's eyes stared at him. Thinking of de Cailly's words on commitment, Richard closed his fingers around the reins and, every sinew and muscle locked, he kicked Solis on. The horse bounded away and the reins were jerked from the Little Lord's hands.

Richard had never felt more focused. He held the reins up and over the Little Lord's horse's head. As Solis accelerated away, Richard held the captured reins out in front of the young Tancarville's horse. The Little Lord now had no reins and no hope of reaching them.

Richard and Solis dragged the horse around the yard in a victory lap. The Little Lord flapped in his saddle, utterly unable to help himself.

'Do you yield?' Richard shouted back as they started their second lap.

'Yes,' the Little Lord cried.

Richard decided to turn sharply, the bit in the mouth of the Little Lord's horse yanked him sideways when the reins went tight. The young Norman nearly came out of the side of the saddle. As the horse stopped he regained his balance.

'I said I yield,' the Little Lord shouted with fury, his face now redder than the matted hair under his helmet.

De Cailly, trying his best to conceal a smile, walked over and took the reins from Richard. 'Do you know why you were defeated?' he asked the Little Lord.

The young man's red face scrunched up. 'Because he cheated,' he said.

De Cailly laughed. 'No, you let anger drive you. You did not let that small brain of yours think. A wise knight practices temperance. Anger only clouds. What do you even have to be angry about?' he said.

'You're as much to blame as the upstart,' the Little Lord spat, 'you're the one who promised your daughter to him.'

De Cailly's faced froze.

The Little Lord cried out for someone to aide him and a stable-boy came and held his lathered horse, which coughed.

'I will have Matilda,' the Little Lord said and dismounted.

'She is promised to the church,' de Cailly said.

'Apparently not,' the Little Lord abandoned his horse to his boy.

Bowman appeared at Richard's side and held up his discarded sword. 'That will need a good clean after lying on the grass,' he said.

'I'll get Sarjeant to do it, just to see his face,' Richard said.

Bowman smiled, but looked over to the Little Lord who stomped away way back in the direction of the keep.

'I do not like the way he walks. Matilda is in that direction,' Bowman said.

The Little Lord strode past his father who concentrated on the stable-boy who walked his horse up and down a patch of grass. Their lord was in conversation with Sir John who was his marshal, that is the officer and keeper of his horses. The Spanish horse could bear weight on the injured foot now, but he limped on it.

Tancarville left Sir John and walked towards Sir Gobble, who was still on his horse in the middle of the yard. Tancarville's mail shirt sounded like angry metal bees swarming as he went, his eyes aflame. 'You,' he stabbed a finger through the air, 'you must control your horse,' he shouted.

'I'm sorry, my lord, it won't happen again,' Sir Gobble said.

'If it does, I'll hang you from the tower overlooking the river, so every ship that sails down it will see your sorry face and wonder what you did,' spit flew from the chamberlain's mouth.

Sir Gobble kept quiet and looked at the floor.

'If he is still lame in a week, I will personally break your leg and make you run around the castle walls, up and down all the steps, and see how you like it,' Tancarville continued.

'My lord,' de Cailly said.

'You,' Tancarville turned to his advisor, 'this English halfwit is your responsibility, if he fails to show the proper respect you will answer for it.'

De Cailly's half smile faded.

Bowman tugged on Richard's mail shirt. 'He has gone into de Cailly's chamber.'

Richard looked up to see the Little Lord storm into a doorway of a stone building near the keep.

'He means to carry out his threat. The face he has on, I have seen it before,' Bowman added.

Richard thought of Adela, of her joy when the manor cat had kittens, and how he'd ridden away from her.

'We have to stop him,' he said and put his hand on the sword.

'No, young lord,' Bowman reached up and put his hand on Richard's, 'you're in enough trouble already, let me go.'

Richard let go of the sword.

Bowman let go of him, nodded, and went unnoticed towards the keep.

'My lord,' Richard shouted at Tancarville, who had returned to berating Sir Gobble.

The Chamberlain of Normandy turned to him. 'How dare you interrupt me, you little turd.'

'Your son is about to do something foolish,' Richard said. There, he hadn't saved his sister, but maybe he could save Matilda.

Tancarville's nostrils flared. 'Foolish? Foolish? You are foolish, boy, how dare you speak over me. You, especially you, do not accuse my son of anything. He is the heir to half of Normandy and he can do as he pleases.'

De Cailly wrinkled his brow and approached Richard. 'What do you mean?'

'He's gone to look for your daughter,' Richard said.

'Nonsense,' Tancarville said, 'and slander will be punished, boy. I think I will break your leg too, and make you and Sir Gobble race around the castle together to see which one of you I shall hang.'

Richard wanted to back his horse away and hide. Tancarville's rage terrified him more than when he'd stood in the chapel with uncle Luke, or even when he turned in the Hempstead alleyway and seen two men who meant to harm him.

'For mercy's sake,' de Cailly started to run towards the keep.

'Stand your ground,' Tancarville shouted.

De Cailly slowed. Then he stopped. Richard thought he knew a little of what went through the knight's head. De Cailly lifted a foot to continue.

'Stand your bloody ground,' Tancarville roared, 'or there will be a race of three around the walls tonight.'

Silence fell in the castle's yard. A flight of waterfowl flew overhead, but everyone watched de Cailly. The Englishman took a step.

Tancarville howled, his face bright red.

Bowman appeared from the doorway. He dragged the Little Lord by an arm. The young Tancarville struggled but Bowman was far stronger.

'Unhand my son, you lowborn filth,' Tancarville shouted.

Bowman came closer and Richard could see that the Little Lord's face had scratch marks across it.

Tancarville noticed too. He froze and the breeze ruffled his red hair. He was either going to burst or shatter into a thousand pieces.

De Cailly ignored him, deliberately didn't look at the Little Lord either, and ran into the keep. Richard wished he'd been able to do the same and felt a surge of admiration alongside a bitter pang of historic regret.

Bowman deposited the red haired young man at his father's feet. His father glowed red from rage. The son shone red too, but Richard hoped from shame. The boy started to cry and grabbed his father's leg.

Tancarville looked down at him, pulled his leg free, then kicked him square in the face. Blood ran from his son's nose. 'You dishonour me, your mother, the family, this castle and everyone in it,' Tancarville said. He breathed for a moment then spoke with cold, hushed words to his son. 'This is the last time, if it happens again I'll throw you off the castle walls myself.'

That chilled Richard even more.

The Little Lord reeled away, blood dripped onto his mail shirt. A gust of wind blew across the yard. It rippled the grass as Tancarville stared down at his son. 'You will spend the next ten days in the chapel, praying for forgiveness. And on the dawn of the sixth day, it will be your leg that is broken, so that you can remember what you have done for as long as it pains you.'

Tancarville left the boy to sob on the grass and walked over to Richard, who met his gaze for a moment but couldn't stop himself and had to look away. His lord's chest moved up and down, the mail rings glittered as the rising sun caught them. 'I am man enough to admit when I was wrong. You showed spirit, a spirit my son unfortunately lacks.'

Richard's ear still rung and he heard the words only under a droning wail. He nodded and didn't dare look up as Tancarville finished,

'But challenge me again, boy, and you will answer for it.'

THE HUNT

The next day's enterprise was a hunt. Tancarville announced it the previous night as dinner had been brought out. Their lord had looked down and seen fish and waterfowl on his table, then looked up and decreed that four hunting parties would go out the following day to catch him a better dinner.

Richard had been excited. Hunting was one thing he could do. He had even followed Sir Gobble's lead and gone to sleep early, curling up along the wall as the teller finished the Song of Roland. Sir Gobble had been less enthusiastic about the hunt than Richard, but he said he would catch himself a nice big deer and eat venison from it for days.

Neither de Cailly nor his daughter had appeared in the knight's chamber that night, and a rumour had gone round that Matilda had been sent back home. The monk's death had largely been written off as a drunken accident, and Richard decided that most of the inhabitants of the castle simply weren't that interested in a monk. Richard's memory of the incident didn't feel real, but he now felt uneasy and unsafe at Castle Tancarville. Another man would surely replace the monk in time, but for now he just had to keep suspicion away from himself. Tancarville's was not a pious household, so that might be possible, he thought. The castle's priest was still unhappy about the death and Brother Geoffrey had been busy all day making enquiries, but no one else cared. The monk had cornered Richard outside on his way to check on Solis. 'When did you last see Brother Thomas?' he'd asked.

Richard replied that he'd last seen him when he left the hall, the same as everyone else.

Brother Geoffrey's eyes lingered on Richard, who maintained his gaze.

'I don't know who would want to kill a monk anyway,' Richard added hopefully. He'd been saved a deeper interrogation when Nicola the merchant had come by and asked to speak to Brother Geoffrey.

The inhabitants of the castle cared much more about the hunt. Sir John led all the knights, and almost everyone else, to hunt in a managed area. They went with nets and spearmen, the prey to be flushed out by hunting dogs. The aspirants were to hunt in another forest altogether, Lord Tancarville's boar-park, and as such their prey was boar.

Horses were saddled and boar-spears handed out. The spears had horizontal spikes which jutted out horizontally just below their long blades. Richard knew this was so a charging boar couldn't run onto the spear and keep charging along it to attack the man holding it. Richard rode out with Sir Gobble and Bowman, but Sarjeant had been dragged off to walk around with Sir John's party.

It was still dark when they rode out of the castle, the morning not yet having fully taken over from the night.

'How big are the boar here?' Richard asked.

'Half the size and weight of a horse if we're lucky,' Sir Gobble answered.

Richard smiled. 'Good, the same as England then.'

'They smell worse here,' Sir Gobble added.

Bowman laughed and scratched his ear, his hand free as no one had given him a hunting spear. 'I am not going anywhere near one. I hate boar. I will leave that to you proud lords,' he said.

'If we can bring back a decent boar, Lord Tancarville might cool his temper,' Richard said.

'We can only pray, I need to stay here long enough to get knighted, which looks far off after yesterday,' Sir Gobble said.

'The Spanish horse will still be lame today,' Richard said.

'I know, that's what I'm worried about,' Sir Gobble frowned, 'I'm not sure even the largest boar in Normandy will appease him, and I quite like my legs unbroken.'

'As long as we spear a bigger one than Simon and the young Normans I'll be happy. I quite like the spot in the hall we have,' Richard said.

They rode through the village at the foot of the castle's hill. It was small and mostly consisted of those who could sell their produce directly to the fortress. A team of blacksmiths started to grow a fire in their forge. Next door a mail-maker held up half a shirt to remind himself of where he'd got to. They rode on along the northern road until the sun heralded its coming with a tendril of orange that split the sky in two.

Silver birches lined both sides of the road and animal tracks occasionally cut through the bushes between the tree trunks. Sir Gobble led them down a small road and Richard started to struggle to keep track of their path.

Bowman spotted some deer dung and tracks after a while. Later he finally pointed out fresh boar prints in the earth. They were near a stream, the wet earth around it the only ground soft enough to leave tracks. These tracks though, around their water source, were fresh.

Clouds began to lazily pass by overhead and birds chirped various songs. Bowman dismounted to examine the tracks. 'Yes, they drank here this morning,' he said.

Sir Gobble laughed. 'Your rude man has some use then,' he said.

Richard smiled until Bowman glared at him as he remounted Pilgrim.

Sir Gobble let Bowman take the lead. Bowman halted every so often and careful considered the environment. It mostly looked the same to Richard, silver birches and grassy ground. But there was no sign of boar that he could see.

Bowman stopped again and pointed off to one side.

Richard halted but couldn't see anything.

Sir Gobble lowered his spear and edged forwards to where Bowman had indicated. Some leaves rustled and a dark shape hurtled at them out of the undergrowth. It grunted, then screamed a high pitch squeal.

Sir Gobble pushed his horse sideways out of its path.

Solis spun away by himself, his rear end rotated out of the boar's way but the palomino kept his front facing it as it ran.

Richard clenched his legs and stayed on.

'Go on then,' Bowman shouted.

Richard was ready and Solis enjoyed a hunt as much as he did. The stallion's ears pinned back and he scrambled in a flurry of hooves to give chase. The birch branches were low but also thin, and Richard stayed onboard as Solis followed their prey as it weaved through the birch trunks. The boar turned onto a track and sprinted as fast as it's legs could go. Its dark brown brush-like tail stuck out behind it.

It was a large boar.

Solis ran much quicker down the track, but the boar turned right just as Richard thought about coming up alongside it. They overshot the boar and had to slam to a halt, turn right, and crash through some branches to get back on its tail.

Sir Gobble cantered behind them but didn't overshoot, so he was now closer to the boar and followed it down a minor animal track.

Branches whipped Richard in the face, but he couldn't hold a hand up to protect himself because he held the winged spear. He kept it low through habit to avoid getting it caught in the foliage. Richard followed Sir Gobble and pushed on to catch up.

Sir Gobble disappeared around a corner of dense undergrowth. The hedge ran in an L shape which Richard could see through the birches. Sir Gobble followed the boar into the corner of the L, so Richard changed direction and headed to the other end of the hedge to cut their prey off.

He smashed his way through the trees and turned to face where he thought the boar would appear from. Through the trees there were flashes of movement that must have been Sir Gobble.

The boar burst out of the bushes. Its big ears were up and Richard's eyes were drawn to the two tusks on either side of its brown snout. They curled upwards into points. That's what you had to avoid, his father had told him, getting above the boar so it could thrust upwards into you.

The boar stopped, surprised by Richard and its body heaved with exertion.

Sir Gobble almost cantered over it, but he still had the wherewithal to attempt a strike with his spear. The boar turned to face the noise behind it and Sir Gobble's horse jumped away when it saw tusks flying in its direction. His horse went left but Sir Gobble had leant right and his spearhead hit the ground. It dug in, and although Sir Gobble let go, it was too late to stop himself from being catapulted from this saddle. He hit the ground and rolled, his tunic picked up leaves and twigs as he thudded into the trunk of a birch.

Solis's instinct made him chase the loose horse, and the palomino leapt after it before Richard could tell him not to.

That left Sir Gobble to face the boar alone.

The boar lowered its head and charged.

Sir Gobble still knelt when the enraged animal reached him and threw its head into an attack. Sir Gobble tumbled backwards and the boar ran over the top of him.

Solis raced through the trees, and as Sir Gobble's horse forgot what had spooked it and slowed, Richard grabbed its reins. He ignored being swatted in the eyes by a bunch of leaves and wheeled Solis around.

Richard returned to Sir Gobble to find him part way up a birch tree, his arms and legs wrapped around it. The boar had its forelegs up the tree, and jumped up on its hind legs to try to reach him.

Richard let go of the other horse's reins as the boar noticed him. Richard started to organise the spear in his hand, but the boar charged and he knew he wouldn't be able to lower it in time.

An arrow whistled through the trees and struck the boar in its rear quarters. It was knocked aside by the impact and squealed in pain. The animal paused, then turned and ran away.

Bowman walked out of the trees with his horse walking behind him.

'If you had not arrived, young lord, I would have hit its heart. I was just lining up a perfect shot,' he said.

Sir Gobble dropped from the tree and started to massage his legs. His face had cut marks down it and his tunic was badly ripped around his stomach.

'Are you hurt?' Richard asked him.

'No, but don't let it get away, we're killing this boar if it takes us all day,' Sir Gobble said.

Richard pressed his calves into Solis and the horse plunged into the trees after the injured prey. Yet more leaves and branches cracked and flapped in his face as they pursued. Richard couldn't see the boar at all. But that didn't matter as Solis knew where it was, and he followed the boar through a bush, over a ditch and onto another animal track. Richard grabbed the front of his saddle and went with his horse.

They exploded out of the trees and into a clearing and Richard could see the boar ahead as it scampered across the open grassland. At one corner of the clearing Richard saw a pair of horsemen. He instantly recognised the broad frame of Simon Martel atop a grey horse, his winged spear in his hand. The boar saw them too and raced back into the woodland away from them.

Solis accelerated, the horse instinctively recognised the chance to catch up. Out of the corner of his eye, Richard saw Simon point his horse in their direction and begin a canter. Richard was not going to let Simon have this boar, it was his. He nudged Solis with his spurs and the horse responded. They closed on the boar, the broken arrow still jutted from its side. It headed for some bushes at the edge of the clearing. Richard realised he wasn't going to get close enough in time and lowered his head to save his eyes from thorns.

Solis reached the bush, but instead of diving through, he sat back and jumped over. Richard was thrown back by the surprise movement and looked up just in time to see that the bush was twice as long as Solis was capable of jumping. The stallion landed right in the middle of the thorns, held his head up to protect himself, and crashed into the foliage.

Wood broke and snapped and flew in every direction where Solis's landing flattened the thorny undergrowth. But the horse kept his footing and a stride later they were on clearer ground. Richard's face stung and something hurt in his leg, but they were still in the chase. Solis strained with effort to charge on.

Richard's arm hurt and he realised in horror that his spear was gone. Richard wondered if the boar knew it, because it stopped and turned. Earth was kicked up by its feet as the beast faced him. Solis halted too, his head down at the level of the boar.

Richard normally enjoyed this part, the dance of the boar. Solis would match its movements, dart left and right to face down the beast. If the boar charged the horse would spring away before turning back to it. If it retreated, Solis would attack with his teeth, giving it no rest. After a time, Richard could usually take over and finish the dance with a thrust of his spear.

But he had no spear.

Solis began the dance regardless and the boar obliged, not aware that its dancing partner was vastly more experienced.

Richard kept his bodyweight low as his horse tired the boar out. The stallion leapt out of the way as it tried to gore him, spun around and gnashed his teeth at the beast. Solis snorted.

Richard concentrated so much he only realised Simon had arrived when he cantered by and thrust his spear at the boar. The point drove in to nothing but air and the boar spun to chase his horse.

Simon turned his mount with some skill, but that gave the boar time to catch up and lunge at him. The tusks connected with a back leg and the horse slipped over. It landed on its side and Simon spilled from the saddle. The horse staggered back onto its feet. The boar attacked it again and the horse shrieked and bolted away. A second later and the horse was gone through the undergrowth.

Simon reached to feel the leg that had been under the horse when it landed on him.

The boar turned on Simon, froth fell from its mouth. The animal launched and rammed him straight in the face. It was a thud, a smash, and a crunch at the same time.

The sound sickened Richard. He pushed that feeling away and drew his sword and pushed Solis on to reach him, but the horse was still in the dance and jumped away from the boar instead. Richard realised he couldn't reach the beast from horseback.

Simon grabbed the boar and the animal fought him, squeals and agonised shouts came from both.

Richard dismounted Solis as fast as he could, trusting the horse would keep itself away from the boar, and ran to Simon's aid.

The boar pushed Simon over and stood over him. It dragged his tusks up his body.

Richard slashed with his sword to get the beast off Simon and it shied away. The tusks were dark red.

Richard stood and faced the boar, and the boar stood and faced Richard. The animal's mouth foamed, its eyes furious, its lungs worked fast.

Richard stepped forwards, hoping the boar would turn and run.

Except it didn't, it charged.

Richard watched as its head lowered and he tried to dodge and cut it at the same time. He failed on both counts as his leg was carried away from under him. Richard hit the ground face first, a twig embedded itself in his cheek. He had no time to brush it aside and sprang to his feet.

The boar skidded around for another strike. It lunged again but this time Richard was quicker. His sword cut into the animal's wiry hide, but he fell as he tried to avoid it. The sword twisted out of his hand. Richard rolled over and got up. The sword lay too far away and Richard could taste blood. Behind the boar he heard hooves and snapping branches. The boar focused on him and attacked. Richard tried to grab its tusks, and he got one, but the second sliced along his left arm. He held on with the other hand for all he was worth as the beast tried to push into him. It shook its head and Richard screamed out as he struggled to maintain his grip. He punched the boar with his free hand, but the free tusk ripped his tunic. The boar pushed Richard over and he felt its feet dig into his leg.

He felt the earth shake beneath him, then the shaft of a spear cut through the air above and sliced into the animal on top of him. A horse flew past and the spear dragged out of the boar, the point flashed past Richard's eye and missed him by only a hand's width. The boar staggered. Richard froze, the image of the spear point before his eyes burnt into his vision.

The boar roared, then its breath rattled. It tried to run away, but instead could only hobble off, swaying side to side into the undergrowth.

Sir Gobble stopped his horse and came back, he looked down

at Richard and over to Simon, who lay still on the earth. 'I've saved you now, our score is settled,' Sir Gobble said.

'You nearly stabbed me in the face,' Richard sat up.

'I didn't though, did I,' Sir Gobble grinned, 'would you have preferred me to wait and kindly ask the boar to not gore your chest open?'

Richard pursed his lips together, then had to cough. His chest already hurt quite enough. His left leg had been trampled by small but pointy hooves, and his left arm had a nasty gash along it that bled through his tunic. The tunic was going to take some repairing.

Sir Gobble dismounted. 'Is he dead?'

'I hope so,' Richard said. Then he realised what he'd said.

Sir Gobble looked at him, his eyebrows raised.

'I mean, I hope not,' Richard said.

'You meant the first one,' Sir Gobble bent down over Simon. A rustle of leaves and branches came from behind them. Richard hoped the boar hadn't come back for more.

The boar was indeed back, but Bowman dragged it. He stopped in the clearing. 'I thought you would catch the beast with less in the way of dramatics,' he looked at Richard then down at Simon. 'Is that the Martel boy?' he asked.

Sir Gobble looked up. 'I'm not sure he's going to survive,' he said.

Bowman sniffed loudly, spat into a bush, then shrugged.

Sir Gobble stood up. 'What am I missing here?' his eyes switched between Richard and Bowman.

Richard picked himself up and tested his leg for bearing his weight. He walked a pace gingerly but it wasn't too bad.

'Don't avoid my question,' Sir Gobble said.

'Don't ask me, I'm just his servant,' Bowman said.

Richard sighed and walked over to Solis, who pulled branches from the birch trees. Richard hung his reins over the saddle so the horse wouldn't get them caught round his feet, then went over to Sir Gobble. He looked down at his bloodied arm and told him everything. Or almost everything, Richard left out the monk who flew from the tower.

'Christ's toes,' Sir Gobble said. The wind picked up and agitated the birch trees. Clouds filled the sky above and the air was cool as the sun found one to hide behind.

'I knew you were strange,' Sir Gobble said, 'but I never thought you were so interesting.'

'That's one word for it,' Richard said.

'You killed the monk, didn't you,' Sir Gobble said. It didn't sound like a question.

'He fell from the tower while dancing on the battlements,' Bowman grinned, 'you know how monks get.'

Sir Gobble frowned.

A gasp of air came from Simon and everyone remembered him.

Sir Gobble knelt down. 'He is breathing. It looks like one of you is going to have to finish him off,' he said with a cheeky grin.

Richard wondered if Bowman would be grinning too, but he wasn't. His face set and he ran his fingers over the hilt of the dagger at his waist.

'From what you've told me,' Sir Gobble raised his eyebrows, 'he knows who you are, and sooner or later he'll remember it. Then one day you'll be dragged out of the hall and someone sent by either your brother or the Martels will slit your throat.'

Richard swallowed and involuntarily reached to his neck. 'Are you serious or just seeing what I'll say?' Richard said.

'Both. If your story is true, it's him or you. No dishonour in it,' Sir Gobble said.

'I can't just murder...'

'What? Someone else?' Sir Gobble laughed.

Richard grunted and looked at Simon.

'Let me,' Bowman's hand gripped the handle of his dagger.

'It's his problem,' Sir Gobble nodded towards Richard, 'why would you kill for him? I've seen you and heard his story, you aren't really his man.'

Bowman grimaced and tightened his hand on the dagger. 'That family have caused hurt to more than just our young lord here. I am long dammed to hell already, I will do this and save the boy from the hellfire,' he said.

'How very noble,' Sir Gobble put a hand on Simon's face and pulled back his eyelids.

'He's bright enough, he's not gone yet,' he added.

Bowman approached and squatted down by the broken body of the young man.

Simon groaned.

'I've never killed a man,' Sir Gobble said, mostly to himself.

Richard thought back to the dead-end alley in Hempstead and the tower with the monk who had never danced. He retched and threw up in a bush.

'Seems you have though,' Sir Gobble said.

Bowman shrugged. 'This needs to be over,' he started to pull out his blade.

Richard wiped his mouth clean. 'No,' he said.

Bowman paused, the point of the dagger clear of its sheath.

'My family must not be known for murder,' Richard shook his head, 'that's the lie being told about us across England and Normandy. I can't make it the truth.'

'It could be too late for that, young lord,' Bowman said, 'if this boy speaks out, you'll be hanging from a tree before long, and your family's name will be hanging with you.'

Simon's eyes opened with a start. He cried out in pain. A pool of blood grew slowly on his mangled chest where a tusk had gouged into his neck. His face was white and his eyes, green before, were hollowed and looked almost grey. 'Where am I?' he mumbled.

'In the woods, a boar got you,' Sir Gobble said.

'We can speak to him,' Richard said to Bowman, 'we can reason with him, he might not speak out.'

Simon went to turn his head but he cried out and couldn't. Blood trickled from his mouth.

'He's dead already,' Bowman raised the dagger.

Simon's eyes caught the point of the blade and he gasped.

'No,' Richard shouted.

'I'm not ready,' Simon cried. Tears fell from his eyes, 'I need a priest first.'

'The boy thinks its a mercy killing,' Sir Gobble said softly.

Richard felt ill and light-headed.

Sir Gobble wiped his eyes, which surprised Richard.

'We aren't killing him,' he said.

'No?' Simon muttered. His eyes strained to look at Richard, then lightened. 'You're the one they're looking for, aren't you?'

Richard staggered over and leant on a silver birch.

'Young lord,' Bowman said.

'No,' Richard pushed himself off the tree. A crow or raven croaked in the distance but he wasn't paying enough attention to notice which. Either meant death. He was sure the bird mocked him, mocked his choice.

'No,' he said again, 'we will take him back. If he dies on the way then it is God's will. Put the knife away.'

Bowman looked down at the Martel.

'Put it away,' Richard said with enough force that Sir Gobble looked surprised.

Bowman slowly slid the dagger back into its sheath. 'I hope God's will is fast and sensible,' he said.

Simon gasped in air.

'I think you need not fear,' Sir Gobble stood up, 'more importantly, we won't speak of the boar to anyone,' he said.

'You mean you don't want anyone to know you hid up a tree,' Bowman said.

Sir Gobble's narrowed eyes answered for him. 'We will never speak of any of this,' he said.

'I agree,' Richard said.

'Come on, we'll drape him over the back of my horse and go home,' Sir Gobble said.

All together they picked the young man up, limp but heavy, and slung him over the horse's rump.

Richard retrieved Solis and then went to look for his spear in the bushes. They rode back quietly and with troubled thoughts. Above them the clouds had blocked the sun and the wind picked up.

Sir Gobble only ate one apple from his bag while they went, his tired horse slowed by the extra weight on it.

The occasional moan and sigh escaped from Simon, but each time Richard thought he'd died, he made another sound. The boy was tough, Richard thought. The more he thought, the more he couldn't find anything actually bad to think about Simon, and the more he wanted him to pull through. Every time he thought that, the cawing of birds echoed in his head.

As they neared the village below the castle, a cart trundled the other way along the road. Solis shouted at the horse pulling it, and it answered back.

'Is that Nicola?' Richard asked.

'Looks like it,' Bowman said.

'So it is,' Sir Gobble smiled. They stopped alongside the cart but Richard had to move Solis away from the mare as he started to try to get closer to her.

'Who have you got there?' Nicola asked.

'Simon Martel,' Sir Gobble said, the body behind him still clinging onto life.

'Get him onto my cart, it will be more comfortable for him on the way back,' Nicola said. They transferred him as gently as they could, and the sacks of wool and cloth were certainly more comfortable than the back of a horse.

'He looks… bad,' Nicola said, 'what happened to him?'

'This did,' Bowman gestured to the boar he had tied to the back of his saddle.

'Mother?' Simon looked up at Nicola.

'I am afraid not, child,' she stroked his forehead, 'your father will not be happy if you die, you need to hold on and think of our lord Christ.'

Richard and Bowman exchanged a glance but kept quiet. Nicola turned the cart around and drove it back to the castle.

Brother Geoffrey stood outside its gate and spoke to the two crossbowmen when they reached it. 'Nicola?' he asked as she approached.

'Change of plan,' she nodded back to her cart, 'the Martel boy is badly injured.'

They rushed inside and made for the chapel. It was a stone building, larger than the one at Keynes.

Richard and Bowman put the horses away while Sir Gobble took Simon in to see the priest.

'Should we go in?' Richard said, looking out of the stable door and across the yard.

'No, young lord, leave him be. The priest will likely kill him anyway so let the boy die in peace,' Bowman said.

Richard watched Brother Geoffrey enter the chapel. A stable-boy led Tancarville's Spanish stallion out of its box and it limped past them.

Sir John walked behind and Richard stepped out of his way.

Richard went out to watch the horse in the hope that it would give him something else to think about.

Sir John de la Londe supervised as the stable-boy walked the horse around. The horse had its nose up in the air and swished its tail. The stable-boy started to run and the horse broke into a trot with him. It was still not sound, its head bobbed up and down when it put its weight onto its injured leg.

The wind pushed the clouds across the sky and when Richard looked up it seemed like it might rain. It tasted like it might rain.

A gust rippled the grass in the yard and the Spanish horse jumped into the air and the stable-boy almost had to let go of it.

Richard walked over to Sir John. The horse tried to run off and dragged the boy a few steps before his leather shoes regained traction on the grass.

'Sir John, the horse doesn't like the wind,' Richard said.

Sir John peered down his nose. 'This horse is no concern of yours,' he said.

A cart entered the castle pulled by a donkey. Laden with cut grass, it squeaked as it went. The wind picked up some of the grass and it flew across the castle. The Spanish horse jumped when he saw it, reared up on its back legs, then launched itself into the air.

The rope pulled from the stable-boy's hands and the stallion burst into a bucking fit around the yard.

'Catch that horse,' Sir John shouted.

The stable-boy ran after it and other boys appeared from the stable building to give chase.

Richard watched them chase the horse for a while before he walked away from Sir John, who cursed them.

Richard went into the stables and loaded some horsebread into a basket. He walked back outside, strode to the middle of the yard, put the basket down and sat down beside it.

The stallion ran away from the stable-boys, who were no closer to it. The horse galloped away from them into empty space and snorted, his head high in the air, his movements rapid and thoughtless.

Richard pulled up a handful of grass and played with it. He heard the horse walk towards him but didn't look up. Richard felt the rush of air from a snort on the back of his neck. Beside him a white nose pushed its way into the basket and took a snatched bite of its contents.

Richard heard the stable-boys shout and run over, but Sir John told them to stand still.

The horse picked up a piece of the hard bread and bit it in half. Half of it fell onto the floor and Richard reached over and picked it up. As the horse chewed its piece, Richard turned and offered it the food. Its eyes stilled and Richard gently picked up the loose rope.

'Good boy,' he stood up. He stroked the horse's neck and led it back over to Sir John.

Sir John took the rope. He frowned but said nothing.

'He could get used to the wind,' Richard looked into the stallion's eyes, 'but he needs to live in a paddock for a bit so he can get to know it. He shouldn't live indoors,' Richard turned and walked back to his basket. He collected the fallen bread and went back to the stable.

Tancarville leant on the doorway. He watched Richard approach and stepped out of the way to let him through.

Richard bowed slightly to his lord as he crossed the threshold, but neither said anything to the other.

Once he'd put the basket away he went to leave the stable. He heard Brother Geoffrey's voice outside. Then he heard Tancarville's, and both voices continued but faded away.

Richard stuck his head around the doorway and saw both men walk off towards the chapel. They walked briskly and Richard remembered what he had been trying to forget. His stomach sank. Richard went to be with Solis and wait for his time to come.

He didn't have to wait long. Brother Geoffrey appeared at the stable and summoned Richard to follow him with a curled bony finger and a smug smile.

Richard walked as slowly as he could across the windswept yard and into the chapel. The leaden sky tried to rain and a spot of water landed on his face. He brushed down his torn and tattered tunic and entered the chapel.

The chapel felt cool and candles flickered in silver holders in each corner. They were taller and thicker than the candlestick wrapped up in Richard's bedding. The priest prayed in Latin and swung some incense over Simon's stricken body. The young Martel lay on a table and Tancarville inspected his injuries with a finger. A boy hovered in the room, the young Norman boy Richard had dragged from his horse the previous day.

'Simon rode into the woods following him,' the boy pointed a chubby finger at Richard, who then recognised him from the clearing, just before Simon joined the chase.

Tancarville sighed. 'It looks like tusk wounds to me,' he said.

'But an accusation has been made. We must find the truth,' Brother Geoffrey said.

Tancarville held a hand above Simon's mouth. 'Still breathing,' he said. The lord turned to Richard and the mail rings of this armour clanged faintly. 'You, what happened?'

Richard told him about the boar and its attack. He credited Sir Gobble with the strike, and displayed his torn tunic as evidence.

'The tunic could be from Simon fighting back,' Brother Geoffrey said.

'That's absurd,' Richard said.

A whine came from a corner of the chapel, and Richard realised the Little Lord was curled up there. 'He's never liked Simon, bloody English boy is probably jealous of him,' the Little Lord said.

'Shut up, boy,' Tancarville snapped at his son, 'but the accusation does need to be answered.'

'We all know the English boy killed him, it's murder,' the Little Lord got to his feet.

'He is not dead quite yet,' Brother Geoffrey said.

'Nevertheless,' Tancarville glanced at the altar, 'we must deal with this quickly. New laws have been made by the king, who says a trial should be undertaken for criminal matters. Trial by water.'

'Ridiculous,' the Little Lord spat, 'he's obviously guilty.'

Tancarville sighed. 'Not another word from you,' he said.

Brother Geoffrey gestured to Tancarville. 'The king's word should be followed, my lord. His law is the law,' he said.

'Be dammed with his law, we live by the old ways in

Normandy. We will revolve that matter by ordeal.'

Richard almost fainted. He didn't notice Brother Geoffrey break into a smile as his eyes studied Tancarville.

'Yes, trial by ordeal,' the Little Lord said with glee, 'put him in the river.'

'No, it will be trial by fire,' Tancarville said.

Fire. Richard's world went black.

His eyes opened and he found himself propped up by the chapel wall.

The Little Lord watched him but everyone except the priest and the wounded Martel were gone.

'You'll hang,' the younger Tancarville said in the quiet chapel. His words stuck in the air.

Richard ran his finger over his head. He found scabs, fresh cuts, leaves and a twig. He felt sick.

'The iron bar will burn your hands, and then you'll hang in agony,' the Little Lord laughed.

Richard pushed himself to his feet with a great effort and opened the chapel door.

'You cannot leave,' the priest said.

Richard looked out across the yard and saw the stable-boys lay out wooden posts in one corner of the grass. One held a post up and a second hammered it into the ground.

Sir John supervised.

'Close the door,' the priest ordered.

Richard sighed and pulled it shut. He looked at Simon, who breathed only faintly. At the table at the end of the chapel a golden cross, decorated with green and red stones, shone in the candle light. The colours drew Richard's eyes.

'You are to do penance, boy,' the priest rubbed his hands together, 'for three days you will fast and you will kneel with your eyes on the cross. Then, on the fourth day, you will face our lord in a trial by fire.'

TRIAL BY FIRE

The first day slipped by painlessly. Richard had always fasted on Fridays, as well as any other days he'd been told to, so the lack of food wasn't a problem. This time though, he'd been allowed just water to drink, but that was an inconvenience compared to the ordeal that loomed before him. The priest stayed on hand all day to give him prayers to recite, and to ensure he stayed on his knees with his eyes focused on the jewelled cross on the altar. The Little Lord watched him from his corner, and made a show of eating the meals that were delivered to him twice a day.

Richard could cope with that, he hadn't been particularly hungry anyway. The prospect of spending two further days with the Little Lord were but an annoyance, and if anything, it was useful distraction.

At the morning of the second day, the sun leaked through the roof, its thatch from the Seine estuary thinner than it should have been. Small shafts of light beamed down into the chapel and shifted around the room as the day wore on.

The door opened and de Cailly entered, the open door flooded the chapel with daylight that stung Richard's eyes.

The sound of steel on steel echoed from the yard, but both the sound and light were slammed out of existence when the door closed.

De Cailly placed a bowl of pottage at the feet of the Little Lord who slept under a pile of blankets, then sat down by Richard. 'How are you?' he asked.

Richard, glad that the priest had gone for his own breakfast, looked away from the cross. 'Hoping my prayers will be heard,' he said.

De Cailly was not in his mail shirt today, instead he wore a rich red tunic with an intricately patterned border around the neckline. A fine blue cloak hung from his shoulders, its inside lined in light brown fur. His dark skin looked softer than usual as the light from the candles rippled over his hunched face.

'Keep praying, I believe they will be answered,' de Cailly said.

'I didn't hurt him,' Richard looked over to where Simon still lay, and somehow still breathed. His wounds had been covered but his face remained ashen and motionless.

'I know, I have spoken to your man. And young William, or Sir Gobble as our wondrous lord likes to call him. They both told the same story,' de Cailly said.

Richard sighed. 'That won't save me from the hot iron though. I've never seen it done, only heard stories,' Richard said.

'Three of every four who carry the iron are shown to be innocent by our Lord, and surely He will ensure your hands do not petrify,' de Cailly said.

'How can you be sure?' Richard asked.

'One can never be sure in such matters,' de Cailly's eyes twinkled, 'although one should always do what one can to ensure the correct outcome.'

Richard looked into his dark eyes and for some reason felt slightly better.

De Cailly smiled.

The Little Lord snored deeply on the chapel floor.

'I must confess,' de Cailly made the sign of the cross, 'I am tempted to make real our little jest about my daughter and marriage.'

Richard felt his face redden and excitement stir within.

'Both of the red-haired tyrants need to learn that they cannot always get exactly what they want. Shouting and stomping one's feet will work for those of us who have no choice but to serve, but it will not suffice for an enemy at war. It will not help if King Henry makes an order Lord Tancarville doesn't like, nor if the King of France makes a request that challenges his loyalty to England.'

Richard nodded, his lips had started to crack and wished de Cailly had brought him a drop of wine.

'Matilda is promised to the church but that can be undone. Do you have family I would need to consult if I decided to poke our lord in the eye?' De Cailly asked.

'I am from Newbury and have no family but Sir Gobble's,' Richard said, one eye on the Little Lord's sleeping place.

De Cailly chuckled. 'Very good, my boy.'

'Did you know Sir Gobble's mother is related to Lord Tancarville?' De Cailly said.

'He has mentioned it,' Richard replied.

'Of course he has. It means that not requesting consent from Lord Tancarville for the marriage would be poking him in the eye on two accounts,' de Cailly said, 'and you show enough promise that I might one day trust you to be in my service.'

'Your service?' Richard said.

'If you married my daughter, you would move into my household. Would you like that?'

Richard's eyes lit up. 'Of course.'

'Interesting. Young Matilda of course wants nothing to do with you, you should know that.'

The brightness faded from Richard's eyes and he glanced down.

'Do not take that to heart, her opinion of you is hardly relevant to the matter,' de Cailly said. The knight stood up and his spurs scraped on the cold stone floor. Richard's knees hurt from the ground, especially his left one since the boar had run through it. That left knee was what most discomforted him. The gash on his left arm had been bound by Bowman, and although it stung, it caused a lesser pain.

'There are no promises, but when you are found to be innocent I will consider the matter,' de Cailly said.

'You mean, if,' Richard said glumly.

'When,' de Cailly walked towards the door. He pulled it open and the world flooded back in. 'Oh,' he turned back, 'your man wanted me to pass on to you that your horse will be well cared for. Although, to be frank he was rather rude, and if you both entered my household, his impertinence would need to be curbed.'

Richard cracked a smile, he could well imagine how Bowman had spoken to de Cailly.

'Of course, Sir Roger,' he said as the knight left the chapel and silence and dimness enveloped him once again. Richard shifted around painfully on his knees to turn back to the cross. He glanced at the Little Lord, saw he was still asleep, then slipped off his knees and sat down. The relief came instantly but he knew it wouldn't be long before the priest returned. Richard didn't forget the bowl of pottage, either. He might have turned pottage down in Kent, but now his stomach gurgled at the sight of it, and the temptation grew along with his appetite. He pulled his eyes away from the meat-free meal and placed them back onto the cross.

The priest came back eventually and instructed Richard on a new prayer to recite. Richard obliged readily and without complaint, so the priest lost interest and left again.

The Little Lord woke up and pushed the spoon around the pottage. 'I'd sooner eat my own toenails,' he dumped the spoon into the now cold liquid and some splashed onto the stones.

Richard ignored him.

'Boy,' the Little Lord said.

Richard continued to recite his prayer.

'English dog,' the younger Tancarville tried, louder this time.

Richard ignored him but chanted louder.

'English murderer, English thief, English rotten waste of flesh.'

Still no response.

'Are you hungry?' The Little Lord picked up his spoon, filled it, and waved it at Richard.

'I'm not hungry,' Richard replied.

'Ah, he does speak,' the Little Lord said, 'for now maybe, soon he'll hang.' He launched the pottage from the spoon as if it were a catapult, the grey liquid with green peas flew through the air and hit the side of Richard's face.

Cold and wet.

Richard restarted his prayers, determined not to give him any satisfaction.

The Little Lord laughed and reloaded his spoon. He took another shot, but it flew wide and hit the wall, splashed off it and peas bounced down onto the floor. The young Tancarville cursed. His round face scrunched up in concentration as he loosed his edible ammunition a third time. The wetness hit Richard in the ear. It had only stopped ringing that morning.

Richard turned and leapt at the Little Lord, whose eyes widened as the English boy hit him and thumped him into the wall. They clattered across the stones and the bowl of pottage spun across the chapel, landing upside down below the table where Simon groaned.

The young Tancarville punched Richard in the stomach which partially winded him, and Richard swung at him and hit him in the side of the face. They grappled on the floor.

The door swung open and light spread across the stones and onto the fighting penitents.

'How dare you,' the priest shouted and slammed the door behind him.

Richard pushed the Little Lord away and scrambled to get back onto his knees facing the altar.

The Little Lord stayed slumped against the corner. He spat on the floor.

'Do not spit in a house of God,' the priest stormed up to them, 'how dare you fight here.'

Richard started to pray with the strongest voice he had.

The priest focused on the Little Lord and towered over him.

'Your father will hear of this and you will both be punished,' he said. The priest, a tall and slender man, kicked a foot into the Little Lord's midriff. The youth cried out and clutched his belly.

'You will suffer for the Lord,' the priest turned to Richard.

Richard tried with everything he had to keep his eyes ahead, but he tensed his body for what might come. The priest bent down. With a finger he wiped across the remains of the pottage on his face. He looked up at the far wall and saw the liquid as it dripped down and onto the floor. He turned to the young Tancarville.

'I care not that you will one day be lord here, for if you despoil the house of God, you will do penance. You will lick that mess off the wall or I will kick you until you can never eat again,' the priest roared.

Richard found himself saying his prayer faster and faster.

The Little Lord hesitated, but when the priest made to kick him again he complied.

Richard didn't dare avert his eyes from the holy cross while the Little Lord carried out his punishment. Richard heard him start to cry and he sobbed as every last drop was cleaned from the chapel.

The priest stayed and watched for hours, but eventually a call of nature pulled him away.

When the door shut the Little Lord stared at Richard. 'If anyone, anyone at all, ever hears about this, you're dead. Not a quick death mind, the slowest one I can think of,' he said.

Richard looked at him and saw a boy rather than a man, frightened and hurt. His face pleaded more than it threatened. Richard decided to concentrate on the cross and pray. He never answered.

The third day came and Richard found himself unsure which day it was. He no longer registered when someone entered to bring food for the Little Lord. Richard had time to think though, and his thoughts intertwined and diffused as the sunlight moved across the room. He closed his eyes and saw Adela being carried off a hundred times over, the images mixed in with his mother falling to her death.

Eventually he opened his eyes and felt a calmness in his mind. He couldn't have saved either of them. He couldn't save Adela now, but one day he would. His uncle would be stopped, the law would swing in behind Richard, and Eustace Martel would pay. He would pay a little if Simon died, although the young man still clung on to life. Eustace would know when Richard took the final payment from him though, Richard would make sure of it. He swore it, and he remembered he'd sworn to take the cross too. He wished he hadn't, but he had, so now he must go east.

But first, before he could do any of it, he needed golden spurs, and he needed to be able to match his uncle with the sword. As Richard thought about this he felt a sense of purpose, a certainty he hadn't had before. And as he thought these things, Simon died.

The Little Lord jumped up when Simon's lungs rasped for the

final time.

Richard continued to kneel and pray, but the young Tancarville ran to his friend and held him.

Richard heard quiet sobs from where he was. It had never occurred to him that the Little Lord could cry. The young man wept for a long time before the priest came back.

The holy man said some things in Latin and then covered the body. He put the Little Lord back into his corner, and that was that. The priest left, Richard thought to bring the grim news to Lord Tancarville, but no one came to visit the body. Richard had no ill feelings towards Simon himself, and for the rest of the day and most of the night he prayed for his soul. He hadn't deserved his fate. But then again, neither had Adela. Nor his mother. Come to think of it, neither did he, not originally anyway. Richard thought about the monk who he had helped to dance his way off the tower. Maybe whatever happened to him after he'd done that would be deserved. The world wasn't fair.

Hunger and dehydration took their toll during the night and Richard's mind wandered through the worlds of the Song of Roland and Eric and Enid. Knights in those tales were brave, honourable, protected the weak and dispensed fair justice. King Eric's words were that a king should not show sorrow, so Richard resolved to keep his suffering hidden from the world. He looked up at the jewelled altar cross and promised that if he ever won his golden spurs, he would be the good sort of knight.

Another day came on the heels of weakness and dizziness. The priest had withheld water as well as food since the pottage incident, and Richard's head ached. It was as if a red hot poke burnt into his skull above his eyes. More than once he found himself waking up on the floor looking up at the roof. Each time the priest picked him up and ordered him to continue his prayers. His eyes weren't working properly either, the world seemed mostly out of focus. Everything felt very wrong. His stomach moved beyond hunger but his limbs felt disconnected, vacant. He could smell the candles though, smell the only sense that wasn't painful, but before long people had filled the chapel and he'd been dragged to his feet.

The burning realisation that today was the day of the trial

went some way to clear Richard's wayward mind.

De Cailly stood next to him, indeed he propped Richard up.

Simon's body had gone.

Richard wondered when that had happened, but in his place lay a thick plank of wood with a black round bar of iron on it. It was the perfect size to be held with two hands.

The chapel door stood open, and outside blazed an iron brazier, full of logs and already aflame. The sun partly hid behind clouds which made it a grey and sullen day in the castle yard. Nevertheless, the open door refreshed the air in the chapel which had grown heavy over recent days.

Brother Geoffrey stood in a corner of the chapel. His previously big round eyes now reminded Richard of a weasel he'd once seen staring back at him one night in the woods.

Sir John attended too, though unlike de Cailly he wore his mail shirt.

The priest started a Latin incantation and picked a golden cup from the altar table. It shone in the faint daylight but Richard couldn't focus on it. The priest picked up some water from the cup and sprinkled it onto the iron bar. He spat words out as the water spat from his fingers.

Black iron tongs picked up the bar and placed it carefully into the centre of brazier outside. The priest started to say mass but Richard only heard muffled words. His eyes were set on the brazier and the end of the iron bar that stuck out of the top of it. Flames licked the bar.

Soon he would have to hold that.

The mass dragged on, and as it did the black iron bar started to turn a dull red.

'Easy, boy,' de Cailly said as Richard noticed his legs held almost none of his weight. The fire raged and spat as a gust of wind took it, and the iron bar started to turn a deeper red. The wait was an agony and Richard tried to imagine what his hands would feel like if they were on fire.

The priest finished and picked up the tongs.

Richard had a sudden urge to run, but his legs didn't respond.

De Cailly gripped him tighter. 'Now, boy, let it happen,' he said.

The priest thrust the tongs into the brazier and embers took off into the wind. The red iron bar was extracted and the priest walked towards him.

Richard tried to back away.

De Cailly held him firmly and whispered in his ear. 'Trust in your innocence,' he said.

Richard fought an urge to give up and pass out. He blinked his eyes open to see the iron bar placed onto the wooden plank on the table again. It seemed to hum that dull red as if it were alive, and he could feel the heat from where de Cailly held him up.

The priest hadn't stopped with his Latin, and his sharp words bounced around Richard's ears like a crazed bird in a cage.

'He has to read a Gospel now,' de Cailly said. Then the knight turned to the priest. 'May I suggest a Gospel for the occasion?'

Richard didn't hear the priest reply, but heard de Cailly say something else.

The priest started in Latin again. He sprinkled more holy water onto the bar. The water hissed and spat from the ungodly metal and Richard almost burst into tears. His hands sweated. He ran his fingers across them and tried to remember what they felt like before they were seared with fiery agony.

The Gospel went on and on.

The priest tried to get through the mass as fast as he could, but it was a very long mass.

Richard's eyes closed and opened again, but he wasn't sure how much later. The priest's rushed words ceased and Richard felt silence linger after them. The priest handled his tongs.

'Spit on your hands, boy, quickly,' de Cailly said.

Richard did as he was told, but they were already clammy.

The priest turned around, the iron bar in the tongs. Still that ominous dull red. 'Walk nine paces then you can drop it outside,' he said, 'if I judge you do anything faster than walk, then we shall do it all again.'

Richard nodded.

'Hold out your hands,' de Cailly said, 'and if you ever want to be a knight, suffer this well.'

Richard swallowed but the urge to run flowed through his body again. He choked it back. De Cailly's words rang in his ears and he remembered his own thoughts. He had to suffer this well. Richard pictured his uncle's face before him and held out his hands. He concentrated on his anger and his sense of injustice, which made him angrier still.

Richard chose that anger over his fear.

The priest held the bar above his hands and the heat radiated down to his skin. The warmth would have been nice had the circumstance been different.

'May the Lord above us show us the truth,' the Priest opened the tongs. The bar dropped into Richard's hands. He looked down at it. His hands didn't look like his own.

'Walk, you can walk,' de Cailly let go of him.

Richard looked up at the priest. 'I am innocent,' he said.

'Walk, you damned fool,' de Cailly shouted.

Richard took one step then another. His fingers wrapped around the bar. He could see the doorway in front of him, but it seemed to be moving. Uncertain, his focus wandered. Another step, then another. Richard walked out of the chapel and into the daylight. The next lung full of air was fresh, crisp and joyous. He walked some more.

'That's nine, drop the bar,' de Cailly shouted.

Richard stopped and turned his head slowly to the priest, who'd followed him outside. Richard looked him right in the eyes and took another two slow steps.

'Drop it, you fool,' de Cailly rushed up to him and pointed at the grass.

'I have nothing to fear from pain,' Richard mumbled. He bent down slowly and placed the bar onto the ground. Richard straightened up and looked at his open hands. They were red, very, very red. In places they were white. The pain, absent until now, rushed, rushed up from his palms up through his arms and into his chest. Richard gasped and blacked out.

Richard was out cold for the rest of the day. Much later, he opened his eyes and found himself looking up at the roof of the chapel. He wondered if the ordeal had just been a dream and he was still waiting for it to happen. Richard brought his hands up to look at them, and they were wrapped in white linen. The ordeal had been real then. Both hands hurt like a horse had stamped on them.

They stung and the pain engulfed him until the initial

burning faded. Only then did Richard noticed he'd been put into his own bedding.

Sir Gobble arrived and sat beside him. 'You're back,' he said, 'I was starting to worry you were gone.'

'What happened?' Richard's head pulsed so hard he could hear his own blood rush through it.

'Here,' Sir Gobble passed him a wooden cup filled with water.

Richard grabbed it with his fingers and thumb and downed the sweetest drink he'd ever tasted. Then he fumbled around in his bedding.

'The silver is safe,' Sir Gobble smiled, 'although I was quite surprised when I found it. I'll ask about it later though,' he glanced over at the Little Lord's corner.

Richard grunted.

'I was watching you know,' Sir Gobble said.

'Watching what?'

'You, possessed by the Devil some are saying. You picked the bar up and stood there, staring at the priest like some crazed demon. I've seen a few ordeals of fire, and the accused walk dammed fast. None of the others ever stood there looking at the priest while a bar of molten iron burnt through their hands.'

'I wanted to show him,' Richard said.

'You showed everyone, do you know Sir John was in the chapel? The first thing he did afterwards was go to his lordship and admit that the paddock for his horse was your idea. You scared him, Richard.'

'I don't remember,' he replied.

'You walked twelve steps. Do you know what that means?' Sir Gobble said.

'That he's a raging idiot,' the Little Lord chirped in from next to the altar where he sat and sulked.

'Undoubtedly,' Sir Gobble grinned. 'But there were twelve apostles, and Brother Geoffrey is telling everyone that you are in fact blessed.'

'The monk is saying I'm blessed?' Richard remembered the weasel eyes and was confused.

'It's odd, I thought he disliked you,' Sir Gobble shrugged. He held a piece of bread up to Richard. He ate it and his stomach growled back at him.

'The priest still thinks the Devil lives in you, he says he saw the fires of hell in your eyes. But everyone saw you hold the bar and take twelve steps. Do you remember gently placing the bar on the floor?'

'Not really,' Richard flexed his bandaged hands which made him wince.

'No one has seen anything like it.'

'It really hurts,' Richard said.

'Good, filthy English criminal,' the Little Lord said.

Richard looked him straight in the eyes. 'Have you got any pottage, William?'

The Little Lord shrank into his bedding and disappeared under his matted red hair and woollen blankets.

Sir Gobble pulled a face.

'Don't ask,' Richard said.

'Very well, but you've got two more days in here before they unwrap those. Best pray your hands stay free of corruption,' Sir Gobble said.

'If they hang me, you can have Solis,' Richard said.

Sir Gobble leant back. 'Really?'

'You're the best rider here, you might understand him,' Richard said.

'Please,' the Little Lord groaned, 'if you're going to sodomise each other with praise, do it somewhere else.'

Sir Gobble threw a piece of bread at him.

'They aren't going to hang you,' Sir Gobble said.

'Are you sure?'

'Not really, but even if they don't, they might stone you to death for sorcery.'

Richard had lost count of which day the next day was. It was better than the previous one though, because Sir Gobble brought him actual meat and watered wine.

'Whys aren't my men bringing me food?' Richard asked him.

'Bowman says he won't go inside a chapel, which I think will get him burnt at a stake one day, and your other man has been passed out from drink since the hunt. They're going to throw him out soon, Lord Tancarville detests those who can't hold their drink.'

'He can hold it,' Richard said, 'the problem is he apparently can't stop drinking it.'

'Either way, Lord Tancarville has noticed and he only hasn't thrown him out already because he's so busy with lawyers and clerks all day,' Sir Gobble said.

'That sounds boring.'

'Speaking to lawyers seems to be what being a lord is really about,' Sir Gobble replied.

Later Richard's evening meal was brought in by de Cailly.

'They saved you a piece of the boar you caught,' he handed him a silver basin with a cut of meat in it.

Richard didn't know if it had been meant in a good or bad way. He was happy to just take and eat it. It certainly tasted good, but it didn't help with how badly his hands stung. They itched too and he was afraid that it was a sign of infection. Which meant a guilty verdict.

'The Spanish horse,' de Cailly said.

'Yes?'

'They are saying the paddock was your idea.'

'It was,' Richard replied.

De Cailly looked over at the altar table. 'The horse jumped around at night to start with, but has now settled down,' he said.

'He just wasn't used to the wind, in his stable he can't hear or feel it,' Richard said.

De Cailly laughed. 'Yes, that may be, but Sir John did not think of it, and he is the marshal here.'

'I just wanted to help the horse,' Richard said.

'It has pleased our glorious lord,' de Cailly said.

The Little Lord squirmed under his covers. 'You can't please him,' the young Tancarville said, 'it isn't possible.'

De Cailly raised his eyebrows to Richard. 'Tomorrow you will be free of this place,' he said.

'My hands itch,' Richard turned them over.

De Cailly picked up the golden cross and looked into one if its bright jewels. 'Do you believe in fate, Richard?'

'I don't know, probably.'

'Fate implies our choices have already been made, which to me suggests our actions do not matter,' de Cailly said.

'Sounds like heresy to me,' the Little Lord muttered.

'You will not hang,' de Cailly said softly, 'and tomorrow at vespers they will unwrap your hands and proclaim a miracle. The gospel the priest sung while the bar cooled was a very long one.'

Richard groaned, he didn't want to wait until the end of the next day, he didn't think his mind could take the tension anymore.

Vespers on the final day came so much slower than Richard wanted it to. He had tried to sleep but it had come only in fits and starts. His senses returned to him fully by the time the priest came in with de Cailly and Sir John.

Brother Geoffrey slid into the chapel later when the priest called Richard to stand. The churchman sprinkled holy water onto his upturned hands and the Latin started up again. The priest started to unwrap the linen.

Brother Geoffrey sidled over and peered over his hands.

'Get out of my light,' the priest told him.

The bandage on the first hand came off, which peeled away some of a blister and a scab.

Richard stifled a cry but it felt like he'd been stabbed.

The priest took the hand roughly in his. 'No corruption,' he said flatly.

Richard thought he sounded disappointed. There was still one hand to go though, and his stomach didn't loosen one bit.

Brother Geoffrey started on the second hand himself. As the last piece of linen came off, Richard looked down and saw no putrefaction.

'Glory be to God,' the priest said.

'Fascinating,' Brother Geoffrey dropped the linen wraps onto the table.

'It was a cheat,' the Little Lord said from his corner, but no one turned to acknowledge him.

'See, my boy,' de Cailly said, his smile clear to see, 'his innocence is unarguable.'

Richard sighed and wiggled his fingers. They creaked, popped blisters stung and the skin hurt, but at least he wasn't going to hang.

'I must confess,' Brother Geoffrey said airily, 'I was expecting a different result, but I have seen this with my own eyes.'

'You are free to leave the chapel,' the priest told him.

'I will be leaving the castle now, young Richard,' Brother Geoffrey shuffled around him in his big black robe, 'but I will see you again.'

Richard ignored him as he left, his eyes glued to his mutilated hands. He couldn't grip anything and he couldn't dress them in fresh bandages himself either, so he went to find Bowman.

The yard shone gloriously in the warm light of day. Even though clouds dotted the sky overhead, the light warmed Richard's face and he looked up at the sun with his eyes closed and let it shine on him. The Spanish horse grazed in its paddock at the bottom corner of the yard, and a team of aspirants faced off against the younger knights in a horseback game of chase.

Richard walked through the middle of the game and the riders all rode around him. They stopped their exercise and left a path clear for him, all kept a distance and watched him as he went. Richard traversed the grass and made for the knight's chamber.

Bowman sat at a table with Sarjeant, a black and white board between them with a number of identical black and white pieces on it.

'Ah, we missed the unwrapping,' Bowman said without looking up, 'my apologies, young lord.'

'It's no matter,' Richard said, although he wasn't sure he meant it. They easily could have walked over.

Sarjeant looked glazed behind the eyes, and he pushed a piece across the board in a wobbly line.

'Are you sure?' Bowman asked him.

Sarjeant looked at the game, but his head rocked back and forth.

'No,' he put the piece back.

'I take it they are not hanging you then?' Bowman pushed a cup of wine in Richard's direction.

'I suppose not,' he said.

'We did watch your little performance with the iron,' Bowman said, 'it is the talk of the castle. Even in the village down the hill they are speaking of the English fire devil. You have scared the absolute hell out of them,' he laughed.

Sarjeant made the same move he'd just undone.

Bowman sighed and played his own to take Sarjeant's piece.

'I would not get too comfortable here though, young lord. This much attention ends in lynchings in my experience, although in these parts I'd wager a burning is more likely.'

'I've had enough of fire,' Richard shuddered, 'Sir Roger spoke of us joining his household, so maybe we can leave soon.'

Bowman looked up from the board. 'Sir Roger? He serves Lord Tancarville and his place is here, which means our place would more than likely remain here too,' he said.

'But it might not,' Richard said and sat down.

'No, it might not,' Bowman said, 'but you may wish to add it as a condition of service if an offer is made.'

Richard nodded. Bowman was right, the castle felt like a dangerous place to be.

Sir Gobble entered the hall. 'There you are,' he said. He carried Richard's bedding, which he dumped on the floor where his bed had originally been.

'Thank you,' Richard held his hands out, 'would anyone be able to wash and wrap these for me?' he asked.

'I'm not doing it, these men are supposedly yours, Richard of Newbury,' Sir Gobble sat down on the table and chuckled.

Sarjeant looked over at the burnt hands. 'I can dress those,' he said.

Bowman grimaced. 'I would recommend that you didn't let him, young lord,' he stood up and walked towards the door. 'Come on, young lord, I'll do it. Sir Gobble likes to win so he can finish our game for me.'

Sarjeant jeered and drank from a cup.

Richard let Bowman dress his damaged hands.

The next morning Sarjeant shook Richard awake. His blue eyes were clear and alert.

'Lord Tancarville has called for you,' he said.

Richard pushed his blankets away. He rubbed his eyes and yawned while Sarjeant threw his leather shoes at him.

Still groggy, Richard had a sinking feeling as they walked out into the yard. A heavy fog lingered, so dense that he couldn't even see the far wall.

'He is waiting in the great hall,' Sarjeant hurried before Richard. They walked up the steep slope that led towards the keep and towards some finely built stone arches that were painted in whites, blues and reds. The climb made Richard's calves ache.

The great hall was on the first floor of the main square keep. Richard thought it was magnificent. Its ceiling stretched high above their heads and its walls were painted even more brightly than the outside had been. A raised area dominated the far end with two large chairs, all painted in red with golden borders. A table stood next to the chairs, silver basins, golden crosses and assorted shiny objects on display.

Richard appeared and bowed before his lord.

A rank of desks lined one side of the room, clerks waited at some and wrote at others. Men in fine tunics and cloaks spoke in a huddle on the opposite side, and Tancarville's large wolfhounds roamed between everyone. The largest was not much shorter than Solis. Tancarville himself sat in one of the high chairs. His fingers drummed on his chair's armrest which rattled the mail on his wrist.

'Did we wake you, boy?' Tancarville asked.

'Yes, my lord,' Richard replied.

Tancarville laughed. 'You are perhaps an honest Devil, then. My councillors have been discussing whether you are of our Lord or the Devil. I thought it best to hear it from you yourself. Which is it?'

'Neither, my lord, I am of House Tancarville,' Richard replied.

Some of the men who wore fancy clothing groaned, but Tancarville burst into a prolonged fit of laughter.

'See, he outwits all of you,' he said.

Sir John stood amongst the crowd, the exception to the dress code in that he wore his mail shirt.

'This Englishman is upsetting the balanced order here, my lord,' he said.

'Sometimes a little disruption is a good thing,' Tancarville said, 'it keeps everyone thinking, improving.'

'Or wasting their time and being distracted,' Sir John's eyes centred on Richard.

'He has potential, you see that, John, he rides nearly as well as Sir Gobble. I will never tell Sir Gobble to his face, but that arrogant English lad has promise. This one standing here still has four years to catch him up, he could be just as good,' Tancarville said.

'If he is taken by the Devil and driven by dark forces, then you are just training up a stronger foe for good Christian men,' Sir John said.

Tancarville shook his head and slammed his hand down on the chair. 'Nonsense, he is nothing but a boy a long way from home. I have a mind to make him a deputy to you, John, a place in the marshalcy seems like the place for a boy with his obvious talents.'

'My lord,' Sir John protested loudly.

'Keep your voice down,' Tancarville said, 'the only person who has the luxury of shouting in this keep is me.'

Sir John snorted and growled at Richard. 'He cannot stay, we will not move on the matter, and Lord Martel's letter was very insistent,' he said.

Richard's heart sank.

'He is just a boy who is good with horses, what if I promise not to knight him for ten years?' Tancarville said.

Sir John stared at his lord. 'You swore that you would break their legs and chase them around the wall if your horse remained lame. And lame he still is.'

Tancarville drummed his chair again and sighed. 'I have made a decision. I will go against my instincts and compromise with you. This boy and Sir Gobble will not have their legs broken, and nor will they leave my service,' he said loudly.

Almost all of the councillors groaned and complained. Sir John swore and threw his arms up into the air.

'Quiet,' Tancarville shouted and the hall settled, 'but they will be banished from this castle. I will send them back to England to the town of Grantham, which I apparently own. They will serve me there for five years, after which they can return. Sir Gobble did let my horse get kicked, five years is a fair punishment for that.'

The announcement was met with whispered exchanges.

Richard wondered what had just happened. He couldn't go

back to England, not yet. If his uncle didn't kill him first, Sir Gobble surely would because his chance of being knighted had been torn away from him.

Being sent back to England would be ruination of all Richard's hopes for the future, too.

Sir John started to speak, but Tancarville stood up.

'Silence. I have spoken, come on, write it down,' he said to the clerks who had been motionless.

One started to scribble.

'You helped my horse,' Tancarville said to Richard, 'but as you can see, these small men will all rebel if you stay here. I need them more than I need you. You and your English friend have today to pack and prepare, then tomorrow you head back to Harfleur. I will give you plenty of coin and letters of introduction to whichever of my men is running Grantham for me.'

Richard's mouth gaped open but no sound came out. It was done, he would be going back to England. Where his enemies might find him.

'You may go,' Tancarville waved him away.

Sarjeant turned Richard's shoulders around and pushed him towards the exit. Richard walked out of the keep in a daze, down the stone stairs and out into the fog. That cold fog suffocated him as he walked through it. It chilled his bones.

The reaction he got from Sir Gobble when he brought back the news wasn't any warmer.

'England? I can't go back to England,' he raged.

'At least no one there wants to kill you,' Richard growled back.

'There are no tournaments in England, how am I supposed to make any money? How am I supposed to show prowess in war, when there aren't any wars?' Sir Gobble continued.

'Children, please,' Bowman shouted.

Sir Gobble collapsed onto the bench and Richard noticed that others in the hall sniggered and whispered. They weren't looking at him, either.

Sir Gobble noticed and went back to beating Sarjeant at their board game, his face red.

Sarjeant was no better at the game sober.

Richard had never seen Sir Gobble like this before. He sat down too.

'We cannot go back to England,' Bowman said, 'we barely went a day there without someone trying to kill or rob us.'

Sarjeant burped loudly.

Sir Gobble looked at Richard, his lips raised almost to a snarl. He thought to speak but pulled himself back.

Richard put his forehead on the table and wrapped his hands around it, although he was careful not to touch anything with his palms. 'It's over,' he mumbled into the hard wood of the table.

'I would prefer taking the cross and taking my chances in the sand and dust over England,' Bowman said.

'How do we get there?' Richard said, still muffled.

Bowman sat back and put his hands on his head. 'I have no idea, young lord, it's a long walk.'

Richard remained still for some time. Had he not prayed in the chapel and had God not shown his favour for his mission? Now he was being punished, but what for? Was it a delayed punishment for the dancing monk? Everything had become jumbled up, how was he supposed to work it out?

'The Lord works in mysterious ways,' Sarjeant said.

Richard lifted his head. 'Why does he? What's the point of being mysterious?' he asked.

Sarjeant shrugged. 'Life either goes your way or it doesn't, my boy. I have found you can only really control how you react to it,' he said.

'So how you turn to drink?' Richard snapped.

Sarjeant raised his eyebrows.

Richard immediately regretted his outburst.

'It is my choice,' Sarjeant said, 'it harms only me. You will turn to the way of the knight and that will harm many. Close your eyes and pray, let God know your intentions and maybe he will listen.'

Richard let his eyelids close and prayed to God that if He would save him, he would go on a pilgrimage to Jerusalem and join the Knights Templar. He swore it on his mother and father's souls. Richard nodded and opened his eyes.

The door to the hall crashed open and a man in a grey tunic

burst in. His face ran with sweat and his black hair stuck to his head with sweat. His long face was redder than Sir Gobble's. 'There's war,' the messenger shouted.

Everyone in the chamber froze and looked over. The messenger took a few gulps of air.

'The Flemings and the Count of Boulogne have crossed into Normandy,' he shouted before he ran out and left the room to take it in.

Richard didn't move.

Bowman laughed. 'Wars need warriors, young lord, maybe there is no need to turn to religion just yet.'

Frantic conversations broke out around the hall.

Sir Gobble's face lit up. 'Thank God for the Flemings,' he said, 'let's go and see what old Tancarville wants to do with us now.'

Richard closed his eyes again and said a prayer of thanks. Then he picked himself up and went to find out if he was going to England, or to war.

WAR

Even though the fog had burnt off and midday came and went, Richard and Sir Gobble still had not learnt of their fate. They stood outside the great hall as the sound of arguments blared out.

'I can't believe we aren't allowed in,' Sir Gobble said as the guard blocked their fourth attempt to enter.

'There is a war on, they're probably talking about that,' Richard said.

'They should discuss us first, at least me,' Sir Gobble replied.

'I'm going back, when they want us, we'll know about it,' Richard said.

Sir Gobble looked back again at the guard but his expression was enough to send him back to the knight's chamber with Richard. They returned to a flurry of speculation and excited discussion. On all sides of the hearth boasts of future deeds mixed with wild talk of marching on Boulogne.

It wasn't long before De Cailly and Sir John entered and all the talk ceased. Expectant eyes turned towards the senior knights and the chatter dried up. De Cailly wore his mail shirt once more and his expression was grim. His hunchback seemed to have hunched a little further.

'Normandy has been invaded. Our lord commands us to prepare to leave for the north east, where Count Matthew of Boulogne and a large number of Flemings have massed on the frontier. Lord Tancarville believes that they are planning to cross the border for a ridden war,' he said.

The room erupted again.

'I'm going to capture me a rich knight,' Sir Gobble said.

'They have no siege equipment, nor hired any specialists for mounting attacks on castles,' Sir John said in his low voice, even throatier than usual, 'we expect them to move fast and to target villages. We will send out three small groups of scouts ahead of our army. These groups will set out today and the main body will leave in the morning once our men from the west have mustered here. It will be a hard campaign, but it is the price we all pay so that others toil in the fields for us.'

'Are we saved?' Richard whispered to Bowman.

De Cailly and Sir John spoke to each other and pointed at various tables.

A few logs were added to the hearth which had almost died, and it crackled and jumped back to life. The two elder knights moved around table by table giving assignments, and de Cailly went to Richard's.

'Sir Gobble, you will be in the northern scouting party under Robert des Ifs, you will lead five squires under him. We do not expect the Flemings to ride north as the coast would hem them in, but do not be complacent. Lord Tancarville is testing you with this, do not mess it up,' he said.

Sir Gobble beamed. 'I won't, you can trust me,' he said.

'You,' de Cailly said to Richard, 'you and your men will go with the central scouting party which will head directly to where we think the invaders are. You and your two men shall be the only squires, you will be with some mounted crossbowmen. Your task is to hold castles along the way overnight ahead of the main body. You ride as far as Neufchâtel-en-Bray and hold the castle there until our glorious lord arrives with his host. Your party is the most likely to get itself into trouble, which I think is our lord's intention.'

'Which knights will lead us?' Richard asked.

De Cailly smiled and his hunchback straightened up for a moment. 'You will not like it,' he smiled.

The Little Lord pushed his way into the hall, back in his mail shirt already. His mail leggings made a metallic rattle with each step.

De Cailly looked at the young Tancarville, then grinned at Richard.

'No, surely not,' Richard said.

Bowman groaned.

'You will do as you are told,' de Cailly half smiled, 'even if he is the one doing the telling.'

'But he's not a knight,' Richard said.

The Little Lord halted. 'What did you say?'

'Nothing but the truth, young William,' de Cailly said.

Richard looked over into the flames as the knight continued.

'His father gives him the command to test him, too. If he fails, he will not be trusted with leadership again, so he needs you,' de Cailly said.

The young Tancarville sneered. 'Do what I say,' he said.

Richard saw a flicker of doubt in the young man's face, his broad shoulders perhaps uncertain on how to carry the weight of responsibility.

'Sir Thomas of Clères will accompany you as a councillor to young William, along with his retinue. He will meet you at Lillebonne castle in the morning,' de Cailly added.

The Little Lord scrunched his face up. 'I don't need a wet-nurse,' he said and walked off to find some food more to his taste than he'd found in the chapel.

'Do not antagonise him, Richard,' de Cailly said.

Richard held his hands up. 'What can I do to him? I can't grip a knife to cut my food, let alone swing a sword at him,' he said.

De Cailly chortled. 'Lord Tancarville is not accepting you back quite yet, this is more of a last chance,' he said. The knight pointed at Sir Gobble. 'And that goes for you, too. Our lord very rarely forgives anyone, and he certainly never forgets. Every time he gets on that Spanish horse, he will remember that you disrespected him,' de Cailly said.

Sir Gobble kept his face still. 'I will have earned golden spurs before this is all done,' he said with his head up.

De Cailly nodded. 'Good. You need to prepare to leave now, the scouting parties have no time to waste. The people must see their lord does not hesitate a moment to defend them. All squires will take shields with Tancarville colours from the store. I am afraid we do not have any extra mail shirts for your men though,' he said.

Bowman sat back. 'Well, the lowborn do not matter, do they,' he said.

De Cailly didn't register the comment. 'Muster as quickly as you can and be ready to leave. You will have to march on your warhorses, I'm afraid, you need to move fast. Remounts and pack animals will be brought in our main force,' he moved on to the next table.

Richard exhaled. 'I've never been to war,' he said. He thought of the idea of Solis being hit by arrows and shuddered.

'You'll be alright,' Sir Gobble said, 'war means opportunity for men like us.'

'Men like you?' Sarjeant said, 'you are both but boys, ignorant of the world. War is great to those who have not seen it,' he reached for a cup.

Richard looked at his wrapped palms again. 'I don't think I can wield a sword, not for at least a few days,' he said.

'That is a good point,' Bowman pushed the wine jug away from Sarjeant, 'they never gave me a new sword after that useless one broke. I am going to see if I can acquire myself one.'

He ran his hands through his blonde hair, looked about the hall, then walked quietly out.

'He's going to steal one, isn't he,' Richard said.

'Of course he is,' Sarjeant reached to the jug and dragged it back to his place, 'he isn't going to find a sword just lying around, is he?'

Serving women walked around with bread and cheese. Sir Gobble flagged one down and tucked in.

'We need to muster,' Richard said.

'Not on an empty stomach,' he replied with a mouthful of hard cheese.

Richard had to grudgingly agree, so he did the same.

Aspirants rolled up bedding and left the hall, and some of the younger knights had brought in shields to re-strap and adjust.

'They always leave that until the last moment,' Sir Gobble said.

'What?'

'Sorting their equipment out, everyone seems to leave it late. It's lazy.'

'I'm guessing yours is perfectly set up?' Richard asked.

'Of course,' Sir Gobble replied.

Richard sighed, he had other things to worry about.

'Do you know who the Martels are loyal to?' he asked.

'How should I know?' Sarjeant checked Bowman's cup to see if it had any wine left.

'Why would you care? Ah, was this Simon's family, the one who took your sister?' Sir Gobble asked.

Richard nodded. 'Simon said his uncle was in Boulogne, so I wonder if Eustace was likely to be with our enemy,' he said.

'I hope so,' Sir Gobble broke some bread, 'then you can kill him and be done with petty family squabbles. Then I won't have to hear about it anymore,'

Richard yet again glanced at his hands. 'I doubt I can, he's huge,' he said. He picked apart half a loaf of bread and ate it. Into the second half of the loaf, he started to carve the words of a charm with his knife.

A rope seller who stopped at Keynes had taught it to him, the rope seller said it would keep a horse safe in war. Richard picked up the charmed bread.

The younger knights got up as a group and started to pack their belongings. The hall emptied.

'Time to go, my boy,' Sarjeant drained Richard's cup for him. He stood up and swayed a little. 'I'm fine,' he said.

Richard and Sir Gobble exchanged a look and decided he was probably right. Richard rolled up his candlestick in his bedding, and carried it over to the stables which buzzed with activity.

Stable-boys groomed horses, picked their feet out and placed wooden saddles on their backs. Horses snorted and shouted at each other.

'They know today is different,' Richard said.

'They do,' Sir Gobble put a hand on Richard's shoulder, 'be careful around the Little Lord, you need to learn more courtesy. Let his insults and insolence wash over you. You need to suffer him well to survive,' he said.

'I'll try, but he is an insufferable fool,' Richard said.

They both laughed.

'May God be with you,' Sir Gobble went to saddle his horse.

Richard found Solis. The horse stood with his head out of the stable, a stable-boy hanging from his mouth via his tunic. The small boy frantically tried to grab a hold of the stable wall, but

Solis swung him from side to side.

'Drop,' Richard said and the stallion opened its mouth and snorted. The boy hit the ground, went to punch Solis, but froze when he saw Richard's face glare at him. The boy ran off.

'You can't do that, Soli,' he opened the stable door. Despite his behaviour, Richard still held out the charmed bread for him to eat.

Richard tacked him up and tied his bedding to the back of his saddle. Then he went to find a shield and lance, which he had to rest on his shoulder to carry. His mail shirt still had damage in its centre, but there was no time to find someone to repair it.

Bowman appeared from the stable next door where Pilgrim now stood ready.

Richard noticed that Bowman wore a fine sword belt of red dyed leather around his waist, a polished pommel and well wrapped handle stuck out of it. He smiled a toothy grin at Richard. 'Do you like it?' he asked.

'I'm sure the previous owner still does,' Richard said.

'No doubt that he did, but he's dead so I expect he has no strong feelings about it,' Bowman disappeared back into the stable.

Richard had to wait for two horses to be led out from his stable before he could exit, then he went outside with Solis. He leant his spear against the wall of the stable building and slung his shield around onto his back. He laced his helmet on and put his foot into the stirrup. He could just about grip the front of the saddle with his fingers, but with the added weight of the mail shirt, he almost failed to mount first time. As he landed in the saddle with a thud he checked that no one had seen his near miss.

Everyone was too busy to care. Men sat on horses, led horses, and shouted commands all around.

Richard picked his spear up from the wall and rested it on his right foot. Then he could lean it on his shoulder and avoid having to grip it with his hand. He took the reins and the palm of his left hand exploded into pain as he tried to close his hand even a little. He swore and fumbled for the little metal ring on the end of his reins. He found it and slid it onto the hook on his belt by his belly button. He was going to have to ride without his hand for a few days, and that was that.

Solis felt excited beneath him and started to walk on the spot.

Bowman appeared with Pilgrim and mounted him. 'I will feel naked without a mail coat,' he said as he looked at Richard's.

'Are you saying you've been to battle with one before?' Richard replied.

'No, I am not,' Bowman shifted his grip on his spear. He had found a felted wool tunic to wear over his normal tunic. The new one was a faded and mouldy looking blue, but it was better than nothing.

Richard noticed him adjust his cloak so it covered the sword.

Bowman looked at him and winked.

Sarjeant walked over on foot, holding a red lance with a banner wrapped around it.

'Where did you get that?' Richard asked.

'I do not want it,' Sarjeant said, 'Sir Roger shoved it into my hands and told me I am the standard bearer now. Standard bearers always get killed,' Sarjeant leant the banner on the wall and went in to get his horse.

Sir Gobble mounted and found his scouting party, which had already nearly gone out of the gate. They shouted 'Normandy' loudly as they went.

Tancarville and a few companions strode down from the cliff under the keep. 'Normandy,' they shouted back at the scouts.

It was enough to make Richard feel confident.

Hooves echoed off the walls and shields banged into saddles. The air buzzed.

Tancarville pointed at Richard. 'Why are you still here, get ready,' he shouted.

Richard thought about replying that he was ready, but wisely declined to voice it.

'Look after my son, boy,' Tancarville came closer, 'if he dies, I will kill you too.'

'Yes, my lord,' Richard replied.

Bowman reached down and checked his cloak was still in place without looking at it.

Tancarville didn't notice the sword belt. 'God smiles at you again it seems. He intervened just in time for you,' Tancarville inspected Solis. He looked up. 'Did you really walk twelve steps?'

'So I'm told,' Richard replied.

Tancarville burst into laughter. 'I do like you, boy, even if you trouble me so much,' he said.

The next scouting party formed up and de Cailly mounted his horse, a large black stallion with fire in its eyes, and rode over to them. The bottom half of his shield was blue, the top green, and the two halves were separated by a thick yellow line. He wore a surcoat, a long sleeveless woollen tunic, over the top of his mail armour, and it had the same colours.

Richard had never seen such a garment before, it shone with colour, and as he watched de Cailly, he knew he wanted to look like that.

'Do you know what my councillors are calling you, boy?' Tancarville asked.

'No, my lord.'

'Some are calling you the Devil's Centaur, they say you talk to horses,' he said.

'I do,' Richard said.

The lord chuckled. 'Indeed, but they are also calling you Leopard's Bane,' he said.

'Leopard's Bane?'

Tancarville pointed to the banner that Sarjeant had just picked up. 'The banner of Normandy, red with two golden leopards.'

'Leopards? Oh,' Richard said.

'It would seem you have terrified them, boy. They hope you fail to return from this campaign. Personally, I do not care either way, but if my son is harmed, it would be better than I never see you again. Am I clear?'

'Very clear,' Richard said.

'Good. Although if you are the devil, I would rather have you on my side. Now go on, you are the last to leave.'

Richard turned, followed by Bowman and Sarjeant, and rode to where the Little Lord waited for them.

'Unfurl the dammed banner,' Tancarville shouted.

Sarjeant groaned and complied. The banner was large and sagged down due to the lack of wind.

Behind the Little Lord were a dozen crossbowmen, including

the two guards Richard remembered from the night of the dancing monk. Those men were as unarmoured as Bowman, crossbows slung over their backs and bags of quarrels tied over their bedding behind their saddles. Half of them had metal helmets, some had long knives, but they were hardly heavily armed.

'Hurry up,' the Little Lord said to Richard.

'We're here,' he replied as the Little Lord spun his horse around. Richard noticed it was the good warhorse that his father had confiscated from him before.

'Normandy,' the Little Lord shouted in his own weak voice before everyone else joined in.

'Normandy,' they all cried as they rode through the walls, out of Castle Tancarville and off to war.

The excitement of their new adventure wore off by the time they'd marched through the village below the castle. Bowman didn't know where their first stop at Lillebonne was, and even Sarjeant, who seemed to have been everywhere, didn't have any idea either. He had been ordered to ride just behind the Little Lord who rode out in front of their column, the flag of Normandy aloft but limp.

Richard rode next to Bowman and both were silent as they traversed the hedge-lined lanes. Richard had begun the journey having to use his fingers to pull back on the reins to keep Solis's walk slow enough, but soon the stallion had settled into his walking mood. He didn't seem to mind being beside Pilgrim either, a horse that Richard felt sure Bowman was starting to like.

'How far did Sir Roger say Lillebonne was?' Richard asked.

'He didn't,' Bowman said.

The crossbowmen behind couldn't hear them, and the Little Lord ahead wouldn't have answered even if he had heard, so they rode on east not knowing how far away their destination was. The road was rutted from the heavy use of carts, with thick woodland on its left side. On the right the country opened up and sloped down into brushland and more trees. It was green, very green. Bird life flew overhead and sometimes flapped in the bushes as they walked past. Sometimes the horses jumped at them, sometimes they didn't. A river appeared to the right of the road and they followed it for a while. The trees on the left changed and became tall thin trees that reached up into the cloudy sky like green spears.

Eventually the column turned north and rode along a ridge that dropped away into a leafy valley. The valley was not wide or deep, but a river ran through it, a thread of blue in the blanket of greenery. A wooden bridge wide enough for a cart spanned the gently flowing river, and a castle kept guard over the crossing. A round tower, several storeys high, stood to one side with a wall and gateway directly leading on to the bridge. To cross the river, one had to go through the castle. The castle sat on Richard's side of the river as they rode towards it, and a queue of carts waited to cross the bridge and continue on their way west.

'No one seems very bothered about an invasion,' Richard said.

Two guards took payments from the carts before they ushered them on through the stone gate.

'They might not know,' Bowman said as they approached the wooden palisade that ran in a semi-circle around the tower and gate, starting and ending at the water. The flag of Normandy hung from a flagpole atop the tower, the tower as white as Castle Tancarville.

The gateway into the castle was guarded by a single spearmen who opened it based on the flag Sarjeant carried, and shouted at the carts to move out of their way. When the Little Lord told him they were there for the night, his eyes widened and he ran inside to tell someone.

They rode into the yard, or bailey, and dismounted. Richard did so with care, he grabbed the saddle with his fingertips and tried to lower himself down much more slowly than he usually would.

The bailey was barely big enough for the company to fit in, and there were enough stables for just four horses. Luckily for Richard and his companions, that meant their horses joined the Little Lord's for the night indoors. The less fortunate crossbowmen had to leave theirs loose to wander around the bailey overnight.

Richard took a drink of water, then watched cut grass being

thrown into piles around the bailey for the horses.

The Little Lord spoke to a short old man with a grey beard. The man had a clean and bright blue tunic, lined in a decent fabric.

The Little Lord dismissed him and returned to the stables. 'The castellan will give us food tonight, but he doesn't have much to go around with no notice,' he said.

'I wager he is holding back,' Bowman said.

The Little Lord grunted. 'Then have a look around,' he walked away.

'He's in a good mood,' Richard said.

'He is in command,' Sarjeant rolled up his banner.

Bowman slipped away to hunt for food and disappeared into the tower.

'This wasn't far from Castle Tancarville,' Richard said, 'we could have gone further.'

Sarjeant put the banner inside the stable doorway. 'This castle holds the river crossing, it seems cautious to wait here for tonight, but Lord Tancarville is known widely as a shrewd commander,' he said.

The crossbowmen unpacked their saddles and left then in a great heap of wood and leather.

'Besides,' Sarjeant unlaced his nasal helm, 'Neufchâtel can't be more than a few days ride from here, if the French and the Flemings rode fast they may not be far away.'

Richard thought about that, he rather hoped they were very far away. To take his mind off the enemy, he climbed the tower and looked out over the scenic river.

Bowman found him a while later as he peered out of an arrow slit that had a good view of the valley to the east. He could see a cart with a brown cover moving westwards over the bridge and into the castle.

Bowman squatted down beside him. 'Here you are, young lord,' he held out some dried fish, 'they do not have much, but this will be better than whatever mouldy bread and rotten cheese that tight castellan decides to give us.'

Richard pulled the fish apart with his teeth and held it gingerly with his fingers.

'How are the hands?' Bowman asked.

'Useless,' Richard chewed.

The first floor of the tower had a chamber that the castellan called a hall, although it was just a round room big enough for a few men to sleep in. A fire smouldered against the wall. There was one wooden table with a single bench, and nothing covered the wooden floorboards. Richard made his bed there, then went up to the top of the tower to watch the sunset.

He looked over the battlements east towards where Sarjeant said Neufchâtel was, but saw nothing but the night creep in. The valley over the river was populated by a few farmer's houses, their fields shaped like long fingers and full of crops not long for harvest. Beyond those lay an area of cleared woods, and after that the road was consumed by the vegetation that was only a dark green blur in the dusk.

Richard walked around the tower and looked back into the village in the direction they had come from. There was an area like a town square, but it sunk into the ground and a set of stone steps fanned out above it, cut into the hillside. This wasn't a simple hillside though, stone ruins ringed it, and they covered a larger area than his wooden castle. Richard could see big blocks of masonry that had tumbled from some ancient structure that had long since decayed from its previous glory, and he wondered what it had been.

'Time marches on,' Sarjeant took up a place beside him and leant on the battlements of the tower, 'if even the great glories of Rome can fall to that,' he added, 'then what will happen to the likes of us?'

Richard watched the shadows of the ruins lengthen as the sun dipped below the ridge and cast them into blackness. Clouds roofed the valley and he soon felt compelled to retreat down into the small hall, leaving a bored looking crossbowman behind on the wall to keep watch over the bridge.

In the hall Bowman snored lightly from under a blanket, and the Little Lord looked over a wooden platter that held some bread and cheese. The bread was stale.

'Have you got any meat?' he asked the servant who held it.

'No, my lord, we will go and bring you some tomorrow,' the servant said.

'Tomorrow we will be gone,' the Little Lord waved the plate

away.

Richard still had half a smoked fish and thought about giving it to the young Tancarville. He went over to his bedding and felt around to ensure the silver candlestick was still there. It was, as was his copy of Eric and Enid. He took the fish, sighed, and walked over to his commander.

'You can have this if you like,' he said.

The Little Lord's round face inspected the fish. He hesitated, but picked it up and started to eat it.

Richard went back to his bed and clambered into it.

The Little Lord swallowed his mouthful. 'I've been thinking, and maybe you were innocent in Simon's death,' he said.

'God showed everyone that,' Richard said.

The Little Lord grunted. 'Suit yourself,' he ripped a chunk of fish away with his teeth.

Richard went to sleep, the sound of the fire crackled away, accompanied for a short time by chewing as the Little Lord finished his gifted food.

Richard woke the next morning with a yawn. Normal traffic already flowed both east and west as he went to take in the morning air. Clouds drifted over and a breeze from the west caused the two leopards of Normandy on the flagpole to stir. The young lord of Tancarville stirred too, and Richard watched from the tower as he saw a lone rider make his way back towards Tancarville.

The Little Lord stood in the middle of the bailey. He shouted a brisk order to the crossbowmen and they started to round up their horses. That meant they would be leaving soon, so Richard went and packed again, where he saw Bowman slip a bundle of what he presumed was food into his bedroll. They descended the tower and prepared their horses, who banged their stable doors and nosed anyone who went by for food.

'Have we got any horsebread?' Richard asked.

'No,' Sarjeant replied and went by to fetch his banner, 'we would expect to be given some in a castle belonging to Lord Tancarville, our host has not been gracious.'

Solis kicked his door so hard that its hinges were almost lifted off.

'Stop it,' Richard said but he carried on regardless. Richard went to find the Little Lord and asked him if he could get some food for the horses.

The young Tancarville nodded. 'Yes, that's a good idea, I'll see the castellan about it,' he trudged off into the tower.

Another horse banged its metal shooed feet into its door, and that set Solis off again.

The Little Lord returned. 'He says they don't have any,' he complained.

'Have you got coin? We can look in the village,' Richard said.

The young Tancarville looked over at the horses. 'We don't have time for that, prepare to leave,' he went to order a crossbowman to groom his horse for him.

Richard swore and walked out of the castle to find some for himself. There were a number of houses both large and small between the castle's wooden palisade and the Roman ruins, and he looked for one with stables.

He walked past a building with a fenced garden where two pigs ate a pile of scraps. Between that building and the next, an alleyway had been covered over by a rough collection of wood, beneath which two figures sat. Richard caught himself staring at them, because although one man was his father's age, he missed one eye and one hand. His eyes were drawn to the stump.

The second man had a deep scar across his face, one that passed through his nose. It looked an old wound, and he was an old man, only wisps of white hair remained on a dappled old head. Both men looked up at Richard and reached out their hands.

'Some coin from the young lord?' the first asked.

'I have no coin, but what happened to you?' Richard asked.

The old man with the scar looked up. 'I was your age,' he croaked, 'about thirty years ago, when a lord from Anjou, I forget his name, invaded. King Stephen's army marched out to fight him, we were half Norman and half Fleming. Those Flemings, you know, they smell something awful. Now what was I saying?' he asked his neighbour.

'You are about to tell him that the two halves of Stephen's army fought each other, and a Fleming split your face in half,' the one-eyed man said.

'Ah yes, he was the last thing I ever did smell. Rotten he was. Did you know I have not smelt a thing in thirty years.' A bony finger reached up and pointed at his mutilated face.

Richard shuddered

'What I am,' the man said in a wobbling voice, 'you will soon be. Do not look away.'

Richard did look away, and then he walked away as fast as his legs could go. He swallowed, flexed his itching hands, and made for a stable block he could see aside a hall. A boy forked straw into the stables and Richard asked him if he had any bread for the horses.

'Yes sir, it has more acorns in that we'd like though,' the boy replied.

Richard requested some in the name of Lord Tancarville, using his grandest voice, and the boy soon brought out a basket full.

'You will bring back the basket, won't you?' the boy said hopefully as Richard left. Richard said he would, then walked back past the veterans, dropped a loaf off for them, and hurried on.

He threw a loaf into Solis's stable and the horse ducked after it, broke off a piece and lifted his head up as he chewed it. Acorn pieces flew everywhere.

Richard dropped some bread in for Pilgrim too, but he picked it up, waved it around a bit, and threw it out of his stable.

'Why aren't you ready yet?' The Little Lord shouted, one foot in his stirrup.

'They need to eat,' Richard held out a piece of bread to him.

The young Tancarville thought about it. 'Fine, might as well as I have to wait for you anyway,' he said.

Richard lobbed it to him then went to saddle Solis.

The column formed up and rode over the bridge, their metal clad hooves clattered over it as the waiting traffic had to clear out of the way.

On the far side of the river, a knight with a faded yellow shield waited for them. A thick diagonal blue line ran through the yellow shield. Sir Thomas Clères sat mounted on a brown courser, his legs straight down in long stirrups and his saddle painted yellow. It was chipped and worn though, and the yellow had half been replaced by scratches from his mail shirt. He looked older than Tancarville, and looked completely disinterested when he greeted the Little Lord. Sir Thomas was arrayed with four squires, mounted with shields that matched his, and another four mounted crossbowmen.

Sir Thomas fell into the marching formation next to the Little Lord, and his squires rode behind Richard and Bowman.

Richard thought that all of them looked tired, their equipment neither polished nor freshly painted. However, the company was now a little larger, and the Little Lord led the way east, to the next castle, in search of the enemy.

YVETOT

Richard formed the opinion that war was actually very boring. The long morning ride through the repetitive Norman countryside threatened to send Richard back to sleep. He appreciated the pace though, because it meant he could leave Solis to walk by himself and not have to interfere with his scolded hands. They still hurt, and although they had started to heal around the edges, big blisters had formed in the centre of each palm. Richard rode with his lance on his foot and shoulder because gripping it was still too painful.

Their scouting party navigated small villages, orchards and streams, the road carried them ever onwards. Midday came and went and they'd only stopped to water the horses once.

'Sir Thomas is pushing us on,' Richard said.

'The Little Lord has never ridden to war before,' Bowman replied.

'I'm glad we have Sir Thomas,' Richard said, because on his feet were golden spurs, and clearly he had been to war before.

'A hare,' Bowman pointed to a big eared animal that stood by the side of the road and watched them pass.

'A bad omen,' Richard said.

'Only if it runs,' Bowman said. The hare hopped a few steps but didn't run.

Across the sky white clouds drifted in the same direction they travelled. Insects started to land on their wrists, necks and horses. Richard twice swatted huge horseflies from Solis's neck. The first time the stallion jumped, but after that he'd ignored the slaps.

'Those biting beasts are bigger here than at home,' Richard said.

Bowman laughed. 'Many things out here are bigger than at home,' he replied.

They rode down a track that meandered through a clump of ash trees. A two wheeled cart rumbled towards them, pulled by a mule, with a thin cow tied to the back of it. A scythe stuck out of the top of a pile of material and belongings. As they passed it, Richard saw the downcast eyes and faces of a young family, a baby cried in its mother's arms.

Once out of earshot Richard turned to Bowman. 'I don't think I've ever seen anyone look so unhappy.'

'Do you not know what they are?' Bowman said.

'Unlucky? Bad farmers?'

'Young lord, those people flee the war. Their lord must be dead if they have left his lands, permission to leave is needed. They will search for a lord in need of tenants,' Bowman said.

Richard realised his mistake and kept quiet until they reached a town. The town was large and Richard thought it could be twice as big as Hempstead. Norman traders, merchants, churchmen and craftspeople inhabited the streets that forked off on either side of the main road. Sir Thomas directed the column to a large church, its stone spire tall and well built. Stone buildings surrounded the holy building, whereas the rest of the town was of predominantly wooden structures.

Richard smelt sewage as well as cooked meat, which reminded him that he didn't much care for towns.

Sir Thomas and the Little Lord dismounted and went inside the church. No orders had been given so everyone else stayed on horseback as the sun walked across the sky and the town went about its daily business around them.

'What are they doing?' Richard asked.

'No idea,' Bowman replied.

Some time later, and just as Richard was about to learn how to sleep in the saddle, their commanders emerged into the daylight and remounted. The column went on the move again and left the town.

The town disappeared behind them over the horizon. The

top of the church spire dipped below and vanished from sight, and a while later Sir Thomas pointed down a smaller track that turned off the road. It led through a large apple orchard.

'I bet Sarjeant is thinking about cider,' Bowman nodded approvingly at the red apples hanging amongst the green leaves. After the orchard came a village that sprawled around a pond. Half the houses needed repair and the village ditches were clogged with mud and vegetation. Beyond the dilapidated houses, and at the far end of the road, Richard saw a fortified manor house.

The central keep was a three storey stone tower ringed by a square stone wall. It had a larger outer bailey set around that stone wall. The outer bailey was fenced in by a wooden palisade, and within that area the company found a wooden stable block.

The roof of the first one Richard checked had caved in months, or even years ago, and his entrance caused a heron to flap out of the open roof. Solis jumped. His iron shod hooves landed in the ground a finger's width from Richard's foot.

The next stable had a solid enough roof, but some panels had fallen off the back wall big enough for a horse to use as a window. Sir Thomas said they were leaving before dark, so Richard felt just about happy enough to leave Solis in it while he went to find him some water.

Richard wandered around in search for the castle's well. He could see large weeds had sprouted up along the bottom of the wooden palisade, and the outer bailey itself had a thicker covering of grass than he'd seen anywhere else. The well was small but its water fresh, so Richard helped to ferry water to the horses. With a wooden bucket full he walked by Sir Thomas telling the Little Lord where to find water.

'This is a foolish errand, I cannot understand why your father wished it. The Lord is older than this castle and the lady is such a distant relation of the Earl of Leicester that you or I are probably closer to him than she is. Then there is the dubious matter of the parentage on her mother's side. I hardly see that this land will yield us a single crossbow bolt, let alone a man who is able to shoot it.'

'It's what father told me to do,' the young Tancarville said.

'Then let us get it over and done with and we can be on our way. Hurry up, squire,' Sir Thomas chided when he noticed Richard was eavesdropping.

Everyone pitched in to throw the horses in the outer bailey some grass, which had to be fetched from the village by some very fed-up crossbowmen. Then the knight and eight squires, which included the Little Lord, all entered the stone walled inner bailey.

Inside that smaller fortification there was at least some sign of life. Smoke rose from the chimney of a wooden hut as well as the stone keep. From the top of the battlements hung a flag of red with a sheaf of golden wheat at its centre.

'I think the gold was probably an ironic choice,' Bowman said. It tried to flutter in the breeze but it fought a losing battle.

The entrance to the keep, as usual, was on the first floor so they had to climb a wooden staircase to gain access. The whole of the first floor was taken up by the hall of the manor, although larger than the small circular hall at Lillebonne, it was hardly luxurious.

Seated at the end of the room, on plain wooden chairs, were the lord and lady of Yvetot. The lord was a tall, thin man with a thick head of grey hair. He had an oblong face with red rimmed eyes, all the more prominent as his skin was a blotchy pale white. His wife contrasted him in every way, and life shone from her.

Each man noticed her first.

The exception was Sir Thomas, who bowed before the Lord of Yvetot. 'Sir Arthur, it is a pleasure to see you again,' he said.

Richard thought Sir Arthur was so old that he could be the legendary ancient King Arthur.

'Lady Sophie,' Sir Thomas bowed to the lady of Yvetot.

'You are?' Her silken voice floated across the room to the men of war arrayed before her. Lady Sophie's skin was pale yet it shone, and her long blonde hair framed a delicate face. She was young where her husband was old.

'Sir Thomas of Clères,' the knight said.

'Are these all your men?' Sophie asked.

'I am the heir of the Chamberlain of Normandy,' the Little Lord said from behind Sir Thomas.

The knight sighed.

Sophie studied the young Tancarville for a moment. 'It is a delight to meet you,' she said.

'Who are you?' the Little Lord asked.

She smiled with her mouth but not her eyes. 'I am the daughter of the Earl of Leicester,' she said.

Her husband coughed and lifted his head up. 'Why are you here? This is a disturbance to us,' he said.

Richard wondered what their arrival could possibly have disturbed.

'The Flemings and the French have invaded to the east. We ride to muster forces to face them,' Sir Thomas rested his hand on his sword hilt, 'we have alerted the militia in the town, and Lord Tancarville asked us to visit you so that you could honour yourself by providing your fee to our army.'

'Of course, my fee.' Sir Arthur coughed, 'why else would you be here?' Even those words sounded like an effort and after each one there came a wheeze.

An old deerhound curled up beside Sir Arthur. It opened its eyes, passed wind, and closed them again. Richard heard Bowman stifle a laugh.

'We shall all eat together. Servants, prepare the room,' Sophie called.

Two servants started to drag four small tables together to serve as a long table. Each of the small tables was a slightly different height, and there were not enough chairs so some of the squires were sent to find logs that were big enough to sit on.

Richard avoided this duty by showing Sir Thomas his hands.

'So it is true,' the knight turned the bandaged limbs over, 'did you have to bribe the priest?'

Richard pulled his hands away and his face must have been one of genuine shock because Sir Thomas actually laughed.

'Fear not, boy, I would rather the Devil fought on my side than that of my enemy,' he said.

'That's exactly what Lord Tancarville said,' Richard had no interest in furthering that conversation, so went and sat down by the fire. The wooden floorboards were stained underneath a sparse covering of straw. Some of the boards even had gaps between them through which he could see light from the ground floor below.

Lady Sophie re-entered the hall. She now wore a long red dress bordered with gold thread. She stood next to Richard. 'This heir to Tancarville, what sort of man is he?' she asked

'I don't know,' he said. He wasn't sure what the right answer was.

'Now, don't be shy,' Sophie said.

Richard could smell her as she leant in closer. 'Is he promised to anyone, or does he want to be?'

'No he isn't, and I've never heard him speak about it,' Richard said, fairly confident that this was at least not the wrong answer.

The fire wasn't large enough to heat the whole hall, but it bathed Richard in an orange glow. He stood so close an ember flew off and went out on his tunic.

'We have been married for five years now, and yet we have no child,' Sophie's voice trailed off.

Richard maintained his gaze into the centre of the blaze as a log broke up and rolled over.

'I have always dreamt of having sons that look like him, or maybe even you. You in a few years, I mean,' Sophie said.

'I confess I don't know what you mean, but I pray that you get your sons,' Richard replied, uncertain if courtesy would allow his eyes to look anywhere other than the hearth.

'I'm not sure prayers are enough,' she left Richard alone by the fire, which relieved him.

In the distance he could hear Sir Thomas and Sir Arthur arguing.

'You owe a fee to de Cailly, he protects you and you serve him. Sir Roger could ride this way himself, do you wish to disappoint him?' Sir Thomas asked.

'I care little for Sir Roger, he has never once done anything for me,' Sir Arthur replied, still sat on his chair as the hall was prepared for food around him.

Sir Thomas walked a small circle. 'Just one squire. Just one spearman. Give us something and Lord Tancarville may spare you his wrath,' his hands gestured in the air and rattled his mail sleeves.

'I am a lord of a manor, of a village. I am not a lord of war. I do not train men to fight. I have no weapons bar my sword, and I have not even laced that on for twenty years. Or is it thirty?' Sir Arthur looked up at the ceiling.

Logs were brought in and planks placed on top of them to use as benches. Watered wine appeared in two jugs. Richard sat down at the table and knew those jugs were not remotely big enough.

'Have you no honour?' Sir Thomas said.

'Honour? What use is honour to me? I need a son,' Sir Arthur's face pulsated with life for the first time Richard had seen.

Lady Sophie said something to the Little Lord, and Richard saw that he turned away from her and his eyes cast down to his feet.

'Little Lord indeed,' Bowman laughed, 'if he acts like that, people will start to ask why he was called the Little Lord in the first place.'

Richard laughed. Bowman sat down and was first to the wine. He poured it but it looked more like water that had been stored in an old wine barrel than real wine.

'Beggars can't refuse,' Bowman drank and Richard did the same.

Lady Sophie left their commander to gaze at his shoes, whispered something in the ear of a servant with a giant mole on his forehead, then sat back down in her chair.

Sir Thomas gave up recruiting fighting men, and sat at the end of the table furthest away from the lord of the castle.

The Little Lord took a place next to Sir Arthur, whose chair was dragged over to be at the head of the uneven long table. The Little Lord started to talk to Sir Arthur, and the servant with the mole on his forehead placed a new wine jug between the pair of them.

Food was served and Richard recognised some rabbit.

'This is better than I was expecting, we might even avoid food poisoning,' he said. He ate boiled eggs with butter, and drank the slightly red water that no one actually had called wine. As he ate, he heard the Little Lord's words get louder and louder.

Sir Arthur slurred his words too, but that could have been

normal. 'I can trace my descendants back to the Northmen over a hundred years ago,' the Lord of Yvetot said to the young Tancarville.

'Probably because for him, that is only one generation ago,' Bowman said.

Richard and the crossbowmen from Tancarville's gate laughed, and Sir Arthur strained his eyes to see what the fuss was about.

'How did they get in here? The hall was only for knights and squire,' Richard said to Bowman.

'They might look dull witted, but they are smart enough to realise that no one was going to notice if they built these benches and just never left,' Bowman said.

The crossbowman with the beard said something quietly to the one with curly hair. Bowman's hearing must have been better than Richard's, because he looked up at them.

'Be quick about it, I cannot drink much more of this hog's piss,' Bowman said.

The bearded crossbowman nodded. 'Alright Jean, make it quick and quiet,' he said.

'I'm always quiet,' Jean got up from the makeshift bench, which wobbled.

'But you're not always quick,' the bearded man said.

Jean left the hall as the servant with the mole entered with an iron cauldron.

Sir Arthur waved his hands around in an attempt to explain something to the Little Lord.

'We serve pottage to you so that you will see that we are but poor folk. We have no one to send with your army,' he burped.

The Little Lord frowned, went to grab his cup but missed and knocked it over. It was empty, but rolled off the table and clattered onto the floor.

Pottage was poured into bowls, although there were fewer bowls than people.

'Weren't we supposed to be moving on from here soon?' Richard waved away a bowl of pottage.

'Looks like we might not if the Little Lord continues as he is. He'll fall off his horse if he tries to ride after that much drink,' Bowman said.

As he looked around for a spoon, Lady Sophie left her chair, floated around the hall, and took Jean's vacant space on the bench.

'It is not appropriate for a lady to be seated at this end of the table,' Bowman said to her.

'I'm quite aware,' the young lady said, 'but the people at the other end of the table are starting to spit everywhere. Besides, I heard your accents and have been meaning to ask, which part of England are you from?'

Richard looked into her blue eyes and started to say, 'Keynes,' before Bowman kicked his ankle and he caught himself. 'Newbury,' he said.

'I'm afraid I don't know it,' Sophie's eyes swept across his face. 'What brought you to Normandy?'

'Bad luck. What is a lady from Leicester doing here on her own?' Richard asked.

Sophie sighed. 'Marriage of course. My father thought it might gain him lands on this side of the sea. But nothing ever happens here and if I don't have a son soon, it will come to nothing anyway,' she glanced back up to the top of the table.

'The most exciting thing that's happened here was when the villagers got excited and put a pig on trial for thieving from my husband. They hung it, you know. They said no one could be allowed to harm their lord. As if he even knew the pig. Sir Arthur is older than all of the villagers so they think he's a saint to be worshipped. We got some news though, a messenger riding from the east already told us the Flemings were on their way. Another from the west told us that Lord Tancarville had given birth to a child of the devil.'

Richard looked at the Little Lord. 'He's hardly from the Devil, my lady,' he said, 'he's just an idiot.'

'No, not him, this message came only yesterday, but we could make no sense of it,' Sophie said.

Richard slid his bound hands under the table.

'What happened to them?' Sophie asked.

Richard stopped and cursed himself for not being quicker. 'A piece of hot metal,' he said.

Bowman chuckled. 'He will not be doing that again, I can assure you,' he said.

Crossbowman Jean returned with two jugs but stopped at the door when he saw his spot had been taken.

Bowman winked at the bearded crossbowman, then got up and left with Jean. The bearded crossbowman followed him and all three of them left, their jugs with them.

Sophie's eyes looked into Richard's. 'Has this young Tancarville sired any bastards?'

Richard choked on a piece of cheese. 'How should I know?' he coughed the cheese back up.

'Or does he prefer men?' Sophie asked.

Richard's mouth opened but no sound came out. 'How can you ask that?' he said.

Her eyes seemed to lose some of their brightness. 'If only you knew,' she said.

Richard looked at the Little Lord and his head of red hair. 'I think Sir Pottage would prefer Sir Roger's daughter,' he said.

The Little Lord, despite being one tall table and one small table away, flashed his eyes at Richard. 'What did you call me?' he shouted.

Richard groaned. He had lasted just one day without antagonising him.

'Nothing at all, my lord,' he said. Richard looked at Sophie as if she could help.

The Little Lord pushed himself up from the table, almost lost his footing and knocked his chair over onto the wooden floor.

'My Lord,' Sophie stood up, 'this young man said nothing important or disrespectful.'

'He has disrespected me for the last time,' the young Tancarville put his hand on his sword.

Sir Thomas sprung to his feet. 'My lord, no,' he shouted.

Richard went to get up too, his eyes on the path to the doorway.

The Little Lord drew his sword with what was either a flourish or a lack of coordination. 'I'll have your head,' he screamed and slashed the sword through the air for effect. Except it didn't go through the air, it caught Sir Arthur in the neck, the curved point of the sword neatly sliced his unprotected wrinkled flesh.

The Little Lord, unaware, staggered towards Richard.

'My lord,' Sir Thomas rushed to Sir Arthur as the old man's hands scrambled to his throat.

Richard turned to run, but the toe of his shoe got caught in a hole between two boards and he fell.

The Little Lord swung the sword through the air again and charged at Richard. He slipped on some spilt pottage, his legs gave way, and his head thumped onto the floor with a crack.

Richard got to his feet as Sir Arthur went limp, a stream of blood dribbled down his tunic as Sir Thomas grabbed his neck and tried desperately to stem the tide.

Richard bent down over the Little Lord, whose chest moved up and down. 'I think he's just asleep,' he said to no one in particular.

Sir Thomas's squires jumped to aid him, but as Sophie approached she saw the gory mess and collapsed onto the nearest man. He put her down gently.

Sir Thomas stood up, his hands bloodied, and looked over to the Little Lord. 'If I was his father,' he shook his head. Blood trickled down his mail shirt too, a great mass of it dripped down from ring to ring.

Amidst the chaos, Richard's single thought was how difficult that was going to be to clean.

'Water,' Sir Thomas shouted and a servant rushed away.

Richard's stomach turned, but that could have been the eggs.

'You, boy,' Sir Thomas pointed at Richard with a red finger, 'we need to bury Sir Arthur, find a priest and have someone dig a grave. This cursed place must have a church somewhere and I want to leave here as soon as we can.'

'Yes, sir,' Richard answered as the smell of iron seeped into his nostrils. He was used to it from animals, but he didn't much like it now. He ran down the wooden stairway and out of the keep. The fresh air smelt clean. He couldn't find Bowman, but found some of Sir Thomas's crossbowmen and ordered them to find the church and dig a grave. They grumbled, but obeyed.

Richard found Sarjeant stood outside the stables and told him what had happened.

'Allow me to find the priest,' Sarjeant said.

Richard nodded because it meant he could go into Solis's stable and hide. It would take hours to dig a grave and he knew certain things were supposed to happen before they buried the old knight, things he wanted no part of. So he curled up in the corner of a rotting stable on a bed of straw that looked older than he was, and went to sleep.

When Richard awoke it was dark. Two owls hooted from somewhere close by so Richard shuddered and said a prayer to ward them off. Solis lay on the straw, his bottom lip drooped and his head bobbed up and down as he dreamt. Richard stretched and felt his palms. They still hurt, but he could almost make a fist before the pain became too much. He left the stable and walked into the outer bailey. Horses grazed from piles of grass in the dark yard and their eyes reflected the flames from braziers around the walls. It was quiet. Two of Sir Thomas's crossbowmen looked out over the palisade in the direction of the village. Richard walked towards the stone wall of the inner yard. A single spot of rain landed on his face and he pulled his cloak around him. With any luck they had buried the old man already and he could go back to sleep. The moon hung in a blur above him, a half crescent that glowed faintly in the night.

Sarjeant met him as he walked through the gate. 'Sir Thomas is with the priest at the church, my boy. A foul business,' he said. His blue eyes reflected the moon for a brief moment before a cloud drifted in front of it.

'Have you seen Bowman?' Richard asked.

'Not since we arrived,' Sarjeant replied.

'Are you guarding this gate?' Richard asked.

Sarjeant nodded and exhaled deeply. 'I am too old for this,' he said.

'For what?'

'War, my boy. Standing on ramparts in the dark and the cold. When I was young I thought it would be better in the east, but the nights are cold even there,' Sarjeant said.

The owls spoke to each other across the countryside again.

'They make me shiver,' Richard said.

'The east has those too. In Egypt they mean death,' Sarjeant said.

Richard nodded, the owls had meant death today. 'Were you

in the Holy Land last year, when my father was there?'

'No, I returned home years ago, I wish to forget it,' Sarjeant said.

The rain tried to force its way out of the clouds, and a cluster of droplets fell onto the stone wall they leant on.

Richard left Sarjeant and went up the wooden stairs into the hall. The Little Lord snored where he'd fallen, alone in the room and amongst fallen benches and smashed pottery cups. Richard's neck tingled when he looked over to Sir Arthur's wooden chair, a patch of blood already half soaked into one of the wooden armrests. He thought Bowman was probably on the level above, having a grand time, so went to find him.

Lady Sophie appeared in the doorway and they nearly collided.

'I'm sorry, my lady,' he backed away.

'Nonsense,' she walked into the hall.

The fire was almost out and sent too much smoke into the room.

'Would you tend to that?' Sophie said. She floated across the chamber and bent down to examine the Little Lord.

Richard threw some small sticks onto the fire and placed a single log over them.

The lady of the castle squatted down by the young Tancarville. 'Why do men ruin everything? Still, it isn't too late. Richard, will you swear to help me and never tell a soul?'

'Of course' Richard said. He knew he was supposed to say that. In stories knights spent most of their time helping ladies who needed it, and that was the sort of knight he'd promised to be in the chapel at Tancarville. Except , he thought, he wasn't a knight yet and her request sounded dangerous.

'Pick him up and follow me,' Sophie instructed.

Richard thought about refusing, but he looked at the lady and his resolve melted. He put his hands under the Little Lord's body, which stung as he picked him up. The boy's red hair hung down from his head limply but Richard didn't much care how uncomfortable it looked for the Little Lord, his hands hurt a lot.

'Good, follow me,' Sophie said.

Richard carried the sleeping lord's body up a storey and into the private chambers of the lord and lady of the castle.

A four posted bed, curtained with faded fabrics, stood as the centrepiece of the room on the back wall. Linen drapes hung down around the bed.

'Put him on it,' Sophie said and Richard hesitated.

'No, you can't,' he said.

'I dammed well am,' Sophie walked up to Richard who shrank back. Her blue eyes blazed. 'You think I want to? I never wanted to come to Normandy, where everyone says I'm common, or worse, English. You know they think the English have hidden tails between our legs? The first thing Sir Arthur asked me was if that was true. Not that I could even understand him properly in those days. Now my husband is dead, and while no one else noticed, I saw what provoked this boy to kill him. He may have been drunk because of *me*, but *you* owe me a debt for the drawing of the sword. Now I must let him draw another sword and fall on it myself so that I can keep this miserable piece of land and its miserable castle. Do you understand?'

Even if he hadn't, Richard couldn't respond to that. He dumped the Little Lord onto the bed. The unconscious body almost bounced off the other side.

'Do I have your word?' she said as Richard turned to leave.

'You do,' Richard felt an urgent need to be in fresh air. He left the chamber and ran down through the now empty hall and outside into the yard, where Sarjeant leant on the battlements of the stone wall. Richard wanted more than anything to plunge his head into a bucket of ice cold water, but instead he went up to the wall and quietly stood next to Sarjeant. He put his elbows on the cold stone and stared out across the lower bailey and beyond. A fog obscured the village now and the night was still.

'If you are here, I'm going to sleep,' Sarjeant patted Richard on the shoulder. He slid down the wall, threw his brown mantle around his body and shut his eyes. Richard couldn't fall asleep that quickly outside, it always took him a while. He gazed out into the drifting fog and owls hooted again. He groaned, but his eyes felt heavy so he thought to rest them for a moment.

Richard's eyes snapped open when a horse pushed its stable door and rattled it. Another horse walked a circle in its box. Solis stuck his yellow head out of his stable and his ears twitched in one direction and then another. Wolves maybe? Or Flemings? Flemings won't be moving around at night, Richard thought. He pushed Sarjeant until he grumbled and woke up.

'What is it?'

'The horses are agitated, something is out there,' Richard said.

Sarjeant pulled his cloak up to his chin. 'How sure are you? I am not getting cold if this is your imagination,' he said.

Richard thought he could see a faint speck of light far away in the fog. 'Pretty sure,' he said.

Sarjeant pushed his considerable frame upright and yawned. His eyes scanned the fog, then squinted towards where Richard could see light. 'Damn this place,' he said.

A spot of hazy movement in the fog caught Richard's eye, it was as if the fog was coming alive. The dark shape seemed closer than the speck of light. A second dark cloud appeared, then a third. The blurs got darker until Richard could make them out as running humans.

'I was hoping for wolves,' he said.

The two crossbowmen by the front gate sprang into life. The cry of 'Alarm' rang out. The crossbowmen fumbled to pick bolts out of their ammunition bags.

The first dark blur ran out of the fog and morphed into the shape of Sir Thomas.

Right behind him, to judge by his robe, ran a priest.

Sir Thomas sprinted and his squires burst out from the fog behind him. The lights grew closer too, they bobbed up and down as they cut through the fog. Richard's hand went to his sword without thought, and he winced as he tried to handle it.

'Someone needs to fetch our brave commander,' Sarjeant said, his voice steady.

Sir Thomas rushed through the open gate as the two crossbowmen on the palisade levelled their loaded weapons at the fog. More figures appeared in the murk and the specks of light morphed into burning torches.

A shiver ran through Richard.

The last squire reached the lower bailey and the gate slammed shut and was barred behind him. The twang of a crossbow reverberated in the still night. Shouts sounded from the tower behind Richard as others realised the danger.

'I'll get him, I know where he is,' Richard pushed himself off the stone wall. He jogged as much as he could on his way back up to Lady Sophie's chamber.

The Little Lord sat on the end of the bed, his head in his hands.

Lady Sophie looked out of a small window that looked over the two walled baileys.

'My lord,' Richard caught his breath, 'there's an attack. We need you armed and on the walls.'

The Little Lord looked up, his red hair ruffled and his eyes blurry. 'I don't know where I am,' he moaned.

'In the tower. You need to be getting your mail on, we need to go now,' Richard grabbed his lord by the arm.

The Little Lord looked down at the bandaged hand that grabbed him.

'Come on,' Richard tugged.

The young Tancarville stood up, but had to put an arm on the post of the bed to steady himself.

'You must not let them in,' Sophie said quietly from the window.

Richard had a pretty good idea of what had happened in the chamber, but wasn't going to ask about it. He helped the Little Lord down the staircase and into the hall.

A squire appeared with a mail shirt and dropped it on a table with a clatter of metal. 'Sir Thomas says to put that on,' he said and ran back out of the room.

There were shouts outside.

Richard held the mail up over the Little Lord's head and lowered it down over him.

Now armoured, the Little Lord walked under his own effort down into the inner bailey.

'They are pushing the wall over. The wood's rotten,' Sarjeant shouted down to them.

Richard left his lord and ran up to see. The wooden palisade was indeed giving way, the wooden posts being pushed backwards and forwards in several places.

Sir Thomas formed his squires up at the points where the wall was being ripped out. Crossbowmen loosed bolts into the darkness, including from the stone wall beside Sarjeant.

Richard couldn't actually see the attackers as they were hidden behind the palisade.

A third part of the wooden palisade started to move back and forth and the castle started to seem a lot less secure.

Sir Thomas saw it as well. 'Too many breaches. Back behind the stone,' he shouted.

All the men in the lower yard left their posts and ran towards Richard and the stone wall.

Sir Thomas was the last through the gate which his squires shut and barred behind him. 'William,' he shouted towards the Little Lord, 'where is your shield?'

'Someone find it for me,' the Little Lord cried. His face drained of colour and Richard looked over the wall.

A crowd of villagers pushed two sections of the palisade down and swarmed into the yard.

The horses kicked, shouted, and banged on their stable doors, and in the distance dogs barked.

The invaders were lightly armed, most wielded axes or farm tools, but some had no weapons at all.

Sir Thomas's crossbowmen took up positions along the stone wall and opened up on the villagers.

Richard saw one peasant take a bolt to the shoulder which sent him reeling onto the ground.

'Form,' Sir Thomas shouted.

His squires, wide eyed but steady, lined up behind him and faced the wooden gate.

Bowman appeared next to Richard. 'What in God's name is happening?' he said.

'Where have you been?' Richard asked.

A shield was handed to the Little Lord, and Sir Thomas dragged him by the neck and pushed him to the front of their small formation.

'Enough with this nonsense,' Sir Thomas shouted. He turned to his squires. 'We cut them down until they run, and we stop at the palisade, clear?'

A chorus of agreement rang out.

Richard was impressed by the difference between Sir Thomas's soldiers and young Tancarville's, which including himself, stood on the walls doing nothing.

'Draw your sword, boy. This time try to not kill anyone doing it,' Sir Thomas said to the Little Lord, who looked like he was about to cry.

'This is your mess, you deal with it,' Sir Thomas unbarred the gate himself. He stepped back to the Little Lord and nodded.

Two squires pulled the gate open to reveal a mob of peasants armed with axes.

Sir Thomas pushed the red headed Tancarville straight into them.

Richard couldn't see what happened, but Sir Thomas waded in himself and his squires followed, swords raised.

'Go with them,' Richard said to Bowman.

'They have this under control,' Bowman replied.

Richard shot him a strong look and held up his hands. 'If you don't, I'll go with these,' he hissed.

'Fine, fine,' Bowman pulled out his sword and slowly walked down the wall.

Before he got there, some villagers started to flee.

Sir Thomas emerged into view in the lower yard, his sword flashed and peasants fell around him, limbs half severed and heads split open.

A man in a green tunic slashed him with a long knife, but protected by his mail, Sir Thomas didn't notice. The man in the green tunic lost his hand to the knight's dancing blade.

The villagers broke and ran.

Crossbowmen on the stone wall loosed bolts at them, two were caught in the back and thrown to the ground as they fled across the yard.

'To the wooden walls, mend the breaches,' Sir Thomas pointed his red sword to where the wall had failed.

The Little Lord trudged back through the gate into the upper bailey. His sword was red too, and he had a shallow cut across his forehead. He sat down with his back to the wall, tossed his shield to the side and put his arms over his head.

The noise of the crowd faded back into the fog, the glow of their torches in turn faded away into nothingness. The only sound to replace them was the sound of wooden braces being used to prop up the fallen palisade. Sir Thomas's men were busy.

Bowman and Sarjeant went to help with the building effort while Richard kept an eye on the Little Lord, at least until he started to snore.

Richard peered out into the blackness of the night but saw nothing.

Sir Thomas ordered more torches to be lit around the lower bailey, and men were posted all along it to keep watch.

Richard stayed on the wall all night wrapped up inside his cloak. He tried to sleep but his instinct was to keep a look out. Snatched sleep came and went regardless, and Richard prayed for the dawn to come quickly and quietly.

Sarjeant joined him sometime during the middle of the night, but Richard's eyes were leaden by then.

When the sun finally started to rise in the east, the fog eased and the world became a shade lighter. Sir Thomas appeared before him, although Richard's focus struggled so much that he could barely tell the colours on his shield.

'We are leaving, mount up, squire,' the knight said.

Richard nodded and said a prayer of thanks. He tacked Solis up quicker than he'd ever done before, and led him into the outer bailey. Squires and crossbowmen rushed to gather equipment and mount horses, and soon the whole company was on horseback and on their way out of the castle. They left behind Lady Sophie, a yard scattered with corpses, and a night they all wanted to forget.

GOLDEN GREED

The greenery of the Norman countryside seemed to go on forever. Before Yvetot, Richard had thought war largely boring. After it, he decided it was boring *and* terrifying. Since Yvetot, the weather had grown darker too. Richard imagined himself sitting by a hearth fire as they journeyed on, instead he was tired to his core from the previous night. The company had continued at pace, Sir Thomas obviously keen to make up some of their lost time.

'I doubt Lord Tancarville and his army is far behind us now,' Bowman said.

'At least the wind is at our backs,' Richard said. It was the afternoon and the first drops of rain hit Solis's coat and left dark yellow spots on it. Richard gave Solis the last of the horsebread in anticipation of bad weather, and soon enough the air cooled. The column marched wrapped in cloaks, braced against what they all knew was an incoming storm. Rain droplets soaked into their wool at an ever increasing rate as the rain began.

They stopped to water the horses at a stream and the Little Lord's horse drank next to Solis. The palomino went to spin his back end towards the horse, and Richard scolded him.

The Little Lord turned to Richard. 'I remember what you said last night. You're the reason the old man is dead.'

Richard ignored him, the sound of the stream as it rushed past mixed with the sound of the rain that hit it, and almost drowned the young man out. The noise made Richard feel strangely peaceful.

'I don't remember doing it, I'm not sure I really did,' the Little Lord held his horse's reins up as it drank.

'You did it,' Richard said.

'I think Sir Thomas made it up,' the young Tancarville hissed.

Richard decided to avoid trouble, and took Solis away from the stream and remounted him. The bandage on his right hand had become threadbare, as well as wet, but the blisters on his palm had popped. A horrible liquid feeling irritated his hands, but he dared not unwrap them to look.

By mid afternoon the rain fell substantially. It poured off the helmets they wore, and drops stuck to the bottom of their metal rims, waiting to be blown into their eyes by stronger gusts of wind. That wind sounded almost like a rattle, so loud that no one bothered to speak. Richard knew his cloak would be waterproof to a point, and that point was reached as they entered some woods later in the day. Every sort of tree Richard knew pressed close up to both sides of the dirt road, which had turned to sticking mud. His cloak smelt of wet wool and his hands were cold even though he rode off his belt and his hands were inside the sodden cloak.

Others fared worse, but everyone understood that marching on was the thing to do. Besides, Richard thought, where was there to hide anyway? Nothing in the environment around them could possibly be dry. Their horses were wet and smelled wet too, although Solis was warm enough from walking that he at least kept Richard's legs from freezing.

Soon it got even darker, and the wind howled as well as gusted. Richard's toes and fingers ached with cold. Undulating hills made a welcome difference to the flat plains, but it just meant walking through the mud was made more difficult by going down inclines. The Norman horses fared better, but Solis wasn't used to it, and skidded more than walked down the hills. The trees grew taller and the road narrowed between them. Sometimes Richard's leg bumped into Bowman's next to him.

Bowman held his cloak up to his eyes and ignored it.

A flash of light split the sky above the trees. A huge rumble of thunder rolled and rippled overhead. Horses jumped, and some spooked off the road and into branches or bushes. Solis jumped on the spot but didn't go anywhere.

Most of the riders wrestled their horses back onto the road. A second burst of bright light filled the air. A tree in the woods exploded to Richard's right and a wave of light almost blinded him. A crack that could have been the earth splitting followed, and for a moment Richard went deaf. It was by far the loudest sound he'd ever heard, and it reverberated in his skull.

The Little Lord's horse bolted forwards at the head of the column.

Richard's hearing returned to a searing scream behind him, and the sound of man and horse falling into the mud together.

Sir Thomas's warhorse followed the Little Lord's in a flurry of hooves, Richard couldn't tell if it was on purpose or not.

Thunder spread out across the sky above them, a roar that seemed to suck the air out of Richard's lungs. The sky itself shattered as the thunder broke right above them.

Sarjeant's horse cantered on the spot, gibbering, and Richard and Bowman caught up with it. A horse with an empty saddle bolted past them, the hooves rapid and the horse wide-eyed.

Solis spun round, and Richard saw squires and crossbowmen disappear backwards or into the trees.

Pilgrim bolted forwards with Bowman in no control and raced off.

Richard grabbed Sarjeant's arms and pulled him and his wild-eyed horse with him. They cantered after Bowman, leaving the rest of the company to their own troubles.

The road forked and Pilgrim and Sarjeant galloped down the right fork. Richard half closed his eyes, the rain dagger-like at such high speeds. He could see Pilgrim ahead, the rain so hard that it almost obscured the trees around them.

Pilgrim gave up and dropped down into a trot.

Richard caught up and all three horses came to a stand, their lungs heaved and their legs and bellies brown with mud. The rain fell and the road ran like a river.

Richard had to shout. 'Where are we?'

'Normandy,' Bowman grinned as his lungs worked to catch up. His cloak had unwrapped during the bolt, and his tunic was now as wet as the road.

'Idiot,' Richard smiled back, 'I'm just happy we're still alive.'

He turned Solis so the wind ran into their backs. 'Should we go back?' he asked.

'Back there? They will have scattered a mile in every direction by now, we should go on,' Sarjeant said between gasps for air. His right hand held his cloak closed under his face. His knuckles were white.

'I can't feel my cheeks,' Richard shook some water out of his eyes.

'We can't be far from Neufchâtel, we can follow this road until we find someone local to point us the way. I want to be in the dry tonight,' Bowman said.

Richard did too. 'Fine, we'll go on then,' he said.

Sarjeant didn't protest as they followed the road, and hoped the thunder had finished.

They rounded a bend into an opening in the forest. A gentle hillside ran down from a plateau, a rushing stream following the treeline down on one side. On top of the plateau Richard could see wooden scaffolding. He couldn't feel his nose.

They rode up the track to the top of the hill where foundations for a large stone building had been laid. Blocks of stone and piles of timber lay scattered all around. Four covered carts were parked in a line, and Richard spotted one small scraggly horse tied to a tree in the distance. A small wooden building stood on the edge of the site. Construction had started on top of one area of foundations, where one stone corner had been raised above head height. A sheet of canvas had been strung up as a partial roof over the corner, and under it huddled a group of people around a fire that blew around in the wind.

'Any room in there?' Bowman shouted down to them.

'If you bring over some dry wood from under that cover,' one builder pointed to what presumably was a pile of wood hidden under a section of canvas.

'Hobble the horses,' Richard said and dismounted. All three horses were hobbled and their saddles and bridles put under the canvas sheet. Richard and Sarjeant collected some of the dry wood, then splashed though puddles into the shelter.

Richard dove into cover as fast as he could and squeezed in next to a building labourer who grimaced as Richard's wet clothing rubbed into his dry tunic.

Bowman and Sarjeant did the same and all three held their hands out to the fire and laughed.

'God, that's good,' Bowman said.

The rain hammered down onto the canvas roof, each drop a loud dull splat. Richard closed his eyes and exhaled. In the darkness of his eyelids the sound reassured him.

'What are you building here?' Bowman asked.

A labourer in a brown tunic raised his head. 'A nunnery.'

'Are there any nuns here yet?' Bowman asked.

The labourer shook his head but smirked.

'At least its dry,' Bowman said, 'have you been in here all day?'

'Almost, the site is too flooded now, if the water ruins the foundations, or floods the crypt, it will be a disaster,' the labourer said.

'What nunnery has a crypt?' Sarjeant asked.

'When the empress says a nunnery is going to have a crypt, it has a crypt,' another worker said.

'The empress?' Richard opened his eyes.

'Old Matilda, she was taken sick back to Rouen yesterday,' a third labourer said.

Richard looked around at the men huddled together in the dry. Except not all of them were men, and a familiar wrinkled old face peered back at him.

'I knew I'd seen that scraggly mare before,' Richard looked out into the rain to see if Solis had noticed it. He hadn't, instead he had his rear to the wind, his head down and eyes closed.

'What are you doing here?' Sarjeant asked, 'we thought you had gone for good.'

Nicola grinned. 'You cannot leave me alone, can you,' she said.

'This doesn't look like a place to sell wool or cloth,' Richard said.

'That is none of your concern,' she replied, 'what brings you out here?'

'Lightning,' Bowman said.

'And thunder,' Sarjeant added, 'which I could hear in the east, which means great bloodshed next year,' he said grimly.

The fire popped, a log split in two and rolled out into the rain where it hissed as the water drenched it.

'We're riding to stop the Flemings,' Richard said.

'And the French,' Sarjeant added.

'Yes, and the French,' Bowman prodded the fire with a stick. The rain ran down the canvas and fell to the ground like a waterfall.

'I saw three other carts, if the fourth is yours,' Richard said to Nicola, 'where are the horses for the other three?'

Nicola sat back into the shadow and Richard struggled to make out her face.

A builder leant forwards. 'Matilda's people used them to take her to Rouen. We think they will come back for the carts,' he said.

'None of you worry about the carts,' Nicola said from the shadows.

Bowman looked at the old trader and then Richard. 'Do you want to look in the carts?' Bowman grinned.

'Maybe when it's dryer,' Richard said.

'Or not at all,' Nicola said.

'You can't go poking around in the empress's things, my boy,' Sarjeant said, 'that is not done.'

'Why do you care?' Richard asked.

Sarjeant hunched his neck down into his shoulders and looked into the fire.

Richard added one of their logs onto it.

'Can't hurt to look,' Bowman smiled.

'It could,' Nicola said.

'If you have something to say to us, go ahead and say it,' Bowman waved his fire-poking stick in the air.

The labourer next to Bowman looked at Nicola, then back again. 'It's treasure,' he said excitedly.

'I'll have your tongue, Michael,' Nicola snapped.

The builder in brown next to Richard had wide eyes. 'Gold, they told us,' he said.

'Gold?' Bowman's eyes gleamed.

'It belongs to powers higher than you can dream of, keep your grubby hands to yourselves,' Nicola said.

'You are no trader, are you?' Bowman said.

'I certainly do trade,' Nicola said.

'But in what?' Bowman got up and dodged the waterfall that fell from the canvas. The rain eased from torrential to steady and the waterfall began to slow.

Richard decided he was wet anyway, so followed Bowman out.

Bowman unfastened the rope that held down the canvas cover on the first cart. It had high wooden sides, and he tried to throw the canvas back but hadn't undone enough rope.

Richard squelched over the mud and helped him. He wondered if his shoes would survive being this wet, although his feet inside them were already soaked.

'Even if there's one gold coin in there, I'll have new shoes for life,' Richard said.

'If there's a couple of gold coins in here for me,' Bowman unthreaded the rope from some more eyelets, 'I might be able to return to the Midlands after all.'

He threw back the canvas to reveal a well stacked pile of wooden boxes. They all had iron bands and iron corners, and Bowman had to fetch an axe from the firewood pile to smash one open.

Richard peered inside once Bowman had thrown back the lid. It was stuffed full of leather pouches with drawstrings. Their newly released leathery smell floated up to Richard's nostrils as he plucked one out. He opened it to find a collection of silver coins.

'Not gold,' he picked one out.

'Still, young lord, these are silver,' Bowman took it and held it up, 'that pouch there could set you up for life.'

Richard's mouth was stunned and his eyes shone in possibilities.

'You would be kings, would you?' Nicola's voice said sternly from behind them. Her pale blue dress spotted from the rain. A deep frown etched into her face. 'You think to take it all, do you? Have you thought it through?'

Richard looked to Bowman, who sharply pulled the drawstring on the pouch tight. 'No, we have not.'

'Have you thought about where it comes from?'

'I do not much care where it comes from. It is here and it is unguarded,' Bowman said.

'And it should be guarded with the French and Flemings about the country. Sir Thomas said they could be anywhere now,' Richard said.

Nicola pursed her lips.

'The boy has a point,' Bowman said.

'There is an abbot in that wooden hut who says this treasure is under his keeping,' Nicola said, 'the empress's men will be back for it, tomorrow, if not later today.'

Bowman grinned at Richard. 'So I think she is saying that we need to get this away from here fast.'

Richard looked at the old woman. 'What is this money for?' he asked.

'Don't get cold feet, young lord,' Bowman said.

'I've already got cold feet,' Richard picked a foot up and tried to shake off some of the mud caked onto the leather shoe.

'These carts are to fund a crusade,' Nicola crossed her arms, 'King Louis of France thinks it is his, and King Henry thinks he owns it instead. The empress is holding it to work out a compromise.'

'Can we tell each king the other stole it?' Bowman grinned.

'How far do you think you will get?' Nicola asked.

Bowman shrugged.

Richard noticed that some of the builders had appeared from their shelter to watch.

'Is there gold?' one shouted.

'You will get as far as a town. A port if you are lucky, but someone will notice. Do you think both sides do not have people looking for it?' Nicola said. She pointed to the wooden hut. 'Go and speak to the abbot, you will need a holy man if you take these carts, because you will be dead men before the next new moon.'

Bowman covered the chests back up with the canvas. 'Shall we see what this abbot has to say? These labourers can be bought off with a pouch of silver each,' he said.

Sarjeant left the warmth of the fire a dry man, his brown mantle had fared far better than everyone else's clothing. 'Think carefully,' he said to both of them, 'you are in the service of a lord, and that cannot be left easily. Money pledged to crusade is sacred too, there would be a reckoning.'

'With a little silver you could spend the rest of your life in drink,' Bowman pushed Sarjeant out of the way and walked in the direction of the wooden building.

Sarjeant watched them, then looked at the carts. Nicola crossed her arms, glared up at them, and he retreated back to the fire.

The building looked semi-permanent. Richard and Bowman went inside and found tools scattered around as well as piles of food and bedding. They also found an abbot sitting on a stool, his brown robes adorned with a golden chain around his neck. He had a slight paunch which protruded forwards while he sat, and an oval shaped face that had a red hue to it. A young boy bounced on his knee and the abbot sung a quiet song to him in Latin. 'Oh, who are you?' he asked.

'Passers by,' Bowman said, 'just looking to get a little shelter from the rain.'

The abbot inspected them, Bowman with his heavy tunic and Richard with a mail shirt under his cloak. 'Passers by?' he squinted at them.

The child, maybe ten years old, stopped bouncing. He climbed off the abbot and went to sit in the corner of the room. The boy wrapped his arms around a heap of fabric that Richard realised was actually another child.

'There is a canvas shelter for common folk, you have probably walked by it, you can go there,' the abbot said.

Bowman shut the door slowly behind him. 'I would like to talk to you about those carts,' he said.

The abbot winced. 'They belong to my monastery,' he said.

Bowman took a quick step forwards and the abbot flinched backwards.

'I see,' Bowman turned to Richard and grinned. 'The threat of force alone will see that he does not trouble us,' Bowman said.

'What's your name, abbot?' Richard asked.

'Abbot Anfroy.'

'Those carts don't belong to you though, do they?' Richard rested his hand on the pommel of his sword.

The abbot's eyes looked up from the weapon. 'No, but I would put them to better use than all the kings who squabble over it. The last shipment was taken by the Templars and I never saw it again. They will take this one too,' his face implored. He was old and Richard thought he may even be telling the truth.

Faint sobs crept out from one of the two children.

'Why are they crying?' Richard asked.

'Them? Never mind them. Just some children from the village, did you ride through it?'

'No. Why aren't they in the village?' Richard asked.

Bowman nudged him. 'I'm all for doing what you're thinking about doing, young lord, but maybe later,' he said.

Richard frowned.

The abbot scratched his eyebrow, which was half grey, and his eyes darted to the shut door. 'I just bounce them on my leg,' he burst out.

Richard looked at Bowman, who threw his hands up. 'What do you want us to do, Richard? The carts need to be taken back the way we came, away from the French,' he said.

'You mean to take the carts?' Abbot Anfroy's eyes twitched.

'Of course we mean to take the bloody carts,' Bowman said.

Richard, bandaged hand on his sword, walked over to the children. The abbot's eyes moved to the hand as he went.

'If that needs treating, come to my monastery and we can heal you. You could bring the carts with you,' he said.

'It doesn't need healing,' Richard held out both hands to the children, 'I can take you home.'

The abbot saw the second bandaged hand, the linen frayed and worn. He looked over to Bowman. 'Have you come from Tancarville?' he asked in a voice that wavered.

Bowman's face stayed still.

The abbot looked back at the two bound hands. 'You, you are the cursed Englishman. They said everyone you touch will die. Don't touch my children,' he cried. The abbot jumped off the chair and pressed himself into the far corner of the storeroom, knocking over a pile of wooden bowls as he fled. 'Leave the children, I beg you, they are precious to me,' he cried.

'That is enough,' Bowman sighed, 'have your way young lord, we cannot leave them here with this bastard.'

The boy looked up at Richard and his outstretched hands. He glanced over at the abbot.

'He can't hurt you,' Richard said, 'we'll take you home.'

The boy untucked his companion, who was a younger girl, and told her it was time to go home. He called her sister. She smiled and Richard thought of Adela, and how she could spend a happy day in the meadow just brushing her horse. He wondered how many sisters he would have to save before he felt better about failing his own.

'Leave here,' Richard said to the abbot.

Anfroy hadn't taken his eyes off Richard's hands. 'I have no horse, I cannot leave until the empress returns,' he said.

'You best start walking then,' Bowman kicked the door open.

Richard shepherded the children out of it, and they all went back into the cleaner air.

'You are soft, young lord,' Bowman said.

Richard smiled at him. 'Not as soft as you,' he said.

When Sarjeant saw the children he shuffled over to make room by the fire. 'What are children doing in a place like this?' he asked.

'Don't ask,' Richard said.

Bowman glanced at the wooden building. 'Do not let them go back in there, keep them by the fire,' he said.

'I see, I shall keep them safe,' Sarjeant said.

Nicola saw the children too. Her eyes crinkled at Richard, and he felt he was being judged.

'Do you have children?' Richard asked her.

'I did. I do,' Nicola eye's hardened. She folded her arms. 'I didn't think you'd bring them out. I wish I could have, but I am just an old woman. Force has its use,' she said.

Bowman had no wish to speak, and walked to the carts which the labourers had surrounded but where not brave enough to touch.

'I know you can take the carts if you wish,' Nicola said to Richard, 'but I think you have a kind heart, so I will give you a fair warning.'

Richard looked for Solis. The horse still slept, his rump and back almost black from the rain.

'Do you remember Brother Geoffrey?' she asked.

Richard nodded.

'He is King Henry's man, and is looking for these carts. In England he followed me because he thought I knew where they were. I led him to Castle Tancarville because King Henry constantly suspects Tancarville of rebellion. I hoped brother Geoffrey would think Lord Tancarville had stolen the gold to fund a revolt, or an invasion of England, which would leave him at the castle while I came here.'

'So whose woman are you?' Richard asked.

'I am no man's woman,' Nicola snorted, 'and it is no concern of yours, but I have a proposal for you.'

'A proposal?' Richard watched Bowman smash open a few other boxes and look inside.

'You have three carts and no driving horses. I have one cart and one horse. If you leave me alive and steal the gold, I can tell both kings who took it, and you will have a very short time left on this earth to enjoy it. However, if you load my cart full and let me leave, I will swear to never speak of today. I shall deliver my cargo and explain to my... sponsor, that I found just the one cart.'

Richard listened and his mind worked. 'Who is your sponsor?' he asked.

'No king,' she smiled.

Richard sighed. He didn't know what that meant but it hardly mattered. 'How do I know that you will keep quiet?'

'You won't, but you do not have the stomach for murder,' Nicola's eyes darted to the children who sat by the fire being fed something by Sarjeant.

If only she knew, Richard thought, and flexed his hands. The stinging pain almost reassured him. 'I agree,' he said.

'Good, then load my cart. I will fetch my mare and we will be on our way,' Nicola said.

Richard retrieved Solis first and tied him to a small tree so that he wouldn't be able to get too close to the mare. The palomino seemed happy enough to strip the tree of its lower branches.

Bowman threw a silver coin at each of the builders and they started to move chests from one cart into Nicola's. They worked quickly, and before long she hitched her horse and was on her way. She rode east, which was not the direction Richard had expected.

Bowman gave out a pouch of coins to each labourer, which

made them all instantly rich, in exchange for leaving the building site and keeping quiet. They took the two children back home with them.

'Will that actually keep them silent?' Richard asked.

'Of course not, most likely they will all murder each other,' Bowman said, 'but we have bigger problems. Our horses are no cart horses,' he said to Richard as they watched the workers disappear along the road into the trees.

Bowman sucked in a deep breath. 'We do not have much time and I can't think how we can move it all.'

'Can we bury it?' Richard said.

'Bury it? How long would digging a hole for this all take? Anything we dig will just flood anyway, you need to do better than that, young lord,' Bowman said. His blonde hair had started to dry out.

'What if someone had already dug a hole for us?' Richard grinned.

The crypt may have already been dug, but it wasn't dry. The low ceiling was vaulted and well built, but the floor lay hidden beneath a foot of brown muddy water, which still trickled down the stairs from the surface. It was also unlit, so after they'd waded a short way into the gloom, Richard and Bowman had to strain their eyes to see. Richard explored the walls with his fingers, found an indent in the wall, and inside that at chest height, was the space for a body. Above it words were carved into a wooden board. Richard moved his eyes close to make it out: Abbot Anfroy.

'I've found the place,' Richard smiled.

Bowmen peered over and grinned back. 'Perfect,' he said.

Sarjeant joined them to haul the precious cargo from the carts into the abbot's future tomb. They lugged the boxes down the stairs and through the waterlogged crypt for so long that Richard lost the feeling in his feet. He had to stop when his fingers could no longer grip the boxes. Instead, he stood at the entrance to the crypt and kept a watch over the eastern road.

Sarjeant took a break beside him. 'Theft is against both man's law and God's law, you do know that?' he asked.

'It's not theft,' Richard said.

'I think it is the very definition of theft.'

Richard shook his head. 'We're saving it from the French and the Templars.'

'The Templars?'

'The abbot said they kept the last shipment due for a crusade for themselves,' Richard said.

'Nonsense. Although, to be truthful, they would have kept it here,' Sarjeant said, 'but only so they can issue letters of credit abroad. The money gets paid out, kings just use the Templars as safe storage places. They are not rich.'

'Why did you leave them if you'll defend them so strongly?' Richard asked.

Sarjeant ignored him. 'The silver is not yours, God will punish you,' he added.

'The money was for crusading, wasn't it?' Richard said.

'Apparently so,' Sarjeant said.

'It will still go towards one, I swear it, so God can rest easy. As can you,' Richard said.

'Whose crusade will get it?' Sarjeant furrowed his brow.

Bowman walked by with two chests stacked in his arms. 'Our young lord's crusade, that's whose,' he said.

Richard grinned. 'You were there. I promised that archbishop I'd take the cross. With this I can pay for it,' he said.

Sarjeant's blue eyes twinkled. 'My boy, you are smarter than I thought. Why not, we shall poke the King of France and the King of England in the eye at the same time,' he laughed.

Richard wasn't sure what that meant, but Sarjeant got back to work, so Richard got back to his watch over the road to the east.

After the final boxes were removed from the third cart, Sarjeant and Bowman descended again to seal up the tomb.

Richard saw movement out of the corner of his eye.

Horsemen approached, but not from the east. They rode from the western road Richard had arrived by. Had the Flemings or the French already got that far around them? He looked down the hill and strained his eyes. The riders bore red shields with a smaller white shield painted in the centre. The group was led by a mail clad rider.

Richard's heart sank. The Little Lord. He would have rather

they'd been Flemings.

'Bowman,' Richard shouted down into the crypt, 'our company is here.'

He heard swear words from down below, and the sound of nails being hammered got louder and more rapid.

The Little Lord seemed to have rounded up all of his crossbowmen, although there was no sign of Sir Thomas or his men. The column rode up the hill towards the building site.

Richard watched the drenched crossbowmen reach the plateau and dismount. They spotted the fire under the canvas and helped themselves to its heat.

The Little Lord rode up to Richard and looked down at him. 'I see you made no effort to find us,' he said.

'We didn't know where to look,' Richard said.

The young Tancarville looked at the opening to the crypt where the sound of legs moving through water echoed up. 'What's going on there?'

'Nothing much, Bowman and Sarjeant were just taking a look down there,' he said, 'just a load of water by the sound of it.'

The Little Lord's eyes rested on Richard. 'I don't believe you,' he said.

Bowman emerged from the crypt. He walked up the stairs with one hand behind his back. He stood next to Richard as Sarjeant followed him up into the light.

The Little Lord watched them. 'What's down there?'

'Down there?' Bowman glanced back at the crypt's entrance.

Richard felt the hammer handle press into his side so he took it.

'Nothing at all,' Bowman said.

'Quite a lot of water actually,' Sarjeant added.

'Not a lot of light though,' Bowman nodded to himself.

A voice shouted from over towards the wooden storeroom. 'Who is that?' Abbot Anfroy yelled as he walked towards them, his robes flapped around him. 'Did the empress send you?' he asked.

The Little Lord looked up. 'Just what I need. Who is that?'

'A local Abbot,' Richard answered, 'don't trust him.'

Abbot Anfroy ran to the Little Lord. 'My lord, thank the almighty that you are here.' He pointed at Richard. 'Do you know who you are speaking too?'

'I'm afraid I do,' Richard tried to keep a straight face, 'although I wish I didn't.'

The Little Lord frowned.

'These brigands have stolen my gold, my lord,' the abbot said, finger still stretched out towards Richard.

'They aren't brigands,' the Little Lord said, then checked himself. 'You said gold?'

The abbot swung his accusing finger over to the carts, but lowered it limply when he saw they were empty.

'What in God's name?' he stammered.

'What's wrong?' Bowman asked, 'God got your tongue?'

'Blasphemy,' the abbot said, 'there was gold in those earlier today. My gold.'

The Little Lord shook his head. 'Do you take me for a fool, you English thieves? There are empty carts and you are splashing around in the crypt. If there is any gold here, it belongs to House Tancarville,' he said.

He shouted to the crossbowmen for one to come and hold his horse. The bearded crossbowmen and his curly haired companion trudged over and obliged.

The Little Lord dismounted, rubbed his hands together and blew on them.

'You will get cold feet down there too,' Bowman said, 'it really is much nicer up here.'

'If there's gold down there, all three of you will hang. Then I will have my own tournament team, one to rival my father's mesnie,' the young Tancarville growled.

'No, my lord,' the abbot interrupted and rushed over to tug on the young man's mailed sleeves, 'the treasure belongs to God.'

'I thought it belonged to you?' Richard chuckled.

'So there really is gold?' The Little Lord said.

Richard winced at himself and the red haired Tancarville pushed the churchman away and strode down into the crypt.

The abbot barely managed to remain on his feet.

'Gold?' the bearded crossbowman said, holding a horse.

Their lord disappeared below ground.

'If you help us rather than that little turd,' there will be a pouch of silver in it for each of you,' Bowman said.

'You hear that, Jean?' the bearded man's eye glinted, 'silver. We'd be rich like lords.'

'Rich. Yes, that's good,' Jean said.

Sarjeant walked over to Richard and whispered. 'A tournament team is more frivolous than even the snivelling abbot's intentions. My boy, it pains me, but you are doing the right thing.'

'There we go, young lord,' Bowman said, 'a churchman even blesses our enterprise.'

'Former churchman,' Sarjeant corrected as the Little Lord stomped back up the stairs, watermarks halfway up both of his legs.

'There's nothing down there, I need a torch to see,' he said.

'So no gold then, my lord?' Bowman said.

The young Tancarville scowled. 'You've done something with it, haven't you? Where is it?'

'There isn't any,' Richard said, 'just some empty carts. They are worth something on their own though, aren't they? You can take the carts.'

'Crossbowmen, all of you, to me,' the Little Lord shouted.

The men reluctantly abandoned the warmth of the fire and slogged over through the mud.

'Ready your bolts,' the young Tancarville ordered.

To a man, the fed-up troops groaned. Their crossbow cords were greased and waterproof, but they'd unstrung them anyway when the rain started. They began to go through the effort of preparing their weapons.

'What do you need to do that for?' Bowman asked.

'To encourage you to speak,' the Little Lord said.

'He won't shoot us,' Richard said confidently.

'Maybe not you, my father likes you, but he doesn't even know your two men exist. When one is bleeding in the mud, and the other has a bolt sticking out of his leg, you will not defy me so readily.'

Richard licked his lips and threw a sideways glance at Bowman and Sarjeant.

Sarjeant took a step backwards and looked for his horse.

'There is no need for this,' Bowman said.

'They are conspiring against you, my lord,' the abbot said.

'Who is?'

'Your guards there, and these demons,' Anfroy pointed at almost everyone.

'My lord, I don't rightly know what he means,' Jean said, 'do you, Rob?'

'No Jean, not the slightest idea,' crossbowman Rob scratched his bald head.

'Lower those crossbows at them all,' the Little Lord's face glowed red.

The rest of his crossbowmen slowly lowered their weapons, but they were unsure of who they should be threatening.

'This is your last chance to tell me where the gold is,' the Little Lord said.

'Tell this slayer of old men nothing,' Bowman spat.

'Leave us be, or the whole of Normandy will hear about Sir Pottage and his slip of fate,' Richard said.

The Little Lord's eyes widened, his lips pressed together, and he reached for his sword.

'Look, down on the road, my lord,' Jean the crossbowman shouted.

Richard still had the hammer, and although he didn't want to clench his fist around it, he would if he had to.

'Is that Sir Thomas?' Sarjeant asked.

Richard hoped so, he would straighten the situation out before someone got a bolt sticking out of their chest.

'Those are not Sir Thomas's colours,' Bowman said before anyone else, 'that is Sir Roger.'

'De Cailly?' Richard squinted down the hill. The company of horsemen moved swiftly despite the mud, the red banner of Normandy fluttered alongside the blue, green and yellow de Cailly banner.

'You probably want to lower those crossbows,' Bowman said.

De Cailly cantered up the hill as his horse found it easier than walking, and came to a halt so close to the Little Lord that his horse was rattled by their sudden stop and stood on crossbowman Rob's foot. He cursed.

'Why are you here? What is this?' the knight shouted. He looked wet and his horse was splattered in thick mud.

'Indeed, what is this, my Little Lord?' Bowman asked.

'Don't call me that,' the young Tancarville said.

De Cailly's eyes burnt into him and he looked around. 'William. Explain,' de Cailly said.

The Little Lord hesitated.

'Why are crossbows levelled at our own men?' De Cailly roared.

The weapons lowered but Richard didn't relax.

'Speak, boy,' the knight demanded. 'Or you,' he shouted at Richard, his hunchback less obvious under the mail and surcoat.

'He thinks there is gold in the crypt,' Richard said.

De Cailly paused. His face cleared and he frowned. 'Gold?'

'That's what they say,' Richard said.

The abbot bowed to the knight. 'My lord, the gold belongs to my monastery, these men have stolen it,' he said.

'Which men?'

'The cursed boy and his henchmen,' his pointy finger singled out Richard.

'Henchmen? Who are you calling henchmen?' Bowman said.

'And why are Tancarville crossbowmen aiming bolts at Tancarville squires?' De Cailly asked.

'Because they won't tell me where the pile of gold is,' the Little Lord said.

'You want me to believe that these three have managed to steal and hide a huge pile of gold out here. Since the thunderstorm? These three together could be outwitted by a buzzard,' de Cailly said. He turned in the saddle and swung his right leg over it. He lowered himself down gracefully.

'I will check the crypt, and when I find no gold, you can tell me what is really going on.' The knight, his wet mail already thinking about rusting, descended into the depths and was gone.

'You're going to need a good story,' Richard said to the Little Lord, who released a muted scream in frustration.

De Cailly returned above ground after only a moment below. 'Obviously the crypt is empty. Enough of this, it will be dark before long and we can still reach the town and sleep in the dry,' he said.

'There is gold, I tell you. Light torches and look again,' the abbot said.

'I respectfully request that you leave us,' de Cailly said.

The Little Lord kicked at a clump of mud which flew past Richard's face. 'Shoot him,' he shouted.

Some of the crossbowmen raised their weapons again.

'I said shoot him,' the young Tancarville pointed at Richard.

'Lower them,' de Cailly said flatly. He stepped towards the Little Lord and punched him squarely in the face.

The boy recoiled, slipped in the mud and thudded into the saturated earth, brown mud coated his mail and stuck to his face.

Richard stood dead still, eyes wide open, his breath held.

The Little Lord felt his cheek.

'Get up,' de Cailly said.

The young Tancarville rolled over and pushed himself up.

'Get back on your horse and get back on the road,' the knight said.

The Little Lord wiped a blob of mud off his face. 'My father will hear about this,' his eyes watered as he snatched the reins back from the crossbowman and remounted.

De Cailly glared at him until he walked out of earshot. 'You,' he turned to Richard, 'do not make me regret this. Get all these men back on their dammed horses and on their way.'

Richard nodded, and everyone made haste to obey lest de Cailly's wrath fell on them next.

Richard felt glad to be back on Solis, but as they rode away, he looked back at the crypt and felt an unease in leaving the silver. If Abbot Anfroy died before they could return, his burial party would get a rather pleasant surprise. He had to pull his eyes away and focus them ahead though, because they were now on the frontier of Normandy and the edge of the war.

They rode on under a gathering of dark clouds, and just over the horizon lay their destination, Neufchâtel-en-Bray.

NEUFCHÂTEL

Half a dozen crossbows pointed from the wooden town wall towards de Cailly's company.

'They aren't expecting us then,' Richard said from his place at the back of the column. The gates to the town were shut and men with spears peered over the wooden walls.

'This feels like a town waiting for something,' Richard said.

The wooden gates swung open and de Cailly was granted entry. His company entered but he stayed outside. The knight held a hand up when the Little Lord reached him.

'Your company can stay outside the walls tonight,' de Cailly said.

'Outside? We have no bedding or food,' the Little Lord said. A purple bruise grew on the side of his face.

'I am quite aware. Your lord is not yet here and there is no room in the town,' de Cailly said.

'He's your lord, too,' the Little Lord said.

De Cailly's stone-like face rested on the young man. 'Sir William Mandeville has taken most of the lodgings, and I took lodging while you were getting lost in thunderstorms. Mandeville's militia and levy are in tents between the town walls and the river, see if you can convince any of them to take pity on you. I care not a bit if your night is cold and miserable, for that is the condition you forced on me by being late and compelling me to go and look for you in the rain,' the knight said.

Richard had seen him angrier than this only once, the time when Tancarville had shouted at him over his daughter.

De Cailly didn't say another word as he rode into the town and pointed them out to the guards.

'No sneaking in tonight then,' Bowman said.

'He's really angry at us, isn't he?' Richard looked to the south where a forest of tents were indeed huddled around fires on the low ground between the River Bethune and the wooden palisade of the town wall.

'There must be hundreds of men here,' Richard surveyed their limited options for the night.

'The rain has passed at least,' Sarjeant gazed up into the clear sky where stars flickered.

'You're fine, your mantle is dry,' Richard said, his own clothes very much on the wet side of damp. His leather shoes were still utterly sodden, and his toes had not regained any feeling.

Bowman looked back at the gate where the Little Lord tried to shout his way into the town.

'Can you get him to help? I don't think I should talk to him,' Richard said.

Bowman nodded and rode forwards. 'My lord,' he said to the Little Lord. 'You could order the crossbowmen to find us some firewood, then we can bargain some space in these tents.'

The Little Lord glowered at him and went to shout at his crossbowmen instead.

'He isn't speaking to us, is he?' Richard said when Bowman came back, 'although I think we're both happy with that.'

Bowman laughed and dismounted.

Richard followed him to a large fire surrounded by three sheets of canvas strung up as a shelter. The men inside wore no armour, and looked barely any better equipped than the Tancarville company's crossbowmen.

'Any room for some strangers offering firewood?' Bowman asked.

Some faces looked up but there was no response. The light of the fire flickered on the eight or so men that sat around it.

'Come on boys, 'I can't see any more wood here, surely you want this fire going on all night?' he said.

'Fine. Move over, Tom,' the eldest of them said from across the fire.

Jean, the Tancarville crossbowman with curly hair, arrived

with an armful of wood.

'That was quick,' Richard said.

'It was, my lord,' he winked.

Bowman told him to drop it under a cover, then to go and find somewhere for their horses to stay. Relieved of the need to hold his horse, Richard sat down and started to hold his cloak up to the fire to dry it.

Sarjeant made a pile of their shields, then took the cloak from Richard and used the shields to hold it up to the fire.

'There, much better this way,' Sarjeant said.

'Are you Tancarville squires or militia?' The man called Tom asked.

'Squires, who are you?' Richard asked.

'I'm Tall Tom and we are Mandeville's militia,' he said. Tall Tom was indeed a tall man, with a long face, sharp chin and pointed nose. He looked young, but still older than Richard. He and his comrades wore undyed tunics of rough linen and their stacked shields were quartered in red and yellow.

'Is he the lord of this town?' Richard asked.

'No, he's the Constable,' Tall Tom said.

Richard looked at Bowman.

'Constable of Normandy, means when there is a war, Mandeville is in charge,' he answered.

Richard nodded. 'I'd wager Lord Tancarville doesn't like that,' he said.

'How long have you fine fellows been here?' Bowman held his hands out towards the fire.

Sarjeant built it up with their extra logs. The new wood steamed as its dampness was burnt away.

'Since yesterday,' Tall Tom said, 'riders have been coming in all day. Sounds like the whole of the frontier is burning. They say Eu has been razed to the ground because the count is here with his army, instead of being there defending it.'

'They say Aumale has been devastated too,' a second Mandeville man said.

'Eu is North, Aumale is east,' Sarjeant frowned, 'they can't both be under attack. There can't be enough Flemings and men from Boulogne in the world to manage that.'

'That's what we've heard,' Tall Tom scratched his face as the fire caught the new wood. Everyone's faces became brighter in the flames.

'There'll be flames all over Normandy soon,' Tall Tom gazed into the inferno, 'a tanner told us that a company from Boulogne robbed a nunnery and raped every nun. Even the old ones. They torched the whole place.'

'God help us,' Richard said.

A few 'Amens' repeated around the fire.

Bowman nudged Richard, shadows and flames from the fire danced on his face. 'Did Simon say Eustace was with the Count of Boulogne?' Bowman asked.

'I think so', Richard said.

'I would wager a pouch of silver that he was at that nunnery,' Bowman's features set firm.

'A pouch of silver?' Tall Tom said, 'do you have one hiding under your tunic?'

Everyone laughed but Richard's was forced. He hoped not too obviously. He turned his cloak over on the shields so the underside could start to dry. It began to steam when the heat hit it.

'I heard the last crusade only happened because King Louis of France torched a nunnery. I hate the French. No offence,' Bowman said.

'None taken, as we aren't French, we're Norman,' Tall Tom bellowed a great laugh. He leant back so much Richard thought he might fall over.

'You are English, aren't you?' The oldest militiaman asked.

'What gave it away, my good looks?' Bowman said.

'What are you doing with Tancarville? He's a murderous bastard, as bad as any Frenchman,' Tall Tom said.

'Lack of choices,' Richard said and everyone laughed.

'I heard Tancarville murdered someone close to the Count of Eu the other year, and the Count hates Tancarville for it,' Tall Tom said.

Richard could believe that. He took off his shoes, cleared off all the mud he could and placed them on top of the cloak to dry.

'A few stories have come from the west too,' Tall Tom leant forward, 'a trader told of a dancing monk who thought he could fly, and a mad Englishman who had been struck by God.'

'I heard he'd been struck by the Devil,' the older man said.

'Yes, it was definitely struck by the Devil,' another militiaman added.

Tall Tom nodded sagely. 'A knight in de Cailly's host told me that an Englishman made a pact with the Devil so he could hold a hot bar of iron for a whole day,' he said, 'and that the dancing monk was hurled from a tower when he tried to exorcise a demon from an English boy. Personally, I think it is likely the same Englishman.'

Richard turned his shoes over, conscious that both of his haggardly bandaged hands were very much on show.

Tall Tom considered the wrapped hands, then looked Richard straight in the eye. 'You wouldn't know anything about that, would you?' he asked.

'Unfortunately not,' Richard retracted his arms. He slowly folded them up within his tunic but all eyes were on him.

'What has this town got in the way of food?' Bowman asked, his eyes darted between Tall Tom and Richard.

'That depends if your boy here is in league with the Devil,' Tall Tom said. Shadows hid half his face.

'This boy?' Sarjeant said, 'this boy is at best over enthusiastic, and at worst naive.'

'What happened to his hands, then?' the oldest militiaman tilted forwards towards the fire.

'I tried to catch a sword,' Richard said without hesitation.

Bowman raised his eyebrows.

'I did say naive,' Sarjeant added.

Bowman burst into laughter, and everyone except for the older man joined in.

'Food then,' Bowman said.

'You'll get nothing tonight. They'll let you in tomorrow and there's food in the town,' Tall Tom said.

'Won't you give us anything?' Bowman asked.

'No, you're English,' Tall Tom said, 'you should be thankful we are even sharing our fire with you.'

Richard slept badly, a night full of incoherent nightmares of wounded horses and men. Ghosts chased him through towns, and cackling monks chanted all around. Church bells from within the real town woke him in the morning, long after day had broken. He was the last one still in bed.

Bowman rolled up his bedding and Sarjeant handed Richard a handful of bread. He ate it almost without chewing and his stomach gurgled. His head ached too. He rolled his bed up around the silver candlestick, and noticed his mail shirt had a large orange patch at the front.

'Damn,' he picked part of it up and some rust dust fell off.

'Tancarville will kill you if Sir Roger doesn't do it first,' Bowman said.

Richard threw down the metal shirt and swore.

Bowman called Sarjeant over. 'Pick up his cloak,' Bowman said.

They lay the woollen cloak out and Bowman threw the armour into the middle of it, where it landed with a metallic thud. Each man picked up an end, and as they both did, the mail shirt rolled around on itself at the bottom of the cloak. A faint grinding noise came from the armour. A moment later they stopped and Bowman picked up the shirt.

'See, young lord,' nothing to worry about.

Richard looked at the area which had been rusty, and saw only the faintest hint of orange. 'Thank you,' he said.

Bowman nodded. 'Remember how to do that. Time to get some food now though,' he said.

They rolled up their bedding and left it under the reluctant protection of Jean and Rob.

Carts of provisions rolled into Neufchâtel as wagons containing people rolled out. Their occupants were glum, in muddy clothing and without conversation. They led whatever animals they were able to. Few of them spoke, and Richard turned his eyes away from them and down to the ground.

After the gates, they walked up a hill and towards the spire of a church which jutted out above the houses and halls that lined the main street. The tall stone keep of a castle also punctured the skyline at the eastern end of the town. Red and yellow quartered banners hung outside several of the larger buildings, especially around the main square in which the main church stood. Men in armour milled around and clustered in front of the holy building. Richard spotted a mailled man with a

Tancarville shield amongst them.

'Sir Gobble,' he pointed. Sir Gobble was part of a crowd around a knight mounted on a bright white horse at the foot of the church steps. A bishop and his entourage stood behind him while he answered those in the crowd. Men on horses rode by and dogs barked.

Richard grabbed Sir Gobble on the shoulder. 'I'm actually happy to see you,' he said.

The tall Englishman laughed. 'Where's the Little Lord?' He asked.

Richard shrugged.

Sir Gobble smiled. 'Too many real lords here for his liking I suppose,' he said, 'but what took you so long? Your patrol had the shortest route yet you arrived after mine.'

'I'll tell you later,' Richard's eyes fell on the small figure of Brother Geoffrey who stood next to a bishop.

As he began to walk over, Bowman moved to Richard's ear. 'Are you sure you want to tell him? If you keep telling people, there will be nothing left to go around,' he whispered.

'Nothing left of what?' Sir Gobble's dark features wrinkled.

Bowman groaned. 'You've done it now, young lord,' he said.

'Me? It was your giant mouth,' Richard said.

Brother Geoffrey smiled at their group when he arrived. 'Good morning, how are you finding Neufchâtel?' he asked with a silken voice.

No one answered.

Richard could smell cheese and beer on his breath. 'I'd be happy to tell you if you could share with us something to eat,' he said.

Brother Geoffrey walked closer. 'I have heard mutterings about you here. Some I knew about already, but some new,' he said.

'We will find somewhere to eat ourselves, then,' Richard said. He noticed the knight on the white horse wore a new surcoat like de Cailly's, quartered in red and yellow.

Brother Geoffrey shoved his soft face with its piercing blue eyes right into Richards. 'Mind your tone, boy, you should be careful not to dismiss me,' he said.

'I know who you are,' Richard ignored the spit that landed on his face.

'I very much doubt that,' the monk said, 'the question you should concern yourself with, is if I know who you are.'

'I know what you are at least,' Richard's voice backed off from the certainty it had begun with.

Bowman forced his way between them, and easily pushed the small monk away. 'You do not have to be a knight to show courtesy, monk, you should try it. Although I would wager you have golden spurs hidden away somewhere,' Bowman said.

Brother Geoffrey rebalanced himself. 'What about you then? A bowman who is rather good at flying birds, I hear,' he said.

'I'm a huntsman, that was my job,' Bowman said, 'I have had enough of churchmen, be they monks who are not really monks, or insufferable archbishops.'

'Archbishops?' Brother Geoffrey asked. He stroked his chin. 'You came through Dover, that much I know. So you journeyed through Canterbury. Becket. Ha. Now I have you,' he said.

Richard looked at Sarjeant, who just shrugged back.

'I'm hungry,' Richard said.

'I can find you something,' Sir Gobble said.

'Of course you can,' Bowman said as the man on the white horse bellowed at a town burgher in a rich blue tunic.

The burgher turned on his heels and ran away.

When Richard's focus returned, the monk already stood by the bishop. He whispered into the holy man's ear and the bishop's eyes turned to Richard.

Sir Gobble pushed his way through the crowd. He might not have been a full man yet, but he was tall, wide and strong. He shouted up at the knight with the red and yellow quartered surcoat. Lord Mandeville, Richard realised.

The lord sent a group of men in a certain direction, briefly considered Sir Gobble, then moved his attention to an older townsman next to him.

Lord Mandeville was a young man with a smooth, clean face framed with curly brown hair. The townsman asked him a question and Sir Gobble elbowed him gently, although the townsman still nearly fell over.

'Insolence,' Mandeville shouted and proceeded to answer the unsteady man's question.

Sir Gobble shouted at him to ask where food was being given out.

Mandeville's gaze swept over him and he listened to another knight's enquiry.

Sir Gobble leant into the knight and repeated his question.

'Who in the depths of hell are you? I have never met such rudeness, begone,' Mandeville said.

'Just point me in the direction of some bread and meat and I'll be gone,' Sir Gobble said. He nudged the other knight over, and the short round warrior turned to him, puffed his chest out and pushed back.

'Enough,' Mandeville shouted, 'who do you think you are?'

'I am the heir to the Marshalcy of England,' Sir Gobble stated in his most official voice.

Richard leant in to Bowman. 'I think he actually believes himself sometimes,' he said.

'You don't even have golden spurs, you are not the marshal of anything,' Mandeville snapped, 'you are nothing but a loudmouth who was never taught proper manners by his neglectful nursemaid.'

Sir Gobble's eyes flared. 'Golden spurs don't make nobility,' he said, his voice high. 'Deeds do.'

'And what deeds have you performed, you spur-less knight?'

'My day is still to come,' Sir Gobble said, 'I will eclipse all others in fame and glory.'

Mandeville's stony face shattered and he guffawed. 'Today's youth are weak and sensitive, yet filled with their own importance,' he said. He pointed to the south.

'Go that way, the victuals are being unloaded by the southern gate,' he said.

Sir Gobble, his chin still raised to the heavens, blinked his thanks and spun around.

'And boy,' Mandeville shouted, 'come back and meet me when you have your spurs, then we shall weigh deeds.'

Richard and Bowman laughed.

Sir Gobble shrugged at them. 'What is it?' he said.

'Come on,' Bowman said, 'before you get yourself in real trouble.'

Richard agreed, but mostly because hunger gnawed at his

guts. Fast days were one thing, and his penitential time in Tancarville's chapel another, but he had never spent one as cold and wet as the previous day, and he could feel it in his bones.

They left the square and turned south, the sun now above the walls and started to shine into their eyes. Horses went by, and troops of armed men clattered along the roads. Street vendors sold cooked chicken and boiled eggs, as well as salted fish, but they had no coins on them, so they had to keep going, their mouths watering all the way.

Richard saw an empty cart with a shaggy little mare harnessed up to it and stopped. 'I've seen this one before,' he said.

'Probably,' Bowman said, 'we have seen a lot of transport lately. Come on, I'm starving.'

'Wait,' Richard went to look at the mare, 'that's Three Legs, that's Nicola's pony.'

'Her cart would not be empty,' Sarjeant said.

Sir Gobble glanced between them. 'Why do you care so much about her cart? Why shouldn't it be empty? Isn't that what they do? They sell the things from their carts,' he said.

'Forget it,' Bowman said to Richard.

'Come on, I'm missing something,' Sir Gobble grinned.

Richard growled to himself. Sir Gobble was a good friend to have in a fight, but he also seemed a bit of a liability when it came to controlling his words.

A horseman with a Tancarville shield cantered through from the gate. He splattered mud onto everyone around.

'God's legs,' Bowman shouted as he looked down at the sticky mud on his tunic.

'Our Lord can't be far away,' Richard said.

They started to walk, except for Sir Gobble. 'You can walk away, but I'm not going to stop asking about it,' he said.

'You do that,' Richard followed the rutted and muddy channel down towards the town wall.

Sir Gobble waited with his hands on his hips. As the other three walked further away he gave up, and ran to catch them.

The town wall to the south consisted of a wooden palisade just like the one to the west. A square lay behind it, and that was now a jam of carts and horses. Men rushed to and fro, some carts being unloaded and others being sent deeper into town. Horses shuffled their feet and called to each other. Children from the town worked in gangs and collected their valuable droppings into sacks. Militiamen from the Mandeville tent village and townspeople swarmed the carts in search of handouts, the noise was incessant.

Richard stopped and watched the jostling mass of life with dismay. 'I don't want to go in there,' he said.

Sir Gobble marched past with his back straight. 'If you want food, follow me,' he said.

'You heard the boy,' Bowman followed in his wake.

Richard's belly rumbled so he went too, and used the space the two men left behind to good effect. Richard bumped into Bowman's back as they came to an abrupt stop.

Men and women all around shouted for food, and the occasional lucky person walked away with a loaf of bread clutched to their body. Some escaped with some other foodstuff wrapped in a cloth but there didn't quite seem to be enough to go around.

Richard squeezed in between Bowman and a townsman who smelt deeply of urine. Richard rather hoped that man was a tanner.

Sir Gobble had indeed led them to the front of the queue, but he soon retreated with two pieces of bread after he'd snatched a whole wheel of cheese from an angry official.

'Can we go now?' Richard's eyes lingered on his companion's haul.

'I think he'll be eating that all by himself,' Bowman said.

Richard sighed and held up his hands. The bandages were more brown than white now, and loose in places.

The potential tanner next to him saw them. 'Are you English?' he asked.

Richard ignored him and called out for food.

'You are,' the tanner said, 'what is that?' he grabbed Richard's wrist.

'Get off me,' Richard pushed the man away. He collided messily with a squire behind him.

'It's the Devil's Englishman,' the tanner shouted.

Richard ignored it but Bowman glanced over. 'It might be

time to go, young lord,' he said.

'He is stealing our food,' the tanner yelled at the top of his voice.

Heads turned.

Bowman grabbed Richard by the arm and pulled him away. As they went, Richard gave up on getting anything to eat and sighed. He left the crowd and more shouts erupted.

Sir Gobble stood next to Sarjeant and tried to eat some bread from his armful of food without using his occupied hands.

Bowman let go of Richard. 'We need to go,' he said, 'they won't follow us outside.'

'Outside?' Sir Gobble said through a mouthful of cheese.

Richard started to jog, but leapt into a run when he saw that part of the crowd no longer hunted for food.

They hunted him.

The guards on the gate, with their red and yellow quartered shields, inspected the contents of a cart closely and didn't notice Richard and Bowman run by.

Sir Gobble watched as the mob chased them and ran around him. He shrugged, happy to be left alone to finish his breakfast.

Richard hurtled through the town wall and smacked straight into the slender figure of Sir Thomas, who he nevertheless bounced off, and landed on his rear in the mud. The mob burst through the gate and swarmed around its prey. It hesitated when they saw Sir Thomas.

The knight, fully equipped in his mail and with his shield by his side, stood over their intended victim.

'What have you done this time, boy?' Sir Thomas said as Richard scrambled to his feet.

His left knee twinged and he cursed the boar that had run through it.

Bowman ran until he was with Sir Thomas's men who stood around by the side of the road.

'Nothing at all,' Richard said.

Sir Thomas frowned at the common people around him. 'Explain,' he shouted, his hand already on his sword hilt.

The tanner pointed to Richard. 'He's the Tancarville Devil, we were going to take him to the bishop for trial,' he said from within the crowd.

'From what I have heard, he already underwent a trial. This is a waste of my time. He is no devil, just an insolent boy. Be gone or I will cut you all down myself,' Sir Thomas said.

The tanner contemplated a reply but dissident whispers germinated in the heart of the mob.

The knight drew his sword, the cold steel drew their eyes and they started to back off.

'That sword has tasted Norman blood,' Richard heard from the back of the mob.

Some started to withdraw back into the town, and the tanner looked back to see his support had dwindled.

Richard heard, 'Yvetot,' too.

Sir Thomas took two steps forwards and raised his sword.

The mob disintegrated and ran.

Bowman laughed and Richard shook his head as they turned tail and fled.

'The lowborn are starting to forget their station,' Sir Thomas sheathed his sword, 'times are changing, and not for the better,' he said.

Richard couldn't comment on that, but instead looked out across the fields and wasteland to the south of Neufchâtel and studied the southern road.

A traffic jam led up to the gate along the southern road that ran away to the south west towards Rouen. The road crossed the River Bethune in the distance, far over open fields dotted with farm buildings. Closer though, a column of mounted warriors crossed the river. Richard had never seen such a sight, was this a whole army? In the distance they were just a thin line over the bridge, but it snaked its way almost up to the traffic jam that Richard stood near the start of. It was headed by dozens of pairs of mailed knights. At the front flew the red banner of Normandy, and alongside it fluttered the red and white banner of Tancarville. The lead rider was Tancarville himself. He wore a surcoat of his colours, bright silver rowels scattered over the red background. Richard saw Sir John next to him. Richard stepped behind Sir Thomas in an attempt to hide behind him.

Tancarville reached them and Richard noticed that not only was he riding the Spanish stallion, the horse with its long mane and arched neck walked soundly.

'Is Mandeville here already?' Tancarville asked Sir Thomas.

The knight nodded. 'He has been here two days since,' he said.

The red haired lord swore. He turned to Sir John and gave an order. The knight spread the word behind and riders broke off to ride down the column to relay it.

'If he has not left me decent lodgings, I will take every single man home,' Tancarville said. The lord walked his horse on, followed by his dozen household knights. The rest of the army, squires and militia, were left in the field outside the walls.

'What are we supposed to do now?' Richard asked Bowman when Sir Thomas walked into the town.

They watched as the Tancarville army fell out and started to make a camp under the walls. Men dragged canvas from carts at the back of the column, and some took digging equipment from carts and spread out around the borders of the camp.

'Follow Sir Thomas,' Bowman said, 'if you stay near him the locals might not set you on fire.'

Richard didn't have a better suggestion, so trudged into the town as close to Sir Thomas's footmen as they could get.

The tanner peered out of a side street, his eyes never left Richard. 'I don't like it here,' he said.

'Now that Lord Tancarville has arrived, hopefully we can all march away, scare the Flemings into going home, then do the same ourselves,' Bowman replied.

They caught up with Sir Gobble, who now held an empty cloth bag and no food. He burped.

'You're a great help,' Richard said.

'What did I do?' Sir Gobble nodded in the direction Tancarville had gone, 'our lord looked angry.'

'He's often angry,' Bowman looked at Richard, 'but maybe we can find a room in his lodgings we can stay in. If this one can stay out of trouble.'

Richard grunted and flexed his hands. He thought he would have to find some fresh linen soon, the old ones smelt offensive now.

Tancarville rode up to the town square, and he and Mandeville had already finished shouting at each other by the time Sir Thomas and Richard got there.

Tancarville led them back to a two storey wooden building near the southern gate. It had stables attached and Richard thought about bringing their horses here, that is before the crossbowmen got bored of looking after them and sold their wards.

The Little Lord stood in the doorway, his arms crossed and his face pouted as his father entered.

Sir Thomas told them to wait outside, so they all went to sit inside one of the empty stables.

Richard didn't mind that, he'd had enough of walking backwards and forwards around the town, so found some dry straw to lie on.

Soon de Cailly arrived and trudged into the building. Later, and as Richard had gotten thoroughly bored, Sir John also stabled his horse and went into the house.

A large Tancarville banner hung out of the first floor window, and guards with spears were posted on either side of the doorway.

Richard lay on his bed of fresh straw, and had firmly fallen asleep when Sarjeant pushed him awake.

'Come on, my boy, that hideous monk has been inside for a while and now they've sent for you,' he said.

A man Richard didn't know stood at the door of the stable staring at him. Richard groaned and pulled himself to his feet.

'Try to not get hung or chased out,' Bowman said from his corner.

Richard followed the servant into the building and up onto the first floor, which was split into two rooms. He entered the hall and could see a door to the lord's private solar at the far end. The hall had a central hearth which two servants were in the process of lighting. All the notable men of Tancarville's court were in attendance and Richard felt very small.

The Little Lord stood in front of his father and pointed at de Cailly. 'We can't allow that sort of behaviour,' his finer moved up to his bruised face, 'I'm the heir,' he cried.

De Cailly had his mailed arms folded, an icy stare his only response.

'My son does speak the truth, a strike to my heir is not acceptable. Even if sometimes I do it myself,' Tancarville said.

A silver basin was brought over to him and he carefully washed his face. He stretched over the basin to avoid water dripping onto his armour or surcoat. After he dabbed his face clean with a cloth, he turned to his senior advisor.

'Roger, if you cannot give me a good reason for it, I shall have to punish you,' he said.

De Cailly remained motionless. As Richard stepped forwards he could see the tension in his grinding jaw.

The Little Lord noticed Richard. 'It was his fault, father,' he said.

The elder Tancarville sighed. 'Do you remember what I told you before you left?' he asked.

His son nodded. 'But he was lying to me, and Sir Roger didn't want me to force him to speak,' the Little Lord said.

Richard felt himself warm up.

'Is that a reason to point crossbows at him? You accused him of something absurd, it was an excuse to fill him full of bolts,' de Cailly said.

Tancarville looked between Richard and his son. 'I am not even sure I care enough to ask what this quarrel was over. Actually, I am sure. I don't care. All three of you annoy me, I have had enough of all of you. This is not the time for petty squabbles. We are at war.'

'If I may,' Sir Thomas raised his thin face, 'that incident may be petty, but the death of Sir Arthur is not. Your son killed your sub-tenant without reason.'

'He was my vassal,' de Cailly said flatly, his voice deep.

Tancarville walked over to the hearth and gave some instructions on how to light it properly.

'I know he had been your vassal, Roger, and I very much regret the manner of his death,' Tancarville turned with a scowl to his son.

'I said I didn't do it,' the Little Lord said.

'Do you call me a liar?' Sir Thomas roared, so loudly that Richard felt it like a punch.

The Little Lord shrank back and his face twitched.

'Never lie, boy,' Tancarville said, 'it is not lordly. You are not lordly. At least Sir Arthur had been old. He did not fulfil his duty so he would have been replaced anyway.'

'Murdering an old knight is not the correct way to replace him though, is it?' De Cailly said.

'Enough, enough, enough,' Tancarville shouted. The fire caught its kindling and small flames burst up which send smoke out into the room.

'You, whatever your name was,' Tancarville gestured to Brother Geoffrey who waited quietly by the wall.

He slid forwards and bowed to Tancarville. 'My lord, I have damming words concerning one of your squires,' he said.

Richard could already feel sweat down his back, but now an icy finger poked deep into his belly.

'This boy,' Brother Geoffrey met Richard's gaze, 'is not who he says he is.'

Richard held his breath.

Sir Thomas turned slowly and studied him quizzically, but de Cailly kept his eyes on his lord, who sighed.

'Tell me why I should care about whatever it is you're so happy about,' Tancarville said.

'He has been accused of involvement in the theft of the king's crusading gold.'

The room burst into conversation.

'This is wasting my time,' Tancarville said over the top of it, 'he has only been gone a few days, none of which are unaccounted for, he's clearly had neither the opportunity nor the brains to turn gold thief.'

'That's what I needed to interrogate him over,' the Little Lord jumped forwards and waved his hands.

'God's teeth boy, I said I didn't want to hear about whatever that was,' Tancarville said.

'It must be investigated,' Brother Geoffrey said.

'Why? He is standing here now still poor. He has no gold. Why have you such a feud against him?' Tancarville asked.

'He cannot be trusted,' the monk insisted.

'Is this all just because he nearly knocked you from your horse that day?' Tancarville asked.

'He did, he nearly killed me,' Brother Geoffrey said through gritted teeth.

'Then you should ride better,' Tancarville said.

The men in the hall laughed and Tancarville grinned.

Brother Geoffrey stepped forwards. 'He has lied about himself to enter your service,' he said.

'So have half the boys who I have in training.'

'He is a murderer,' Brother Geoffrey said, the words flew out with spit.

'Do you take me for a fool, monk? He underwent the trial by ordeal, we all saw. This prattle is exhausting me,' Tancarville said.

'My lord, that is not the murder I speak of.'

Richard wondered if he could run out of the door before anyone caught him.

Tancarville looked into the flames of the fire as more wood caught and they grew.

'Tell me why I should care, and do it quickly,' he said to the monk.

'The story of the flying monk did not sit well with me, so I questioned the guard who was on the tower that night. On reflection, he saw neither the dance nor the fall. What is more, the monk who was killed was searching for a boy named Richard, who had killed his own mother. This boy,' Brother Geoffrey unfurled his finger in Richard's direction, 'mercilessly threw a man of God from a tower to keep his identity hidden.'

Richard felt eyes scrutinise him. Sir Thomas's glassy face fixed on him, and Tancarville tilted his head to one side and peered at him.

'I have had this conversation before,' Tancarville said, 'there are many Richards in England and Normandy, and I wager a few who have killed their own mothers, too. The trial by fire shows beyond doubt that God saw no sin at the time, which was after both of these deaths.'

'The boy was being chased by the townspeople,' Sir Thomas said, 'they think he is the Devil, or some other nonsense.'

'The Devil works through the actions of others,' Brother Geoffrey said eagerly.

Richard's stomach gurgled and he crossed his arms.

'How can you trust him?' The monk asked.

'He helped my horse, why would the Devil do that?'

'The Lord works in mysterious ways,' Brother Geoffrey said.

'I thought we were talking about the Devil?' Tancarville said.

The knights in the room laughed.

Richard could feel clamminess down his back, and wanted to stick his head out of the window. He walked over to it.

'No need to jump,' Tancarville said. He made his way over to Brother Geoffrey and pressed his finger right between the monk's eyes.

'There is a war coming, and it might be a long war. If it is, I need every sword, lance and man to wield them that I can find. If he manages to survive it, then we can have this conversation yet again.'

The monk backed away. 'When the king hears about his gold, this matter will come back to haunt you,' he said.

'I do not care what the king does,' Tancarville said, which caused Brother Geoffrey's eyes to narrow. The monk spun and made a rapid exit from the hall, his robe streamed behind him.

'Do not think I am letting you off,' Tancarville said to Richard, who had at least got close enough to the open window to feel a slight breeze on his face.

'I nearly lost my horse in that thunderstorm. A flash of lightning caused many horses to rear and bolt, but mine recovered his senses quickly. Sir John has put that down to your paddock suggestion. Mind, he also says you are a malign spirit and wants rid of you. Roger, did all your men muster to you?'

'They did, save for Sir Arthur,' de Cailly replied. His expression was cool but his hands were behind his back and Richard could see they gripped each other tightly.

'Then you would be ready to take a company to find the enemy,' Tancarville said. He wasn't asking.

'I would,' de Cailly replied.

'Take Richard with you, I want him out of the town so he doesn't distract us all by getting himself burnt at the stake. There is trouble wherever he goes, so it might as well be away from me, and if people are going to keep dying around him, some of them might as well be Flemings.'

'Yes, my lord, we will leave at once,' de Cailly said.

'Good, and I do not want to see you all again unless you bring me back a prisoner with golden spurs. Is that clear?'

'Perfectly clear,' de Cailly beckoned Richard to leave the hall with him.

Richard jumped at the chance and ran down the stairs after the knight.

De Cailly got out of the building, turned to Richard and poked him in the chest. 'Sir Arthur was a good man, once, and he did not deserve to die in the manner that he did. One day, that sorry excuse for a Tancarville will pay for what he did, but I need you to learn your place. You do not antagonise him, and you do as you are told. If you want to survive this war, never hesitate to obey me. Our lord has made you my problem, and we now ride to war. You will have to wrap those miserable hands around a lance, however much it hurts, because we need to capture a noble prisoner, and that could be a bloodbath. Do you understand?'

Richard nodded because he did understand, and the pangs of fear he had felt upstairs returned to his stomach.

'What are we doing?' Bowman asked as de Cailly stormed by.

'We ride to war.' Richard's stomach tightened.

Bowman groaned. 'You'll be the death of me, young lord. What did you say this time?' he said.

'Nothing.'

'Do we have time for breakfast?' Bowman asked.

Richard shook his head for he was no longer hungry. He was riding to war, not the distant war of the past few days, but a real one, one where the killing had already begun.

FALLENCOURT

Fallencourt burned. Richard could see fields ahead on both side of the road, and they were on fire. The crops were tall, just a few weeks from harvest, and despite the previous day's rain, they were now all ablaze. De Cailly led his men along the road, the smoke drifted over them and choked their breathing. Richard could feel the heat warm his face but what lay ahead soon took his attention.

'Is this what the end days will look like?' Richard asked. The air tasted of ash.

'I am afraid this is all the work of men,' Sarjeant said.

Wooden barns and outbuildings were already charred ruins that billowed clouds of black smoke.

Richard could see into the middle of the small village, and saw figures running. A mounted figure cantered after them and disappeared from view behind a mill. Men ran into the mill with burning torches. The realisation of what lay just before him struck his guts like a knife made from ice.

Richard gripped his lance in anticipation, so intense were his other feelings that he didn't notice his hand's pain. This was it. War. An urge to relieve himself bubbled up inside.

An order must have given up ahead, because de Cailly and his bannerman, mailed knights, and assorted squires broke into a canter.

'That's us then, young lord, off we go to war,' Bowman pressed his legs onto Pilgrim's sides.

Richard urged Solis on too and followed, although his instinct told him to go back and hide in the trees. They cantered past de Cailly's archers and crossbowmen who were busy stringing their weapons, and followed the Norman shock troops. Solis locked on to the squires in front and Richard caught them up. Before he knew it they were centre of the village. Orders may have been given, but Richard had heard nothing.

Riders with de Cailly shields spread out in groups, he guessed to hunt down the raiders. Richard headed for the mill where de Cailly aimed. They cantered through a trail of corpses, men and women with their head's sliced open or arms half severed, and anger replaced some of his fear. A dozen invaders ran out of the mill, threw their torches back into it and drew their swords. They formed a wall of kite shaped shields. Shields of a red and yellow chequerboard pattern.

'By the grace of God, I'll kill every last one of them,' Bowman screamed a war cry so loud that Richard almost recoiled from him.

De Cailly and three knights cantered into the formation, and infantrymen flew to the ground. Before they could wheel round and finish the job, Bowman couched his lance and spurred Pilgrim into the mix. The lance connected with the top of a Martel shield, slid up it and speared its owner straight between their eyes.

Richard lowered his own lance and aimed it at a foot soldier. Just as the moment of impact neared he did what he'd been taught to, he applied his spurs and gripped the lance. Solis responded to the spurs and rode straight and true. Richard applied his full energy to the lance and his palm exploded in pain, the surprise of it made his hand let go of the lance. The discarded weapon still punched into the shield of its target, but did nothing more than push the man back a step as Richard rode by.

De Cailly and his knights turned and crashed over their opponents a second time, some were trampled under foot and others fell skewed by lances.

Bowman's lance was broken, and Richard saw him attack someone with it anyway.

Richard wheeled Solis round and drew his sword. Prepared for the pain this time, he held it as the agony seared him.

Richard launched his horse at an enemy spearman whose weapon pointed right at his face. Richard batted the spear aside. He tensed his core up to slow Solis enough that he had time to strike. The blade hit the spearman's conical helmet hard and slid down it, the tip nicked the man in the shoulder before Richard went by.

Another spear appeared from his left, and he felt his shield take a blow. He pushed Solis towards it, and saw his stallion's head lash out, followed by a scream. When he turned the horse round again, all the spearmen were on the floor. The one Solis had bitten lay on the ground, his lower jaw lay bloodied on the earth a few feet away from his head.

Bowman dismounted and knifed a fallen enemy in the neck. 'Check they are all dead,' he shouted to no one in particular.

De Cailly's horse came to a halt next to Richard. 'Finish that man, it is the Christian thing to do,' he said and rode off.

Richard looked down at Solis's victim, who clutched this throat and face. He started to choke on his own blood, the hole left by the missing jaw a mangled mess. Richard couldn't look at him, let alone kill him, and turned Solis away so he didn't have to do either.

Bowman slashed the throat of a man Richard was sure was already dead, and looked over. 'I will shut him up,' he said, 'go and find more.'

Richard cast his eyes around the village.

The mutilated man behind him screamed as Bowman's blood red knife drew near.

Richard spotted a huddle of villagers tied together near an animal enclosure on the far side of Fallencourt. Two Martel soldiers sat on their horses as a formation of spearmen mustered before them. De Cailly and most of his horsemen were already headed in their direction, so Richard followed.

The enemy spearmen braced for impact, which came in a splintering of wood, the scream of horses and falling of men. Their organised resistance was shattered by the charge.

Richard reached them and flashed his blade. The metal dug into a spearman's hand. He cut over to his left side as someone tried to grab his reins. The man's head was full of shaggy black hair and he had a moustache. As Richard's right arm swung, he looked into the man's eyes. They looked back and widened. Richard almost pulled the blow, but instead he thought of Adela. He drove home the sword which cut into hair, skin and skull, just as his sword had done in the alleyway that wasn't an alleyway in Hempstead.

Solis's movement knocked the man over and Richard urged him towards the captives. They were inside a low walled enclosure. Martel soldiers fighting with de Cailly and his men blocked the gateway.

Richard rode up to the wall and stepped off his saddle on to it. He hopped off the wall and jarred his left leg when he landed. The villagers fled away from him into the far corner of the enclosure.

Richard ran at the footsoldiers in the gateway who had their backs to him, busy fighting de Cailly's squires. Richard pushed the one on the left with his shield, and at the same time delivered a cut into the neck of his comrade. The man sunk under the blow, but Richard's sword twisted out of his hand as he went. The other solider regained his balance and turned to spear the weapon-less Richard.

De Cailly's spearhead burst through his assailant's face from behind, and his horse nearly pushed Richard over as it halted in the gateway. The speared man hung limply on de Cailly's lance. The knight lowered it and the body slipped off and crumpled to the ground.

'Get mounted,' de Cailly said, 'let none escape.'

Richard recovered his sword and used the wall to remount Solis, who had used his free time to start weeding the enclosure wall. Richard ignored the dandelion that stuck out of his mouth and looked around for new targets.

Close by, and partially obscured by smoke, a mounted man with a Martel shield tried to wrench a young woman from the grips of two other women. Their house was on fire behind them, and a pig lay dead in the doorway in a pool of blood.

Richard wanted to hurt the man. Solis covered the ground at speed. Tears streaked down the woman's face, her hands clawed at her attacker. Richard could canter by and swing his sword, but he might just as easily hit her. Instead, he pulled Solis up more harshly than he'd ever done before. Richard threw himself from the saddle, cursed as his knee almost buckled, and ran to save the woman. He raised his sword, and the horseman was so busy with the struggling girl he didn't notice.

Richard tripped over a loose stone, jarred his knee on the ground again, and his shield snapped away at the bottom. A clump of earth stuck in his mouth but he spat it out and rose. His sword wasn't in his hand, but the woman had been hauled up onto the front of the warrior's horse.

Richard leapt and grabbed her by both shoulders. He used his body weight to pull her down and they both thumped into the earth. The horseman swore and looked up to see de Cailly bearing down on him. He pulled his horse around in an ugly fashion and spurred it away.

De Cailly gave chase, but his horse wasn't fresh, and at once he realised he wasn't going to catch him.

'Are you hurt?' Richard asked the crying woman. She looked about his own age. She had a freckled face, and what must have been her mother frantically pulled her away from Richard.

'You should have pulled him from the horse, not the girl,' de Cailly shouted as his horse walked back.

Richard went to find his sword. The blade had sliced into the ground, so when he picked it up a clump dark earth clung on to it. Blood already congealed further down its length. He felt extremely ill and cold, and threw up next to the dead pig. Luckily, he'd eaten almost nothing for two days so it was quick.

Sarjeant rode over and waited next to Solis. 'You have done your father proud,' he said when Richard took his horse's reins back.

Richard's eyes started to water, so he remounted and told Sarjeant he'd been hit in the face.

'You got off lightly then,' Sarjeant gestured behind, 'there's one dead squire back there and another one with a bad cut on his hand.'

'What about these people?' Richard cast his eyes around, every single building in the village either burnt, smouldered or smoked.

'These things happen in war,' Sarjeant said.

Richard looked back at the freckled girl who cried in a heap beside the house. Fire roared from its roof. One of the walls collapsed in a shower of embers and flames, and half the wooden roof caved in with it. If this was war, Richard thought, he didn't want to see more.

As Fallencourt died, de Cailly's company regrouped in its heart. The squires exchanged stories of what they'd just done, and Richard stared off into the inferno of the mill. The ash in the air blocked his nose.

Bowman looked up to the hills that rose to the east of Fallencourt. 'My lord,' he shouted.

De Cailly was busy and didn't hear him, so Bowman rode over.

'My lord, up on the hill,' he said.

Two banners crested the horizon, although only just visible because dusk had ambushed them, and it was hard to see out of the village.

'The light from the fires has disguised the end of the day,' Richard said.

'We must not take the road back, they will follow us, and our horses are not fresh,' de Cailly shouted.

'What about the people?' Richard said to Sarjeant.

'They live on a frontier, so their villages burn,' his eyes looked sad, 'however regrettable that is, it is the same everywhere.'

'We ride north,' de Cailly bellowed, 'stay close, once it's dark and they cannot track us, we will slow down.'

'Say some prayers, my boy, this could be a long night,' Sarjeant said.

De Cailly's horse sprung into a canter.

The villagers who had left the enclosure stood and waited to see what would come over the hill. What came over the hill was a stream of riders, and they moved fast.

Richard didn't want to be there when they arrived. Solis obeyed the push of his pelvis and cantered after the squires.

'Stay close, Richard,' Bowman shouted, 'if anyone gets lost, head west.'

Richard had no intention of getting lost. He put his faith into Solis, who stayed close to the squire in front, so close that he bit the tail of his horse more than once.

They left the village and its flames and fire and plunged into the cold darkness of the woods. The trees were wide and well spaced, so the company could ride fast between them. It was even darker under the leafy canopy, and Richard focused his eyes to duck branches.

The company cracked and snapped branches ahead of him. He swerved out of the way of a tree, and his shield caught a branch and almost threw him off his horse. Richard righted himself and the column splashed across a stream. The icy water hit him in the face like a wave of pin pricks.

Richard didn't have a chance to look back until they entered a clearing full of tree stumps. A derelict charcoal burner's hut quietly occupied one corner. They pulled to a halt and de Cailly ordered silence. That was an easy order to follow as every rider wanted to catch their breath. Horses panted and snorted.

Pilgrim shook his head and his bridle rattled in the dark, for the sun had long gone.

Richard could barely see the opposite side of the clearing for the moon was slight.

'No one will have followed us through that,' Bowman said, 'not until the sun comes up.'

A command passed around the company with a whisper.

Sarjeant heard it first. 'Sleep on the far side of the clearing just inside the woods. Half of us sleep now, the other half later. No fires, no disarming, no untacking. Horses to be held ready and bridled all night.'

'Soli is going to hate that,' Richard said.

Richard and Sarjeant made their ways to their sleeping spot, but Bowman was sent back the way they'd come to listen for signs of pursuers.

Sarjeant offered to keep watch first, so Richard gave him Solis's reins and tried to find a patch of moss that might almost feel comfortable.

Richard did not sleep well. Solis occasionally broke off branches from the nearest tree, and ate one sapling entirely. Richard rolled onto his side so he could look across the clearing, out towards where Bowman stood watch. As soon as Richard finally fell asleep, he was jogged awake by Sarjeant who handed him the reins to their horses. Solis stood motionless, apart from his bottom lip which flapped away. His eyes were half closed. Sarjeant took Richard's sleeping spot and Richard spent the rest of the night shifting his bodyweight around to keep his feet from going numb.

The sun started to filter through the treetops when Bowman burst into the clearing. Pilgrim cantered through spears of light being cast down through the cloudy sky.

'That doesn't look good,' Richard kicked the sleeping Sarjeant.

'Whose there?' he yelled and sat up.

'A bad dream by the sound of it, but we need to mount up,' Richard said.

Bowman thundered over to where de Cailly slept, then rode back over.

'There are horsemen coming this way, Sir Roger wants to ambush them here. We're to go over there,' he pointed to a part of the clearing.

'Come on, my boy, say some more prayers,' Sarjeant swung himself up into his wooden saddle. His horse bowed slightly as he landed on its back.

'He needs a rest. Or you need a new horse,' Richard said.

'I know,' Sarjeant turned his horse to go to their ambush spot.

Richard and Bowman followed and hid in the treeline to one side of the clearing. Their tracks from the previous night ran from their left to right, and would be clear to any pursuers. Richard patted Solis on the neck and wished he'd been able to recover his spear from Fallencourt, where it still lay by the smouldering mill.

A horseman emerged from the woods to their left. He slowed, and his head searched the clearing as he crept across it. A full company of riders appeared behind him.

Bowman's eyes were glued to them, but from their angle they were on the wrong side to check the shields of their prey.

'That's a Martel flag,' Bowman whispered.

Richard's fingers squeezed his sword hilt. The image of de Cailly's spear bursting out of the Martel warrior's head the day before had plagued his fitful night. It was all Richard could think about. It had happened in an instant but his mind wouldn't leave it alone.

The Martel column neared the edge of the clearing. Their lead rider pointed ahead and shouted.

A flurry of arrows and bolts broke from the treeline and flew into the front of the company. The scout fell from his horse, and the standard bearer lurched forwards and dropped his banner. A large man in mail lowered his lance and charged. The squires behind him broke into canter to follow.

De Cailly's foot-bound squires stepped into the gaps between the first row of trees, and formed defensive lines between them. A second volley of arrows were loosed. Richard saw one bury itself in the chest of the big man's horse, but it was just one arrow and it kept charging.

Bowman looked past the enemy and into the wood behind. 'Look,' he said.

De Cailly led his knights and squires out of the trees on the opposite side.

'Now,' Richard said and walked out of the trees. He pushed Solis into a canter.

The rearguard of the enemy company saw them coming and broke into confusion. Some turned and fled. Others rode out towards Richard, who drew his sword.

Bowman screamed his war cry again.

Sarjeant lowered his lance as the three of them charged in line. The first Martel squire who lined up to attack them rode at Sarjeant. His lance struck the right of Sarjeant's shield, but he attacked too early and the point skated away. Sarjeant's lance was higher and hit the middle of his opponent's nasal helm with a clang.

Richard lined up a squire who headed straight for him. The Martel man spurred his horse on to attack, eager to close on the lance-less Richard.

Richard held his sword forwards, aware that if he mistimed, he was dead. His hand pulsed as he closed his fingers around the weapon, and Richard screamed to keep his grip. The lance point flashed at his eyes. Richard caught the shaft and cast it aside before he dug his blade into the neck of the enemy squire. Richard let it cut and felt the force of its bite. He very nearly dropped the sword again.

'Wheel right,' Bowman shouted.

Richard eased Solis's pace and turned him to the right until they faced back towards the main battleground. The Martel horsemen had crashed into the treeline and came back out again. They formed into a stationary group with Normans circling around them in all directions.

De Cailly's mounted knights and squires held a good line amongst the large tree stumps and charged them. Richard squeezed his thighs and joined the melee. Solis bumped into the press of horses, and Richard swung his sword at the nearest carrier of a red and yellow chequerboard shield. It glanced off.

Something hit his own shield. A lance flashed at his face but missed.

Richard saw an enemy knight who faced away from him, so Richard cut at his back. The blade didn't cut his ringed shirt and Richard rode on. He glanced left and saw a knight stab at him from overhead with his broken lance. The point half hit the top of Richard's shield, slid along the back of his neck and ripped some rings open. His head jolted. The attacker rode into Richard and their legs collided. Richard sensed that his leg was about to get carried away from him as he cut at the knight. The sword dug into the shaft of the lance, but not before it went through some fingers first. The knight howled and his horse carried him away.

Knights and squires on every side battled, maimed and died. Richard watched Bowman jam a broken sword blade into the face of an enemy squire. Not once, but five times. The large Martel knight who had led the charge rode in the middle of the press. Richard saw his shield and his piercing green eyes at the same time.

Eustace Martel.

Richard's heart raced and a hatred seared through him. Richard spurred onwards but Sarjeant attacked Eustace first. He lowered his lance and aimed for his chest. Eustace parried it with his sword and cut at Sarjeant, who ducked almost out of the way but received a cut above the eye. Sarjeant ducked too far and fast, lost his balance and tumbled from his saddle as his horse span the wrong way.

Richard shouted Eustace's name as the knight hacked into the shoulder of one of de Cailly's squires.

Solis ran chest-first into Eustace's horse from the side. The stallion's chest cracked bones in Eustace's horse with a snap. Solis gnashed out and grabbed Eustace's right arm. The stallion came away with a mouthful of mail and wool.

Richard swung his sword, but Eustace somehow managed to raise his own to parry it.

Richard didn't think. 'William Keynes,' he shouted.

Eustace blinked and looked at him, frozen for a split second.

In that split second Richard punched him. His hilt connected with Eustace's helm. Eustace was stunned for a moment and unaware of de Cailly closing behind him.

The Norman knight attacked from Eustace's left side and clouted him around the head so hard that his helmet fell down over his eyes. Richard punched again, which pushed the helmet into Eustace's face, the nasal guard dug into his chin.

De Cailly hooked his arm around the big man's neck, kicked his horse on, and dragged Eustace clean out of his saddle. De Cailly let go, and the Martel knight landed on a tree stump. He didn't get up.

Bowman charged by, sword-less. He rode up behind an enemy squire, pulled him down off his horse by his shield, then leapt from his saddle on top of him. Bowman used the man's own helmet to batter his face into a shapeless mess.

'Enough,' de Cailly shouted.

Bowman buried the helmet into the man's face one last time with a squelch.

A few surviving Martel squires fled to the trees.

Richard took a deep breath. The air tasted warmer that it should have, it was full of horse sweat and the tang of iron.

Bowman walked from body to body on the uneven ground. He used a scavenged dagger to finish off squire after squire.

De Cailly looked down at Eustace and noticed Richard did the same.

'That knight hesitated. The way he fought, I did not expect that error,' de Cailly said.

'He knew me,' Richard said.

'The Martel family, they are a bad sort. Disloyal.'

'This man stole my sister,' Richard said.

De Cailly inspected the fallen knight who coughed and

groaned. Two of de Cailly's men removed his weapons and shield.

'Your man seems to share your animosity,' de Cailly said as Bowman stood tall and searched around for any Martel that had escaped him.

'His motives are his own. I do not know them,' Richard said.

Sarjeant limped over with his grey horse in hand, blood dripped from his forehead.

De Cailly's dismounted men emerged from the trees, some helped others walk, some dragged fallen comrades or held horses.

'Which Martel is this one?' De Cailly asked.

'Eustace. I think he knows what really happened to my father,' Richard said.

'Ah, I remember,' the knight replied. His squires rounded up loose horses and tied them together into small groups. Swords and daggers were stripped from the dead, as was a mail shirt from the only enemy knight to have been killed.

'I think your man has earned that mail shirt,' de Cailly said, 'if he can keep his knife away from our prisoner, that is. Do I need to worry about that?'

Richard nearly lied. 'Yes,' he said instead.

'Very well, I will keep the prisoner behind my bannerman and the three of you can stay at the rear.'

'Of course,' Richard replied.

The clean-up operation concluded quickly. The wounded men were helped onto horses if they could ride, or slung over them if they could not. Richard looked at those who bled or staggered around with pity, and feared for himself.

A Martel squire lay on the ground beside him, his arm attached to his torso by a mere thread, the stump still leaked blood even though the man had died.

'What shall we call this battle?' De Cailly asked Richard.

'The Battle of the Stumps,' Richard's eyes were glued to the squire's arm.

De Cailly laughed. 'Perfectly named, young man. These tree stumps made for a most interesting encounter,' he said.

Eustace opened his eyes. 'Damn all Gods,' he ran his hand over his head. He looked up at de Cailly and studied his shield.

'At least you are a man of some fame, not some whimpering Norman nobody,' he said.

'How much are you worth?' De Cailly asked him.

'A thousand gold solidus to you,' Eustace inspected the gaping hole in his armour and clothing left by Solis's bite. A deep red gouge marked his skin underneath.

'I think you mean solidi, not solidus. But Gold, of course. Richard, are you supposed to have stolen that much gold?' De Cailly chuckled away to himself.

Richard thought he looked happy.

Eustace's face froze and shot up to Richard, where memory and recognition flooded back. 'You're dead. They said you were dead,' he said.

'Well here I am. What did you do with Adela?' Richard replied.

'Who the hell is Adela?'

'My sister,' Richard's temper simmered. What sort of man forgets that. Or did he even ask her name?

'Oh, that,' Eustace pushed himself to his feet. He was almost at Richard's eye level despite not being on a horse.

'Did you kill her?'

'Kill her? I'm not a monster,' Eustace said, 'I just took my payment for my work.'

'Payment? My sister was payment?'

'It isn't so unusual for a man to sell a niece or nephew. Even a daughter. I put her in a convent afterwards, which is a better life than you or her uncle were going to give her.'

'What did you do to her first?'

'Took my payment,' Eustace repeated.

Richard drew his sword but Eustace didn't flinch.

'Richard,' de Cailly held his hand up.

Richard stilled the sword but kept the naked blade drawn.

Eustace sighed and flexed his right arm. 'That is going to be sore. Mind you, boy, you probably killed my horse so I think we are even on your sister.'

'You compare my sister to a horse?' Richard said.

'Of course, but truthfully I think my horse is worth more.'

'Richard,' de Cailly bellowed.

Richard caught himself just as he'd raised his weapon to

strike.

'If you kill a man in cold blood, some will believe the other tales being told about you,' de Cailly said.

Richard slowly, very slowly, put the sword away. 'Which convent?' he asked. A convent was not what Adela had planned for her future, but then she had never thought about it.

At least she lived.

'Halve my ransom and I will tell you,' Eustace replied.

De Cailly's men had almost formed up into marching order. A string of captured horses were brought together.

'We need to leave,' de Cailly said.

'My father, how did he really die?' Richard asked.

Eustace looked Richard right in the eyes, then smiled. 'Get me a horse, then,' he shouted.

'Get to the back, Richard. There will be plenty of time for this when we are behind town walls,' de Cailly said.

Richard cursed under his breath, and walked Solis to the back of the company where Sarjeant followed.

Sarjeant commandeered a Martel horse to ride.

'They are calling this the Battle of the Stumps,' Bowman said when they joined him. He was out of breath and covered in too much blood.

'I know,' Richard said. He sat in silence as the company moved off. They travelled back the way they had come, because no one knew exactly where they were. The column soon found the stream they'd crossed the previous night, and the parched and worn out horses were at least allowed to drink from it.

De Cailly navigated through the big beech trees which looked friendlier in the daylight. At a walk, it was easy to avoid being whipped in the face by branches, too.

Two scouts roved far out ahead until Fallencourt came into view. The village still smouldered and smoke rose from the buildings. The fields were a charred graveyard of crops and Richard couldn't see any sign of life. The windmill had collapsed into a pile of black rubble and bodies littered the ground.

'Where is everyone?' Richard asked.

'The men we fought this morning would have come through here first,' Bowman said.

That was answer enough, but some movement at the edge of the village caught Richard's eye. He gripped his sword, but then realised that the movement was a body that swung gently from a tree.

De Cailly led them through the centre of the village towards the tree. The smoke from the mill billowed and caused Richard to cough. A thick smell stuck in his nose, it was one of death and destruction.

De Cailly reached the tree and shook his head. He pointed to it and one of his squires drew his sword and approached the victim. As a cloud of smoke blew out of the way, Richard made out the red freckles on her face. His face dropped, it was the girl he'd rescued.

'No, no, no,' Richard said.

'A horrible sight indeed,' Sarjeant said.

'I caused that,' Richard said. The girl wasn't just hanging from a tree, an owl had been nailed to her chest.

'The Devil's bird,' Richard's eyes watered, 'how did they even know to do that.'

'Surely just a coincidence, don't take it to heart,' Sarjeant said.

De Cailly's squire cut the rope. Her body hit the ground, and the owl rolled off her into the mud.

'God will damn those Christians who make war on Christians. This is not your doing, my boy,' Sarjeant said.

An order travelled down the company: look for surviving villagers.

'You can find your lance,' Bowman suggested.

Richard searched around the husk of the mill as riders scattered out around Fallencourt. He dismounted next to the lance he'd dropped and retrieved it.

He glanced back towards the hanging tree just in time to see Eustace, whose reins were being held by a young squire on another horse, move the horse sideways towards his captor. Eustace, whose hands were tied, wrapped them over the boy's neck.

The boy's eyes shone with frozen terror.

With a tug, Eustace pulled him straight off his horse. The boy hit the earth head first. With a great crack his skull split. Eustace grabbed his horse's reins.

'Take him,' de Cailly shouted from the other side of the village.

Eustace kicked his horse on. Squires from around the village turned and raised the alarm.

Richard put his foot in his stirrup and mounted but Eustace already galloped his horse towards the edge of the village. A mounted archer had left his bow strung, and fumbled for an arrow.

Richard urged Solis on, Eustace still had much to tell him. An arrow flew at Eustace, it hit him in the back of the shoulder, but the mail he wore stopped penetration and it hung out behind him trailing like a flag.

Richard knew Solis was fast, but he was also tired and had barely eaten for two days. The stallion gave Richard his effort anyway, and galloped up the slope out of the village. Richard kept going, and crested the hill to leave the smoke of Fallencourt behind him.

Solis sweated, and Richard heard his nostrils flare as they pursued Eustace north. If anything, the gap grew between them even more, and Richard felt his stallion's legs slow. He thought about giving up.

The knight disappeared below the horizon as Richard climbed another hill. He reached the top, and looked into a valley that stretched away into the distance. Eustace was between him and the forest, and he was going to get away.

Richard slammed Solis to a halt. Not because he had failed to catch the Martel, but because between Eustace and the forest, in a sprawling camp, looked to be the every fighting man from Flanders and Boulogne.

A cluster of large painted tents stood tall in the centre of the camp, hundreds of smaller canvas tents stood like a forest around them. Fires flickered away all over, and plumes of grey smoke drifted up so thickly that they had merged into a low cloud over the valley. Parties of men felled trees at the edge of the forest and horses were everywhere.

Richard almost panicked. His heart thumped and his palms, painful from the last few days, sweated. He swallowed the panic and started to count tents. He got to thirty before Eustace reached the camp. Men ran over to him and the Martel knight pointed straight up the hill at him.

Richard swore and wheeled Solis around. He said a prayer to Saint Eligius and touched his spurs to his horse. Solis reached a gallop in a few quick strides, and Richard shouted at him to urge him on. He imagined the scene behind him of riders assembling to hunt him down and his panic returned. Riders on fresh horses, he imagined, with sharp swords and pointed spears.

Richard cantered back into Fallencourt on an extremely tired Solis.

De Cailly had found no survivors and had mustered his company in the village square.

'The army is over those hills,' Richard shouted. Solis stopped of his own accord, his whole body heaved and lathered in white foam. The horses's head dropped nearly to the ground.

'An army, or another raiding party?' De Cailly asked.

'Hundreds of tents, and yellow banners with red circles on them,' Richard swallowed and tried to catch his breath.

'Boulogne,' de Cailly said bitterly, 'very well, we ride back to Neufchâtel. Quickly.'

Richard apologised to Solis and joined Bowman and Sarjeant at the rear of the company, which headed south west. Beyond the hill the enemy followed, a mass of fighting men intent on burning Neufchâtel to the ground.

THE BATTLE OF NEUFCHÂTEL

Hooves clattered through the stone gateway into the castle at Neufchâtel. De Cailly's company filled the entire courtyard and dismounted for the sake of their weary horses. Richard's legs were dead when he hit the ground. His thigh muscles had tightened up and he felt as if he couldn't stand up straight.

De Cailly walked up the wooden staircase to the first floor of the keep, where Mandeville appeared out of the doorway. A hurried conversation erupted between them as de Cailly explained what headed their way.

Richard wanted to hear them, so handed Solis to Sarjeant and walked closer. Braziers around the courtyard flickered and threw light onto the white painted keep. The shadows of the company's men and horses cast great moving figures up onto its walls.

'Not a raiding party then,' Mandeville said.

'Boulogne's colours were there. This is the main thrust,' de Cailly replied.

'If they burn Neufchâtel, defending the frontier will be much harder for a decade,' Mandeville said, 'this is a bolder attack than I had expected, but we shall meet it nonetheless.'

'Is Lord Tancarville inside?' De Cailly asked.

Mandeville wore a dark red tunic with gold trim. He smiled. 'His lordship wished to sleep with his men, so he is playing peasant in the fields,' Mandeville said.

De Cailly nodded. 'Then that is where I must go. The enemy could be here by midday tomorrow if they ride half as hard as we did. They are many, more than we are, make sure you see to our defences.'

'You mind your company and I'll mind mine,' Mandeville replied, 'I am not a boy any longer.'

'No, you are not, but you are not yet a blooded knight either. I have squires who have seen more of battle than you. Some of those in this courtyard have won more horses today than you have yet in your life.'

Mandeville cast his eyes down into the yard. 'You have captured many horses, I'll grant you. That is a tidy profit. Although I see no prisoners,' he said.

'We took the knight leading the company, but could not hold him. Most regrettable,' de Cailly said.

'Well, you shall get another chance in a few days when they arrive, Sir Roger. Go and rest your horses, tomorrow your men can eat well and recover their strength. I will send scouting parties out at first light and we shall see how many days we have,' Mandeville replied and returned to his bed.

De Cailly shook his head and descended the stairs, his mail cost clinked on the way down.

'Richard,' de Cailly said, 'we retire to Lord Tancarville's camp to the south of the town. We have enough new horses that everyone in this company can switch to a captured one if we need to ride tomorrow. The Constable of Normandy thinks we have a day or two to prepare, but I am not so sure. Pass the word along.'

Richard nodded and did.

The company led their horses on foot out of the castle and into the town, deathly quiet in its nightly curfew. Curious faces peered out of doorways and windows to see who rode about at such a forbidden hour.

The town militia let them out of Neufchâtel and towards the Tancarville camp. Fires dotted the field, but it was pitch black outside the town which made the smoke from them invisible, although Richard could taste it in the air. The camp had its back to the river, and Tancarville had posted sentries far out on the hill to the north. Richard could make out the distant light from their braziers, glowing spots on the high ground. There were guards closer to the camp too.

'Not that way, my lord,' one of them said to de Cailly as they approached the camp. 'Pits that way, you want to take the horses in closer to the river.'

The company obliged and once in the camp, Richard was happy to surrender Solis to Sarjeant to find a place for him. Richard, sleep overwhelming him, unrolled his blankets somewhere near a fire and closed his eyes. His back ached, his head hurt, his stomach grumbled and his hands now itched badly, but Adela was alive. Eustace terrified him still for sure, but with a little help he'd been able to defeat him. Whenever the battle came, Richard would look for the red and yellow chequered shields.

The sun had already soared into the sky by the time Richard's eyes prised themselves open. He felt groggy at first and wanted to go back to sleep, but there was too much activity around for him to relax. He was sure he'd never been this tired before in his life. Militiamen finished their breakfast and adjusted their war gear around him. It was quieter than the night they'd arrived, conversations between men were short and tense.

Bowman sat next to him. 'I have never been glad to see him before, but there's a first time for everything,' he said as Sir Gobble appeared before them. He carried four wicker baskets and Richard didn't need to be told what they contained.

The tall man dropped them and sat down. 'I heard you had quite an adventure yesterday,' he said. Excitement etched his dark face.

Richard pulled out some boiled meat from a basket, caring not from which animal it came, and ate it.

'Proper food,' he said with a mouthful, 'I cannot thank you enough for that.'

'The Battle of the Stumps they're saying. Tell me everything,' Sir Gobble said.

Richard had no inclination to, so Sarjeant told Sir Gobble what he needed to hear. The young man listened to the story unfold with a child-like glee.

'I will have the sin of envy to confess whenever I next find myself in a church,' Sir Gobble said as the story finished.

'Fear not, the next story will have you in it. There are plenty of opponents for you on the way,' Richard said.

'If I see this Eustace, I will capture him for you,' Sir Gobble's chest puffed out.

Bowman chuckled. 'If you were a lord, your device would be a peacock,' he said.

'Never,' Sir Gobble replied, 'I shall have a lion on my banner.'

'You are not a great lord. You aren't even a knight yet, so you can't even have your own colours, let alone an animal on them,' Richard said.

'Not yet, not yet,' Sir Gobble picked up a basket and passed it to Richard.

'I even brought horsebread,' Sir Gobble added.

'You're being helpful. Do you want something?' Richard's eyes narrowed.

'Just the story,' Sir Gobble replied. He put down an empty basket that he'd emptied entirely by himself.

'I might have a little sleep now though,' Sir Gobble said.

Richard couldn't feel as relaxed or happy as his friend did. He got to his feet and looked to the hills to the north. The lookouts were still there, but Richard felt uncomfortable not being able to see over the ridge himself.

Bowman joined him. 'You heard the senior peacock last night, he is sending scouts out. Until they come galloping back over that hill you can get some rest,' he said.

Sir Gobble curled up under a canvas shelter and looked up at the sky with his hands behind his head. He burped.

'He really was born for war,' Richard said. He was about to lie back down when a horseman rode through the camp to them. 'Are any of you the young William Tancarville, William Marshal, John de Colleville or Henry the Green?' he asked.

Sir Gobble opened his eyes. 'Who is asking?' he said.

The horseman, a short little man with a sour face, looked down a pointed nose at him. 'Lord Tancarville.'

'Why?' Sir Gobble sat up.

'How should I know? You should watch your insolence. You are one of the English boys, yes?' The messenger spat onto the ground by Sir Gobble's legs.

Richard watched to see how the youth would respond. Sir Gobble stood up, his face lit with a smile. 'Where is our lord?'

'Go to the church in the square,' the horseman turned his horse by pulling the reins to one side. He kicked the horse and it walked off awkwardly. The horse's head went up as it turned and both Sir Gobble and Richard winced.

'He doesn't even know how to ride,' Sir Gobble said.

'Doesn't deserve to sit on a horse at all.' Richard shook his head, 'any idea what Lord Tancarville wants with you?'

'No,' Sir Gobble said, 'do you fancy going over with me to find out?'

Richard thought about the alternative, which was lying around in the camp thinking about the army that marched towards them.

'Yes,' he picked up the basket of horsebread. He could at least feed Solis first, then find the best of the captured horses for himself.

Neufchâtel teemed with life but tension hung over it like a cloud. Richard rode into the town square with Sir Gobble. Bowman and Sarjeant ambled behind. A convoy of carts had their supplies unloaded into what looked like a warehouse, and a column of armed riders rode up towards the castle. Lord Tancarville stood at the entrance to the church, clad in his mail. Over it hung his red and white surcoat, the silver rowels gleamed in the morning light.

Mandeville spoke to him, not in his armour but wearing a fur lined cloak over a tunic that seemed to be mostly made out of something golden.

'Peacocks indeed,' Bowman said.

The Little Lord already waited there, in his mail, he stood at the foot of the steps to the church.

A bishop came out and spoke to Tancarville.

Sir Gobble dismounted and asked Sarjeant to hold his horse. Richard did the same.

'I'm not going in,' Bowman said and made an act out of settling into his saddle.

Richard shrugged and followed Sir Gobble over to meet his fate.

'Young William,' Tancarville shouted down as Sir Gobble stood next to the Little Lord, who ignored him.

'My lord?' Sir Gobble said.

'He has no idea, does he?' Tancarville elbowed Mandeville and roared with laughter.

'I told you he was an idiot,' Mandeville said, 'rude and ignorant, too. I cannot fathom why you are willing to do this.'

'He is only rude when he's hungry,' Tancarville glanced down as Sir Gobble, whose face twisted in confusion. 'Although that is most of the time.'

Mandeville laughed. 'Very well, I cannot stop you. I think he is a poor investment, but it's your gold,' he said.

'Gold,' Sir Gobble grabbed Richard's arm.

'Gold?' Richard said.

'Gold Richard, this is it. Finally,' Sir Gobble said.

Richard noticed what dangled from Tancarville's hands. Four pairs of golden spurs.

'Knighthood,' Sir Gobble straightened his back and held his head up.

Richard was quite sure that tears formed in his eyes. 'Congratulations,' he said through gritted teeth.

'Come now, boys,' Tancarville said, 'give me your sword belts and inside with you. Richard, you can watch,' he said.

Sir Gobble unlaced his sword belt and handed it over. He beamed and pulled Richard by the hand up the stone steps and into the church.

It might not have been Canterbury Cathedral, but it was a large church nonetheless. At the far end hung a huge stained glass window. Its bright blue background flooded the interior with light, as biblical figures in bright reds and greens acted out their scenes. A choir sung and various unarmoured knights walked out having just heard mass.

Tancarville led the young men along the nave and up into the chancel of the church. The roof was arched and tall, the space immense and ornate. The inside was almost as tall as the castle tower.

Tancarville stopped before the altar and pointed onto the stone floor before it. 'Kneel,' he said.

The Little Lord and Sir Gobble knelt where they were told,

and looked up at their lord.

Richard could see the smile stretched across his friend's face.

Tancarville girded the Little Lord with his sword belt. He said some words to his son that Richard couldn't hear, then went behind him, knelt down and fixed a pair of golden spurs to his feet. Tancarville hung a red silken cloak with a squirrel fur lining around his neck. He then walked around the Little Lord, stood tall, and promptly slapped him around the side of his face.

The Little Lord reeled and had to put a hand to the floor to keep his balance. The choir still sung, their soaring notes almost brought Richard to tears.

Tancarville moved on to the second candidate and repeated the process. The blow this time was not as hard, and nor was it for the third young man. Three knights created, Tancarville stood before Sir Gobble.

A nobleman pushed in front of Richard, and he had to find somewhere else to stand. When he saw Sir Gobble again, golden spurs glinted on his heels, his sword belt had been laced onto him, and a shining green silk cloak covered his back.

Tancarville rushed through the process, but when he raised his hand to deliver the blow, Richard saw him raise it further than he had for his son. Tancarville grinned. He struck Sir Gobble as hard as he possibly could in the side of his face.

The new knight reeled, his head snapped sideways and his body almost toppled over. His left leg raised from the ground and he wobbled on one knee. Sir Gobble hung in the air. The crowd gasped and he nearly teetered over, but he refused to put a hand down for balance. The new knight called on all his strength, and his airborne leg landed back on the ground under full control.

'Arise, Sir Wobble,' Tancarville burst into so much laughter that he started to cry.

Richard decided that Sir Wobble was just as funny as Sir Gobble, and laughed as the four new knights stood up and congratulated each other.

The Little Lord skipped over Sir Wobble and went to his father, who glowed red in the face and gasped to catch his breath.

Sir Wobble left the chancel, his smile toothy and carved onto his expression. 'I told you, Richard, it is my fate,' he said.

'Watch for the sin of pride,' Richard answered, 'unless you are collecting the full set of sins?'

Sir Wobble laughed. 'It'll be lands and glory that I collect.'

'Don't get ahead of yourself,' Richard said as they left the cool air of the church.

The scene that greeted them outside was not as peaceful. A group of lightly armed riders waited outside on their horses, who breathed heavily and were covered in sweat despite the cool start to the day.

Mandeville left the church, and asked the riders why they had already returned.

'My lord, the enemy are on the hills around the town. They are already here,' a scout said.

Mandeville didn't say anything as Tancarville pushed past Richard to join him.

'What was that?' Tancarville shouted.

The scout repeated his report.

'Ha. Not so clever as you thought,' Tancarville said quietly to Mandeville.

The younger man sighed. 'You can gloat later. Muster everyone,' he said.

Tancarville shouted. 'To arms. Every man, to arms,' at the top of his voice. He nodded to one of his men who waited outside the church. The messenger mounted his horse and cantered along the street towards the Tancarville camp.

Sir Wobble put his arm around Richard. 'We had best get into our mail,' he said. He still smiled, and Richard wondered if the smile would ever leave his face.

Richard didn't share his happiness. Men were about to be killed, and he thought back to the crippled veterans at Lillebonne. That could be him by tomorrow. Normans rode out of the square in every direction, this was it. Richard and his knightly companion mounted their horses.

'He is going to be insufferable now, isn't he,' Bowman said as Richard settled in the saddle. His borrowed horse was brown, thinner than Solis, and much quieter. He looked much older, too.

'He's Sir Wobble now,' Richard replied.

'Wobble?'

'I'll tell you later,' Richard pushed his new horse on.

Richard slipped his mail shirt over his head and wriggled into it. The mail shirt de Cailly had given Bowman was a very tight fit on him, but he somehow slipped easily into it. The first time Richard had put on his father's mail shirt he'd got stuck in it, despite only being a boy.

De Cailly mustered under his banner at the edge of the camp, an array of horsemen around him.

'I suppose we're still with him,' Richard said.

Bowman nodded. 'I do not much like this new horse.'

Richard chuckled. 'I hope he likes you,' he started to walk over towards de Cailly.

'What are you naming yours, then?' Bowman asked.

'I'm not, it's not mine to keep,' Richard said. The horse responded to the movement of his hips well enough, but he didn't know its strengths and weaknesses. He didn't know what it would do when faced with danger.

Tancarville and his household knights cantered out of the town gate, the drumming of their hooves alerted Richard to their approach

One of the lookouts up on the ridge started to ride back to camp at full speed.

'It begins,' Bowman said.

Richard's mouth dried up.

'Finally,' Sir Wobble rested his lance on his foot in the stirrup. His green silk knighting cloak hung over his mail.

'Why are you wearing that? Someone will ruin it,' Richard asked.

'So everyone will notice my deeds,' Sir Wobble replied.

Tancarville's horse raced down the road into camp. The cry went up to form, and de Cailly rode to meet his lord. Richard flexed his right hand on his lance, and realised he hadn't changed the dressing yet. He wanted to be sick. His bowels needed to empty.

De Cailly cantered back through the tent village to his company. 'Flemish knights have ridden round to the west gate.

We ride to push them away from the town,' he shouted.

'The west gate?' Richard asked.

'Outflanked already,' Bowman sighed.

Richard looked over to the corral where Solis and the other spare or resting horses were being kept. It looked worryingly undefended as all the knights and squires flocked to Tancarville's banner outside the camp.

De Cailly and his bannerman rode up to join him, then a seething mass of horsemen pressed forwards out of the camp, seemingly with little order. Banners jostled, and knights with different shields mixed up.

Richard followed Sir Wobble as he pushed his horse to the front of the press.

Tancarville rode in the first rank, a bannerman on either side of him. With a great cry the army marched on up the gentle slope into the town.

De Cailly left his company to join the first line.

Sir Wobble spurred his horse to join them.

Tancarville noticed him there at the front of their advance. 'Sir Wobble, get back, do not be so hot-headed. Let these knights get through,' he shouted.

Sir Wobble held his horse up and dropped back next to Richard. The new knight's face shone bright red despite his natural darkness, and Richard thought his bottom lip quivered.

Bowman shouted over to him. 'Looks like the peacock is not quite ready to spread his tail.'

Richard didn't laugh. An unknown knight to his right banged his shield into his right arm, and his spear almost flew from his hand. A horse bumped into the back of him and his new horse kicked out at it. The hooves made contact and the other horse squealed, but he couldn't dwell on that.

Richard reached the town gate and had to squeeze through a traffic jam of horses and armoured men. They burst through into Neufchâtel and flew along the streets. The few people around dove out of the way. The army cantered through the square and past the church. Richard reached Sir Wobble, who was only a few horses behind Tancarville and his banners. The de Cailly banner fluttered somewhere behind them.

They all turned town the road that led out of the west gate, filed through that gate, and out of the town.

The road was wide enough for two carts. It was lined with animal folds that ran out into the suburbs, and towards the bridge over the river ahead. Richard was surrounded by horses, men, and metal so he didn't see any of it.

A cry went up ahead.

He caught a glimpse of what must have been enemy of horsemen at the end of the road. They were inside the suburb's barricade and headed his way. Richard wanted to hide but he couldn't.

The knights in the front rank couched their lances. There wasn't enough space to spread out, as all the knights and squires strained to be the first to engage. Sir Wobble put some room between himself and Richard, who worried for his knees.

Richard saw the enemy banners but knew them not, and stopped caring as the two sides clashed at fighting speed.

Tancarville's lance smashed into a Fleming who reeled in his saddle. The unfortunate man rode straight into the gap between Sir Wobble and Richard.

Richard shouted his father's name, clenched his lance and lowered it. It caught the Fleming under the helmet, stuck in his face and ripped it open. Richard cantered on.

Sir Wobble's lance broke near its tip on an enemy's shield. He lowered it at a second oncoming knight anyway, and the already broken lance snapped in two on the man's shield.

The second Fleming to ride past Richard came too quickly for him to recover his lance to aim. Their knees collided in an explosion of pain.

Richard slammed to a halt as too many horsemen crashed together in the street and the rush of the charge gave way to a stationary slogging match. Richard was only aware of those directly around to him. He dropped his lance as a mailed Flemish knight was already too close for him to use it. The Fleming did the same. Before he could duel with Richard, Sir Wobble jammed his sword down onto the man's sword arm. The mail armour didn't give, but the blow landed so hard that the bone underneath probably did.

The man howled and started to turn his horse away.

Richard, sword drawn, tried to push his horse to follow the

Fleming. His new horse was sluggish to obey, and the knight got away. Momentum ran with the Normans, and more and more Flemish knights turned and rode back the way they'd come.

Tancarville and his knights pursued, and Richard saw a Mandeville banner a few streets away above the rooftops. He could see a multitude of foreign banners raised all over the suburbs when he looked for them, but he had no idea how the battle fared elsewhere.

Richard's horse joined the chase of its own will, but other squires overtook him. They charged with their lances and smashed into the Flemings who had got caught standing still at a junction. Men and horses went down in sickening crunch, followed by screams and shouts. Richard juddered to a halt as the horses ahead of him stopped and the battle generated into another static melee.

A cry rose up from their rear, and Richard turned to see an unknown banner move towards them from a side street.

They were being flanked. Terror filled his soul.

Enemy horsemen, lances down, charged into the side of the Tancarville force.

'They're on both sides of us,' Richard said.

'Follow me,' Sir Wobble shouted as he pushed his horse through the flimsy gate of one of the animal folds along the road.

It was big enough to hold a dozen horses, so Richard followed him and Bowman appeared a moment later. Richard couldn't see Sarjeant.

'We can't attack, we have to wait,' Sir Wobble said.

Tancarville and his leading knights hurtled back along the road, chased by fresh Flemings with unbroken lances. The sheer mass of the retreating Normans forced the flank attack back into its side street.

Richard went forwards to leave the fold and join his comrades, but the Flemings who chased Tancarville rode past the gate before he could leave.

'Wait,' Sir Wobble shouted.

With the company of Flemings gone towards the town, Sir Wobble led them back out onto the suddenly empty road.

Empty except for the fallen men and broken lances that littered it.

'We should attack the enemy who chase Lord Tancarville,' Richard said.

'No, follow me,' Sir Wobble shouted and cantered off the other way along the road away from town.

'Damn him,' Bowman followed the new knight.

Four surprised enemy squires stood motionless in their path, Sir Wobble had chosen to pick them off rather than aid his lord.

Bowman lowered his lance.

The Flemings realised they were under attack, but it was too late. The first young man died as Bowman's lance penetrated his chest. The lance snapped in his ribs.

Richard cut at a boy who was younger and smaller than him. Richard was stronger too, and struck him three times with his sword. The boy made no move to defend himself and slumped in his saddle covered in blood.

Sir Wobble despatched the final two riders with two brisk sword cuts, the accuracy of which Richard could barely dream of.

'Who else is there?' Sir Wobble shouted across the streets.

Richard saw the distant Mandeville banner fluttering next to an unknown one, the sound of iron smashing into iron and wood echoed all around.

'Behind us,' Bowman shouted and they all turned.

The Flemings who had chased Tancarville now charged right back at them. There must have been thirty of them. A wall of horseflesh and metal the width of the road, and many ranks deep. This was his death, Richard knew it in his bones. Maybe he could flee, he thought, and quickly turned his head towards the edge of the town.

'We can't go that way, young lord,' Bowman said.

'But we can't survive them all,' Richard said.

'No we can't,' Bowman said, 'but we can show these Normans how the English die.' Bowman pushed his horse on.

Sir Wobble laughed.

Richard was surrounded by madmen.

'Attack,' Sir Wobble shouted and Richard spurred his horse.

Richard swung his sword at an enemy knight who parried it.

Two squires collided with Richard's horse and nearly dragged him over. They didn't stay to fight, instead they rode by. Two more squires pressed into Richard, one hewed a chunk of wood from the top of his shield. In a flash the enemy had all gone right through them, the three Englishmen left in the middle of the road to grin at each other.

'I suppose I owe God a prayer,' Richard said, but before he could utter it, Tancarville knights cantered down the road after the Flemings. Richard ducked into the animal fold again to get out of their way.

Bowman and a beaming Sir Wobble joined him.

A knight unhorsed by Sir Wobble crawled on his knees in the road. He was trampled by de Cailly's standard bearer as the Normans rushed by.

Richard stood still and caught his breath. 'I thought we were dead,' he smiled, 'I really did.'

'The day's still young,' Bowman said.

Two Tancarville squires led four captured horses back up towards the town gate and disappeared inside.

Richard heard a noise from the side street. A Flemish knight and a pair of squires cantered along it, then turned onto the main road in order to attack Tancarville from behind. As they reached the animal fold, Sir Wobble launched his horse out from their stone resting place and directly into a squire. A pommel strike to the side of his head caused him to drop his sword.

Richard joined in.

The enemy knight cut at Sir Wobble, sliced into his shield and banged his helmet. Sir Wobble cut back, hit the knight's blade hard and it snapped.

Richard attacked the second squire, who couldn't lower his lance in time, and Richard was able to knock it out of his hands. The young man was lithe but strong, and he tried to grab Richard's shield to drag him down. Richard cut at the fingers which grasped his shield and at least one sliced off.

The man screamed and flailed at Richard with his bloodied hand.

Bowman delivered a cut down onto his neck from behind. 'That will do him,' he said.

The Fleming lurched sideways and his horse bolted. The body fell from the saddle but a foot caught in the stirrup. The bolting horse dragged the corpse away from the fight.

Sir Wobble shouted at his opposite number to surrender.

The enemy knight kicked his horse and burst free to make his escape, leaving the road suddenly devoid of anyone left to fight.

De Cailly rode back towards the town, two of his squires leading a bound knight still on his horse. De Cailly himself led another horse which had no rider. 'That was impressive,' he said as he rode by, 'but you do not have much to show for it, do you.'

Sir Wobble withdrew back into the animal fold. 'Next time we'll capture one,' he breathed hard.

Richard felt tired. Different parts of him started to hurt. His left knee had a constant dull ache, and his head felt like someone had bashed his helmet in with the back of an axe.

A pile of dead mean littered the road, for any fallen fighters who hadn't been killed by weapons had been finished off by hooves. Richard looked around the rooftops again but still couldn't see the Martel banner. The Mandeville banner however, had been pushed back but still floated above the town.

The Little Lord rode back from the end of the road where his father fought, and stopped outside their animal fold. 'What are you doing here you cowards, the fight is up there,' he shouted.

'We are manning Castle Peacock,' Bowman replied. Someone else's blood had dyed the right arm of his tunic red.

'Castle Peacock,' Richard couldn't help but laugh.

The Little Lord's armour had no blood or oil on it, and he still had his lance intact. He walked his horse into the stone fold. 'The fight is over there, go to it,' the young Tancarville demanded.

'Why are you over here, then?' Sir Wobble stretched his sword arm out and winced.

The Little Lord growled back. He spun around because a new group of horsemen burst onto their road from the same side street as before.

The Little Lord spun his horse and left Castle Peacock.

Richard and Sir Wobble joined him on the road to face the

attack.

The Little Lord lowered his lance, but he only rode at a walk and it glanced off a squire's shield. That boy's lance hit his shield in return. The force of man and beast broke the back of his saddle with a snap, and the Little Lord barely avoided toppling backwards onto the ground.

Richard did what his father had told him never to do, and ducked an incoming lance. While he was down, he sliced his sword across the mailed leg of a knight on his right.

The man shouted and accidentally pulled his horse to a stop. Sir Wobble punched him in the helmet with the hilt of his sword. A second blow stunned the knight, and Richard closed on the Fleming and pushed him towards Sir Wobble.

The new knight caught the confused Fleming, hooked his sword arm around his neck, and backed his horse up. Sir Wobble pulled the knight right out of his saddle. His trailing leg caught in his stirrup, which dragged the horse along with him. The animal reared up and spun which dislodged the foot from the stirrup. Free of his rider, the horse ran off down the road.

The Little Lord took blows from a knight and two squires who fought to get close enough to steal his reins. One dropped his sword and grabbed at the young Tancarville's sword arm.

'Help me,' the Little Lord cried.

Sir Wobble ignored him, and dragged his captured knight into Castle Peacock.

Bowman duelled with a lance-armed squire who rode a horse so agile that Bowman couldn't get inside the lance-tip to attack with his sword.

Richard rode towards the Little Lord who took a cut across the chest.

Richard cut at the squire and sliced into the padding on his arm but didn't harm him. The second squire grabbed the reins from the Little Lord and jerked them from his grasp.

'Help, God curse you if you don't,' the young Tancarville shouted.

The Flemish knight who desired his capture turned to intercept Richard.

Richard tried to turn away from him at the last minute, but his new horse didn't respond and the horse collided with the knight's mount. Both horse's tangled legs and bridles. The stallions screamed and tore at each other, their legs and teeth drawing blood as the fought. The knight's horse backed away with a bad limp on a front leg, red bite marks on its face and neck.

The Little Lord threw down his sword, and made to throw himself from his broken saddle in an attempt to evade capture.

Richard kicked his horse on, the horse grunted and tried to chase the Little Lord, but it was clear he couldn't catch up.

The young Tancarville preferred pain to capture, and ejected himself from his broken saddle, landed on his shoulder, and rolled into the wall of a wooden house.

Bowman's opponent darted away from him on his fine horse, and charged at the Little Lord while he looked the other way.

'Watch out,' Richard shouted, but it was too late.

The Flemish squire couched and lowered his lance, but just as he struck, his horse tripped on a body and the lance tip brushed the Little Lord's left arm and ripped the shield from his body instead. The Little Lord was sent spiralling to the ground.

The squire, now on his own, turned his agile steed away and cantered back down the side street where he'd come from, abandoning his knight to Sir Wobble.

The Little Lord picked himself up and staggered back into Castle Peacock, the earth inside it now chewed up.

Richard rode his horse back in too, but the limp worried him.

'You left me. My father will hear about that,' the Little Lord said. He checked that his golden spurs were intact. 'You're lucky they aren't broken,' he clutched his left arm and winced.

Sir Wobble dismounted to bind the legs of his captive. 'I will capture some more and take them back together,' he said.

The knight stood up, but could do nothing except shuffle about and looked around at his captors. He was in his late forties and had a worn, round face.

'I have been taken by boys,' he said in such a strong accent that Richard only just understood it.

Tancarville and his company cantered back past the animal fold. 'Thomas, head down there and get around them,' Tancarville shouted to Sir Thomas, whose company followed him down the side street the Flemings had repeatedly tried to outflank them from. Tancarville kept going, leaving Castle Peacock as a bastion against the invaders once more.

Richard's horse shivered in the fold. It held a front leg up in the air.

'Doesn't look great, young lord,' Bowman said.

Richard dismounted and tied the horse to the back of the fold. His left knee hurt to walk, so he leant against the fold where it backed on to a building. He hoped the pain would fade after a rest.

The Little Lord threw up in a corner of the fold.

'You're despoiling my little castle,' Sir Wobble grinned.

The Little Lord spat and turned around, his face dark. 'You won't have those spurs once I've told my father you left me to be taken,' he said.

'Your lack of prowess offends me. Be better,' Sir Wobble said.

Bowman looked around the corner of the neighbouring building and down the street. 'We are about to have company,' he said. He walked his horse backwards. 'Infantry,' he added.

'Castle Peacock is about to become a peacock trap,' Richard said.

'We can't fight a horde of infantry from in here,' Sir Wobble agreed.

'We aren't going to have time to leave though,' Bowman said as a swarm of footsoldiers appeared. They surged along the street, a wall of excited sound, for they knew a couple of trapped Norman knights could make them rich.

There was no time to escape, and Richard hobbled towards the entrance of the fold with his splintered shield raised.

The Little Lord joined him even though he didn't have a shield, and the two of them attempted to form a barrier in the gateway.

The Flemings wore their normal civilian clothing, an array of greens, whites, greys, oranges and yellows. They had no shields and only a few had spears. Axes were the weapon of choice.

They ran at Richard and the Little Lord, two men swung axes at them. One bit into the top of Richard's shield right in front of his eyes.

The Little Lord swung his sword but cut nothing but air.

Richard hacked at an arm in the air and his sword cut it. The owner of the arm disappeared. A spear jabbed next to his face. Richard ducked it, but an axe battered him down onto his left knee. Pain shot up it. He slashed his sword and it dug into a thigh. Another axe blow penetrated his shield, the axehead cut though it enough that the blade jutted out the back by Richard's face. It pushed him over, and he tried to roll out of harm's way.

The Little Lord fell back under many blows, and Bowman and Sir Wobble counter-attacked on their horses as the Flemings flooded through the undefended gateway.

Richard cried out as he got back to his feet, his leg a mix of heat and stabbing pain. He was also dimly aware of blood above his left eye, which threatened to drip down and blind him.

A Fleming tried to climb over the stone wall to get behind them.

Richard hit him in the neck and he fell back down the other side.

A spear thrust at Bowman's horse and caught it in the chest, but the point wasn't driven home. Bowman spun the horse, leant sideways over the militia, and hacked down at their exposed heads.

Two Flemings acquired a fire hook, a long pole with an iron angled end used to clear roof thatch off houses that were on fire. They waved it at Sir Wobble. He batted it away once as Bowman split heads beside him.

Richard engaged the infantry who had singled out Sir Wobble. The fire hook was thrust by two men together at the new knight. The rusty blade dug into his shoulder, ripped the green cloak, hooked his neck, and pulled him from his horse. Sir Wobble landed on Richard, who hit his head on the ground. The impact undid the lace that held his helmet on and it rolled away.

Sir Wobble yelped in pain but scrambled to his feet.

It had become a fight to survive.

A spear found Sir Gobble's horse, and it went up on its back legs and turned away as the shaft snapped.

Richard got up on his knees, and swung his shield around just in time to block another axe blow. It sheared off a part of the now shattered shield and wood splintered into his face.

The Flemings pressed their attack, and he saw Bowman's

horse hop backwards, a front leg bent the wrong way, before an axeman connected with its skull and the animal fell to the ground. Bowman went down with it, but Richard couldn't watch because Sir Wobble struggled to fend off three Flemings by himself.

The knight's shoulder wound stopped him raising his shield enough to defend himself while a Fleming swung a broken lance like a quarterstaff at Richard. He blocked a strike with his sword, but not quickly enough, and his blade was knocked from his hand. The Fleming smiled, his teeth cracked and brown, and prepared for a killing blow.

Richard thrust the shield at him which forced him to jump back and bump into one of Sir Wobble's attackers, which gave the young knight a chance to slice off one of his ears. The other attackers jumped onto him, and he fell backwards with them on top of him like a pack of wolves.

Richard picked one up and went to throw him away, but his bandages slipped, and he tripped at the same time. Richard sprawled onto the earth with the man he'd tried to throw.

The Fleming got back to his feet first, stopped, and turned his head towards the town. Then he ran out of Castle Peacock.

Richard picked up an axe from the ground and hacked it into the back of the man that grappled with Sir Wobble. The axehead sunk into the man's back and he froze.

Sir Wobble finished him off.

The Little Lord bled from the head, neck and hand as he fought a Fleming. His opponent also disengaged, turned and fled.

Richard heard cries and shouts in Norman French as a handful of crossbow bolts spun through the air and hit some of the Flemings in the road.

The rest ran. A heartbeat later and the street was full of only wounded and dead Flemings.

From the direction of the town, infantry under a Mandeville banner charged over the top of them. The advancing Normans slit the throats of every last one, whether they were already dead or not. Like a wave they flooded by, leaving Castle Peacock just about in the hands of its defenders once again.

Sir Wobble looked over to the rear of the fold, but his captive knight had gone. As was part of his fine green cloak, now torn and tattered. He went to move, but the mail on his shoulder lay torn and blood oozed out. He cried out half in pain and half in frustration.

'I think we need to go,' Richard said.

Bowman flexed his leg. 'That is going to hurt later. This is why I hate horses, they are large animals to fall on top of you,' he said.

All four of them staggered out of Castle Peacock. Richard decided to leave his lame horse tied there as everyone else was on foot anyway. They picked their way around the corpses and limped back towards the town walls. They were a mess.

Richard put a supporting arm round Sir Wobble, who had gone white.

Sir Thomas and his company trotted back from the side street, their horses frothed and men just as winded.

'Give them horses,' Sir Thomas ordered and his youngest squires dismounted.

'Help us get him into the town,' Richard had to take most of Sir Wobble's weight.

'We will get him to the church,' Sir Thomas said, 'quickly now.'

Sir Wobble was given a horse to ride, led by the squire on foot who had donated it, and they made their way into the town. The gates were unbarred and slammed shut again behind them. Guards looked out nervously over the palisade, fingers twitched near the triggers of their crossbows.

Richard helped Sir Wobble off the horse outside the church in the square, and carried him inside. He was assured the knight would be cared for, then left to rejoin Sir Thomas.

A few of his squires displayed a shield with his colours, that of a yellow shield with a diagonal blue line, but many had Tancarville shields or other colours that Richard didn't know. The company moved off again as one regardless.

Richard's new horse was a young grey horse, not yet fully trained, and he had to close his fingers on and off the reins to maintain a sensible pace. Richard wondered if its mind was still in the fight.

The company rode back out through the southern gate. The

plain opened out with the Tancarville camp to their right, and Richard looked up to the hills on their left. At least twenty horsemen rode down the hill towards the camp. Leading their charge were two banners, banners Richard had seen at the camp near Fallencourt.

One was red and yellow.

'There is a God after all, look young lord, we get another go,' Bowman said.

Richard, Bowman and the Little Lord had been given the lances the squires hadn't broken yet, and Richard gripped his as he saw a large man next to the Martel banner that must have been Eustace.

'This time, I'm keeping him,' Richard said.

'Who are you talking about?' The Little Lord asked.

Sir Thomas shouted. 'Into line,' before Richard could answer.

Richard pushed his horse on away from the road, so that he could take his place in formation as the whole company rode into one long line and rode away from the walls.

The knights of Martel and Boulogne couched their lances and held them half lowered as they cantered on. They saw the pits dug into the ground, and the formation broke up as knights either jumped them or slowed to go around them.

The Tancarville infantry formed a long but thin spear wall to await them. In front of them, crossbowmen aimed their weapons at the oncoming horsemen. They loosed their bolts. Richard wasn't close enough to hear, but he saw them fly. Some riders fell, and some horses spun in pain and surprise. The missile volley irritated the attackers, but it didn't stop them.

Once over the pits, the knights launched into canter, and their disordered formation homed in on the middle of the Tancarville line.

Sir Thomas pulled ahead at the centre of his company. and Richard had to let his new horse go to keep up.

The knights from Boulogne fully lowered their lances at the spear wall.

Some of the infantry took a step back as a wall of horseflesh ploughed into them. The knights crashed through the spearmen without so much as slowing down. Lances broke and wood flew into the air. In the wake of the horsemen, broken bodies lay on the earth.

The Tancarville force split in two either side of the breach, and the surviving spearmen clumped together for safety at each end. The Martel banner and half a dozen horsemen headed for the spearmen furthest away from Richard.

Sir Thomas instead aimed his force at that of Matthew of Boulogne's. Richard couched his lance. He could feel his right hand sticky and wet inside his torn bandage. The knights from Boulogne never saw them coming. Richard's lance buried into the side of a mailed chest. The force pushed the lance back out of Richard's armpit, and it wrenched from his grip. His grey horse lurched forwards, fighting Richard and wanting to go faster. He used his now empty hand to wrestle back control of the horse, and in a whirl he spun it around and leapt back into the battle.

Richard drew his sword. He wondered when the day would end, and rode into the chaotic melee.

The Little Lord's lance broke off two thirds of the way down, so the young knight swung it like a club.

Bowman rode into a French knight, and with his sword hand he punched him in the face, the crossguard left a dent in the helmet. Bowman grabbed the knight and dragged him off his horse.

The Little Lord rode up to the man as Bowman rode away to another victim. The Little Lord looked down from his horse over the fallen knight. 'Do you yield?' He shouted.

The French knight held his arms out and shouted that he did.

Richard grimaced because knew the young Tancarville was going to take full credit for the capture later. He pushed his horse towards the hedgehog of spearmen who moved onto the attack now that Sir Thomas's men were helping them.

'Capture them,' Sir Thomas ordered his men.

The Count of Boulogne's standard bearer and some knights broke away as Richard reached them. They jumped over the pits and galloped up the hill and away from the battle.

The second group of Tancarville's infantry were still under attack. Eustace Martel had pushed into their defensive hedgehog and rained his bloodied sword down on them. Two of his fellow knights pushed in behind him.

The Tancarville crossbowmen fled into the tent village.

Sir Thomas lifted his attention from his local victory. 'Follow me,' he shouted.

His standard bearer alongside him, they made to rescue the battered spearmen who fought for their lives.

Bowman got there first and found a squire with Martel colours and battered him with his sword. The young man tried to shelter under his shield, but the look on his face showed he already knew his fate.

Richard let his horse go and it drew level with Sir Thomas.

Eustace cut his way right through the panicked spearmen as they broke and ran in all directions.

Richard pointed his horse just past an enemy squire and raised his sword. His horse accelerated just before they made contact, leapt through the air, and Richard missed his attack. The squire didn't miss him though, his sword caught Richard's right hand.

Richard dropped his sword. 'Not again,' he shouted. He used his free hand to get his horse back under control.

'Give me your spear,' he shouted at a spearman who ran by. The footsoldier obliged happily, and Richard couched his new lance and looked for Eustace.

Eustace Martel killed two spearmen with two blows.

Sir Thomas picked him out too, and he aimed his lance at the big man's horse. The speed of impact drove the lance deep into the neck of the animal, and it was pushed backwards on its hind quarters before it toppled over. Eustace spilled from the saddle.

The few spearmen still nearby stopped their retreat and ran over with their spears lowered at Eustace now that he lay on the ground.

Richard had his lance, but needed to take Eustace alive. He aimed for the man's red and yellow shield instead of his body.

Eustace sprung to his feet and batted a spear away with his sword. His next stroke cut across a Tancarville man's face who reeled backwards in agony.

Richard kicked his horse on. It cantered to Eustace and Richard leant his bodyweight down into the spear tucked into his armpit. The spear hit the middle of the shield, Eustace unaware of its approach, and sent him back down to the grass.

Sir Thomas, sword drawn, rode up and stopped. 'Do you yield?' he asked.

Eustace, aware that he was now alone on the battlefield, did not. He clambered to his feet yet again and ran at two spearmen. He punched one in the face with his shield, and cut into the shoulder of the second.

An infantryman managed to dig a spear into his belly, but the mail stopped penetration and Eustace turned and attacked him. As that man fell, Richard jumped off from his unruly horse. His knee sent the now expected pain up his body again, but he wielded his spear in two hands and pointed the wickedly sharp tip at Eustace.

Sir Thomas's company, at least those not chasing the enemy, stopped and watched.

Eustace Martel was trapped.

'Gut him quickly,' Bowman pulled his horse up.

'He is a knight,' Sir Thomas replied, 'and he shall not be killed.'

Eustace's eyes caught Richard's. The Martel knight took a violent step towards the spearmen and they all jumped backwards.

Eustace laughed. 'Why even bring footmen to a battle?' he said.

Richard edged closer, his spear point high and trained at Eustace's face.

'Killing you will be sweet,' Eustace said, 'I will ride back and tell your sister that she needs to pray for your wretched soul.'

Richard lunged. He stabbed at Eustace's face but the big man swatted the spear away like a twig.

'You are still a boy, and you will die like one. You will die like your father, in a pool of your own blood.'

Richard stabbed again, but this time it was a feint. When Eustace went to bat it away, Richard had already pulled the blow. He pressed home. He stepped into his thrust and the spear dug into Eustace's shoulder. The spearhead prised apart mail rings, which pinged open and let the point through.

Eustace's eyes widened as the strike spun him around, but somehow he kept his footing. He stepped back and looked at the wound. He tested his sword arm and he grunted as it moved slowly. 'I'm still strong enough for the likes of you, boy,' he said. Eustace came at Richard fast.

Richard back-pedalled to keep Eustace in front of his spearhead, but the big man advanced.

Eustace grinned. 'You are mine,' he started to jog.

Richard couldn't move backwards any quicker, so he jammed the spear down into the earth between Eustace's legs. With the spear in both hands, he took a step to the side and levered the knight's now tangled legs.

Eustace tripped and lost his sword as he hit the ground. His own shield smacked him in the face and blood poured from his nose when he looked up.

Richard's spear had fallen from his grip too, so he picked up his battered and split shield in two hands, put a foot on Eustace's throat and raised it up. Richard's eyes blazed like the fires of Fallencourt.

'Yield now,' Sir Thomas said.

That cry snapped Richard out of the moment.

Eustace looked up at him.

Richard paused.

Eustace fumbled for something.

Richard brought the shield down.

'I yield,' Eustace shouted and shut his eyes against the shield and its dagger-like splinters.

Richard stopped the shield above his face, shards of wood so close to his eyes that his eyelids flickered on them.

'I yield,' Eustace repeated, eyes closed.

Death didn't come so he opened one eye.

Richard stepped off his neck and backed away, his heart pounded in his ears.

'Clear him,' Sir Thomas ordered.

Spearmen descended on Eustace, pulled off his shield, his sword belt, and the knife his right hand was on. Spears levelled at him the whole time, the infantrymen were rough with him as they picked him up.

Richard walked away so Eustace couldn't see his face. He dropped the spear. He stepped over a Tancarville militiaman who groaned faintly on the earth, an eyeball hanging from his face by a thread. An urge to vomit simmered in Richard's throat. He set his eyes on his borrowed horse and choked back the tears that threatened him. The stench of iron and spilt bowels filled his nostrils, but he had Eustace Martel, and he was still alive, so when Richard had recovered, he could talk.

AFTERMATH

Richard hugged Solis's yellow neck. The stallion sniffed him, snorted, and went back to the pile of cut grass on the ground of the corral. Richard lied down right there next to his horse. He looked up at the sky and said prayer of thanks for the effectiveness of the bread-based horse charm he'd fed to Solis in Castle Tancarville. One small twist of fate, and he would have ridden Solis into battle that day. Richard closed his eyes and tried to relax. His back, shoulders and arms all ached, for the battle's tension hadn't left them yet.

Bowman shook him awake before he knew he'd even fallen asleep.

Solis licked mud from his leather shoe.

'I can't have slept all afternoon?' Richard blinked himself to life.

'After battle, some men sleep and some men drink. Seems that you sleep,' Bowman said.

'What about you?'

'Drink,' Bowman smiled, 'and luckily for me, there's a victory feast for the knights, and we're invited. You don't skip those,' he said.

Richard yawned. 'I would rather sleep more, it's nearly dark anyway.'

'Nonsense, you need to eat after a battle,' Bowman hauled Richard up.

Richard brushed himself down and followed Bowman out of the camp. The bearded crossbowman and his comrade guarded the entrance.

'Did you two even notice there was a fight going on?' Bowman said.

'We did our bit, didn't we, Jean,' the bearded guard stated.

'We did, I killed at least three knights. It was all under control until you horse-boys showed up and ruined everything.'

'Right, whatever you say, Jean,' Bowman patted him on the back and left.

'Have you seen Sarjeant?' Richard asked as they entered Neufchâtel.

'I have, he went to help Sir Wobble get from the church to the hall. Apparently his shoulder is worse now, but I think he is just looking for sympathy and better quality food.'

'Probably,' Richard said.

They walked through the square with the church. Men lay on blankets outside as they waited to be treated. Some lay still, some moaned, a few screamed into the evening.

Richard shivered. 'That is a horrible sound,' he said.

'It is the sound of your trade,' Bowman said and flexed the leg his horse had fallen on.

Richard turned his head away. The sound of the wounded faded as he hobbled towards their feast.

The town's largest hall was a fine building with a grand high roof. Its open doors radiated song and light out onto the dark street. Richard started to walk in, but Bowman held him back. 'That feast is for the squires,' he said, 'we are going to the feast in the castle.'

'The castle?'

'Our great hero, the wobbling peacock, dines in the castle with the lords because he is newly knighted, and apparently the toast of the town. He has named us as his retinue because he will look rather foolish as the only knight sitting there on his own,' Bowman said.

Richard hesitated.

'Never turn down good food, young lord. We also need to stop Sarjeant from drinking all the good wine by himself,' Bowman added.

Richard laughed, which felt good and loosened his stomach a bit, so they went to find the castle's hall.

That hall was in the great stone tower, up some stone stairs, and was just as noisy as the feast in the town. A hearth roared in the centre of the cavernous room, and tables were placed around in a huge wooden square.

At the far end, Tancarville sat next to Mandeville. A number of faces he didn't know surrounded them, except he did know one.

Eustace.

'The high ranking captives dine with the lords, as a courtesy,' Bowman said.

Richard clenched his jaw and looked for Sir Wobble. He sat far away from Tancarville and Eustace, and Bowman went to sit down opposite him with his back to the fire. Richard sat next to Sir Wobble and looked at his shoulder.

'How bad is it?' Richard asked

'It ruined my cloak,' Sir Wobble said, 'and I will have to get my mail fixed.'

'What about your shoulder?'

'It will be fine, look,' the new knight rotated it in demonstration, although he winced when he tried to hold the arm up.

Sarjeant, who was sat on his other side, went to stop him moving. 'Stop doing that, keep it still,' he said.

Once Sir Wobble went back to eating fish, Sarjeant pushed some cups across the table.

Richard peered into one, saw a dark red liquid and took a drink. 'That is strong,' Richard smiled. 'Thank you, Sarjeant. What happened to you today?'

'I was carried away with Tancarville's company. When we ran into a Mandeville company and I got mixed in with them. I was ordered to take a captured knight to the castle for safe keeping, then saw this wounded fool in the church,' Sarjeant said.

'You went into the church instead of back into the fighting?' Richard said.

'Of course,' Sarjeant said, so firmly that Richard took another drink instead of pressing the issue.

An empty silver plate sat on the table already, but a servant brought a fresh one over. It contained a whole roasted peacock, head and all, and its tail had been reattached, bright feathers of blue and green.

'You won't get this with the squires,' Sir Wobble eyed the dish. One of the feathers brushed by Richard's nose as it was placed onto the table, which made him sneeze.

'How will it feel to eat one of your own?' Bowman said.

Sir Wobble sneered at him and ripped a leg from the bird. The long feathers flew out all over the table.

Sarjeant ignored the food, and poured himself another drink from the large jug of wine by his side.

'I never went back for my horse,' Richard realised, 'I hope it isn't still tied up in Castle Peacock.'

'Someone will have claimed it by now, although he was broken and worth nothing,' Bowman said.

'I don't have a horse at all now,' Sir Wobble said.

'I'm really sorry about him,' Richard held his cup up, 'to your horse.'

Sir Wobble raised his cup, and Richard was sure he could see a hint of water in his eyes.

'I'm a knight without a horse,' he emptied the cup and slammed it onto the table.

'Not really a knight at all then,' Bowman grinned at him, 'just a peacock eating his own kind.'

'Not now, Bowman,' Richard said, 'Lord Tancarville will give him another horse. I thought you get a horse when a lord knights you?'

'I hope so,' Sir Wobble said, 'I will ask him later. I defeated many knights for him, so he should be grateful.'

'We did hold Castle Peacock,' Richard grinned.

'Just,' Bowman said, 'but I thought I was gone when my horse went over.'

'How is your leg?' Richard asked.

'Better than yours, you barely got here,' Bowman replied.

Sir Wobble chuckled as Brother Geoffrey sat down next to Richard and all their smiles faded.

'What do you want? You are not welcome here,' Richard said.

The monk had red cheeks. 'I wanted to apologise for my accusations earlier today. God has indeed signalled his acceptance of whatever it is you have done,' he said.

Richard ignored him and poured himself some more wine.

Brother Geoffrey put down an empty cup.

Richard didn't fill it so the monk sighed. 'There is still the matter of the gold,' he said.

Bowman took a long drink.

'I'd like to know about that, too,' Sir Wobble said.

'So you were not a part of it?' Brother Geoffrey asked.

'No, I have no idea what everyone is talking about.'

'There isn't anything to talk about,' Richard put his already empty cup down on the table. A little too hard.

The monk looked at the cup. 'Really.'

'Really. Tell me, who actually saw any gold?' Richard asked.

A knight fell off his bench on the far side of the hall and those around him cheered.

'I heard word today that the old Empress died in Rouen. I wonder if her heart burst when she was told the carts holding the crusading funds were now empty,' Brother Geoffrey said.

Richard focused on the peacock that Bowman now attacked with a knife.

'It is men like you who spread sin around our realm, your thieving kills royalty and will end in murder. Mark me, that much money is too much for common men to handle. You will all kill each other over it,' Brother Geoffrey said.

'There isn't any gold,' Richard said, 'can you go and torment someone else?'

'Very well, Richard from Keynes,' the monk stood up. He clattered into a passing serving girl who carried a platter of bread. White loaves spun across the wooden floor. The whole hall cheered, and Brother Geoffrey's cheeks turned even redder. He brushed himself down and shot a glance at Richard.

'I will be watching every step you take,' he said.

'Do not mind him, young lord,' Bowman said, 'he is just jealous that you are not an uptight, prudish, boring, foul smelling and ugly old man.'

Richard laughed as Brother Geoffrey stalked away in the direction of the bishop's table.

A group of musicians set up in a corner of the hall with some drums, a flute, a lute and some other instruments that Richard didn't know. The song they started to play was fast, the instruments layered over each other and crafted a rich sound that bounced off the walls and raised the hairs on Richard's neck.

Sarjeant burped and poured more wine from the jug, except that it was empty and nothing came out.

'Was that full when they gave it to you?' Richard asked.

Sarjeant nodded and cast his eye around for a new one.

'I think he's had enough,' Bowman said.

'I will decide when I have had enough. It is not yet,' Sarjeant said. He raised his voice. 'Wine, bring me wine.'

'Quiet your squire,' Tancarville shouted from the high table, 'He forgets his place.'

'Is he talking to me or you?' Richard asked Sir Wobble.

'I don't think it matters,' he replied. Sir Wobble delicately cut himself half of the peacock's breast off for himself.

Mandeville laughed and turned to Tancarville. 'What was his name, the rude boy?'

'William, but we call him Sir Wobble,' Tancarville said.

'Sir Wobble,' Mandeville shouted across the hall, over the music, and the knights laughed.

Sir Wobble looked down at his peacock, sighed, then got up. He approached the high table, his tattered green cloak still hung from his shoulders.

'Your broken peacock feathers hang round your neck like you've been mauled by dogs. I heard great things about you today, Sir, what was it again?'

'Wobble,' Tancarville said.

'Sir Wobble. Hilarious,' Mandeville continued, 'I heard you felled many a knight and hundreds of squires completely unaided.'

Bowman snorted.

'I was victorious over some great knights,' Sir Wobble said.

'He loves this, doesn't he?' Richard said.

Bowman nodded.

'Well then,' Mandeville said, 'out of friendship, would you care to give me a gift?'

'Of course, what would you like?' Sir Wobble asked.

'Perhaps a bridle, or even just a single breastplate taken from one of your many victories. Such a rich and successful knight can surely spare one small item for a gift?'

'My lord,' Sir Wobble's dark face grew a rosy colour and his hands fidgeted.

'Well, boy?' Tancarville said.

'I have no spares of those things, my warhorse was even killed from under me,' Sir Wobble said.

'My young knight, I am sure you defeated as many knights as you claim. I am sure I saw you take forty, nay, sixty knights yourself, surely you were not neglectful enough to fail to capture a single one of them?' Mandeville beamed. His eyes twinkled in the hearth light.

The knights around the room chuckled and whispered between themselves. The fast and upbeat music cut across the air as Sir Wobble stayed silent.

Mandeville turned to the red haired lord next to him. 'I thought you were the Father of Knights? Yet you raise them up like this? Do you not teach them the very basic lessons of knighthood?'

'Hold your tongue,' Tancarville said, 'and be careful what you accuse me of.'

'I don't think it is an accusation. Your new knight showed prowess, I will not deny that, but he profited not the slightest from it. Very unknightly,' Mandeville said.

'My knights are the finest in Normandy, the finest in Christendom,' Tancarville's nostrils flared and his fist thumped down on the table.

'Better than the king's?' Mandeville flinched not at all from the heavy blow on the table.

'Of course, one day I will prove it too, on the field of iron,' Tancarville said.

'That sounds a little rebellious to me,' Mandeville's mouth hinted at a smile, 'I wonder what our king will make of your boasts?'

'They are no idle boasts,' Tancarville said, 'my knights won this battle, not yours.'

'That is a matter of opinion,' Mandeville said.

Sir Wobble took a step backwards.

'I didn't say you could go,' Tancarville said.

'No, my lord.'

'Why did you fail to capture a knight?'

'I did capture one, but the Flemish militia appeared and

recaptured him,' Sir Wobble said.

Mandeville burst into laughter. 'Footsoldiers? The great Sir Wobble was bested by men who don't even own a horse.'

The hall rippled with amusement.

Richard almost felt sorry for him, but Bowman joined the laughter.

Sarjeant put his arms on the table and nestled his head in them.

'They killed my horse,' Sir Wobble said.

'Why should I care?' Tancarville said.

'I was hoping that you would replace my horse as I lost him in your service.'

'Do you? The Constable of Normandy seems to think I have failed to teach you the way of things. Maybe you need a final lesson to see you on your way in this world. You should have captured horses instead of glory. I will not replace your horse. Walking around like a commoner will burn that lesson into your thick skull,' Tancarville said.

'I can't walk back all the way to Castle Tancarville,' Sir Wobble said.

'You do not have to,' Tancarville got to his feet. He waved at the musicians and they ceased their playing. The hall fell to silence except for the roar of the fire in the centre of the room.

'The Flemings will not come this far south again for years,' Tancarville announced, 'and the French were given such a bloody nose that they will not dare set foot in Normandy for a generation. Any knights or squires in my service who wish to find their glory elsewhere have my licence to leave.'

Murmurs filled the hall.

Sir Wobble's face furrowed. 'Are you releasing me from your service?'

'No. You damaged my horse so I am not replacing yours, which makes us even. If you can or want to make it back to the castle before the leaves turn yellow, then you are still mine,' Tancarville said.

Mandeville laughed and waved back at the musicians who started to play a new, slower song.

'You can go now,' Tancarville motioned him away.

Sir Wobble slumped back down at the table and picked up his

slice of peacock. He dropped it back down. 'The only thing of value I have is my cloak.'

'Shame it isn't new any more,' Richard said.

Sir Wobble flung it round and examined it. 'It will fetch a few shillings at least, but I need a horse. Any horse will do, hopefully someone will have captured too many to take home,' he said.

'You should have left the cloak behind, even the Little Lord did not wear his knighting cloak into battle,' Bowman said.

Sir Wobble growled but didn't reply.

'Not going to eat that?' Bowman said as Sir Wobble picked up the peacock again.

'No, I don't think I want any more peacock,' he said.

Richard laughed, but stopped when doing so made his head ache. He rubbed it. 'Can we leave whenever we want?' he asked.

'I would suggest not to be the first to,' Bowman turned his head to the high table, 'although if they are drunk enough you would be fine. Is that your Martel knight?'

'Yes,' Richard said.

'I am surprised you are not over there trying to torture some sort of confession out of him. This isn't England, it's legal here,' Bowman said.

'I'm surprised you aren't over there stabbing out his eyes with your knife,' Richard said.

Bowman laughed and turned over his eating knife in his hands. 'I have satisfied myself for today at least,' he said.

Eustace caught Bowman's eyes, and must have spotted Richard, for he rose and approached.

Richard clasped his knife and Bowman stood up as the large knight smiled at them.

'I never thought you low born nobodies would be in the lord's chamber tonight,' Eustace said.

'Low born?' Bowman said. His shoulders matched Eustace's, although the Martel man was bulkier.

'Obviously. I don't know you, but your spurs are iron,' he said.

Bowman checked his reply but stood his ground, eyes wide.

'Why are you here?' Richard asked. He couldn't hold back a yawn. 'I want to talk to you, but not tonight,' he said.

'I'm here now, what have we to talk about?' Eustace said.

'What have we to talk about? Are you goading me?' Richard said.

Eustace's green eyes shone back at him. 'I thought we had already established that your sister was worth one mediocre horse,' he said.

'Don't let him get to you, young lord,' Bowman said.

Richard gripped his cup tightly. 'Which nunnery is my sister in?'

'I don't rightly remember,' Eustace grinned. The big man picked up Sarjeant's empty jug of wine and looked inside.

'What do you want so that you'll tell me?' Richard asked.

'You have nothing I want. When you do, boy, ask me again.'

'What about my father, what really happened to him?'

'Ask your uncle,' Eustace dropped the empty jug onto the table where the pottery cracked in two.

'I'm asking you,' Richard said.

'Ask the Templars.'

'The Templars?' Richard asked.

The big man sighed. 'This is tiresome, why do you want to talk of dead men?'

'Just tell me how he died, and I'll stop asking questions,' Richard said.

Eustace sat down on the bench and put his arms on the table. They were thick. 'He broke an oath and turned down an offer. Ask your uncle, and ask the Templars in Jerusalem.'

Sarjeant lifted his head from his arms, his eyes red. 'I can find them for you, my boy, but do not expect me to go inside the Temple. I will complain about it the whole journey, too,' he put his head back down.

Bowman still stood behind Eustace, and his eyes burnt into the back of the Martel's head.

Eustace turned around slowly, his eyeline rested on Bowman's bright red sword belt. His eyes looked at the sword and then to the belt. 'I know that belt,' Eustace said.

Bowman's face froze.

'But I don't know the sword,' Eustace said, 'where did you get the belt?'

'I don't remember,' Bowman said.

Sir Wobble tilted his head. 'That does look familiar, actually,' he said.

Richard kicked him under the table and glared at him.

'That's Simon's belt,' Eustace looked around the room, 'but he's not here, where is he?'

Sarjeant burped and lifted his head. 'Poor boy was gored. Died in agony.'

'Gored?' Eustace said.

'A boar,' Richard said.

'I know what being gored means, but why do you have his belt?' Eustace said to Bowman. The Martel man peered into Bowman's face. His eyes widened. 'I know you.'

'I don't think you do,' Bowman replied. He rested his hand on the pommel of his sword. 'Many men have red sword belts, especially those who fight for Norman lords. If I had taken your Simon's belt, I'd have his sword too.'

Eustace rose to his feet. They stood nose to nose.

Richard banged his cup on the table. 'This matter has been investigated, speak to Lord Tancarville if you want to find out about Simon,' he said.

Eustace whirled around. 'Quiet boy, you have nothing to do with this,' he said.

'Actually, he was accused of his murder,' Sir Wobble waved a peacock leg around.

Richard kicked him under the table again, and the new knight yelped.

Eustace blinked at Richard. 'Murder? Not a boar then? Are you all liars?'

'Not at all, I never lie,' Sir Wobble smiled.

'You could sometimes just keep quiet, though,' Richard said to him.

'It was you, wasn't it? It makes sense now, the stories they are telling, the binding on your hands, and all these lies,' Eustace said.

'I didn't kill him, and God proved my innocence,' Richard said.

'I swear on my own immortal soul that I will have vengeance on you, boy. I will kill you,' Eustace's face darkened.

Bowman drew his knife. He put one arm round the Martel man's neck and held the point up to his throat. 'Now, we aren't going to be doing that,' Bowman said.

'Release him at once,' Tancarville shouted from his table.

The festivities stopped and eyes turned to the knife. 'You break my hospitality, how dare you,' Tancarville said.

Bowman looked at Richard.

'Let him go,' he said.

Bowman withdrew the knife and pushed Eustace away. He knocked his shins on the bench and swore.

'Get out,' Tancarville shouted, 'now, before I gut you myself.'

'I don't want to be here anyway,' Bowman said.

'Richard, here, now,' Tancarville roared.

'Peacocks,' Bowman muttered, and left the hall.

Eustace rubbed his throat and retreated back to his place on the high table.

'Thanks a lot,' Richard mumbled to Sir Wobble as he pushed himself up. The knights in the hall grew bored, and went back to their drink.

Richard stood before Tancarville.

'I forget. Are you Richard from Newbury, or Richard from somewhere else now?' he said.

Richard looked at Eustace as he retook his seat. Knights told the truth, he thought. Besides, he was sick of running and hiding.

'I am Richard of Keynes.'

'I have lost track,' Tancarville said, 'so you are the boy everyone is accusing of murder in England after all?'

'I am who I am,' Richard said.

'One small skirmish, and the boy thinks he's brave,' Tancarville laughed. His table laughed with him.

Richard noticed de Cailly sat at the end of it, sullen.

The Little Lord had sat himself on his father's side, and watched with a smug expression. 'He didn't try to help me when I battled against three Flemings,' the young Tancarville said.

'Three?' Richard , 'it was two, and I did help you.'

'I'm not a liar,' the Little Lord's smugness turned into anger.

'I don't really care,' Richard said. He felt tired and glanced over to the doorway.

'I captured a knight,' the Little Lord said.

'You didn't defeat him though, Bowman did that, you just claimed the prize,' Richard said.

The Little Lord jumped up and pointed at Richard. 'Lies, this boy is a liar, kick him out too.'

His father sighed. 'It matters little who did what, it only matters who took the man captive. Richard, if your man ever disrespects me again, I will cut you from my service and cut his head from his body while I'm at it.'

Richard nodded.

'Send him away, he shouldn't eat from our tables,' the Little Lord said.

'I'm sure I can find a table to serve me pottage,' Richard said. He regretted it as soon as he'd said it.

The Little Lord screamed and drew his sword. His eyes wild, he stepped up onto his bench and went to jump onto the table to get at Richard. A golden spur stuck on the bench and he tripped.

Richard stepped aside, and the young knight fell head first onto the reed covered floorboards.

'Enough,' de Cailly shouted.

Tancarville raised his eyebrows. 'Have you something to say?'

'Enough blood has been shed today,' de Cailly said. Unlike his lord, he was out of his armour.

The Little Lord sat up and looked around for his sword. It was on the table, embedded in a peacock.

Richard picked it up, the roasted bird stayed attached and Richard lifted it into the air.

The Little Lord looked up.

Richard smiled because the new knight wasn't sure what Richard was going to do next.

The elder Tancarville laughed. 'The boy is getting cocky, maybe we can make a knight out of him,' he said.

Richard raised the sword.

The Little Lord put his arms up in front of his face and braced.

Richard flicked the sword down and the peacock flew from the blade and thumped into the Little Lord. It left a smear of grease on his expensive tunic.

Tancarville burst into laughter.

The Little Lord went bright red and scowled at Richard.

'You really need to keep better control of your sword when we're eating,' Richard said. He flipped the sword round and offered the handle to the Little Lord.

'I'm going to kill you with that,' the young Tancarville reached for it.

'My lord,' de Cailly said loudly and stood up.

'What do you want?' Tancarville said.

'These two boys are going to kill each other,' de Cailly said.

'I'm not a boy,' the Little Lord grabbed the sword and got to his feet.

Richard stood his ground and let go of the blade.

'You are a boy,' Tancarville said, 'you may have been knighted, but you act like a child, and are not even married yet.'

'That's his fault too,' the Little Lord spat the words in Richard's face.

Richard remained unmoved.

'I am not marrying my daughter to your son,' de Cailly said.

'You damn well will if I wish it,' Tancarville said.

The Little Lord sheathed his sword and smiled.

'My lord, that is a matter for another day,' de Cailly said, 'your son and this Englishman are going to kill each other. Let me help you by taking this Englishman into my service. Make him my problem. I will gift you one of the horses I captured today as a guarantee,' de Cailly said.

Tancarville frowned. 'Why in God's name would you do that?' he asked.

'Because he wants to marry his daughter to Richard,' the Little Lord said.

'I swear I will not do that,' de Cailly smiled.

Richard wasn't sure what was happening.

Tancarville folded his arms. 'Why? You do nothing without a reason,' he said.

'Give me the boy, to do with as I please, save to marry Matilda, and you can have the best of the horses I took today. I will be responsible for him,' de Cailly said.

Tancarville glanced at Richard.

Richard shrugged.

Tancarville picked up his golden cup and raised it. 'Very well, it is done. Leave us,' Tancarville waved Richard away.

'Boy, come here,' de Cailly said.

Richard left Tancarville and went to the end of the high table.

'Why did you do that?' Richard asked.

The knight straightened his hunchback and smiled. 'Come with me,' he got up.

Richard followed de Cailly around the hearth as it spat embers at him, and out of the hall. De Cailly took Richard by the shoulder and walked him out of the castle and down the hill towards the church square. The sky above was black and dotted with bright stars.

'Where are we going?' Richard asked.

De Cailly smiled. 'I am going to make a man out of you,' he said.

Richard saw the church, light spread onto the dark stones outside its open door. Richard thought of his rolled up parchment.

'What does being a man mean?' he asked.

'For us it means looking after yourself, your family and your reputation,' de Cailly said.

Richard thought about that as they entered the church. That didn't seem like a good enough answer to him.

De Cailly stopped him on the church steps. 'Untie your belt,' he said.

Richard paused. 'Are you going to...'

'Yes, Richard, I am,' de Cailly said.

The sound of running feet echoed from up the street.

'You can't do that,' the out of breath Little Lord shouted, 'he doesn't deserve it. My father will be furious.'

'Let him be,' de Cailly said.

Richard undid the leather lacing that held his sword belt up. He passed the sword and belt over to de Cailly.

The Little Lord joined them and gulped down some air. 'My father hasn't sanctioned that,' he said.

De Cailly shrugged, a motion that with his posture had a hint of menace. 'I can do what I like with my man,' he said.

'You can't knight him, my father doesn't allow his tenants to keep households of their own,' the Little Lord said.

'I know,' de Cailly flashed a toothy grin at Richard.

Richard felt lost, but the English knight took him by the hand and dragged him into the church. Candles shone along the nave and threw patterns of light onto the wounded men who lay there. Richard followed de Cailly by the silent and less silent men.

One wailed as they went by, a wail that bounced off the walls. He only had one hand. Luckily the Little Lord hadn't followed them in.

'Has he gone to tell his father?' Richard asked.

'I care not,' de Cailly said, 'I am breaking no bonds or oaths here. Kneel.'

Richard knelt where Sir Gobble had become Sir Wobble.

De Cailly crouched down and took off his own golden spurs.

Richard decided this wasn't a dream, but in the dim light it didn't feel real. For him to be a man he had to be a knight, he was sure of that. For him to reclaim his lands he had to be a knight, too.

Richard nodded.

'Hold your hands out,' de Cailly said.

Richard clasped his bandaged hands together.

'You really need to change those,' the knight said.

'I know,' Richard said.

De Cailly put his own hands around Richard's and asked him to swear his loyalty to him as his new lord. Richard wasn't sure what the consequences of what was happening were going to be, but he knew he was too far along now to pull out.

'I do, I swear it,' he said.

He was no longer in Tancarville's service. Now he served de Cailly.

The English knight picked up Richard's belt and laced it around him. Then he went behind him and took off Richard's iron spurs.

Richard felt new spurs being placed onto his heels, and the leather strap being done up. De Cailly put Richard's iron spurs onto his own feet.

He smiled. 'Be dammed with all of them, I'll wear iron spurs for the rest of my life,' he grinned. De Cailly stood before Richard. 'I will find you a knighting cloak, a horse and mail for your legs,' he said. Then he slapped Richard in the face.

It stung and Richard's left eye went black for the briefest moment.

'Sir Richard,' de Cailly said.

Richard felt his cheeks heat up and a tingle ran down his spine. He wanted to cheer and he wanted to cry.

'You serve me, then Tancarville, then the king, and then God. In that order.'

'Why knight me?'

'At the Battle of the Stumps you fought well, and I heard good things about today, too. You have a fraction of the training of the other squires, and you could barely use your hands, yet you showed genuine prowess for your age. You will never match Sir Wobble with a sword, but your instincts are almost as good as his,' de Cailly said.

Richard cast his eyes down to the stone. 'Do not be shy, Sir Richard. Now you have to pretend you know what you're doing, at least until you do.'

'I don't understand,' Richard looked up, 'I thought Lord Tancarville doesn't like his knights to have their own knightly retinues. He has to approve this, or is the Little Lord wrong?'

'He's not wrong,' de Cailly said.

The stained glass window looked bleak without sunlight to illuminate it. The knight smiled at Richard, his teeth white. 'I am not adding you to my retinue,' de Cailly said.

Richard's left knee ached, so he stood up. He looked down at his heels and saw the golden spurs stick out. 'I still don't understand,' Richard said.

'Come now Richard, you are relatively sharp of mind.'

'If I married Matilda it might work, but you promised that wouldn't happen,' Richard said.

'Indeed, and I am a man of my word. You are not far wrong though, young knight,' de Cailly waited for him.

Richard frowned.

'There is the matter of your name,' de Cailly said.

'Richard?'

'No, Keynes,' de Cailly said, 'it is trouble. You have been marked by rumour and superstition. I heard talk of a Devil's Centaur yesterday. Today I heard of a Lion's Bane.'

'I heard it was Leopard's Bane,' Richard said.

'That is precisely my point,' de Cailly said, 'our king has taken to using a lion for his badge, I doubt he will take kindly to anyone known as Lion's Bane. As for Leopards, our Lord Tancarville is always looking for traitors. Men see in others the faults they themselves are most prone to. Therefore, the Chamberlain of Normandy sees rebellion in others. If the people call you Leopard's Bane, then you best be far away and uninteresting to him.'

'Being in your household would still put me at Castle Tancarville,' Richard said.

'Open your thick skull, I have already said that you are not joining my household. You are also no longer Richard of Keynes,' de Cailly said.

Richard sighed. He was tired. 'What am I then?'

'Richard of Yvetot,' de Cailly's eyes smiled and he flashed a toothy grin.

'Yvetot?'

'Yvetot,' de Cailly's grin grew wider.

'Why?'

'Sir Arthur's murder left an opening for the lord there. He was my sub tenant, so I will appoint a replacement without Lord Tancarville's approval. He won't like it, but I can do it. I am doing it,' de Cailly said.

'Yvetot?' Richard remembered what had happened in Lady Sophie's chamber. Or at least what he thought had happened.

'I know it is run down, and the income is only enough for one good warhorse a year if the harvests are good. But it is still land. A knight with land is above those who serve in the households,' de Cailly said.

'But, Lady Sophie?' Richard said.

'Yes, I know she is hard work, and a bit old for you, but I am sure you can find a way to enjoy being the Lord of Yvetot,' de Cailly somehow smiled even more.

Richard felt his cheeks getting hot again.

'If you can be more successful than Sir Arthur at making yourself an heir, I could even make Yvetot's title hereditary,' de Cailly said.

Richard's mouth flapped open. The Little Lord was already angry, when he found out about this he was going to be out for

His blood.

'Why me?' Richard asked.

'Because this may teach our irreproachable lord that he should be more courteous in his actions, and that he cannot shout at his greater men without cause. I'm using you to poke him in the eye, Sir Richard, Leopard's Bane,' de Cailly said.

The older knight had never seemed more alive.

'Can I go back to camp and go to sleep?' Richard asked.

'You can do as you please now,' de Cailly said, 'that is what it is to be a lord.'

'What is it to be a man?' Richard asked.

'I told you that already. Look after yourself, your family and your reputation. From what I heard of Yvetot, you will want to be worrying a lot about looking after yourself. Heaven knows why, but they loved Sir Arthur. I am giving you a chance, Richard. This is a test. You ask what a man is. For a nobly born man, you must run the manor of Yvetot well. Look after its people and its animals. Show that you are a man of worth.'

'A man of worth,' Richard said to himself. That sounded better, that sounded like something he might have heard in the Song of Roland. He could be a man of worth, at least he could with land. A landed knight with a few squires and a hidden hoard of silver might be able to pay for a few knights who had no pennants on their lances, too. Then he could wreak vengeance on the Martels and his uncle.

Maybe he could get his lands back, avenge his mother and save his sister.

Richard left the church and went to see Solis. The horse whinnied when he saw him and Richard fed him an apple. Richard ran his fingers down one of the rolls of parchment still plaited into the stallion's mane. The plaits were frayed. He gripped it and thought.

Richard nodded to himself and tugged on the roll. It came loose in his bandaged hand, and he held it up to the flames of the nearest brazier. The parchment crackled and smoked, then took light. The flames crawled up the roll until it reached his fingers.

Richard thought of the iron bar, and held on until the yellow flames licked his fingers and the parchment was all but gone.

Then he let go and blew on his fingers as the ash from the parchment floated up into the cold night sky.

He knew what he had to do, and that Richard decided, was what being a man meant. The second parchment would have to stay rolled up and free from fire for a little longer. If he could recover the silver he could take the cross, go to the Holy Land, and uncover the truth about his father. Richard left his horse and went to sew a cross onto his tunic. He unwrapped the bandage from his hand and cut a cross from the stained fabric. Richard nodded. Tomorrow would be his first day as a knight. He would be the lord of a castle.

Then he smiled, for he couldn't wait to tell Sir Wobble, who was going to be extremely jealous.

Next up - Book 2 in The Legend of Richard Keynes series:

Brothers-in-Arms

Including an added Historical Note, where you can find out just how much of Golden Spurs was based on real events

You can also investigate the author's non-fiction work:

The Rise and Fall of the Mounted Knight

www.clivehart.net

Printed in Great Britain
by Amazon